Henry Nutcombe Oxenham

Short Studies in Ecclesiastical History and Biography

Henry Nutcombe Oxenham

Short Studies in Ecclesiastical History and Biography

ISBN/EAN: 9783337013103

Printed in Europe, USA, Canada, Australia, Japan

Cover: Foto ©Raphael Reischuk / pixelio.de

More available books at **www.hansebooks.com**

SHORT STUDIES

IN

ECCLESIASTICAL HISTORY

AND BIOGRAPHY

SHORT STUDIES

IN

ECCLESIASTICAL HISTORY

AND BIOGRAPHY

BY THE

REV. H. N. OXENHAM, M.A.

LATE SCHOLAR OF BALLIOL COLLEGE, OXFORD

London

CHAPMAN AND HALL, LIMITED

1884

Bungay:

CLAY AND TAYLOR, PRINTERS.

TO

The Very Rev. John Oakley, D.D.,

DEAN OF MANCHESTER,

IN GRATEFUL RECOGNITION OF A VALUED FRIENDSHIP

LASTING FROM OLD OXFORD DAYS,

This Volume

IS WITH MUCH REGARD AND AFFECTION

INSCRIBED.

PREFACE.

THE following Essays are reprinted, by the kind permission of the Editor, from the *Saturday Review*, with
some corrections and additions, and the occasional omission of matter of merely temporary interest. In one
or two cases portions of different articles bearing on the
same subject have been incorporated. It was of course
inevitable in dealing, under the necessary limitations of
space, with themes of wide and varied import, on many
of which whole volumes might be written, that a method
of treatment should be adopted suggestive rather than
exhaustive, with a view to bringing out the salient points,
and thus refreshing the memory or stimulating the minds
of those who may lack leisure or opportunity for more
serious study. And in a busy and restless, which is
also a reading age, but is somewhat apt to regard "a
great book, as a great evil," the author ventures to hope
that to many readers such aids to their own reflection
may prove not unacceptable.

While however he has thought it most suitable to

the character of the work to avoid, as far as possible,
all display of learning, and not to load his pages with
references, which to some might appear wearisome and
to others superfluous, it must not therefore be supposed
that the judgments expressed have been lightly formed,
or are based on authorities which have not been carefully
verified.   It has been his aim throughout to offer an
honest, if but a modest and fragmentary, contribution,
as of a single stone, towards the building up of the
great temple of historic truth.

May 1, 1884.

CONTENTS.

SHORT STUDIES

ECCLESIASTICAL HISTORY AND BIOGRAPHY.

I. CHRISTIANITY BETWEEN TWO FOES.

IN an address which he delivered some years ago before a religious Congress at Munich, Dr. Döllinger starts from the assertion that by the cradle of Christian theology stood two mighty foes, heathen philosophy and the heretical gnosis, with both of which it had to contend, and from both also had much to learn. No student of ecclesiastical history will question the correctness of his statement. But a still broader truth is conveyed in a remark we came across the other day, which applies, not only to the early Church, but to the whole course of Christian history from the beginning until now. Christianity, it was observed, has in every age been confronted by two rival religions; its morality has been threatened by the higher Paganism, or worship of beauty; its doctrinal system by a scientific Theism, or worship of what claims to be pure and absolute truth. With both of these it has always been in conflict,

B

and yet to both it has been constrained to own its obligations; and this mutual interchange of blows and courtesies
was never more conspicuous than in our own day. A
distinguishing feature of the last half-century has been the
revival of artistic taste and culture in the service of religion
throughout Europe, of which the so-called Ritualistic
movement is one subordinate phase; but alongside of this
ecclesiastical restoration there has grown up a religion of
art, independent of all theological restraints, and looking on
them much as the Roman and Florentine *literati* of the
Renaissance looked on the reforms of Savonarola. Meanwhile the dominant scientific school is impatient of any
Deity that cannot be resolved into an impersonal abstraction, and declines to proffer more than "a silent worship
at the altar of the Unknowable and Unknown." Yet, at
the same time, the exponents of the extremest form of
scientific Atheism loudly assert their claim to be the
prophets of a new and exclusively true religion. And,
however much we may smile at the half-grotesque details
of the Comtist creed, with its elaborate mimicry of the
hierarchy, the discipline, and the ritual of Catholicism, no
one can fail to be struck with so unexpected a homage to
the inextinguishable cravings of the religious sentiment,
which it as fully recognises as it entirely fails to satisfy.
Nor can the Church, which has in former periods accepted
the services of an Augustine, an Aquinas, and a Pascal,
affect to ignore in our own day the need for scientific
champions of her cause. It may perhaps be said that
these opposite forms of faith or scepticism, in whichever
light we choose to regard them, are now more confident
and impetuous in their assault than has usually been the

case before, and that they more distinctly assume the functions, not of mere negative criticism, but of rival creeds. Whether or not Mr. Mill could be fairly considered a Theist—and his nearest approach to it appears to have been a kind of revived Manichean dualism—he inculcated a kind of religious and ethical system of his own, often borrowing the language, if not the ideas, of the historical religions which he rejected. This may also be said of some living writers who would be classed more or less in the same category with him. And thus again the artistic religion of Paganism finds a passionate apologist in Mr. Swinburne. But if there is some difference in their methods of warfare, the same triangular duel, so to call it, between Christianity and its two powerful rivals has been in progress continually since the first preaching of the Gospel. The two mighty antagonists stood, to repeat Dr. Döllinger's language, by the cradle of the nascent faith; but the infant Hercules proved strong enough to coerce, if not to strangle, them, or rather succeeded in bending them to the service of a power yet mightier than themselves. Some change there has been no doubt in their relative importance, as mankind has gradually advanced from what has been termed the mythological to the physical stage. Pagan art was a far more formidable opponent to reckon with in the first century than Pagan philosophy; the opposition of science, which cannot always be thrust aside as false, gives much greater trouble to the apologists of Revelation in the nineteenth. Let us begin with art.

From the earliest period of which any records remain, art has been a powerful factor in the religious development of mankind. It has been by turns the instrument and the tyrant of the national faith, or sometimes both together. Greek religion, which was the worship of natural beauty, expressed itself in those unrivalled artistic forms which have riveted the admiring gaze of successive generations for above two thousand years; but the chisel which wrought so marvellously in its service was tracing the lines of its corruption. Its most exquisite art was the efflorescence of decay. The gods who were worshipped with sincere devotion were the deities of Homer, not the creations of Pheidias, and it was only by crushing the genius of its artists that Egypt so long preserved the sombre grandeur of its hereditary faith. Christianity could afford to be less jealous, although the early fathers betray an uneasy suspicion of whatever had been associated with Paganism. And accordingly the Catacombs, which were the first homes and workshops, as well as the sepulchres, of the new religion, are profusely ornamented with sculpture borrowing the imagery of existing forms of art. A refined and graceful Christian symbolism was by degrees superinduced on these ancient models; but it showed nothing of that darker and sterner aspect of Gospel teaching which was afterwards so abundantly exhibited in churches and cemeteries; there were no representations of hell or purgatory, or of the Last Judgment; and, what seems stranger, there were at first no representations of the Passion. The fiery persecution, through which so many of those who were thus piously commemorated had passed to their reward, was but distantly alluded to in an occasional picture of Daniel among the lions, or the three holy children walking unharmed amid the flames. All this was changed of course at a later date, and, in spite of the triumphs of mediæval architecture, it is true to say that, as the purely religious sentiment attained its ascendency in the "ages of faith," æsthetic art on the whole declined, to revive with the irreligious, or at least non-religious, outburst of the Renaissance. Yet Christianity never forgot, like narrower and more artificial creeds, that its world-wide mission imposed on it at once the capacity and the obligation of embracing every genuine product of the human intellect and heart. The contrast is strikingly exemplified, if we turn for a moment to Mahometanism, which could only hold its own against the inroads of idolatry by sternly proscribing art. The Arabian prophet, it has been truly said, could not prevent his disciples from worshipping images, except by absolutely forbidding them to make any ; and thus "he preserved his religion from idolatry, but made it the deadly enemy of art," as it has remained ever since. The same criticism applies, in a more limited sense, to the illogical compromise by which the Iconoclastic controversy was eventually settled in the Eastern Church, permitting pictorial, but prohibiting sculptured, representations of sacred subjects. On the other hand, the Renaissance was not a religious movement. In its artistic development there is a close analogy to what has already been noticed in the case of ancient Greece. Instead of using his art to do honour to religion, the painter made religious conceptions subservient to the display of his artistic power. The devotional and the æsthetic temper are distinct, though not incompatible, and seldom predominate in the same class of minds. It was perfectly natural that an ardent reformer like Savonarola should head a crusade against a classical revival which had brought, not only the arts, but the tastes, the sensuality, and the

scepticism of classical Greece in its train.   It had already
been strongly denounced, and indeed forcibly suppressed,
by Paul II., though his successors in the Roman See for
some time afterwards by no means followed his example in
this respect.   But neither Pope nor preacher could permanently arrest the degradation of religious art which rapidly
followed, and the course of which may even be traced in a
comparison of the earlier and later pictures of Raffaelle.
There cannot be said to be a school of religious painters in
the present day, though some of the earlier works of the
præ-Raffaellites may have suggested an anticipation not
destined to be realised.   In another department we have
indeed witnessed a remarkable resuscitation of distinctively
religious art, for it is quite true that Gothic architecture
and the love of it are intimately connected with the
Christian, as contrasted with the Pagan or secular, habit
of mind ; and Mr. Lecky is certainly right in saying that
"we mainly owe the revival of Gothic architecture to the
Catholic revival of the present century," though a party
powerful of late in the Roman Catholic Church have
betrayed their instinctive aversion to history by opposing it.

In the early Christian centuries physical science was not
sufficiently advanced to present any serious difficulties to
the Christian apologist.   St. Augustine could easily dispose
of Manichean objections to the Mosaic cosmogony in a
fashion which would never occur to a very inferior class
of thinkers now ; and in the sixth century Cosmas Indicopleustes—the special butt of Mr. Matthew Arnold's raillery
—carried public opinion with him when he argued against
the antipodes, in his *Topographia Christiana*, for this reason,
among others, that St. Paul speaks of all men living "on

the face of the earth," which proves that it is flat and not round. It is right to add that when Virgilius, two centuries later, maintained the existence of the antipodes, Pope Zachary declined to condemn him, and he became a bishop, and eventually a canonized saint, but the religious world of the day, which found a mouthpiece in St. Boniface, was profoundly scandalized. We need not stay to dwell here on the critical instance of the Copernican controversy, but it is notorious that there has been a chronic feud between theologians and men of science, which one class of writers is fond of representing as the gradual triumph of science over a dwindling supernaturalism. This is the leading idea, for instance, frequently avowed and always implied, which runs through Mr. Lecky's *History of Rationalism*. On the other hand, as was pointed out before, if the Church has been jealous of scientific, as of artistic, encroachments on her own domain, she has numbered great philosophers as well as brilliant artists among her most devoted servants. In the fifteenth century, Christianity appeared to be engaged in an internecine struggle with the Pagan revolt against her ethical code ; in the eighteenth, a Deistic philosophy questioned the primary articles of her creed. In our own day the controversy has passed into a new phase, and arguments which were unanswerable in the mouth of Bishop Butler fail to convince disputants who repudiate, not his reasoning, but the premisses admitted in common at the time by himself and his opponents. It is not unreasonable, however, to believe that a religion which has survived so many open or insidious attacks will still be equal to the crisis. A way may be found in the future, as in the past, for acknowledging the legitimate claims of science, without resolving into a beautiful but visionary *Aberglaube* the faith which has ennobled the life and consoled the last hours of sixty generations of Christians. Meanwhile it is significant that the great master of the positive philosophy in France should have passionately proclaimed the indestructible necessity of a religion, while the chief upholder of a similar system in England has left on record his conviction that the Christian religion has certainly been useful, if not indispensable, hitherto, and in part at least may not impossibly be true.

II

CHRISTIAN AND PAGAN ART.

IT has been said, with some truth, that art is the bloom of decay. There are two senses in which this may be understood, political and religious. The zenith of Athenian art coincided with the decay of political power; and in modern Europe the highest artistic rank has been attained by that country which was popularly said, till lately, to be a "geographical expression," and which has over and over again been the battle-field but never the leader of the nations. Of ancient Rome, on the contrary, the poet's words were emphatically verified; her "arts" were those of conquest and of empire; what she borrowed in her later days from the conquered Greece never became more than an exotic growth, and served but to grace the decadence of her imperial might. There is of course one obvious explanation of this phenomenon. A people whose energies are absorbed in political or military struggles lack both the time and the taste for artistic niceties; while it is natural, on the other hand, that where there is less of the stir and grandeur of national life, intellectual and artistic cultivation should be more eagerly pursued, as the resource of faculties that might otherwise lie dormant. This is no doubt, for instance, one reason why German scholarship and

literature are in many departments so far superior to our
own. But there must be some other explanation of the
fact, if such it be, of religious art—and art has been in all
ages closely dependent on religion—illustrating the decay
rather than the vigour of religious faith. To a certain
extent this is especially true of ancient art. The oldest
and most profoundly reverenced images of the gods were
little more than hideous blocks. The beautiful creations of
Pheidias or Praxiteles were admired, but not worshipped, by
a people who, to say the least, sat very loosely to their
mythological belief. Mr. Ruskin has a remark somewhere
about Christian art, which points in the same direction.
He says that, so far as he has observed, the pictures which
excite popular devotion are invariably staring daubs, while
the masterpieces of Raffaelle or Perugino are gazed at with
critical appreciation by the cultivated few, and neither
appreciated nor reverenced by the vulgar. So much as
this may at least be admitted in either case, that art is
necessarily self-conscious, whereas the natural atmosphere
of devotion is unconscious awe. It was not till they had
begun to theorize about their gods that the Greeks could
make elaborate sculptures of them ; and, with a polythe-
istic religion, to theorize means to rationalize. This need
not, of course, be the case with Christianity. Frescoes of
the " Good Shepherd," and other typical subjects of Christian teaching, were traced on the walls of the Catacombs
in the ages of martyrdom. Yet we can hardly conceive,
under any circumstances, the " Transfiguration " or the
" Sistine Madonna " being painted in those days of early
faith. It is not simply that the genius for it was wanting,
but that, if there, it would have been differently employed.

That profound sense of the unseen which made the beings of another world almost a visible presence to the primitive Christian, and taught him to listen in each fresh political convulsion for the tokens of the approaching Judgment, could hardly consist with a minute attention to the details of artistic effect. There is a great step even from Fra Angelico to Raffaelle, and we feel at once that the artist has triumphed over the saint.

But if in this respect there is some analogy, though it must not be pressed too far, between Christian and Pagan art, there are some very observable differences. The fact, which has so often been dwelt upon, that sculpture is the special glory of ancient, as painting is of modern, art, is at once suggestive of some deeper contrast than meets the eye at first sight. Many reasons may be given for the change. The higher and more scrupulous standard of purity introduced by the Gospel, and which shrank from the exhibition of the nude form, is of course one of them. Another may be found in the dread of a relapse into idolatry, which long exercised so marked an influence over ecclesiastical discipline and worship, and of which we have a permanent record in the prohibition of sculptured images, as distinguished from "icons," or pictures, still maintained in the Greek Church. But explanations of this kind evidently do not go to the root of the matter. An observation of Winckelmann's, quoted by Mr. Lecky, suggests what is probably the real solution of the problem. "The supreme beauty of Greek art," he very justly insists, "is male rather than female." Strength, freedom, masculine grace are its prominent characteristics. And this was only to be expected, for all genuine art is the expression of a moral ideal, and the moral ideal of Paganism in its best days was essentially masculine. Courage, independence, constancy, patriotism, were the qualities it most highly honoured; the softer virtues of charity, gentleness, meekness, benevolence, kindness, it either despised or ignored. Stoicism was the loftiest Pagan conception of excellence, and Cicero expressly distinguishes it from all other philosophical sects "as males differ from females." Christianity reversed all this. Without discrediting, except in a relative sense, the masculine virtues, it gave a wholly unprecedented importance to the feminine type of goodness. Compare the Beatitudes with the moral standard of Stoicism, or of the best classical literature, whether poetry or prose, and they read almost like an explicit condemnation of it. Of all the qualities which Christ pronounced "blessed," there is not one which the Pagan ideal would recognise as virtuous; there is more than one which it would reject as simply contemptible. And the ethical ideal in either case inspired the artistic. Sculpture was instinctively chosen by the Greeks as best suited to the expression of masculine grace. There was a further reason, partly growing out of the former, which it is impossible to dwell upon, though it cannot be passed over. The public games and the exercises of the palæstra, which accustomed the Greeks to the habitual contemplation of the nude human form, tended to foster the masculine ideal of beauty and the peculiar forms of vice with which it was connected in the ancient world. And the taste thus generated sought both expression and aliment in contemporary art. The type, as well of courage as of passion, which the Greeks desired especially to idealize is sufficiently illustrated by the fact that the first statues erected by Athenians to their country-men were those of Harmodius and Aristogeiton. It is not a little curious that the type should have been so well pre-served in the days of Rome's lowest moral degradation in the perfect purity of the Antinous.

The reasons which made sculpture the chosen vehicle of artistic utterance to the Pagan are precisely those which led Christian art to eschew it. It gave but inadequate scope for the expression of those virtues which Christian sentiment had learnt to canonize, and it suggested an ideal partly indifferent and partly abhorrent to the new religious sense. Painting, on the other hand, was admirably adapted for bringing out those feminine attributes of tenderness, purity, and patience which belonged to the Christian saint, and which mediæval piety found most perfectly embodied in the Virgin Mother. Take as typical instances the Sistine Madonna and the Belvedere Apollo. The one as com-pletely satisfies the Pagan as the other satisfies the Chris-tian ideal. Both in their respective ways are of matchless beauty, but the one expresses devoutness, the other strength. To the mediæval Catholic the Belvedere could be no more than a curiosity, and the Sistine Madonna would have been wholly unintelligible to Greek taste. It is a striking con-firmation of this view that, so far as the artist is dominated by the Christian or the classical sentiment, does he fail to give expression to the other. Michael Angelo's representa-tions of our Lord in the Sistine Chapel are as conspicuous a failure as Perugino's frescoes of the ancient heroes and sages. His figure of Cato, says an observer, "almost approaches the type of St. John." Nor can it be accidental that a poet of our own days, whose artistic sympathies are intensely classical, also rebels fiercely against the ethical standard of Christianity. We may again borrow an illustration from ancient and modern poetry, where the same sort of difference reappears. With a few trifling exceptions, which only bring out the general fact more clearly, there is nothing tender or subjective in classical poetry. Thus, for instance, no single ancient poet ever dwells on his childhood, while scarcely any modern poet of note has failed to do so.

If we turn from sculpture and painting to architecture, we shall find something of the same contrast, though other considerations also come in, which it would take us too long to enter upon here. It may be true, as a great judge has said, that, properly speaking, "there are only two fine arts possible to the human race—sculpture and painting," and that "architecture is only the association of these in noble masses." But for practical convenience, at all events, it requires to be separately treated. And Gothic, which was the creation of mediæval Europe, may be fairly called the specifically Christian type of architecture, as bearing the intellectual impress of that period of modern history when men's minds were most exclusively and powerfully ruled by purely religious influences. Speaking broadly, then, we may say that size and symmetry are the dominant characteristics of the Grecian; delicacy, tenderness, and reverential awe, of the Gothic style. The one is calculated to exhibit the greatness of man, and the other to suggest that there is a God above him ; the one to rouse admiration and a feeling of pride, the other to inspire humility. It is quite in accordance with this, if the story be true, that Louis XIV., who was so great an admirer and promoter of the Renaissance style, should have expressed himself shocked at hearing that Christ spoke the language of the humble and poor. The heroes and philosophers of antiquity would have entirely agreed with him. We need not carry out the comparison into its details here, but the low doors and lofty roofs, the elaborate carving, even where least likely to be seen, the disregard of mere symmetry, and the subdued light, which are characteristic of Gothic churches, will serve to illustrate our meaning. There is a further point to be borne in mind in reference both to Christian painting and architecture as distinguished from Pagan. The former was designed to teach, but not the latter. Greek art was indeed mostly religious, that is, consecrated to the commemoration of gods or heroes; but, like the priesthood and worship of Paganism, it had no didactic office. Even under Judaism the functions of the priest and the prophet were kept separate, and the latter had no existence elsewhere in the ancient world. Christianity for the first time presented the priest and the preacher in the same person. And Christian art, from the rudest frescoes on the walls of the Catacombs to the most finished compositions of the great mediæval painters, was designed not simply to " charm," like the sculpture of the Pheidian period, but also, or rather chiefly, " to strengthen and to teach." Painting is obviously more available for this purpose than sculpture. So far as ancient sculpture had any reflex action on popular morality, it would tend, as was observed just now, to foster the ethical conceptions which gave it birth. Painting and architecture in later times would do the same; but this kind of influence is probably much less widely felt than we are apt to imagine,

and would be pretty well confined to the cultivated classes
—the immense majority of citizens perhaps in ancient
Athens, but a small minority in any modern State. It was
by the personages, scenes, and stories represented that the
picture and the painted window were expected to convey
direct instruction to the multitude. What has been the
actual effect, both in nature and extent, of these appeals
oculis subjecta fidelibus, on the faith and devotion of Christendom, would be an interesting subject of inquiry for the
historian of religion or of art. But the question has been
so darkened and perplexed by the rival zealots of image
worship and iconoclasm, from the days of Charlemagne
downwards, that it is far from easy to disentangle fact from
fiction, and arrive at the requisite data for a trustworthy
decision.

III.

CONFLICT OF EARLY CHRISTIAN AND PAGAN THOUGHT.

AT the opening of a paper in the *Contemporary Review* (for May, 1879), on "Origen and the Beginnings of Christian Philosophy," Dr. Westcott touches on the great struggle between the Pagan and Christian systems of philosophy during the first three centuries of our era, which is at once a deeply interesting and a much neglected subject of inquiry. We are apt to speak, or at least to think, in a loose sort of way of the conversion of the Empire, as though up to the year 313 A.D. Christians were undergoing a chronic and almost unintermittent persecution, until suddenly the whole edifice of Greek and Roman Paganism collapsed, like the walls of Jericho before the trumpets of Joshua, and thenceforth the Church was co-extensive with the civilised world. It need hardly be said that a view more grotesquely unhistorical could hardly be conceived. Christianity, in spite of frequent outbreaks of persecution, very unequal in duration and intensity, was carrying on an active and continuous conflict, and on the whole making a steady advance, during the time of trial which preceded its public recognition. On the other hand, Paganism after the formal conversion of the Emperors still

C

retained its hold on a large proportion—at first a decided majority—of the population under their rule ; and even its outward forms and splendour—its priesthoods, endowments, and ceremonials—maintained a protracted, if somewhat precarious existence, long after it might have been supposed that imperial edicts or popular sentiment would have suppressed all public manifestations of a defeated and decaying faith.   The history of the first three centuries, as Dr. Westcott puts it, is the history of a threefold contest between the rival forces of the new and the old creed, closed by a threefold victory.   "They met in the market and the house; they met in the discussions of the schools ; they met in the institutions of political government." There were, in other words, conflicts in the region of life, of thought, and of the State ; and the victory in the world of thought, with which we are at present chiefly concerned, was the second, not the first.   "The victory of the soldiers" —the common mass who supplied the multitude of martyrs, confessors, and humble examples of Christian faith and practice—came before "the victory of the captains of Christ's army," who vindicated the philosophical claims of the conquering creed.   The period during which this second conflict was waged Dr. Westcott defines, "roughly speaking," to be "from the middle of the second to the middle of the third century"—the special age of what are called "the Apologists," which precedes the age of "the Fathers."   Of course the discussion really lasted much longer, but for its immediate purpose the limit of time is correct enough.   And one of its leading characteristics was this, that, in the words of another recent writer, it "was a moment in the history of the human mind when East and

West were blending their traditions to form the husk of Christian creeds and the fantastic visions of Neoplatonism," while moreover its "whole creative and expansive force lay in the despised Christian sect." The peculiar centre and point of contact of these diverse influences, at once conflicting and yet converging, was found at Alexandria, "the forge of fanciful imaginations, the majority of which were destined to pass like clouds and leave not a wrack behind, while a few fastened with the force of a dogma on the conscience of awakening Christendom." Mr. Lecky is not far wrong when he says that "the influence which this [Alexandrian or Neoplatonic] school exercised over Christianity forms one of the most remarkable pages in [early] ecclesiastical history," though he certainly exaggerates it, in suggesting that Neoplatonic modes of thought are reflected in St. John's Gospel. No one familiar with Dr. Newman's *Arians of the Fourth Century*, one of the earliest and greatest of his works, can be ignorant of the important part played by the Alexandrian school in the development of Christian doctrine. After referring to the "cosmopolitan" tendencies of the age, Dr. Westcott adds :

As a necessary consequence, the teaching of the Bible accessible in Greek began to attract serious attention among the heathen. The assailants of Christianity, even if they affected contempt, showed that they were deeply moved by its doctrines. The memorable saying of Numenius, "What is Plato but Moses speaking in the language of Athens?" shows at once the feeling after spiritual sympathy which began to be entertained, and the want of spiritual insight in the representatives of Gentile thought. Though there is no evidence that Numenius studied or taught at Alexandria, his words express the form of feeling which prevailed there. Nowhere else were the characteristic tendencies of the age more marked than in that marvellous city. Alexandria had been from its foundation a meeting-place of the East and West—of old and new—the home of learning, of criticism, of syncretism. It presented a unique example in the Old World of that mixture of races which forms one of the most important features of modern society. Indians, Jews, Greeks, Romans, met there on common ground. Their characteristic ideas were discussed, exchanged, combined. The extremes of luxury and asceticism existed side by side. Over all the excitement and turmoil of the recent city rested the solemn shadow of Egypt. The thoughtful Alexandrian inherited in the history of countless ages, sympathy with a vast life.

And he goes on to cite the testimony of a prominent personage of philosophical tastes, who has indeed sometimes, though on grounds absurdly inadequate, been credited with being actually a Christian, the Emperor Hadrian. Hadrian had himself disputed with the professors at the Alexandrian Museum, and it is a curious fact that the practice of magic was already coming into vogue there ; Celsus, according to Origen, " compared the miracles of the Lord with the feats of those who have been taught by Egyptians." Dr. Westcott naturally interprets this as showing that " there was a longing among men for some sensible revelation of the unseen, and a conviction that such a revelation was possible." Incredulity had reached its extreme point in the Roman Empire during the period immediately preceding and following the commencement of the Christian era. From the middle of the first century a reaction began to set in, and there was a growing desire for some positive religious belief. The expiring Paganism made desperate and sometimes temporarily successful efforts to satisfy this desire, and it is remarkable that in doing so it was constrained to borrow, consciously or unconsciously, from the powerful rival whose advance it was striving to arrest. One startling example of this, which helps to support Dr. Westcott's argument, though he does not notice it, is closely connected with the name of Hadrian. A recent writer has traced out with much care and ingenuity the true significance of what he calls "the canonization of Antinous," which has proved a standing puzzle to historians. Milman speaks of the act as "tending to alienate a large portion of the thinking class, already wavering in their cold and doubtful polytheism, to any purer or more ennobling system of religion," and quotes a prediction from the Sibylline (probably Christian) poet about Hadrian :—

παιδὰ θεὸν δεικνύσει, ἄπαντα σεβάσματα λύσει.

This, however, was by no means the immediate effect of the procedure, which served rather to bolster up than to shake the tottering fabric. There was nothing of course out of the way in itself in the deification of an imperial favourite. These posthumous compliments were a common fashion of the Empire, and strangely enough lasted on into Christian times ; there were fifty-three of them altogether. But what is at first sight very perplexing—especially considering the circumstances as commonly reported— is the exceptional duration and tenacity on popular senti- ment of a cult which may in the first instance have sprung from a mere personal whim of the reigning Emperor. This might account for the fact of the city near which the death of Antinous occurred being rebuilt and named after him, and a new constellation which appeared about the same time being identified with his glorified spirit. It will not account for the rapid spread of his worship throughout

the provinces of the Mediterranean, and its survival for
some three centuries. Medals were struck and countless
works of art produced to perpetuate his memory; public
games were periodically celebrated at Antinoe, at Mantinea,
Eleusis, Athens, and elsewhere, in his honour; he had
temples, priesthoods, oracles, miracles; great cities wore
wreaths of red lotus on his feast day. His worship
extended not only over Greece and Asia, but into Italy
also, where his name is frequently found in Roman and
Neapolitan inscriptions, and his statues in various cities of
the Campagna. No other imperial apotheosis took such
a hold on popular belief. What was the secret of its
success? It is needless here to follow Mr. Symonds into
his elaborate discussion of the different versions of the
legend about the death of the Bithynian slave boy, and the
comparative evidence on which they rest. But he seems
to have clearly established the actual *motif*, so to say, of
his cult as it came to be generally accepted. It was
adopted as supplying a nobler and more spiritual element
to the effete forces of the ancient Paganism. "Here and
there, in the indignant utterance of a Christian Father,
stung to the quick by Pagan parallels between Antinous
and Christ, we catch a perverted echo of the popular
emotion upon which his cult reposed, which recognised his
godhood *or his vicarious sacrifice*, and paid enduring tribute
to the sublimity of his young life untimely quenched." In
short, "the most rational conclusion seems to be that
Antinous became in truth a popular saint, and satisfied
some new need in Paganism, for which none of the elder
and more respectable deities sufficed." The belief in the
value of vicarious suffering, of which classical literature

presents so many illustrations, and to which Christian preaching had given a fresh and powerful impulse, attached itself to the new demigod, and this appears in process of time to have become more or less distinctly recognised by Christian Apologists. Prudentius, Clement of Alexandria, Tertullian, Eusebius, Justin Martyr, Tatian, all inveigh against the base adulation of the worship of the imperial favourite—which however will not explain its maintenance and increase long after Hadrian's death ; but Origen treats the matter more seriously in his controversy with Celsus. Celsus had deliberately put forward the self-devotion of Antinous in rivalry with the sacrifice of Christ. Origen replies, justly enough, that there is no real parallel between the lives thus strangely compared, and that the alleged divinity of the favourite is a fiction. But it is clear from the method of treatment on both sides how the name of Antinous had become endeared to his Pagan votaries, and formidable, or at least odious rather than simply contemptible, to Christian Apologists. His cult, however it originated, had been adapted, by a kind of plagiarism very characteristic of the age, for the satisfaction of cravings which the Christian doctrines of self-devotion and immortality had awakened throughout the Roman world.[1]

Alexandria, at the opening of the third century, offered an epitome of the old world which Christianity aspired to quicken in all its parts. And there too the·first attempt was made, in the second century, to give a philosophic form to the Christian solution of the problems of the age. To the questions uppermost in men's minds at the time

[1] This curious problem is discussed more fully in the Third Excursus of my *Catholic Doctrine of the Atonement*.

three types of answers were being returned, the Gnostic, the Neoplatonist, and the Christian.   As against the Gnostic, the teachers of the new faith maintained that the universe was created, not by any inferior demiurgus, good or bad, but by the one Supreme Deity, and that evil is not inherent in matter, but due to the misuse of free will by the creature.   As against the Neoplatonist, they insisted on the separate and true personality of the Deity, and the reality of the Incarnation and its results.   As against both alike they maintained that the Creator is distinct but not alien from the world He made, which was originally good, and that man is the crown and end of creation.   Moreover, while Gnostic and Neoplatonist were agreed in despairing of the world as it is, and saw no salvation for the multitude, the Christian was content to appeal not to the few but to the many, and claimed to be the bearer of a message addressed, in virtue of a common divine faculty, to all alike who bore the stamp of the Creator, and were the subjects of a common redemption.   But while his answer to the difficulties propounded was a widely different one, the Christian teacher was prepared to meet the Pagan philosopher on his own ground.   He "did not lay aside the philosopher's mantle in virtue of his office, but rather assumed it"; so literally indeed was this the case that convert philosophers continued to wear the cloak or mantle which had been the outward badge of their former calling. "At Alexandria a Christian 'School'—the well-known Catechetical School—arose by the side of the Museum," and from the first they were connected with each other by more than mere local proximity, as was curiously typified in later days by the intimate relations of Hypatia with

Synesius, both before and after his conversion and elevation to the episcopate. Both Pantœnus and Clement, the first great names in the Catechetical School, were led to embrace the Gospel through the study of philosophy, and both of them carried on their philosophical studies as Christians. Origen, the most famous of them all, was born of Christian parents, and trained from the cradle in the exercise of piety and faith. He was but sixteen when his father was martyred, and before he was eighteen he became a teacher in the Catechetical School. Nor did he shrink from attending the lectures of Ammonius Saccas, the founder of Neoplatonism, whose lessons appeared to him to unveil fresh depths in the Bible; and in after years, when charged with listening to the opinions of heretics and heathens, he defended himself by the example of Heraclas, his fellow disciple in the school of Ammonius, who, "while now a presbyter at Alexandria, still wears the philosopher's dress and diligently studies the works of the Greeks." He exhorted his theological scholars to study first the philosophers and poets of every nation. Yet he never faltered for a moment in his Christian steadfastness, and it was not his fault that the torture and imprisonment inflicted upon him in the Decian persecution were not consummated by a violent death. But this is not the place to enter into a discussion of the life, writings, and opinions of Origen. As a great master of the Alexandrian Catechetical School, he may be taken to illustrate the points as well of contact as of divergence between the Pagan and Christian modes of thought at the beginning of the third century. It is true, as was observed before, that "the victory of common life" preceded in the long struggle of the early Church "the victory of thought," and of "civil organization." As St. Augustine said afterwards, *domuit orbem non ferro, sed ligno*, by patient suffering, not by outward force. The martyrs came before the Apologists, and the populace were already being won over before philosophers and statesmen would lend an ear to the teachers of the new religion. In Dr. Westcott's words, "the discipline of action precedes the effort of reason," just as, we may add, the process of reasoning precedes the elaboration of the formal rules of logic. But the second stage is not less indispensable than the first. The triumph of Christianity in the world could never have been assured if it had not proved itself able to satisfy the intellectual no less than the moral cravings of mankind.

IV.

RELIGIOUS ATTITUDE OF THE EMPEROR HADRIAN.

AN article on " the Emperor Hadrian and Christianity," from the pen of M. Renan, which appeared some years ago in an American periodical, deals with a vexed question of acknowledged historical interest, though it can hardly be said to throw much new light on the subject.[1] That Hadrian has usually been reckoned by Christian writers among " the good Emperors " was of course notorious. But moreover, a notion has prevailed in some quarters that he was not only " an earnest man endowed with rare virtues, who devoted the best and finest part of his life to mankind," but was at least more than half a convert to Christianity himself. The two main grounds for this belief, so far as appears, are, first that he caused certain temples to be erected in which no images were placed, and which—in the absence of any description, dedication, or known object— he was not unreasonably supposed to have intended for Christian churches ; and secondly, that a policy of toleration was consistently pursued during his reign. Of these two facts there can be no doubt; the question is how they are ·to be explained. And it will perhaps be found that the same explanation, based on a careful estimate of the

[1] See *North American Review* for May, 1878.

Emperor's character and tone of mind, will sufficiently
account for both alike without having recourse to what,
without some better evidence to support it, would be, to
say the least, a somewhat violent hypothesis. When indeed we are told that " even Hadrian's relations with
Antinous became a theme for Christian apology," it is
difficult to restrain a smile. " Such a monstrous act," adds
the writer, " seemed to be the culminating point of the
reign of Satan. ' This last demon (does he mean Satan or
Antinous ?) of whom every one had heard was employed
to overthrow the other gods, which were more ancient and
less easy to reach." Certainly, whatever version of the
story of the death of Antinous be accepted—whether it
was an accident or an act of heroic self-sacrifice or a selfish
immolation—the subsequent deification and cult of the
departed favourite is sufficiently startling, nor would it
have appeared at all more tolerable to the early Christians
from the fact of its having bequeathed to us one of the
most perfect models of ancient sculpture. Emperors and
their relations, wives, and favourites had often, it is true,
been deified before. Caius assigned these posthumous
honours to his sister, Claudius to his grandmother, Nero
to his father and his wife Poppæa, Vitellius worshipped
Narcissus and Pallas, favourite freedmen of his uncle.
But Antinous obtained a far higher and more permanent
place among the gods than any previous subject of imperial
apotheosis. The city of Antinoe or Antinopolis was built
over the spot where he died; temples were erected and
games celebrated in his honour at Mantinea and elsewhere;
he had prophets, priests, and oracles all over the Empire;
coins bearing his likeness are still found in Greece, Syria,

Asia, and Egypt; and astrologers were not long in dis-
covering a new constellation which represented his glorified
spirit. What is still stranger, this worship was so far from
ending with Hadrian's reign that it lasted for centuries
afterwards, especially in Egypt, where the new deity continued to work miracles which both Christian and Pagan
writers have noticed. An explanation of this remarkable
phenomenon has been suggested elsewhere[1]; but it is not
one that would occur to contemporary Christians, who in
fact regarded this abnormal development of polytheism as
providentially designed for a *reductio ad absurdum* of the
whole system, and this is distinctly implied in a passage
of the Eighth Book of the Sibylline Oracles; but they
could hardly attribute any such intention to its author, and
it must have been with important reservations that they
spoke of him as an earnest and virtuous man.

The fact remains that Hadrian discountenanced persecution of the Christians. But persecution in those days, to
use a phrase of Mr. Goldwin Smith's, was "tribal" or
"political" rather than theological. Its motive was superstitious among the vulgar, prudential among their rulers.
There was little real belief in the gods of Olympus surviving in either class, but the populace were shocked at the
open defiance of the established worship, which was so
inextricably mixed up with all the main incidents of civil
and social life, and the magistrates suspected the loyalty of
men who deliberately disobeyed the law. To both alike
there was something "uncanny" about such stubborn and
exceptional perversity. Hadrian, who was of a speculative
and intellectual cast of mind, felt probably little sympathy

[1] Cf. *supr.* p. 22.

with these sentiments or fears.   He took indeed an exceedingly practical view of the interests of the Empire, as was
shown in one of his first acts, when he withdrew the Roman
garrisons from Mesopotamia, Armenia, and Assyria, and
once more made the Euphrates the boundary of the Roman
world.   Nor can it be doubted that the Empire flourished
under his sagacious rule.   His vast and active genius, as
Gibbon says, embraced at once the most enlarged views
and the minutest details.   But it is equally true, as the
same writer proceeds to observe, that the ruling passions of
his soul were curiosity and vanity.   His curiosity may not
improbably have led him to inquire about the Christian as
well as about other forms of contemporary belief, but if his
letter to Servianus is genuine, in which Christianity is studi-
ously confounded—whether from ignorance or, as Milman
thinks, sarcasm—with the worship of Serapis, the result of
these inquiries cannot have produced any very deep effect
on his mind.   However, he issued a rescript to the procon-
sul of Asia forbidding Christians to be punished in deference to popular outcry, without a formal trial and conviction of some legal offence, and ordering the punishment of
all false accusers.   And as a matter of fact the Christians
were left unmolested during his reign by the Government,
though they suffered horrible tortures at the hands of the
Jewish insurgents, which may have helped to open the
eyes of their Roman masters to the distinction between
rival religionists whom they had been accustomed loosely
to identify as members of the same sect.   At all events,
when Hadrian rebuilt Jerusalem under the name of *Colonia
Ælia Capitolina*, Christians flocked into the new city,
which the Jews are said to have been forbidden to enter,

and certainly did not approach; perhaps the dedication of a temple to Jupiter Capitolinus on the site of their own ancient temple would alone have proved a sufficient deterrent to them. But it was neither on Jerusalem nor on Rome but on Athens that the affections of the philosophic and cultivated Emperor were concentrated. He spent a winter there enjoying to the utmost the *strenua inertia* of learned dilettantism, disputing, conversing, legislating, building, and endeavouring to reproduce a kind of shadowy "Panhellenism" on the old historic site. He founded innumerable philosophical chairs; he fused the laws of Draco and Solon into a new Athenian constitution; he completed the unfinished Temple of Jupiter Olympius and rebuilt the city, one quarter of which received the name of Hadrianopolis; he chose to be initiated in the Eleusinian mysteries; and he solemnly assumed the ancient titles of "archon" and "agonothetes." At Athens he was regarded as not only philosophical but very religious—somewhat in the sense in which St. Paul applied the term to the Athenians of his own day—and the spirit of discussion which his tastes led him to foster did undoubtedly give rise to a new development of Christian literature, though it cannot plausibly be maintained to have inspired him with any Christian belief. His mind was in fact essentially sceptical, in the strictest sense of the word; he neither accepted nor denied any religion or philosophy, but balanced one impartially against another, or rather played with each in turn. The very levity of his dying apostrophe to his "*animula, vagula, blandula*" marks the character of the man as truly as the savage blasphemy of his last recorded words marks the very different spirit of the

Emperor Julian two centuries later.   M. St. Croix says of
him :—" Il parut constamment livré à cette incertitude
d'opinions, fruit de la bizarrerie de son caractère, et d'un
savoir superficiel ou mal digéré."

We have said that Hadrian's policy gave occasion to a
novel species of Christian literature.   Christianity had
already borne fruit at Athens as at Rome ; but the secular
contrast of the two great centres of ancient Pagan civilisation was reproduced in their relations to the Church.
None of the early Popes were men of any intellectual or
literary distinction ; the very names of several of them are
still open to dispute.   But from a very early period something of the old imperial instinct seems to have taken
possession of them, and whereas Eastern theologians and
prelates were exercised on the subtlest questions of the
Divine nature and attributes, the first official utterance of a
Roman Pontiff—towards the close of the fourth century—
enjoins the observance of clerical celibacy.   It was the
speciality of Athens, as M. Renan words it, to produce
" individual Christian thinkers," and among these thinkers
were found the first " Apologists."   The " philosophers "
who from time to time embraced the Gospel did not feel it
necessary to abandon their title or the peculiar dress which
was its outward symbol ; being writers and orators by profession they naturally became the doctors, disputants, and
advocates of their adopted faith.   Hitherto Christianity
had never been put on its defence, argumentatively that is.
Its strongest and only available arguments had been written
in the blood of martyrs.   Even had the advocates been
prepared, there was no one ready to listen to them.   No
previous Emperor had challenged such explanations or

would have deigned to read them, and *Christianos ad leones* was a method of attack that did not admit of controversial rejoinder. But Hadrian's inquisitive temper and known love of free discussion invited overtures, which till then would have been scornfully ignored; his very vanity was flattered by an appeal to his superior discernment. To him accordingly was addressed the first Apology on record by one Quadratus, who is said to have been a disciple of the Apostles. It is lost, unfortunately, but we know that at the time it was highly esteemed; the author is reported to have refuted the calumnies of "evil men" against the Christians, and to have dwelt on the miracles of our Lord, insisting that men whom He had healed or raised from the dead were still alive. The Emperor had probably heard of these miracles already from his secretary, Phlegon, who was familiar with the subject. Another convert philosopher, Aristides, also presented an Apology to Hadrian, of which we only know that it was not less admired than that of Quadratus. That these writings made some impression on his mind there is no reason to doubt. They must at least have confirmed his conviction of the perfect harmlessness of the new religion, and there is some evidence of his having shown signs of genuine respect for it. He ordered, as we have seen, the erection of a number of temples or basilicas, which were never dedicated, and the precise destination of which is not distinctly known. When in the next century Alexander Severus expressed a desire to build a temple to Christ, the Christians asserted, not without plausibility, that Hadrian had entertained a similar design, and had only at last abandoned it on account of the response of the oracles that, if such a temple was built, all the others would be deserted, and the world would become Christian. They pointed in proof of this to the singular omission of placing any images in these temples, and the alleged ground of Hadrian's pausing in his design is quite in accord with all we know of his character. Several of these *Hadriana* were in fact turned into Christian churches after the conversion of the Empire. Still all this in no way proves that Hadrian ever meditated becoming a Christian, but only that he was disposed, like Severus, to provide a niche for the Founder of Christianity in his comprehensive pantheon.

V

HELLENISM AND ITS REVIVAL.

IN the short and very imperfectly reported address which he delivered at the close of M. Renan's last Hibbert lecture, Dr. Martineau drew out what he conceived to be the moral of the whole course more pointedly than the lecturer had cared to do himself. He considered that, as in the early Christian ages, Paganism—or what he preferred to call Hellenism—and Atheism were apparently engaged in a death struggle for religious supremacy in the Roman Empire, which however resulted in the triumph of a third form of belief ignored or trampled on by both alike, so in our own day, when the future of religion seems to lie between the rival forces of Christianity and Agnosticism, a third solution of the problem might eventually be found; and his hearers were left to infer that this *tertium quid* would be a purified and enlightened Theism. Whatever may be thought of the analogy suggested between the traditional Paganism of the Empire and the traditional Christianity of to-day, or of the proposed Church of the Future, Dr. Martineau had good reason for tracing in the present unsettled and fluctuating condition of religious thought something analogous to the restless temper of the age when a corrupt and exploded Paganism was gradually

D 2

succumbing to the nascent faith of the sect that was everywhere spoken against. He might indeed have gone further,
and have shown how one of the most curious among the
moral and intellectual phenomena of our own day is a kind
of spurious revival of " Hellenism," recalling in its darker
rather than its brighter features the Renaissance of the
fifteenth century. But that Renaissance did not end in
the common absorption of the Hellenic and Christian
elements into some newer, and presumably nobler, phase of
creed or culture, but in the great schism of the sixteenth
century, and the striking revival of spiritual life, under
somewhat different forms, which followed it, in both
divisions of Western Christendom. We need not essay
prediction, but no fairly intelligent observer can have failed
to notice that peculiar classical or Pagan revival of our
own day which is a present and a patent fact, revealing
itself at once in art, in literature, and in social life. A
recent Catholic writer has not inaptly described it as " the
reappearance of a passionate love for, and a desire to rest
in and thoroughly sympathize with, mere nature, accom-
panied by a more or less complete and sympathetic rejection of the supernatural, its aspirations, its consolations,
and its terrors." One of the leading prophets of the new
evangel, of whose high classic and literary culture all
must desire to speak with respect, Mr. J. A. Symonds,
does not widely differ from this external estimate, when he
reminds us (to the discredit of the former) that " modern
[*i.e.* Christian] morality has hitherto been theological, and
has implied the will of a Divine Governor," whereas
" Greek morality was radically scientific ; the belief on
which it eventually rested was a belief in φύσις, in the order

of the universe"; and accordingly, while the motto of the one system is contained in St. Paul's words, "To me to live is Christ, and to die is gain," the other may be summed up in Göthe's well-known lines, "Im Ganzen, Guten, Schönen resolut zu leben." Göthe may indeed be fairly taken as the typical representative or precursor of this revived Hellenism. It is recorded of him that "repugnance to the supernatural was an inherent part of his mind"; and therefore on the approach of death "he only calculated the chances that might still remain to him of life and enjoyment, and the means he might employ for increasing them, among the foremost of which he placed care in keeping at a distance all gloomy thoughts," and when the end was close at hand his last words were, "Open the shutters, that more light may come into the room." Conspicuous in our own day among the literary exponents, in prose or verse, of this Pagan or naturalistic reaction, though differing widely from one another, are writers like Mr. Pater, Mr. Symonds, and Mr. Swinburne, the latter of whom strikes the keynote of the movement in such poems as the "Hymn to Proserpine" and "Our Lady of Pain," while we recognise in the obscene rhapsodies of Walt Whitman —which are as dull as ditchwater and a good deal dirtier— the shout of its drunken helot. It would be going much too far to say that "all able authors are avowed and aggressive atheists," but it is quite true that "a good many writers make it a condition of ability to exclude the Unknown Factor, . . . and in fact to speak from the Agnostic standpoint."

This last extract is taken from a paper on "Debased Hellenism and the New Renaissance" in the *Church*

Quarterly Review (for April, 1880), containing much interesting matter, though one could wish the writer had drawn
out more fully and distinctly than he has done the signs
and characteristics of the movement he so earnestly con-
demns. We quite agree with him that, if the worst vices
of Greek civilisation and art were repeated, and if possible,
exaggerated in old Rome, the tendency of some of our
own schools, both of literature and art, seems to be to
repeat them now, and that a protest is accordingly needed.
That this new Renaissance should emulate, as indeed that
of the fifteenth century did, the lower and debased rather
than the higher moral tone of Greek art and culture, was
perhaps inevitable, and is certainly the fact. Those who
would revert from belief in a Divine Ruler of the world to
belief in Nature—to adopt Mr. Symonds's account of the
distinction of the two systems—are not in the same position
with thinkers of an earlier age who, like some of the
greatest among the old Greek poets and philosophers, were
really "looking through nature up to nature's God." It is
an echo of the baser, not the better, Hellenism that bids
men exchange the "lilies and languors of virtue for the
raptures and roses of vice," and calls on the dethroned
goddess of lust to "come down and redeem us from
virtue." There is moreover a fatal defect inherent in this—
to apply a phrase used in another connection by Cardinal
Newman—"bad imitation of polished ungodliness." Every
attempt at the galvanized revival of a defunct form of
civilisation is necessarily unreal, but the unreality is
doubled in this case, for it is not merely an imitation but
an imitation of an imitation. We have to measure the
descent first from Pericles to Politian, and then from

Politian to the modern pretenders who ape his worst extravagances.

It has been already shown that any attempt among ourselves to revive "the delighted animalism of Greek life" is a very different thing, both morally and intellectually, from what the pursuit of their cherished ideal was to those old Athenians, who had never known or rejected any better and purer faith. But that is not all. We have learnt from boyhood to gaze in something like a rapture of admiration on that wonderful product of human genius, the Athens of Pericles and Pheidias and Socrates, of those unrivalled orators and poets who being dead yet speak, and whose glowing words have rung music in the ears of some seventy generations of mankind. And our admiration is a perfectly natural one; the spectacle is unique, for history has not such another marvel to record. As a recent poet puts it :—

"Every thought of all their thinking swayed the world for good or ill,
Every pulse of all their life-blood beats across the ages still."

But then we must remember that there was also a darker side to the picture, from which, as Professor Jowett—no prejudiced or unfriendly critic—observes, "we should have turned away with loathing and detestation." And that darker side—not of course in its naked deformity, which would be felt to be intolerable—is what some of our classical revivalists, like their predecessors four centuries ago, seem constrained or determined to unveil.

Two prominent causes of the moral decline of Athens may be specified, the disorder of sexual relations and slavery. The critical significance of this last point is rather apt to be overlooked. It really divides the Greek from every variety of modern life by an impassable gulf, and renders all social or political analogies to a great extent nugatory or misleading. When we recollect that all mechanical labour, whatever was esteemed βάναυσον, or unfit for a gentleman, was devolved on a helot class immensely outnumbering the little community of free citizens, it becomes at once evident that the Athenian democracy in its most democratic days was, as compared with any form of political life we are familiar with, in one sense, a close and oppressive aristocracy. On the moral degradation of Greek, and still more of later Roman society, to which this absolute domination over a subject class offered such fatal facilities, we need not dwell here. Nor was that by any means the only cause of the evil. On one part of the subject it is difficult for an English writer to speak in detail. It has been treated with great tact and discrimination, both in its darker and its nobler aspects—for he shows that it had a nobler side—by Mr. Mahaffy in his *Social Life in Greece*. But we may observe here that it has a direct bearing on one prominent contrast of Christian and classical art. As Winckelmann remarked, "the supreme beauty of Greek art is rather male than female," and sculpture is as far superior to painting in the capacity of expressing masculine vigour and beauty as painting is superior to sculpture in the expression of feminine grace. This is undoubtedly one reason why sculpture has always been regarded as distinctively Pagan, and painting as distinctively Christian, the Pagan instinct delighting rather to glorify the masculine and the Christian instinct the feminine qualities, both moral and physical.

Here again our modern Renaissance naturally manifests its unmistakable preference for the Pagan or Hellenic as distinguished from the specifically Christian type of excellence. It is not of course the recognition of masculine virtues, which must have their place and value under every system, but the depreciation—amounting both in ancient Greece and Rome almost to simple contempt—of the feminine type, which is in fault. This one-sided conception of excellence culminated philosophically in the hard and pitiless Stoic ideal, while it lent itself no less readily to the popular canonization of Harmodius and Aristogeiton. And there are not wanting ominous signs of a tendency in the bastard Renaissance of our own day to reproduce the twin characteristics so inseparably united under that old civilisation which is its prototype—reckless cruelty and unbridled license. Both forms of selfishness, for they have a common root, were abundantly exemplified in the literature and the life of the Italian Hellenists of the fifteenth century; the latter is exhibited with an almost incredible shamelessness, far exceeding the worst passages of Ovid or Martial, in the *Lusus Quinque Poetarum in Venerem*, notably in the *Hermaphroditus* of Beccadelli, which nevertheless was much admired by contemporary scholars. Both have found at least literary expression in the "debased Hellenism" of our own. It might not even be a difficult, however ungracious, task to point to ugly revelations which suggest that in some quarters these neo-Pagan aspirations are beginning already to be translated into act. But it must suffice to have struck a note of warning, not at all before it was required.

VI

THE ROMAN EMPIRE AND THE CHURCH.

AN interesting paper by Professor Zeller of Berlin, on the "Contest of Heathenism with Christianity as reflected in Greek and Roman Literature,"[1] bears on a cognate question to that dealt with by M. Renan, both in his Hibbert Lectures and in a review article already noticed on the Emperor Hadrian. Considering that the period referred to includes the golden age of Roman, which is itself a borrowed reflection from the golden age of Greek literature, it may seem strange at first sight that any such "contest" should occur. For the literature of an age expresses and represents its highest civilisation, and in Greece and Rome posterity has agreed to recognise the representative civilisation of the ancient world. But Christianity and civilisation unquestionably have much in common in their idea, their methods, and their history. Christianity, it has been justly observed, waited till the world had attained its most perfect form before it appeared, and it soon coalesced and has ever since co-operated, and often seemed identical, with the civilisation which is its companion. Both alike are based on common ideas, have common

[1] See *Contemporary Review* for May 1877.

views and principles, and a common standard of appeal, for the classics and the studies rising out of the classics are to the one what Scripture and the Creeds are to the other. If Christianity has its patriarchs and apostles, Homer may be considered the patriarch, and the great Greek poets of a later age the apostles and evangelists, of the typical culture of the human race. We must say Greek, for the fact, already referred to, that the best Latin literature and philosophy were mainly a transcript from the Greek, seems to indicate that—according to the familiar saying of Horace — the Attic writers were destined to be, as they have in fact proved, the teachers and schoolmasters of all future generations. Civilisation, to use theological language, is in the natural what Christianity is in the supernatural order, and there surely need not be, and ought not to be, any clash or "contest" between them. Nevertheless, while in the long run they have coalesced and co-operated, their aims are not identical, and as every power has an inevitable tendency to encroach beyond its own legitimate boundaries, there have often been quarrels between the two. The almost chronic conflict of Church and State, though it involves other questions also of a purely dynastic kind, is in a wider sense part of the same great dichotomy. But the differences, whatever they be, between Christianity and culture, and between the ecclesiastical and civil order, which are constantly reappearing in various forms, have never since culminated in so violent and radical a divergence as during the first three centuries of our era, when the brilliant but deeply corrupted civilisation of the mighty Empire, already sinking into premature decrepitude, was pitted against the vigorous and growing life of the nascent Church. It is to that contest, so far as it is reflected in the literature of the period, that Professor Zeller would call our attention, and there is much that is fresh and suggestive in his handling of a familiar theme.

He begins by pointing out—what naturally follows from what has been already said—that the new religion was not without many points of contact with the mental tendencies and needs of the age. It had really in some respects more in common with Hellenic culture than with Judaism; and it certainly had much in common, in spite of important contrasts, with the Stoic philosophy, whence the story became current—for which there is no real evidence, nor even the slightest probability—that Seneca, if not secretly a Christian, was at least partly indebted to the teaching of St. Paul. It is thus the more remarkable that Christianity should have appeared to all classes of Roman society something simply and unmixedly abhorrent. "The Christians in the first place were Atheists"; and "Down with the Atheists" was the cry which rung round St. Polycarp's martyr stake at Smyrna. Being atheists, they were of course obnoxious to the charge of every form of atrocious crime, and hence the horrible and grotesque fables of their worshipping an ass's head, their Thyestean banquets, and their orgies of nameless obscenity. Even the great critical historian Tacitus thinks it perfectly natural that "a sect universally hated for their shameful deeds" should be credited, though untruly, with the burning of Rome. But to him, as to his more intellectual contemporaries generally, their original sin was not atheism but superstition, though they were not the less for that "the enemies of the human race." Atheism and fanaticism were indeed only different forms, suited to the capacity of the vulgar or the learned, of conveying the same indictment; the real offence was that Christians were monotheists. We have heard of a modern writer, whose zeal considerably outran his knowledge and his logic, beginning his attack on the doctrine of eternal punishment with a disclaimer of any desire to adjudicate between the opposite alternatives of Universalism or annihilationism, though he might have known that the rival theories are, if possible, more absolutely incompatible with each other than with the doctrine they are intended to supplant. In the same way the Romans did not seriously care to discriminate between the merits of atheism and polytheism; the latter was the established cult; the former, if we may trust Juvenal, was in his day the general belief. But whether it was more reasonable to worship many gods or to reverence none, it was equally opposed to reason and to "civism"—to adopt a later phrase—to believe in One God. It was, as Professor Zeller rightly observes, its monotheism that placed Christianity in undisguised enmity to the national religion.

But the root of this enmity lay deeper than any purely theological ideas in the national mind. We have seen that Tacitus considered the Christians a sect of loathsome and criminal fanatics, though he admits their innocence of the particular crime, of setting fire to the city, for which they were being executed. Pliny, who knew better, did not share this opinion. He had no special fault to find with the Christians, except the one unpardonable sin of resisting the State religion, to which they opposed their own

"strange and absurd superstition"; but for this treason-
able conduct he thought they deserved death, when it was
judicially brought home to them.   And Trajan, whose
mandate governed for a hundred and fifty years the policy
of Rome in the matter, approved his view of the case.
All other religions were compatible with the established
worship; this one alone maintained a resolute isolation,
and Christians, whatever their virtues or their vices, "could
not be permitted to break the laws against making proselytes and against unauthorized societies."   The way in
which they held together among themselves, and their care
to hold aloof, as far as possible, from the heathen world
around, conveyed to an outsider, educated or uneducated,
the impression of a secret society, a conspiracy against
the established order of things.   And that feeling was
deepened among the higher classes by their well-known
practice of recruiting their ranks from slaves, freedmen,
and artisans, with whom they associated on terms of
equality, but whom their masters looked down upon with
a contempt which is but faintly reflected in the feelings
of a Southern slaveowner in former days towards his
niggers.   Here we touch at last upon the root of that
hopeless estrangement between the Empire and the Church
which, if it occasionally smouldered, broke out again and
again into fierce energy during three centuries of more or
less persistent persecution.   A true, though at first unconscious, instinct taught the ruling classes that there was a
vital antagonism between the new faith and the existing
national order, which must sooner or later issue in the
destruction of one or the other.   And therefore a well-
known remark in Dr. Arnold's *Lectures on Modern History*

must be regarded as only a half truth, though it may seem to a casual reader to be partly endorsed by Dr. Döllinger in his *First Age of the Church*. That the Christians "were punished, not as men who might change the laws of Rome hereafter, but as men who disobeyed them now," is true of the conscious and immediate motive of the early persecutors; it is only very partially true of the later and more intelligent representatives of the same policy. Dr. Döllinger says, with his usual accuracy, that "the authorities and philosophers did not *for some time* understand clearly how completely the Christian Church was the rival of the Roman State, or they would not only have persecuted by fits and starts"; but the very form of expression implies that they began to discern this after-wards. And so only can we account for the startling fact, at first so perplexing, that Marcus Aurelius, the best of the Emperors and one whose character and belief had much of moral and even religious affinity to Christianity, was the severest of persecutors, and denounced the constancy of the Christian martyrs as proceeding from "mere defiance."

If we come to later Roman writers, we find the sceptical and worldly Lucian content to sneer at the foolish and fanciful fanaticism of the Christian sect. His Platonist friend Celsus takes a much more serious view of the matter, and charges them and their Founder with deliberate imposture; but the head and front of their offending is still, as in the days of Tacitus—though it is expressed in less vehement language—their exclusiveness, their want of patriotism. Originally apostates from the national faith of Judaism, they were accused of remaining indifferent or hostile to the welfare of the Roman State. After the middle of the third century the antagonism to the new faith took a somewhat different form with the rise of the Neoplatonic philosophy. Philostratus and Porphyry and Hierocles display more of the critical and carping tone of modern sceptical writers, and are obliged to admit a good deal of truth in the system they assail. The brief and highly artificial attempt of Julian to galvanize the moribund Paganism into a new life was in fact based on an elaborate plagiarism from the despised "Galilean" superstition, which he both hated and feared, and, even had his reign not been prematurely cut short, was doomed from the nature of the case to inevitable failure. When St. Cyril wrote his ten books against Julian the last hope of Paganism had sunk into the grave with him, and thenceforth even literary attacks on Christianity gradually diminished. It is quite true, as Professor Zeller points out, that the heathen polemics have been revived by many recent assailants of the Gospel, but that is too wide a subject to enter upon here.

VII.

UNITY AND VARIETY IN CHURCH AND STATE.

THE problem and puzzle of all Governments, whether in Church or State, has been to combine authority with freedom, or in other words, variety of action with unity of principle and aim. For since individual judgments, tastes, and tendencies must always differ widely, a dead level of uniformity is the sure sign of stagnation or of tyranny. There is no necessary opposition between order and liberty, though they are popularly supposed to represent contrary if not incompatible ideas. There has been a good deal of talk of late years about Imperialism, but in its proper sense the word may be said to be obsolete. We have indeed in our own day seen the rise and fall of Empires so-called, both in the Old World and the New, and there are no less than three Emperors in Europe at this moment, but the distinction between a King and an Emperor is now little more than a verbal one. A King may be absolute like Louis XIV., and the powers of an Emperor may be strictly limited by constitutional checks, as is now the case in Austria. The last shadow of the old Imperialism disappeared, in the memory of some who are still living, with the formal extinction of the Holy

E

Roman Empire; the reality had departed centuries before.
For in truth Empire in the old sense—the sense in which
the Romans, from whom we have borrowed the term,
understood it—means a power that is or at least aspires to
become universal; and hence the difficulty common to all
governments of reconciling liberty and authority is under
such a rule enormously increased. It was this universal
domination which "the King," as the Greeks called the
Persian monarch, aimed at in his assault on their liberties,
to the acquisition of which Alexander, for whom "one
world was not sufficient," devoted the energies of his life,
and which was in large measure carried on for centuries,
though with very various degrees of stability and vigour,
under the sway of imperial Rome. And the rule of the
Cæsars was reproduced in theory and in name in the
Holy Roman Empire of mediæval Europe, which suggested
the ideal of Dante's *De Monarchiâ*, though it was never
more than an ideal very imperfectly realised. The counter-
acting principle of liberty was supplied then not only by
the action of independent States, but still more by the
spiritual power, which through the long strife of Guelf
and Ghibelline represented, on the whole and in the long
run, the cause of moral and intellectual freedom as opposed
to brute force. The *imperium* and *sacerdotium* were regarded in mediæval theology as the opposite poles of a
great cosmopolitan system for the government of mankind.
All later attempts to revive the scheme of universal empire,
which was supposed to be the best guarantee for universal
peace and happiness, have been temporary and spasmodic,
and have passed away with their authors. It was certainly
the ideal of Charlemagne and of Napoleon, possibly of

Charles V., and of Maximilian. But the conditions of the modern world are fatal to its success.

There is one institution, however, which has survived the wreck of dynasties and empires, and which from the nature of the case can hardly help laying claim to this cosmopolitan character; that is the Christian Church. One of Cardinal Newman's old Oxford Sermons is entitled " The Christian Church an Imperial Power," and he explains in the discourse that by a kingdom is meant "a body politic, bound together by common laws, ruled by one head, holding intercourse part with part, acting together " ; and that this particular kingdom or empire was to be international and coextensive with the world, including all that is ordinarily involved in the idea of a great empire—extended dominion, warfare on its enemies, aggression, acts of judgment and the like. And such no doubt the Christian Church has shown itself in history. It follows then that the same problem which has perplexed civil governments, and has proved fatal to the continuance of a system of universal dominion, will recur here also. Nor can any student of ecclesiastical history fail to observe the constant struggle carried on, in various forms and with very various alternations of success, between the rival principles of authority and independence. The conflicts of national Churches with the sovereign jurisdiction of Council, Pope, or Patriarch claiming their allegiance, of religious orders with bishops or Popes, of heretics or reputed heretics with ecclesiastical tribunals, and of " the lay element " generally with the clerisy, are all examples of the same standing rivalry. It is obvious of course that, when the contest is pushed on either side beyond a certain point, it becomes fatal to the maintenance of unity. After several centuries of intermittent conflict and compromise the Eastern Patriarchates finally repudiated the advancing claims of the Papacy, and a similar contention issued at a later period in the disruption of Western Christendom into its Latin and Teutonic elements. With the theological or controversial aspect of these questions we are not here concerned. The rival but complementary principles which in this relation may for convenience sake be designated Catholic and Protestant, the centripetal and centrifugal forces, must ever coexist in the Church as in the State, and in either sphere the great problem of sound statesmanship is to harmonize the two without sacrificing the due interests of organization on the one hand or of liberty on the other. But it is a common temptation of rulers ecclesiastical and civil to imperil both alike by confounding uniformity with unity. This is one of the stock charges of Protestant controversialists against the Church of Rome, but it has in fact a wider application. The French Minister of Public Instruction who boasted that at the same minute, which he could tell by looking at his watch, the children in every school in the country were learning the same lesson, and the French bishop who boasted that his clergy was an army to which he had simply to give the word of command, "March, and they march," betrayed a common addiction to the regimental method of administration. Uniformity was their notion of unity.

It has been for many years past a cherished object of Ultramontane zeal to suppress every lingering trace of diversity, whether in great matters or small, within the Roman pale; and accordingly during the last pontificate,

in deference to such wishes, all the various diocesan " uses "
in France—many of them in the opinion of competent
judges very superior to the Roman use—were suppressed
one after another. The Paris Breviary, well known to
liturgiologists without as well as within the Latin Church,
was buried in the grave of Archbishop Darboy. Yet three
centuries ago not even St. Charles Borromeo, the saintly
and strictly Ultramontane Archbishop of Milan, would
consent to sacrifice the Ambrosian rite, which may be
witnessed there to this day; and the Eastern Uniates
may perhaps prove equally firm in refusing to surrender
rites, which are more distinctive and probably older than
the Ambrosian. But we merely refer to the matter here
in illustration of a general principle. If national and
local specialities are not to be tolerated, even in ritual
minutiæ where confessedly no difference of doctrine is at
stake, we may recognise at once the narrow and impolitic
temper which pursues uniformity at the risk of schism.
The Church, which is described in prophecy as *circum-
amicta varietatibus*, was not weaker but stronger for all
important purposes when it included in one visible body
a variety of disciplinary and liturgical arrangements, as
well as of nationalities, and the attempt to enforce a
rigid uniformity of detail has ended in creating a diversity
of communions and creeds. In the State, as we have
seen, the scheme of an ecumenical empire has long since
been abandoned as impracticable, however plausible in
theory. In the Church, as the organ of a religion which
claims to be universal, the principle must always be upheld, but it has now and again been so applied as to limit
her range of comprehension by snapping the cord till it

broke. To use theological language, Catholicity has been
sacrificed to Ultramontanism. How far precisely the contrast between the Christendom of the early ages and the
modern "spirit of disruption," which not only acquiesces
but glories in "the Protestantism of the Protestant religion
and the dissidence of Dissent," may be due to this cause is
too wide an inquiry to be undertaken here. But we cannot
be wrong in assuming that what has proved a fatal difficulty of imperialism in the State has also very seriously
affected the policy and fortunes of the Church.

In this respect, as in some others, a certain analogy may
be traced between the Greece and Rome alike of ancient and
of modern times. That imperial instinct, which the great
Latin poet claimed as the proud prerogative of his people,
reappears under new conditions in the steady advance and
strong hand of the Roman pontificate ; there is the same
political temper, the same tenacity of purpose, the same
subordination of the abstract and ideal to the practical, the
same stern intolerance of rivalry or opposition ; the *Ponti-
fex Maximus* of the new order inherited the sceptre of the
Cæsars. Greece, on the other hand, in the classic age was
the home of philosophy, not the seat of empire ; it was split
up into a number of rival States, jealous of their separate
independence and refusing all common organization, till
they fell under a foreign yoke. And the Greek Church in
like manner was the fruitful mother of speculative theology,
not the "mother and mistress" of an ecclesiastical commonwealth ; its several Patriarchates were independent of
each other, and would acknowledge none but an honorary
primacy either in the Old or the New Rome ; its schools
were the hotbeds of heresy as well as the nurseries of

sacred learning; it aspired to shape the thought, not to rule the destinies, of Christendom. There have been Greek theologians and preachers who might rival the subtlety of Plato and the eloquence of Demosthenes, but no line of imperial pontiffs has sat on the thrones of Alexandria or Constantinople. If the instinct of dominion has been the ruling principle of the Latin Church, the secret alike of its weakness and its strength, the energies of the East have been absorbed and often wasted in controversial discussion ; it has produced no Hildebrand and provoked the opposi⁻ tion of no Luther. And as ancient Greece, from lack of internal coherence and power of organization, fell a prey first to a Macedonian and then to a Roman master, so has the Eastern Church too often succumbed to the despotism of the Sultan or the Czar. But we need not pursue the parallel further. Enough has been said to show how, alike in secular and sacred history, East and West exhibit the con⁻ trast of an individuality tending to anarchy and a central⁻ ization hardening into despotism. An imperial *régime* that shall combine the excellences and avoid the faults of both extremes has been the dream of philosophical statesmen, since Plato imagined a republic where philosophers should reign, and Aristotle sketched the idea of the παμβασιλεὺς who should be absolute in power as in justice. But the world has long since resigned all expectation of seeing the ideal carried out in practice; "the balance of power" has replaced the *Monarchia* of Dante. It is not so easy for religious minds, familiarized with the old conception of a *Civitas Dei*, to abandon all hope of witnessing in the Chris⁻ tendom of the future the harmonious co-ordination of principles which in their divorce have been subject to so much perverse exaggeration. This perfect consummation however belongs as yet to the region of unfulfilled prophecy; perhaps we must wait for St. Malachy's *Pastor Angelicus*—who ought to come fifth in succession from the present Pontiff—to make it a reality.

VIII.

LATIN CHRISTIANITY.

DEAN MILMAN'S well-known history of the mediæval Church is entitled the *History of Latin Christianity*. There is a fitness in the title, though in one sense it is open to exception. The author uses it to distinguish the Western from the Eastern Church, and he has no doubt purposely chosen a term which indicates that the distinction is something more than a geographical one. It is true that for several centuries the Christian Church received its impress, as it had derived its origin, mainly from the East. The great majority of the early Fathers and theologians, and several even of the early Popes, as Dr. Milman has pointed out, were Greeks. All the seven Councils which met before the great schism were assembled in Eastern cities, and occasioned by Eastern heresies. Pelagianism was the first heresy that stirred the West, and characteristically enough it concerned, not the nature of God, but the free will of man. On the other hand, the mediæval Councils of Western Christendom were concerned much more with discipline than with doctrine. The subtleties of Greek theology and of Greek heresy were alike alien to the sterner and more practical spirit which the Roman Catholic Church inherited from the Republic and the Empire.

The first Eastern Council was summoned to define the nature of the Trinity; the first recorded decree of a Latin Pope, about half a century later, was to enjoin, what the East had never admitted, the celibacy of the priesthood. The words of the Roman poet describe no less the distinctive genius of the Roman Church than of the Roman people :—

> Tu regere imperio populos, Romane, memento;
> Hæ tibi erunt artes.

And accordingly, from the first, if Eastern influences were most powerful in shaping the creed, it was left to the West to organize the polity of Christendom.   M. Guizot says somewhere that the Church is a great idea ; the dominant aim of the Papacy has been to make it a great fact.   It is not, therefore, without a special meaning that the history of the mediæval Church is called the history of Latin Christianity.   As the old intellectual civilisation of the East succumbed before the inroads of the barbarians, there were no renovating influences at work to give it a fresh lease of life.   Action had never been its strong point, and from the time of Photius, in whom the expiring flame shot up with a bright but evanescent radiance, its vigour of thought seems also to have died out.   Thenceforth Eastern Christianity presents at best a spectacle of sterile conservatism ; we have to look to its rival for that capability of progressive development and adaptation to successive emergencies which is an inseparable attribute of all healthy life, whether mental or moral.   If we compare either the monasticism or the theology of the two great divisions of Christendom from the eighth century onwards, the same conclusion is forced upon us.   There may be much that is open to criticism in both systems, but no one who will contrast the dull stagnation of an Egyptian Laura, or the passive immobility of the peopled solitude of Mount Athos, unbroken still by the revolutions of ages in the living world around, with the studious labours of Monte Cassino or St. Maur, or the active zeal of a Jesuit or Franciscan community, can fail to note the radical difference between them. There is an almost ludicrous perversity in the popular Protestant misconception of the cloister, as a mere refuge of broken hearts, fainting spirits, and crushed affections. It is certainly true that the most prominent characteristic of the Western monks was *power*, and that the cell was to them as really a battle-field as the world they had in one sense abandoned. And it is therefore a mistake of Montalembert's to attribute the origin of the monastic life, as far as they are concerned, solely, or chiefly, to a desire for solitude. Bernard from his cell at Clairvaux was the adviser of popes, the healer of schisms, the mouthpiece of synods, the protagonist of Catholic orthodoxy, and helped—alike in matters ecclesiastical and civil—to control the destinies of Europe. Such was mediæval monasticism in its Latin form. Nor can the later Eastern Church offer any parallel to the huge edifice of scholastic theology, which tasked and tested the logical acuteness of contemporary thinkers in the West, however limited may have been the permanent result. St. John of Damascus in the eighth century was her last theologian.

These considerations abundantly suffice to explain, if not to justify, Dr. Milman's use of the term Latin Christianity. But, without explanation, there is serious danger of its misleading us. It must not be forgotten that, if the Roman Pontiffs inherited much of the imperial and organizing spirit of the Cæsars, to whose throne they succeeded, there would have been little opportunity of giving practical effect to their policy, had not a very different element come into play to supplement and regenerate the decaying energies of the Latin race. The barbarian hordes who swept down from the North, and, like the ancient Romans in their conflict with Greece, were vanquished by the civilisation of those they had conquered in war, added much more than a merely numerical force to the Church of their adoption. Little of the stern old Roman spirit survived among the Italians of the fourth and fifth centuries. They retained the passive virtues of submission and obedience, but the vigour, the energy, the self-reliance to which, quite as much as to the organizing genius of Rome, Christianity owed its noblest conquests in the middle ages, were the contribution of the Teutonic nations to the religion which had reclaimed them from barbarism. And, broadly speaking, the Teutonic and Latin elements parted company at the Reformation. While, therefore, we may in one sense speak all along of the Latin as synonymous with the Western Church, it is, at least as true to say, in another sense, that the Roman Catholic Church became the Latin Church after the Council of Trent. At that period, in the words of the great, historian of the Papacy, it "owned the circumscription of its dominion; it gave up all claims upon the Greeks and the East, and Protestantism it repudiated with countless anathemas." No doubt, as Ranke immediately adds, "in thus limiting the field of its operations, it concentrated its strength and braced up all its energies." But the limitation, both morally and materially, was a very important one.

In his work on *The Church and the Churches*, published in 1861, Dr. Döllinger observes that, " as each new and vigorous population enters into the Church, she becomes *not only numerically but dynamically enriched.* Every people, in whatever way gifted, contributes its share in religious experience, ecclesiastical customs, interpretations of Christian doctrine, in its impress on life and science. It adds thus to the great Church capital which is the product of former times and older nationalities." Cardinal Newman says, in the *Apologia*, with still more direct reference to our immediate subject :—" The multitude of nations who are in the fold of the Church will be found to have acted for its protection against any narrowness (if so be) in the . various authorities at Rome. . . . It stands to reason that, as the Gallican Church has in it an element of France, so Rome must have in it an element of Italy. It seems to me that Catholicity is not only one of the notes of the Church, but, according to the divine purpose, one of its securities. . . I trust that all European races will ever have a place in the Church, and assuredly I think that *the loss of the English, not to say the German element,* in its composition, has been a serious misfortune." In other words, the combination of various races, with their diversities of national character, contributed not only numerically but morally—or, as Dr. Döllinger words it, dynamically—to the strength of the great whole whereof they became constituent portions. And in this sense " the Teutonic element " was lost to the Roman Catholic Church at the Reformation. It is true that several million Germans and several million English-speaking Celts, as well as a small fraction of Anglo-Saxons, still remain in her communion.   But the merest tyro in Church history is aware how infinitesimal since that date has been the influence of the Teutonic mind on her intellectual or moral life.   In the middle ages, as we have seen, the Teutonic peoples supplied the very life-blood of the body they joined on their con-version.   It was the German Emperors in the eleventh century whose aid was invoked, and who, by procuring the election of German Popes, largely contributed to raise the Papacy—after that " iron age " when it was currently said that " Christ was sleeping in the ship "—to the highest point of authority over the conscience and convictions of Europe it has ever attained.   The reforming Councils of the fifteenth century were convoked and carried on, and the Council of Trent was summoned, under German influences. But the latter came too late to arrest the Protestant revolt, and the Church tightened her grasp on the Latin race, in despair of recovering the Teutonic.   The German element would count for little in a General Council now ; German Catholic divines, however eminent, have long been viewed with something more than suspicion by the authorities at Rome.   For the last three centuries of the Latin Church, her administration, her theology, her devotional literature, and the ruling spirit of her whole religious life, have almost exclusively represented what Cardinal Newman calls the Italian element.   And this dominant Italianism it has been the persistent aim of the Ultramontane school to import into England ; even the Italian language has been extolled as peculiarly sacred, or Catholic, or "dear to Catholic hearts."

One cause which has largely contributed to the prevalence of this exclusive spirit in the Church, is the fact that for three centuries and a half none but Italians have sat in the chair of St. Peter—Adrian VI. was the last foreign Pope—and that hence also the great majority of the Cardinals, who are the special Senate or Privy Council of the reigning Pontiff, as well as the electors of his successor, have also usually been Italians. And there was at least a plausible ground for this while the Pontiff was an Italian Sovereign. But it is noteworthy here that there are already signs of change. Of the twenty Cardinals named by Leo XIII. nine are non-Italian, one of them being Cardinal Newman, while of the fifty-eight members at this moment composing the Sacred College no less than twenty-six—between half and a third—are also citizens of other States than Italy. Of these last three are English, one Irish, and one American, giving a much larger proportion of English-speaking Cardinals than at any previous period either before or since the Reformation : there has seldom indeed been more than one at a time. Much will probably depend in the future of Catholicism on the influence of the Teutonic element among the advisers and electors of the chief Pastor of the Church.

IX.

RISE AND GROWTH OF ULTRAMONTANISM.

FEW things are so remarkable, when we penetrate at all beneath the mere surface aspect of events, as the silent revolutions of history, and the unnoticed and seemingly insignificant or accidental agencies on which they so often depend. No doubt there are occasional cataclysms in the moral as in the material universe; but for the most part what Newton said of the order of nature is true equally of the progressive sequence of national, as of individual, life— *Continuo, non vero per saltum.* The most momentous changes in the character of a society or an institution are accomplished quietly; the old order passes and the new succeeds, but it " cometh not with observation," and is only recognised long afterwards in its results. We can point to the Edict of Milan as marking the precise date of the public recognition of Christianity, yet it did but proclaim and sanction the ultimate issue of a process which had been secretly working for centuries. Had that recognition of the triumph of the new faith over the old civilisation come from Marcus Aurelius, instead of from Constantine—and it looks like a mere accident that it did not—who can calculate the difference it might have made in the subsequent history of Christendom? We can point our finger again, if

not to the exact year, to the very decade, somewhere
between 835 and 845, when the Isidorian forgeries were
compiled in the province of Tours, and palmed off on the
patient credulity of an uncritical age; but it was not for
centuries that their full significance was revealed in the
altered relations of the Papal See to the hierarchy, and the
final estrangement of East and West.   It is not, however,
to the spurious Decretals—still less, as is popularly but
most mistakenly imagined, to Hildebrand—that Ultramontanism owes its rise.   Gregory VII., whatever his faults,
was far too great a man, both morally and intellectually, to
stoop to the vulgar ambition of ruling as a despot over
willing slaves; and the system so often associated, both by
his admirers and his enemies, with his name, can lay no
claim to so venerable an antiquity or so distinguished a
parentage.   He sought to work out in practice, imperfectly
enough, no doubt, but honestly and in accordance with the
needs and circumstances of his day, that ideal of the " City
of God " which had floated as a glorious vision before the
greatest mind of the ancient Church.   It was no part of
his aim to convert the Church into a vast bureaucratic
despotism, with a well-drilled episcopal police obedient to
every intimation of the unseen hand that pulls the wires at
the Vatican.   He left it for lesser men and a later age to
essay the Tarquinian policy of cutting down all the taller
poppy-heads, and importing into the ecclesiastical government that vicious centralisation which has been the bane
of so many secular States.   Gregory desired to strengthen
the hands of metropolitans and primates, whose influence
it afterwards became the policy of his successors to
depress, partly by curtailing their privileges, and partly by

F

multiplying their number; so that at the present day there is one archbishop on an average for every four or five bishops of the Latin rite throughout the world, nor is there—since the suppression of the old Gallican hierarchy —a single province containing as many suffragans as were originally assigned by Gregory the Great to the primates of Canterbury and York.   But we are anticipating.

The etymology of the term "Ultramontane", as indicating a party or principle dominant "beyond the Alps," meaning an Italian one, sufficiently reveals its Northern origin, in the theological application which for the last four centuries has attached to it.   At an earlier period it had been used in Italy, but in a purely geographical sense, to describe nations lying to the north of the Alps.[1] In the century immediately preceding the Reformation, when the demand, more loudly uttered from day to day, for "a reform of the Church in her head and in her members" had become the watchword of all serious men, there was passing over her whole spirit and constitution one of those silent changes, the origin and growth of which it is not difficult to trace, but which has not yet attained its final issue.   The "seventy years' captivity" of Avignon in the thirteenth century, and the schism of the anti-Popes which followed directly on its close, had forced on practical men the important inquiry, where the supreme authority of the Church must be held to reside?   Was it in a Pope or a Council?   The question received an authoritative answer when, in 1409, the Council of Pisa, acting in the spirit of

[1] Thus, e. g., Urban VI., in 1378, "openly avowed his design to make so large a nomination (of Cardinals) that the Italians should recover their ascendency over the Ultramontanes." (Milman, *Lat. Christ.* viii. 42.)

Gerson's famous work *De Auferibilitate Papæ*, deposed both the rival Pontiffs, and appointed Alexander V. in their place; and again, eight years later, when the Council of Constance, having deposed two Popes and extorted the resignation of a third, proceeded to elect Martin V. to the chair of St. Peter. Had the principle then affirmed been consistently upheld—and, above all, had not the Council of Constance, against the urgent reclamations of its most earnest members, elected first to appoint a new Pope, who at once dissolved it, and leave the reformation of the Church to be taken up afterwards—the future of Christian history might have been very different from what it actually was. In checking all reforms that did not emanate from themselves exclusively, and in drawing continually tighter the reins of the central autocracy, Martin V. and his successors were at once sowing the seeds of Ultramontanism and of the Reformation. From that time forward the depression of national Churches, the exaltation of purely Papal authority, and the fatal plan of seeking to get rid of scandals not by correction of abuses but by silencing complaints, became the normal policy of the Roman Court. It has been said, with substantial if not with technical accuracy—and we are of course exclusively concerned with the matter here in its historical, not its theological, aspect—that whereas hitherto the Popes had claimed extraordinary, they henceforth claimed ordinary, jurisdiction over national Churches.

This may be illustrated from the history of the English Church during the century which intervened between the Council of Constance and the complete severance with Rome under Henry VIII. Indeed the struggle between the rival systems, though seldom breaking out

into open antagonism, forms the chief element in the
ecclesiastical history of the period. The appointment of
Cardinal Beaufort to the purple, without consent of the
Crown, and the attempt to make him legate *a latere*, was
the first encroachment, and was resisted, with only partial
success, by Archbishop Chicheley. When, soon afterwards,
Kemp, Archbishop of York, was made a cardinal, the Pope
ruled that he should take precedence, as such, of the
Primate of all England, on the curious ground that the
Cardinals were "those venerable priests mentioned by Moses
in Deuteronomy, and that they were afterwards instituted
by St. Peter"; which reminds one of M. About's equally
remarkable statement, at the opening of his pamphlet on
the Roman Question, that "the Catholic Church is governed by a Pope and seventy Cardinals, in memory of
Christ and the twelve Apostles." Thenceforth till the
Reformation, some bishop — who was usually, but not
always, the Primate—was made legate *a latere* in England,
and three of the Archbishops of Canterbury—Kemp, who
was translated from York, Bouchier, and Morton—were
also Cardinals. It was as Cardinal Legates, not as national
Primates, that they were to exercise supreme ecclesiastical
authority in the country; and this of course immensely
increased the actual power of the Pope, who began to interfere much more than before in episcopal appointments and
other matters. The last effective resistance made to the
new system occurred in Henry VI.'s reign, in the case of
Pecock, Bishop of Chichester, whom Foxe, with characteristic blundering (probably in this case ignorant rather than
dishonest), has metamorphosed into a Protestant martyr.
He had, in fact, excited general opposition by his extreme

Ultramontane views, as we should call them now; maintaining among other things, what was then a startling novelty, though it has since been revived by some of the Jesuit divines, that the Papacy is the sole Divine institution in the Church, and the Episcopate a creation, not of Christ, but of the Pope. Pecock was charged with seeking to change the religion of England, and was censured for heresy and imprisoned; but his leading principles afterwards prevailed. It was by Papal authority only that Archbishop Morton and Archbishop Warham assumed the visitatorial functions which served to expose but not to remedy the crying abuses of the existing monastic institutions. In Henry VII.'s reign indulgences were publicly hawked about for sale in England, under sanction of a papal bull, by one John de Gigliis, for all sorts of crimes, including simony, theft, murder, and uncleanness. Meanwhile in Italy Pius II., who had abandoned the opinions as well as the name of Æneas Silvius on ascending the papal throne, condemned in a bull with the ominous title of *Execrabilis* the appeal from a Pope to a General Council, thus annulling on his own authority the principle affirmed at three General Councils held during his own lifetime.[1]

[1] The claim of Pisa to be reckoned among the General Councils has been subsequently called in question by Ultramontane writers, and is still made matter of dispute, but no doubt was entertained about it at the time by the Council itself, by Pope Alexander V., whom it elected in place of the two rival claimants it deposed, or in Europe generally. The decrees entitle it "Sancta et Universalis Synodus, Universalem Ecclesiam repræsentans," and the Bull of Alexander sanctions them as "Universalis Ecclesiæ auctoritate et corcordiâ facta." Milman justly describes it as "the most august assembly as to the number and rank of the Prelates, and the Ambassadors of Christian Kings, which for centuries had assumed the functions of a representative Senate of Christendom" (*Lat. Christ.* viii. 114). Bishop Maret (*Du Concile Général*, i. 380) says, " Légitime dans sa convocation, le

In Spain the practical fruits of the new system were exhibited in the establishment of the Inquisition ; the earliest
auto-da-fè was held at Seville in 1481, and no less than two
thousand heretics were burnt in that year.

The first epoch of Ultramontanism, which commenced
with the Council of Constance, closed with the Council
of Trent. For a while the two principles hung in the
balance, and had the counsels of men like Pole and
Contarini prevailed, who strove to avoid by timely con-
cessions the consummation of the religious schism, there
can be little doubt that a *bonâ fide* reformation of at
least the graver practical corruptions would have followed,
and the Teutonic element would have conquered for
itself its natural place and recognition in the development
of the Catholic Church. But it was not to be. The
movement which rent half Europe from the obedience of
Rome riveted the chain of Latinism all the more tightly
on the half which retained its allegiance. If the Isidorian
Decretals of the ninth century had done much to pre-
cipitate the severance of East and West, and in doing so
paved the way for the growing pretensions which culminated in the Ultramontane movement of the fifteenth, that
movement, in contributing to the success of the Reformation, was also preparing its own temporary ascendency

Concile de Pise fut général dans sa composition, car il représenta vérit-
ablement l'Eglise Universelle. *On ne peut douter de cette universalité*,"
&c. Hefele indeed declines to acknowledge it, but on grounds the
reverse of convincing, and which would prove equally fatal to the
claims of other mediæval Councils (such as Constance, *e. g.*) whose title
has not been seriously impugned in the West. Even the Ultramontane
Bellarmine, while he abstains from positively committing himself, was
too much of an historian not to call it a General Council, and he gives
very sufficient grounds for so regarding it.

within the more limited area still left to it. When the
Catholic became virtually the Latin Church, the victory
of Ultramontanism was an inevitable sequel, even if it
had not been avowedly one of the first aims of the
master mind of Ignatius, in organizing those indefatigable
"prætorians of the Papacy," of whom it has been said—
not by their enemies, but their admirers—that "for the
last three centuries the history of the Jesuit Order is the
history of the Catholic Church gone into Commission."
As the old methods of persecution became obsolete, the
new methods of spiritual terrorism and pious frauds came
in to take their place. It was dangerous to question any
doctrine asserted in the name of the Church, though it
might be merely the private opinion of an individual or
a school; and equally dangerous to admit any estimate
of facts discreditable to the Church, or to those who
claimed to represent her. Historians, like Rohrbacher,
or Audin, or Dom Guéranger, too plainly show that the
favourite temptation of theological partisans of all schools,
to lie "for the greater glory of God", has not yet lost its
charm. In one Roman Catholic country the struggle
between the rival systems was continued for two centuries
after the Reformation, and the great name of Bossuet is not
more illustrious for his eloquence than for his bold vindication of the national as opposed to the Ultramontane theory
of Catholicism.[1] But, in this as in other respects, the Revolution sealed the work of the Reformation, and with the
fall of the old Gallican Church the last corporate protest

- [1] Ultramontanism, in its contest with this later phase of Gallicanism,
has been defined by an impartial critic, as "a jealousy of liberties,
stimulated by an equal jealousy of authority."

against the modern pretensions of the Papacy was extinguished. A national Church's necessity is Rome's opportunity; and though the devout and high-minded Pius VII. deeply resented the pressure put upon him by Napoleon, and only yielded unwillingly at last, and to avoid greater evils, it is not the less certain that to sweep away at one stroke of the pen the hierarchy of a thousand years, and substitute another in its place, was an exercise of Papal power which as yet its extremest advocates had scarcely dared to claim. In an age like ours there could not well have occurred a contingency more favourable to the progress of those principles which the Church of Bossuet so resolutely resisted, but which the Church of the French Empire was content to make her own.

The Ultramontane movement gained a fresh impetus, not only from the incidents of the French Revolution, but from the line adopted by the reactionary school of Catholic apologists to which it gave birth, of whom De Maistre and Lamennais, in his orthodox phase, were the chief representatives. The latter, according to Bishop Maret, was, " even more than De Maistre, the true founder of modern Ultramontanism," and he illustrated in his later career what has too often proved the effect of such opinions on a sensitive nature and keen intellect. Of De Maistre Maret justly observes that "his mind was essentially and eminently *political*," and that his leading aim was to restore the principle of authority or sovereignty in the Divine order. Hence " the political dictatorship of the Popes, the theocracy of the middle ages, appeared to him the ideal of Christian society," and he advocated an extreme view of Papal infallibility—which had not then in any sense been authoritatively proclaimed—on grounds neither theological nor historical, but because "infallibility is identical with sovereignty." If the Pope was not infallible, room was left for an appeal against his judgment, whether to a Council or to conscience mattered little, for any appeal against the supreme authority savoured of revolution. It was therefore necessary in the nature of things that it should be infallible, if his argument is to be consistently applied, alike in Church and State. Indeed, he says expressly that "infallibility in the spiritual order and sovereignty in the temporal are terms perfectly synonymous." But to carry out these principles in detail was the work of a very different class of minds from De Maistre's, who would have turned in scorn or disgust from the petty jealousy of all local or personal independence which busies itself, *e. g.*, with the suppression of national liturgies, or the gagging of writers, however eminent, and however sincerely and intensely Catholic, who cannot frame their lips to re-echo its peculiar shibboleths. In an age when education is general, and the Inquisition is out of date, this sort of Ultramontanism can make little way with thoughtful minds. Already, indeed, a reaction has visibly set in against it, not from a sceptical or a Protestant point of view, but among the devoutest believers and deepest thinkers in the Church.

X.

LATIN HYMNOLOGY.

IT has been justly observed by a recent writer in the *Quarterly Review*,[1] that not the least important side of the history of the Christian Church is written in her hymns, that is of course the history of her internal development and religious life. "It is with a hymn that it opens, the sublime Canticle of the Incarnation, *Magnificat anima mea Dominum;* and in the Apocalyptic vision which presents the last glimpse of the City of God the glorious company gathered in adoration around the Immaculate Lamb have 'a new song' in their mouths." And hence, we may add, the *Benedictus* and *Magnificat*, the two great prophetic hymns of the Incarnation, have held from an early period a prominent place in the Lauds and Vespers respectively of the Latin Breviary, from which they were transferred to the English Prayer-book. Nor is it only the history of the Church, but the history of every great religious move-ment in the Church, that has been marked by a fresh outburst of hymnology. Two of the ancient Creeds, the Nicene and the *Quicunque vult*, are hymns as well as creeds, and may be said to celebrate an epoch in the onward march of the Church as well as in the elaboration of her doctrinal system. Thus Cardinal Newman speaks of the *Quicunque* as "the war-song of faith," celebrating

[1] *Quarterly Review*, July, 1882.

a triumph over its Arian assailants; "it is a psalm or
hymn of praise, of confession, and of profound, self-
prostrating homage, parallel to the canticles of the elect
in the Apocalypse; it appeals to the imagination quite
as much as to the intellect." And Dr. Arnold used to
call the Nicene Creed a "triumphant hymn of thanks-
giving," and made a point of having it always chanted
in the services of Rugby School Chapel. To come to
later times, the German Reformation owed quite as much
to the hymns of Luther, with their captivating double
rhymes, as to his translation of the Bible. The Wesleyan
revival again was largely indebted for its early successes
to the hymns of its founder, and it would be difficult
to exaggerate the influence of the *Christian Year* in
popularising the spirit and teachings of the more important movement which succeeded it. It is not indeed
too much to say that every religion, Christian or not, relies
more or less on its hymnology, as may be exemplified in
the Vedic songs of our Aryan ancestors, just as ballad
poetry, like the songs of Tyrtus, is a power in the early
history of almost every nation, whence the familiar saying,
"Give me the making of a nation's ballads, and I will
leave you the making of its laws." Our present concern,
however, is with what the *Quarterly* Reviewer calls the
mediæval, but what it is more correct to call the Latin
hymnology of the Church—for its origin dates from the
fourth century—or as Dean Church puts it, "that wonderful body of hymns to which age after age has contributed
its offering, from the Ambrosian hymn to the *Veni Sancte
Spiritus* of a King of France, the *Pange lingua* of Thomas
Aquinas, the *Dies Iræ* and the *Stabat Mater* of the two

Franciscan brethren, Thomas of Celano and Jacopone."
His predecessor, Dean Milman, observes that it "has a
singularly solemn and majestic tone." The late Mr. C.
Hemans, by the by, considered the *Stabat Mater* to be
more probably the composition of Pope Innocent III., a
century earlier, than of Jacopone. It is only natural then
that the great ecclesiastical revival of our own day should
have drawn the attention of learned writers, both German
and English, to this splendid treasure-house of old
Catholic devotion, the principal English contributors to
the subject being Cardinal Newman and the late Mr.
Isaac Williams, who both edited and translated the greater
part of the hymns as well of the Roman as of the Parisian
Breviary, Archbishop Trench, Mr. Digby Wrangham, who
has translated the poems of Adam of St. Victor, and the
late Dr. Neale, who both edited and translated many of
the Latin Hymns and Sequences, and discussed the general
question in a paper on "the Ecclesiastical Latin Poetry of
the Middle Ages" in the *Encyclopædia Metropolitana.* How
far indeed, and in what relative degree, these translations
or any of them are satisfactory, or how far again translated
hymns are as a rule suitable for use in public worship, are
questions which we cannot do more than glance at here.
All translation, and notably translation of poetry, is confessedly a difficult problem, and there can be no doubt that
the Latin hymns present peculiar difficulties to the trans-
lator, from the obvious fact that they are cast in the mould
not only of another language but of another age. It is
not easy to avoid the opposite dangers either of literal
exactness, which produces a stiff and pedantic version
wholly unsuited to popular singing, or of substituting

paraphrase for translation. And, as to the latter, it may be questioned whether original hymns embodying the same ideas would not really possess for English congregations more of the spontaneity and verve of the originals; to transfuse the spirit and idiom of a Latin hymn, whether of the fourth century or the twelfth, into a modern English hymn is—certainly not impossible, for it has sometimes at least been achieved, notably by Cardinal Newman and Dr. Neale—but is a task where failure is much more common than success. And here it may be well to put on record the righteous protest of John Wesley against the reckless and inexcusable—in many cases illegal—manipulations to which the makers of hymn-books, almost without exception, are wont to subject the compositions, original or translated, whether of living or departed authors, whom it pleases them to fancy they can adapt or improve :—

Many gentlemen have done my brother and me, though without naming us, the honour to reprint many of our hymns. Now they are perfectly welcome to do so, provided they print them just as they are. But I desire they would not attempt to mend them, for they really are not able. None of them is able to mend either the sense or the verse.

Both Dr. Neale and the late Dr. Faber, the great hymnologist of the day among English Catholics, and many of whose pieces have found their way into various Protestant compilations, found reason to make similar complaints, as well as other and less illustrious composers who have suffered from the same fraudulent dealing. But to return to the Latin Hymns.

It would be a complete misapprehension to look on the hymnology of Western Christendom as a corrupt and

deteriorated excrescence on the silver, or post-silver, age of
Latin Classicalism. It really represents a new language
created by the Church. Dr. Döllinger has called attention, in his *First Age of the Church*, to the change which
passed over the Greek language when "the richness,
depth, and speciality of Christian ideas constrained them
[Christian writers] to form a new terminology, not so
much by coining new words as by giving a new sense to
old ones." The Latin tongue, which became the vehicle
of theology and worship for the most powerful and energetic portion of the new community, underwent a yet more
thorough transformation, and nowhere perhaps does this
revolution show itself more conspicuously than in the
contrast between classical and Christian poetry. The
poetry of ancient Rome in its best estate had been a more
or less skilful imitation and adaptation of Greek models ;
poetry was not in any form germane to the Roman genius,
and could only flourish as a delicate exotic ; its graces
were artificial, and appealed exclusively to the learned
and the refined. There is no clear proof, begging Lord
Macaulay's pardon, that even in their national infancy the
stern nurslings of the she-wolf had any ballad poetry of
their own deserving the name. And a type of literature
so unreal in its origin and its form was the least fitted
for the exigencies of a popular religion. The leading
characteristic of Latin ecclesiastical poetry, from which all
its other peculiarities were ultimately derived, is the intense
and essential popularity of its construction. The strength
of the Gospel in those days of its early struggles and
advance lay not so much in the power of intellect, or the
force of logical demonstration, or the prestige of authority,

as in its appeal to man as man, to the *testimonium animæ naturaliter Christianæ;* in the answer it offered to the immemorial yearnings of our common humanity. It was therefore not in obedience to any external arbitrary law, but in mere fidelity to her mission and from the nature of the case, that the Christian Church gradually, and to some extent unconsciously, evolved a literature of her own, which in its passionate directness and vigour set little store by graces of diction, and was too stern in its objective sublimity to hanker after the studied prettinesses of foreign imitation. The process was necessarily a gradual one, for the Church could only utilise the materials placed ready to her hand, and infuse, as time went on, her own spirit into their somewhat effete formalities. The *Quarterly* Reviewer therefore is right in observing that mediæval Latin is no uncouth *patois*, but a real language, with definite rules and principles of its own and " can no more be judged by Augustan standards than Westminster Abbey by the rules of Vitruvius."

The first great change, not so much adopted perhaps as unconsciously evolved, was the substitution of accent for quantity, as better meeting the needs of public singing or recitation in the Church service, where, as Archbishop Trench remarks, " the classical or prosodical valuation of words would have been clearly inappreciable by the greater number of those who it was desired should take part in the worship. . . . Quantity, with its value so often fictitious and involving so many inconsistencies, could no longer be maintained as the basis of harmony. The Church naturally fell back on accent, which is essentially popular, appealing to the common sense of every ear, and in its

broader features, in its simple rise and fall, appreciable by
all." The next and still more important transition, to
which this change led the way, was consummated by the
full development of rhyme, which, however, began in mere
assonance of vowels, and hardly reached its perfection
before the age of Hildebert and St. Bernard. Dr. Neale
distinguishes two great periods of Latin hymnology, the
first chiefly marked by a decay of the old life, and ending
with Gregory the Great, the second illustrating the growth
of a new and better life, and beginning with Venantius
Fortunatus, who, however, only survived Gregory by five
years, dying in 609. To the former period belongs St.
Ambrose, the reputed author of the *Te Deum*, and "father
of Latin hymnology," to whom, by the way, not more than
nine of the twenty-one hymns traditionally ascribed to him
can with any confidence be assigned ; those which rhyme
regularly, or display a want of metrical exactness, though
rhyming is not infrequent in his undoubted poems, must
be certainly rejected. The noblest of his compositions,
Veni Redemptor Gentium, is too well known to need quotation here. To the same early period belongs Prudentius,
who in his fifty-seventh year first devoted himself to the
production of the ecclesiastical poetry which has conferred
on him an enduring fame. And last, but not least, comes
Gregory the Great, at its close, in whose undoubtedly
authentic hymn, *Primo dierum omnium*, the growing
tendency towards rhyme manifests itself. Venantius
Fortunatus, who had been, as Archbishop Trench puts
it, "a master of *vers de societié*," but became afterwards
Bishop of Poitiers, opens a new epoch in hymnology.
His two grandest poems, *Vexilla Regis prodeunt* and

Pange lingua—not to be confounded with the Sacramental *Pange lingua* of Aquinas—are both embodied in the Passion-tide offices of the Breviary, and have become familiar to English readers and worshippers in Dr. Neale's excellent translation. The second, beginning

Pange lingua gloriosi lauream certaminis,

from which the following characteristic stanzas are extracted, is a fine specimen of the rolling trochaic tetrameter which had been once or twice incidentally used before, but which he was the first systematically to arrange or adopt :—

Crux fidelis, inter omnes arbor una nobilis,
Nulla talem silva profert fronde, flore, germine ;
Dulce lignum, dulci clavo dulce pondus sustinens.

Flecte ramos arbor alta, tensa laxa viscera,
Et rigor lentescat ille quem dedit nativitas,
Ut superni membra Regis miti tendas stipite.

Sola digna tu fuisti ferre pretium sæculi,
Atque portum præparare arca mundo naufrago,
Quem sacer cruor perunxit fusus Agni corpore.

Between the rise of the new school in the seventh century and its culmination in the verse of Adam of St. Victor in the twelfth, we have, besides several striking hymns of unknown authorship, such masterpieces as the *Veni Creator* by Charlemagne, the *Veni Sancte Spiritus* by King Robert of France, the *Chorus Novæ Hierusalem* of St. Fulbert, and a hymn on the Joys of Paradise, attributed to St. Augustine, but which is really the work of St. Peter Damiani, and later on the *Jesu, dulcis memoria* of St. Bernard, and the exquisite hymn by his contemporary and countryman, Bernard of Morlaix, which has attained a wide popularity in Dr. Neale's ringing translation,

G

"Jerusalem the Golden." The introduction of "Sequences," sung between the Epistle and Gospel in the Missal, of which in their earlier form of "proses" the *Victimæ Paschali* for Easter is a notable example, is ascribed to St. Notker Balbulus; it was left for Adam of St. Victor— "the foremost among the sacred Latin poets of the middle ages," as Trench calls him—to develop the rhythmical Sequence. It must suffice to mention in passing the four great hymns composed by St. Thomas Aquinas for the newly-instituted festival of Corpus Christi, the greatest of which, *Lauda Sion Salvatorem*, has been familiarised to modern ears by the noble music to which Mendelssohn has wedded it. About fifty years after Adam of St. Victor comes Thomas of Celano, the author of what has been regarded from his own age down to that of Göthe and Sir W. Scott—who died with its murmured words on his lips—as the masterpiece of ecclesiastical poetry, while it is also the solitary extant example of the triple rhyme in which it is composed; the solemn and pathetic *Dies Iræ*, too well known to require citation here. Two specimen stanzas, however, shall be cited from a hymn of Adam of St. Victor on the four Evangelists, a finer one even than his Sequence on St. Agnes, quoted in the *Quarterly* :—

> Jucundare, plebs fidelis,
> Cujus Pater est in cœlis,
> Recolens Ezechielis
>   Prophetæ præconia ;
> Est Joannes testis ipsi,
> Dicens in Apocalypsi,
> Vere vidi, vere scripsi
>   Vera testimonia.
>
> Circum throna majestatis,
> Cum spiritibus beatis,

> Quatuor diversitatis
> Astant animalia ;
> Formam primum aquilinam,
> Et secundum leoninam, .
> Sed humanam et bovinam
> Duo gerunt alia.

From the close of the thirteenth century the old founts of Christian inspiration, in poetry as in theology, and even in architecture, were beginning to run dry. "Sinai and Calvary were deserted for Parnassus and Olympus," and under the blighting influence of the Renaissance "imitation took the place of invention, pedantry of inspiration." Nor was the evil a purely negative one. It seemed good to Renaissance Popes and poetasters, like the Medicean Clement VII. and Zacharius Farrerius, to whom he committed the ignoble task, to replace the splendid heritage of old Breviary hymns by a new series of pseudo-classical compositions made to order, in the style of the following Horatian doxology :—

> Unus est divûm sacer Imperator,
> Triplicis formæ, facie sub una,
> Qui polum, terras, tumidosque fluctus
> Temperat alti.

The volume containing this collection of mongrel monstrosities was actually published with Papal approbation and authorized for use in the Divine office, but by some happy and rather unaccountable accident the clergy declined to avail themselves of the proffered boon. The ecclesiastical authorities, however, were not so easily to be balked of their pet scheme, and if they could not get rid of the existing hymnology altogether, they determined to reform it on classical models, and the charge was finally

G 2

entrusted by Urban VIII. to three Jesuit fathers, among
the most approved pedants of their day, of reducing the
old hymns "ad bonum sermonem et metricas leges," and
adding some new ones to the Breviary. A French ecclesiastic of the present day, the Abbé Pimont—whose work
on the *Hymns of the Roman Breviary*, it is fair to say,
was published with the express imprimatur of the late
Pope—has justly complained how in this revision "under
the pretext of elegance or clearness the correctors have
too often, alas! on the whole, merely sacrificed, for the
sake of classical expressions, the primitive words which
were nearly always rich in symbolism and a profound
mysticism." In his Introduction the Abbé insists at
length on the very important point already referred to,
that "Christianity created a new Latin language for
the expression of ideas to which classical forms were
inadequate." He might, further, with advantage have
made some reference to the collection of hymns, decidedly
superior on the whole to those of the Roman Breviary,
which till within the last few years were sung in all or
nearly all French churches. The ruthless scythe of that
ultramontane centralising movement which culminated
under the last pontificate has swept away the Paris
Breviary, in common with many other local or national
"uses," but it may be permitted to the Christian scholar
and ritualist, as well as to those who scruple at the many
fabulous legends, still left after several prunings, in the
Roman lectionary—touched with a gentle hand in Lord
Bute's translation—to deplore its fall. Not least among
its merits were the preservation in their pristine form of
ancient hymns which Urban's correctors had done their

best, to use a phrase of Ruskin's, " to polish into inanity, and the wonderful beauty of some of the modern ones of comparatively recent date, which were not unworthy to stand beside them. There are few, *e. g.*, among the shorter Latin hymns of any age to equal, still fewer to excel, the musical rhythm and sublime simplicity of the lines beginning

O luce qui mortalibus
Lates inaccessa, Deus,

which some may recollect hearing sung at Sunday Vespers in France, and will regret to know they can have no opportunity of hearing again. But this is not the place to enter on a discussion of comparative hymnology.

XI

FOURTEENTH BENEDICTINE CENTENARY.

IN the year 1880 there was observed throughout the whole Benedictine Order, and especially at the famous Abbey of Monte Cassino, which was the cradle and is still the centre of its organic life, the fourteen-hundredth anniversary of the birth of its illustrious founder, St. Benedict, in 480. The celebration was a natural one. Benedict may justly be styled the father of Western monasticism, which received its first impetus and its mould from his informing hand, since all later religious orders, or at least all established before the Reformation, are directly or indirectly modifications of his rule. To celebrate his centenary is in fact to keep the birthday of monachism in the Latin Church. And the institution is one to which, apart from all theological or ethical differences of view, Protestants need not be, and of late years have not been, slow to acknowledge their indebtedness. It is not only, as Mr. Lecky has rightly pointed out, that to the monks, and especially to the Benedictines, we owe it that the dignity of labour came to be appreciated, as under Pagan forms of civilisation it never had been appreciated, in modern Europe. Nor was the rapid spread of monasticism due simply to the popular belief—a belief not difficult to

account for in a rude and barbarous age, when "conversion" seemed almost to imply seclusion from the world—
that the cloister was the sole or the shortest road to heaven.
It had other and more sublunary attractions for many
classes of minds.   It combined the elements of aristocratic
and democratic power in the princely position and prestige
of the abbot, who ranked with the highest of the land, from
whom indeed he was often sprung, and the vast commonwealth of monks, where peasants and emancipated serfs
found a secure·refuge, and took their place side by side
with the tonsured knight or noble, in the choir and chapter
house or at the plough.   There too was seen the corporate
influence of vast wealth—generally, it is fair to remember,
expended with discretion and benevolence—combined with
the merit of individual poverty.   And thus to the ambitious,
the philanthropic, and—in Benedictine houses especially
—to the studious, the cloister offered attractions hardly
less inviting than to the devout.   Monasteries were the
nurseries not only of labour but of learning ; they were the
great eleemosynary institutions of the age ; and mitred
abbots made their voices heard in courts and parliaments.
Of this vast and comprehensive system St. Benedict of
Nursia was the founder, and from him it derived, as has
been intimated already, not merely its origin, but the
shape and form which, throughout all variations of detail,
it has substantially preserved from his day to our own.   If
it be true that "the Benedictine statutes still remain a
living code, written in the heart of multitudes in every
province of the Christian world," that is partly due to the
remarkable union in the person of their author of those
opposite characteristics, active and passive, which usually

divide mankind; he had the instincts at once of a worker and a thinker, a ruler and a recluse. And his whole nature was dominated by that fervent yet profound enthusiasm without which no man in any age—least of all in such an age as his—can hope to exert a lasting influence over his fellows.

Benedict was born at Nursia, in the duchy of Spoleto, in 480, of respectable parents, and, if we may credit Mabillon, gave early presage of his future sanctity by singing eucharistic hymns in his mother's womb. He was sent to Rome for his education, but the sensitive boy fled from the vices of the capital and took refuge in a cave near Subiaco, which is still pointed out to travellers, not far from the site of Nero's villa of *Sublaqueum*, and here he was wont, like St. Jerome, to subdue his animal passions by rolling his naked body among the thorns and sharp points of the rocks. At length his hiding-place was discovered, and the fame of his sanctity led a neighbouring convent of monks to choose him for their head, in spite of his earnest remonstrances. They soon tired, however, of the severity of his rule and attempted to poison him, but the cup miraculously broke in his hands, as the Breviary assures us, and after calmly reproving their wickedness the youthful abbot returned to his old solitude. But solitude was no longer possible for him. Little communities of monks or hermits grew up around his retreat and under his government, including some noble youths from Rome who were drawn thither by his growing reputation, one of whom, Maurus— afterwards known as St. Maur, founder of the Order in France—began very soon to share his gift of miracles. There was another attempt to poison him, the culprit this

time being a priest named Florentinus, who was envious of
his fame, and then at last, about his fiftieth year, Benedict
left Subiaco, never to return.   He travelled to a hill over-
looking the fountain head of the Liris, Monte Cassino,
where an ancient temple of Apollo is said to have been
still standing, to which the ignorant peasants brought their
offerings.   Benedict converted them, destroyed the idolatrous temple, cut down the grove, and raised a monastery
on its site; and here, to use Milman's words, "arose that
great model republic, which gave its laws to almost the
whole of Western Monasticism."   But even in this final
retreat he was not left undisturbed.   The storm of war
swept over Italy, and Totila, the Gothic monarch, came to
visit him, when the saint rebuked him for his cruelties, and
predicted his conquest of Rome and his death after ten
years.   We are told that the last days of Benedict were
darkened by a vision of the destruction of his abbey by
the Lombards, which happened forty years afterwards, but
consoled by another vision, which also came true, of the
extension of his rule throughout every part of Europe.
He died March 21, 543, and was buried in the oratory
of St. John the Baptist, which stood on the site of the
demolished sanctuary of Apollo.

The Benedictine Rule is of course bound together, as its
animating principle, by the threefold cord of monastic
perfection—poverty, chastity, and obedience; and the three
occupations into which the Benedictine day is apportioned
are divine worship, study, and manual labour, the last two
of which found no counterpart among the cœnobites of
the East.   Monte Cassino was not a reproduction of the
Egyptian Laura, or the model of Mount Athos.   But the

comprehensive vigour and wisdom of his polity, which has
made it the model for all subsequent institutions of the
kind in Western Europe ; the skilful adjustment of abbatial
dominion with universal suffrage of the monks, at once
concentrating power and diffusing it ; and that prescient
insight into the human heart, which has moulded some
forty generations of men and women (for there are Benedictine nuns also) into voluntary and submissive instruments of his will—all this does certainly show a legislative
capacity in the founder which, as Sir James Stephen
observes, may well appear to those who reject the theory
of supernatural guidance "a phenomenon affording ample
exercise for a liberal curiosity." And we may further
agree with him that, great as are the services rendered
by the Benedictine Order for many centuries, by their agricultural labours, their marvellous architectural achievements,
and their priceless libraries, their greatness is most signally
attested by the names of so many worthies illustrious alike
for active piety, for administrative wisdom, for profound
learning, for devout contemplation, and, we may add, for
missionary enterprise. The names of Lanfranc and Anselm
would alone suffice to show the influence produced by
mediæval Benedictines on English history and theological
thought. The dying vision of St. Benedict was indeed
fulfilled with a rapidity which he could scarcely have foreseen. In Italy houses of his Order began at once to rise,
increasing as time went on in spaciousness and splendour,
from Calabria to the Alps, and to this day, or at least till
the recent changes, scarcely a town of any size was without
its Benedictine convent. His monks, as an abbot of Monte
Cassino expressed it, "swarmed like bees," and began

everywhere to plant new monasteries. Yet it is hardly in Italy that they have won their highest reputation. Before the death of Benedict, his faithful disciple Maurus had crossed the Alps, and the first French Benedictine abbey rose at Glanfeuille on the Loire near Angers. It was the first of many rich and noble foundations, famous for their learning, and still "the name of St. Maur is dear to letters." During the seventeenth century no fewer than a hundred and five writers of that Congregation shared their literary renown, and to them we owe the best editions known of the works of many of the Fathers, both Latin and Greek, as well as of some later celebrities, not to speak here of the gigantic task accomplished by Mabillon alone in his *Spicilegium*, his *Acta Sanctorum*, his *Annals of the Benedictine Order*, and other works.

To English readers it may be more directly interesting to remember that with St. Augustine the rule of St. Benedict passed into this country, and, we might almost say, took possession of it. To quote Milman once more, " In every rich valley, by the side of every clear and deep stream, rose a Benedictine abbey, and usually the most convenient, fertile, and peaceful spot in any part of England will be found to have been the site of one of them." It may be generally assumed, till evidence appears to the contrary, that an English monastery belonged to this Order, for the Cistercian was only a stricter reform of the Benedictine rule. Far the greater number of our old abbeys, several of our cathedrals, and many parish churches were in Benedictine hands. The names of Canterbury, St. Albans, Westminster, Glastonbury, and Tewkesbury in the south, of Wearmouth, Yarrow, and Lindisfarne in the

north, will recall many others to those familiar with our
ecclesiastical history or our ruined shrines.   So strongly
indeed were the English Benedictines rooted in the soil,
that after the suppression of their houses at the Reformation they resolved at least to retain in the Order all their
old titular dignities, in the hope of better days.   And we
believe that at this moment Dean Bradley has a rival in
existence somewhere—though it is not on record that he
has ever claimed his seat in the Upper House—in the
shape of a mitred Abbot of Westminster.   In mediæval
England, as on the Continent before the rise of the Jesuits,
the education of youth was conducted chiefly in the schools
attached to Benedictine monasteries.   To this day indeed
these schools are frequented by Roman Catholics of the
upper classes, many of whom prefer their milder and more
liberal discipline to that of the Jesuit teachers.   But in
the present stage of civilisation, religious orders, whatever
their permanent merits from an ascetic or theological point
of view, are hardly likely to reconquer the wider influence
or reputation that once belonged to them.   They still of
course have their uses, but their glories must be sought
rather in the past than the present.   And a community
which has flourished already for nearly fourteen centuries,
and shows no signs of decay, may afford to repose on its
laurels and dwell with a pardonable pride on the memory
of a founder whose name is honoured and his will obeyed,
amid all the social and moral revolutions of later ages, by
a multitude of men and women throughout modern Europe
and beyond it.   To a thoughtful observer this abiding
influence in a world so full of change will perhaps appear a
greater miracle than any of those which his biographers

have recorded.   It would have amazed John Knox and
his associates to know that, three centuries after "the
rookeries had been pulled down, and the rooks had fled,"
a large Benedictine monastery and school would be erected
in the heart of Presbyterian Scotland, on the banks of the
Caledonian Canal ; while another, not without architectural
pretensions, has arisen almost under the shadow of Here-
ford Cathedral, and as the centre of a rival See, to say
nothing of the more ambiguous establishment set up by
"Father Ignatius" at Llanthony.   It may at least be
granted, by friends and foes alike, that St. Benedict has
more than earned the honours of his fourteenth centenary.

XII

PROPHECIES OF THE CHRISTIAN ERA.

THERE has never probably been a period or a nation in the world's history that has not borne witness to that craving for a knowledge of the hidden future, which seems to be an ineradicable instinct of the human mind, whilst it is doomed by the limitation of human faculties to inevitable disappointment. From the savage who reads in a thunderstorm or an eclipse the anger of his offended Deity, or the somewhat more systematic reasoner who argues, *cometa fulsit, bellum erit,* to the most elaborate organization of "wizards that peep and mutter," all are dominated by a common feeling of hopeless curiosity and a common desire to gratify it. Even Saul, who had been so zealous in destroying witches, bows down in the cave at Endor. In our own day the spirit-rapping superstition counts its votaries by thousands among the educated classes, and has even formed in America the basis of a religious sect ; while, on the other hand, science, if the Positivist theory is to be accepted, proposes to establish by natural methods that prescience in which so many rival claimants to preternatural power have competed and failed. There is, however, this distinction, broadly speaking, between the prophecies of the ancient and modern, or rather, let us say,

the Pagan and Christian world—for with Jewish prophecy
we are not concerned here—that the former was purely
national, referring mainly to wars or approaching political
revolutions, while the latter has also wider bearings, and
often points to a more distant future.   The nations of
mediæval Europe, without losing their separate individuality, felt themselves to be parts of a great religious commonwealth, in which, moreover, the three leading nations—
Germany, France, and Italy—were supposed to have distinct and special offices to fulfil.   To Italy was committed
the chief priesthood, to Germany the Empire, to France
the leadership of intellectual culture.   We may again make
a fourfold division of the subject-matter of Christian prophecies, which are either purely religious, or dynastic, or
national, or cosmopolitan.   Under the last head would
come those bearing on the fortunes of the Universal
Church—predictions, *e. g.*, of a great reformation, or of the
reunion of separated bodies—which, however, have often
a secular as well as an ecclesiastical aspect, in so far as
they affect the history of the principal civilised nations.
And if we turn from their subject-matter to their origin,
these prophecies seem sometimes to be a kind of sponta-
neous product of the soil or of the temper of the age,
sometimes to be deliberately framed with a view to pro-
moting their own fulfilment, and sometimes to be due to
the predictive glance of genius, inferring the future from
the past.   Prophecies with a purpose, which may be called
" prospective history, as history is retrospective prophecy,"
are such as John of Bridlington's poem in the reign of
Edward III., where a bitter satire on contemporary vices
is disguised under the form of a prediction.   So again a

good specimen of dynastic prophecy may be found in the
old English proverb of Elizabethan days,

> When hempe is spun,
> England's done;

where the five letters of the word "hempe" stand for the
five Tudor monarchs (Henry VIII., Edward VI., Mary and
Philip, Elizabeth), and the chances of invasion or revolution at Elizabeth's death are indicated.   Such, too, is the
old catalogue of mottoes for successive Popes, ascribed to
St. Malachy, who died in 1148, but first heard of in 1595,
which begins with Celestine II. in 1143, and extends to
nine Popes still to come.   Sometimes it has had a curious
felicity, as in giving Pius VI. the motto "peregrinus apostolicus," and Pius IX. "crux de cruce"; while a more
far-fetched interpretation may adapt "aquila rapax" to
Pius VII., who was torn from his throne by the French
eagles.   To Leo XIII. is assigned the appropriate title of
"lumen in cœlo."

These remarks are partly suggested by a short treatise
on *Prophecies of the Christian Era*, published in 1871, by
Dr. Döllinger—one of those little satellites, so to speak,
like the *Papstfäbeln*, thrown off from his larger works in
the process of composition, and bearing similar evidence to
the wonderful range and minute accuracy of his information.   In it is given a sketch of the course of popular
prediction in successive Christian ages, which is of course
in some respects a measure of the course of popular feeling and belief.   It must be remembered that the early
Christians inherited from the Jews the Sibylline books,
composed partly before, partly after, the time of Christ, to

which both alike attached a high authority, and whence the Christians inferred the triumph of the Church over the Pagan Empire. For many ages indeed the chief subject of Christian prediction was the reign of Antichrist and the end of the world, which last, in the tenth century especially, was believed to be very near at hand, but—as was gathered from the Apocalypse — could not ensue till Antichrist, who was expected to be a Jew, had appeared, and tyrannized for three years and a half over the afflicted Church. It was not of course till later, when Christendom was shaping itself into separate States, that there was room for national prophecies to spring up, which, so far as they are not distinctively religious, seem usually to be the expression of the common hopes or fears of the people. Often they cannot be referred to any known author; and then some mythical personage, such as Merlin, "the British Orpheus," is usually credited with them, and comes to be accepted as an historical reality. English chroniclers testify to the high repute in which Merlin was held by their frequent use of such phrases as "tunc impletum est illud Merlini," or "ut impleretur Merlini prophetia." Galfridus, who has incorporated Merlin's prophecy into his work, is open to the reproach of having altered the legend about him by making a *dæmon incubus* his father, and thus sanctioning the dark superstition, afterwards raised almost into a dogma by Aquinas, and even authorized by Popes, which cost the lives of so many thousands of innocent persons. The tough hold which national prophecies get on the popular mind may be illustrated from a contemporary Irish writer, O'Curry, who says, in his *Lectures on the Manuscript Materials of Irish History*, that "he himself knew

H

hundreds, including highly-educated men and women, who neglected the ordinary means of obtaining provision for life from faith in predictions of a great restoration in Ireland, for which, however, no fixed period was assigned." In the middle of the seventeenth century the first preacher in Portugal, the Jesuit Vieira, wrote a *History of the Future*, announcing that Portugal was to be the centre of a fifth Empire of the world. But he paid dearly for his patriotic zeal, for the Inquisition of Coimbra scented out some occult heresy in the book, and, after a year's imprisonment, compelled him to recant.

Among the most copious at once and most interesting of mediæval prophecies are those relating to the city of Rome, which has been for above two thousand years one of the chief factors in the history of the world. In its heathen period it was called the " Eternal City," but the early Christians, like St. Jerome, thought this was the name of blasphemy written on the brow of the apocalyptic harlot and designating " Babylon the Great."   St. Benedict of Nursia in the sixth century foretold that Rome would be destroyed, not indeed by foreign invasion, but by tempests and earthquakes.   St. Bridget predicted that it would be wasted by fire and sword, and the plough should pass over its barren site. St. Frances of Rome at one time believed that her intervention had arrested the impending woe, but afterwards she had another vision of the destruction of the city. An English monk of the fourteenth century predicted that its fall would coincide with a general separation from the Roman Church, on account of its gross corruptions.   In 1519 an English prophecy was brought to Venice, that Charles V., then just elected Emperor, would

subdue all nations, and reduce the Mahometans to subjection to the cross, but would first burn Rome and Florence ;
a prophecy fulfilled in spirit, though not in letter, eight
years later, when Rome was taken by his army. Rome had
already been identified with the Babylon of the Apocalypse,
and is indeed called Babylon by St. Peter, and there were
prophecies as early as the fourteenth and fifteenth centuries
of the seat of the Papacy being removed elsewhere, while
Rome, the adulterous city, was given over to destruction.
The whole Jesuit Order accepted this view, which is
found in writers like Bellarmine, Suarez, and Cornelius a
Lapide. Prophets, it must be observed, were not supposed
necessarily to be saints, nor were saints always right in
their predictions. St. Bernard was unfortunate in his promises of a victorious crusade, and the announcement of
St. Vincent Ferrer, that Antichrist was already nine years
old, and would appear shortly after his death, was not
borne out by the event. St. Catherine of Siena was equally
at fault in her predictions of a vast crusade of the whole of
Europe, and of a thorough reformation of the Church. On
the other hand, St. Bridget, who spoke of the approaching
ruin of the Church and the rents in its walls, had her words
verified in the Reformation. Indeed two conflicting streams
of prophecy, one of the downfall, the other of the cleansing
and restoration of the Church, arising from a common
sense of the urgent need of reform, permeate the literature
of the fourteenth and fifteenth centuries. Both feelings
find expression in the burning words of Savonarola. On
all sides the conviction prevailed that a free Œcumenical
Council, superior to the Pope, was the only available
machinery for effecting the necessary reforms. Cardinal

Nicholas of Cusa predicted that the Church would sink still deeper, till it seemed to be lost, but would again emerge triumphant. One of the earliest of these stern censors of hierarchical and Papal corruptions was St. Hildegarde of Bingen on the Rhine, whose prophecies were examined and solemnly approved at a large Council assembled under Eugenius III. She was consulted by three Popes, two Emperors, and innumerable bishops and abbots. Yet she was not afraid to predict, in the true spirit of Teutonic indignation against prelatical greed and ambition, that princes and peoples would strip the Papacy of its power because of its faithlessness to its trust, that some countries would reject it altogether, and that the Popes would have only Rome and its environs left under their rule. St. Bridget of Sweden in the fourteenth century was no less outspoken than St. Catherine of Siena in denouncing the judgment of God on the crimes of Popes and Cardinals, some of whom she described as "like unto Lucifer, more unjust than Pilate, more cruel than Judas, more abominable than the Jews," while she roundly declared several previous Popes to be in hell. Her namesake, the Irish St. Bridget, had a vision seven centuries earlier not very flattering to her countrymen, but which subsequent history cannot be said to have disproved. "She inquired of her good angel, 'Of what Christian land were most souls damned?' The angel showed her a land in the west part of the world [Ireland]. She inquired the cause why. The angel said, for there is most continual war, root of hate and envy, and of vices contrary to charity; and without charity souls cannot be saved."[1]

[1] Froude's *History of England*, vol. ii. p. 248.

Passing over several kindred predictions, and only pausing to note that in Roger Bacon we have the first hint of the *Pastor Angelicus*, destined to reform all abuses, so often promised since, but so long in appearing, we come to the striking series of "Joachimite" prophecies, so called from the Abbot Joachim, who founded a monastic congregation in Calabria towards the close of the twelfth century. He, like St. Hildegarde, was much honoured in his lifetime. Three Popes exhorted him not to keep back what God had revealed to him; Richard I. of England, and many French and English prelates, sought his advice; and after his death Honorius III. affirmed his orthodoxy, and he was venerated as a saint in Calabria, and numberless miracles were ascribed to him. He told the English King and bishops that Antichrist was already born, and would hereafter sit on the Papal throne; and, indeed, the profound corruption of the Church through the poisonous influence of the Roman Curia was the keynote of his predictions. These were multiplied after his death by the publication of spurious works in his name, issuing from the "Spirituals," as they were called, in the Franciscan Order, and thus a Joachimist school came to be formed. Its characteristic principle was the distinction of history into three periods: the Old Testament period, or that of the Father, before Christianity, the Petrine period; the New Testament period, or that of the Son, up to A.D. 1250, the Pauline period; and that of the Holy Ghost, after 1250, the Johannean period. The Church, through the evil rule of the Popes, had been made into a brothel and a den of thieves, the people were deceived and corrupted by their pastors, and Rome was the very centre and focus of all

impurity and corruption in Christendom, and was to be
overthrown by the Saracens and the German Empire. Then
would come the conversion of the heathen and the Jews,
and the restoration of the Church by means of a new Order
of Eremites. This teaching was maintained for a long
time in the Franciscan Order, and many hundreds of the
"Spirituals" suffered death or imprisonment under John
XXII. in consequence of it. The commentary on Jeremiah,
attributed to Joachim, had foretold long before that "the
Curia should itself be murdered as it had murdered others";
and as Boniface VIII., the author of the *Unam Sanctam*,
had been openly denounced as "a new Lucifer," for his
tyranny and unchastity, the fate of the uncompromising
prophets excites less wonder than regret. The tribune
Rienzi, and his Laureate, Petrarch, combined with their
political aspirations an ardent faith in the Joachimist predictions of the *Papa Angelicus* and the coming age of the
Holy Ghost.

The tone of prophecy from the fourteenth century to
the Reformation is not very different from that of the
Abbot Joachim. St. Bridget and St. Catherine of Siena,
already referred to, are the great visionaries of the period;
their denunciations are not less sharp than his, and yet, like
him, they were honoured by theologians, Cardinals, and
Popes. St. Bridget prophesied that the sovereignty of the
Pope should be confined to the Leonine city—a prediction
which Italians of the present day have naturally not forgotten. The nearer we approach the outbreak of the
Reformation, the more threatening becomes the language
of these prophets. In a similar spirit Bishop Grostête
had declared on his deathbed, in 1253, that only by fire

and sword could the maladies of the Church be healed, and Machiavelli did but repeat the same sentiment in other words when he said that either ruin or bitter chastisement must overtake the Roman Church.   It must suffice here to note in passing the unique grandeur of the character and position of Savonarola, whose political foresight—if it was nothing more — was seldom at fault, while his visions of the future glory of the Church still await their adequate fulfilment.   With the Reformation Dr. Döllinger closes his record of Christian Prophecies, from which these examples are mostly taken.   The subject is one which would well repay the closer study of historians.   What has been said of a nation's ballads is perhaps even more true of its prophecies.   If men's characters may be judged from what they love to remember, they are at least as clearly exhibited in their hopes and fears.   And prediction, putting aside supernatural claims, which we are not here concerned with, is the record of the highest aspirations or the darkest anxieties of a nation or a Church at any particular stage of its existence.

XIII

LATER CHRISTIAN PROPHECIES.

THE treatise by Dr. Döllinger noticed in the last essay, *Das Prophetenthum in der christlichen Zeit*, ranges from the first age of the Church to the Reformation. But it must not be supposed that the passion for peering curiously into the future, which seems to be an ineradicable instinct of humanity, has died out since then, or that the demand has ceased to create a supply. The second-sight of which Sir Walter Scott has told us so much, and many of the best authenticated dreams and ghost-stories—of which we may hope to gain some further knowledge through the labours of the Psychical Society—bear witness to the persistent desire of mankind to pierce the veil, and to their robust faith, in spite of all former disappointments, in the possibility of gratifying it. Indeed the very use of the word "prophet," which has come in ordinary apprehension to be simply identified with seer, or foreteller of the future, is a significant indication of this. In Latin the same word is employed for prophet and poet, and the Greek term προφήτης, so largely employed in the Septuagint and the New Testament, does not, strictly speaking, mean a foreteller of coming events at all. Liddell and Scott rightly translate it, "one who speaks for another," and especially "one who speaks for God"—an "interpreter"—and give as its New Testament sense "an interpreter of Scripture, a preacher." This is also, of course, its Old Testament sense. The Jewish Prophets were the interpreters of God's will, or preachers to the people; their predictive or "prophetic" function, as we have come to limit the sense of the word, was entirely subordinate to this. When Dr. Newman styled one of his early Anglican works *Lectures on the Prophetical Office of the Church*, he was as accurate as he always is in his choice of language. But there can be little doubt that nine-tenths of ordinary Christians, and probably a good many Christian ministers, if they were asked who the Prophets were, would reply at once, without any hesitation, that they were persons who foretold future events; so completely has that one incident of the office which they discharged in the Jewish Church obscured all recognition of their other functions in the popular mind. And the enormous multiplication of the prophets of Baal who "with one mouth declared"—that is, predicted—"good things unto the king," but who do not seem to have greatly concerned themselves about any moral or spiritual instruction, shows that this one-sided estimate of the prophetic office is by no means of merely modern growth.

It has been observed that the stream of Christian prophecy by no means dried up at the Reformation, while there are, moreover, many predictions of an earlier date still eagerly canvassed, as being unfulfilled, or only partially fulfilled. Many of these, which were not long ago popular amongst Legitimist and Ultramontane circles in France, had reference to a *Monarcha fortis*, who was at one time identified with the First or Second Napoleon, and was afterwards supposed to be the Count of Chambord, though the circumstance of his being sometimes described as "a young prince" rather complicated that application latterly. With the great King was usually associated a great Pope, who is called in the prophetical catalogue ascribed to St. Malachy, which is really about three centuries old, *Pastor Angelicus*. The monk of Orval, who died in the middle of the sixteenth century, and whose written prophecies were buried with him, but were dug up in 1793, and afterwards published—whether with or without being tampered with it is now impossible to say—adds some further particulars. According to him, three great Kings—whom the *Times'* Correspondent some years ago specified as the Czar, the King of England, and a German Prince—are to be converted to Catholicism, and two island nations also are to embrace the true faith. This is indeed a favourite topic of these later seers, and a famous vision, said to have been related by Edward the Confessor on his deathbed, is interpreted in the same sense. He saw, we are told, a green tree, representing England, cut down and moved to a distance of three furlongs from its own root, after which it was replaced. This is explained to refer to the separation of England from Catholic unity for the space of three centuries, and therefore to point to its speedy conversion. Still more elaborate was the prophecy of St. Hildegarde, who lived in the twelfth century, and foretold that "in distant ages the Christian nations would very generally depart from the fear of God, wars would increase and become more destructive, vast multitudes would perish by the sword, and many cities be destroyed; but, at last, mankind, purified through heavy tribulations, would return to the practice of the laws of Holy Church." The language, as so often happens in such cases, is sufficiently vague, but it no doubt lends itself readily to the antecedents and out-break of the Reformation and the religious wars which followed in its wake. The prophetess goes on to describe the reign of righteousness and peace which shall follow the repentance of the nations and usher in the Second Advent, partly in language derived from Isaiah, and the conversion of the Jews. A century and a half later St. Gertrude expatiated in more general terms on the glory reserved for the latter days of the Church. Far more explicit are the predictions of the hermit Bartholomew Holtzhauser, nearer our own day, who foretold in detail the reunion of Greeks and Latins, the return of England and Germany to Catholic unity, the fall of the Turkish Empire, and that "all idolatry and unbelief shall be rooted out, and the nations enjoy a general peace, while all arts and sciences shall be brought to perfection, and the promises of the inspired Prophets of the Old Testament shall receive their full accomplishment." There are strange stories of predictions of the kind current even in our own days, of which a specimen may be given here, taken from a work published in 1857 by the late Mr. De Lisle of Garendon Park, Leicestershire, on the *Future Unity of Christendom.* He was travelling in Wales at the time, and, in the course of conversation with the priest at whose chapel he had been hearing mass, asked him whether he thought England would ever again become Catholic :—

The good priest said with much earnestness that he believed it would. And he added a most remarkable his-tory that tended to confirm his opinion. About a hundred and fifty years before that time there was a saintly Catholic gardener in that very town, who was a man of extraordinary virtue and prayer; indeed his life was one continued prayer, and next to his own sanctification no object occupied so prominent a place in his multiplied petitions to the throne of grace as the return of his own dear country England to the unity of the Catholic Church. One morning, three years before his happy death, he had received the holy communion, and all at once he was rapt in spirit, and Jesus, whom in the Sacrament of His love he had just received, manifested Himself to His humble servant, and with a sweet and gracious aspect said to him, "My son, I have heard your prayer so often poured out before me; I will have mercy upon England." At these words, the poor gardener, overwhelmed with gratitude, exclaimed: "When, Lord, oh! when?" "Not now," replied our Saviour; "but when England shall build as many churches as she destroyed at the change of religion, and when she shall restore and beautify the remainder."

The narrator of the tale proceeds to quote a contemporary authority to the effect that about three thousand churches had then (in 1857) been restored, and nearly two thousand new churches built, in Great Britain during the present century, and he considers that there is "a mysterious relation between the facts and the prediction."

The prophecies already mentioned chiefly concern the fortunes of the Church, and indeed there are few of the mediæval predictions, many of which emanated from monks and nuns, which have not a religious bearing, though they often include political references also, and especially where Rome, the home both of an ecclesiastical and a civil sovereignty, is concerned. There are also many vaticinations about Paris, which was looked on as the second centre of Latin Christendom, and these not many years ago seemed to be still exerting a perceptible influence, if we may credit statements as to personages of high family in France who were then said to be holding aloof from the capital at the

moment, from dread of being involved in its imminent
destruction. Still more frequent, as is natural, are the
predictions about Antichrist, who, according to some
authorities, is to be born of the union between a Jew and a
Mahometan. It would be interesting to examine how far
many modern and Christian prophecies may be traced to
a Pagan source. The Christian apologists of the early
centuries, as is well known, invariably recognised a genuine
prophetic element in Paganism, as well as in Judaism,
and boldly appealed to it. And Neander insists that, as
" Christianity is the end to which all development of the
religious consciousness necessarily tended," they were fully
justified in doing so. But he also admits that, with their
lack of critical taste or skill, they made many mistakes,
especially in using all sorts of spurious or interpolated
writings which passed under high-sounding mythical
names, as of the Grecian Trismegistus or the Egyptian
Thoth ; and it seems that Christian as well as Jewish
writers freely interpolated the Sibylline oracles themselves.
Celsus at least publicly reproached them with doing so,
and Origen could only answer that the earlier Sibylline
writings were also full of interpolations. The tendency to
fabricate predictions and the tendency to credit them,
which necessarily react on one another, spring in fact from
a common source. It is easy to classify the prophets and
their disciples as knaves and fools, and a generation or
two ago such a rough and ready classification would have
passed current in educated society as exhaustive. There
are no doubt still persons who regard Swedenborg or
Joanna Southcott, or even Edward Irving, as mere vulgar
impostors, and their followers, past or present, as idiots or

stark mad. But psychology and history alike rebel against this process of coarse rationalizing. It is very doubtful if any impostor ever gained a following who was not at least half an enthusiast, and it is certain that nine-tenths of the followers in such cases are much more of enthusiasts than of fools. The feverish hankering after a knowledge of futurity may be as irrational as the ready credence accorded to any one who offers to satisfy it is often purely superstitious, but denunciation will do little to dispel a curiosity which repeated disappointment seems wholly powerless to diminish. It was just as unreasonable to feel an exceptional dread about the result of the Prince of Wales's illness on the anniversary of his father's death, and an exceptional sense of hopefulness when the day was over; yet it is probable that not one in ten even of the educated classes was altogether exempt from such a feeling, and far from unlikely that it was shared by the Royal Family themselves. How many persons are there of sound digestion and well-stored mind, and not exclusively ladies, who will never, if they can help it, start on a journey on a Friday or sit down thirteen to dinner! Yet this is much more irrational than to attach some weight to a prediction, not in itself absurd, coming from a man of apparently saintly character who believes himself to be inspired from above. And belief is of course more natural, though not therefore more reasonable, when the prophecy happens to jump with a surmise or a wish of our own. Archbishop Laud was not perhaps a wise politician, but he was certainly very far indeed from being a visionary or a fool, as is sufficiently attested by the fact that he has left his mark on the English Church to this day. The late Professor Mozley observes: "That we have a Prayerbook, an Altar, even our Episcopacy itself, we may, humanly speaking, thank Laud . . . that any one of Catholic predilections can belong to the English Church is owing to Laud."[1] Yet Laud attached what is now considered a ridiculous importance to his dreams, and was not ashamed to avow it. It is the privilege of a well-regulated mind to regard all such matters with a lofty indifference, but we are not sure that the privilege may not be too dearly purchased. Man is not only " a rational animal," as the logic manuals tell us, and according to the deduction drawn by the same authorities, " a cooking animal," but he also possesses what Bishop Butler rather unceremoniously designates "that forward delusive faculty" of imagination, which plays to the full as important a part in the mental development of most men as the reason. And as long as that "delusive faculty" holds its place, there will always be plenty of men and women, who are neither knaves nor fools, so organized as to have a capacity for seeing visions and dreaming dreams, and a vastly greater number eager to listen to their tale, and more than half inclined to believe it.

[1] *Historical and Theological Essays,* vol. i. p. 227.

XIV.

PROPHECY OF ST. MALACHY.

UNDER the title of *Corona Catholica*, and in a gorgeous binding of scarlet and gold, Mr. Charles Kent has "offered at the feet of the Successor of Peter" an epigram in fifty languages, ancient and modern, and from as many different hands, on his accession to the pontifical throne, which he considers a suitable method of testifying reverence for the eminent virtues and learning of the "Ruler of the world." The original English stanza, which is subjoined, is neat, if not particularly striking. The Latin version is so involved as to be rather difficult to construe; the Greek, by Professor Paley, as might be expected, is pure and classical. On the greater number of translations it must be left to more accomplished linguists to pronounce a critical judgment, but such names as those of Professor Sayce, Max Müller, and Renouf may be accepted as vouchers for the correctness of the Assyrian, Sanskrit, and Egyptian. The English original runs as follows :—

> Through the Cross on Cross of Pius,
>   As through Mary's Dolours Seven,
> Lo! from Death what Life emerges,
>   Joy from anguish, Light from Heaven.

It will at once be observed by connoisseurs that the two mottoes of the late and present Pope respectively in St.

Malachy's Prophecy—*Crux de Cruce* and *Lumen in Cœlo*—
are worked into this epigram, and indeed the actual words
occur in the Latin form.   And it appears from Mr. Kent's
preface, which is headed "S. Malachy, Archbishop of
Armagh," that his main object is to rehabilitate that curious
document, which he evidently believes to be genuine.   We
are reminded how St. Malachy flourished in the first half
of the twelfth century, and was an intimate friend of the
great St. Bernard, who wrote a Life of him—which is
hardly perhaps considered generally "to be one of his
most finished masterpieces."   But St. Bernard, while
crediting his friend with miraculous and prophetic gifts,
says nothing at all of this "most renowned of all the
visions and prophecies attributed to him," which was in
fact never heard of, as Mr. Kent candidly admits, till four
centuries and a half after his death.   It is true, no doubt,
though it scarcely seems a sufficient explanation of this
long silence, that the art of printing was not invented till
the latter half of the fifteenth century ; but a good century
more had to elapse before the first publication of the
Prophecy of St. Malachy by a learned French Benedictine,
Arnold Wion, in 1595.   Under these circumstances Mr.
Kent prudently declines to "insist upon its authenticity,"
but he thinks it bears a certain analogy to "that mysterious Fourth Eclogue of Virgil," in which the Advent of
our Lord and His birth of a Virgin were predicted forty
years before the event, and to the Sibylline acrostics.   So
it does, but on that point a word shall be said presently.
Several fresh editions appeared during the seventeenth
century, and in 1675 one in two splendid quartos was
dedicated by permission to the reigning Pope, Clement X.,

I

and "formally authenticated by the notable words, *con licenza dei superiori.*" To Mr. Kent's mind this dedication seems to be conclusive evidence of authenticity, though he does not exactly say so. A certain Jesuit Father Menestrier did indeed in 1689 venture to express the first doubt as to the authenticity of the document, and in 1859 the Rev. John O'Hanlon published a *Life of Saint Malachy*, in which he reiterated that doubt. But their scepticism is rendered innocuous, if not excusable, by the consideration that Father Menestrier either ignored or— let us charitably hope—was ignorant of the fact that Pope Clement X. had scarcely two decades before deigned to accept, as Pontiff, the dedication of those "two splendid quartos, in which the authenticity of the predictions was formally maintained," while Father O'Hanlon frankly acknowledges his regret at having been unable to obtain a sight of "that most remarkable publication." It seems clear, however, that the condescending approval of Clement X. did not go for much with Father O'Hanlon, whatever he might have thought of the arguments. Finally Mr. Kent urges that these Prophecies "present from first to last a series of astounding coincidences," of which he thinks, however, it will suffice to mention four. Three of these four, we may observe, all of comparatively recent date, are invariably selected whenever it is desired to illustrate the striking coincidences in St. Malachy's Prophecy, from which it is only natural to infer that they are somewhat exceptional, even if the exceptions cannot be said to prove an opposite rule. These four are the mottoes of Pius VI., *Peregrinus Apostolicus;* of Pius VII., *Aquila Rapax;* of Pius IX., *Crux de Cruce;* and of Leo

XIII., *Lumen in Cœlo*. We shall perceive that the fourth Pope after his present Holiness is to be *Pastor Angelicus*, and this is a personage who had figured in earlier vaticinations, being first mentioned by Roger Bacon.

The fact is that St. Malachy's Prophecy, whatever may be the exact date of its composition—and there is no shred of evidence for its existence before the time of its first publication in 1595—belongs to a vast family of visions and predictions, running through the whole course of Church history. Some years ago Dr. Döllinger published a little work on the subject, already noticed, giving copious examples from the beginning of the Christian era to the period of the Reformation. And there have been various later illustrations, coming down to our own day, of this ineradicable human instinct for prying curiously into the future. It is not of course at all confined to the Christian era; thus a special gift of prophecy was attributed to virgins, both among the ancient Greeks and Romans, and in India, as Clement of Alexandria testifies. In referring to the Sibylline oracles Mr. Kent recalls the earliest, most long-lived, and most famous of all these Christian prophecies, but with more than questionable discretion for his own purpose of helping to authenticate St. Malachy. It is very possible that the first of the fourteen Sibylline Books formerly in circulation, eight of which we now possess, may have suggested the strangely Messianic colouring of the Fourth Eclogue of Virgil. But what is the origin of the Sibylline books, so far as it has been as yet clearly ascertained? The earliest of them was probably composed by an Alexandrian Jew, at the beginning of the second century, B.C.; it closes with predictions

of the future coming of the Messiah, borrowed from Old
Testament prophecies, and may have become known to
Virgil. The second and third books also betray their
Jewish authorship, but must have been composed after the
destruction of the Temple of Jerusalem, somewhere about
the end of the first century of our era. The next five
books are evidently of Christian composition, and are
assigned by most critics to the third century. That
fragments of the old Pagan oracles are embedded in them
is more than probable, but they can only be regarded on
the whole as deliberate impostures. The acrostic on the
titles of our Lord, to which Mr. Kent refers, as well as
another on the Cross, quoted by St. Augustine, occur in
the eighth book. The acrostic form seems to have been
adopted because it was a known characteristic of the
original Sibylline verses. For some sixteen centuries
these pretended oracles were accepted as genuine throughout Christendom, without a shadow of a misgiving. They
were habitually cited from the first in controversy with
Pagans by the most eminent Christian Apologists and
Fathers, such as Tatian, Athenagoras, Justin Martyr,
Clement of Alexandria, Lactantius, and the great Augustine
himself. Justin Martyr ascribed the Pagan prohibition to
read them, under pain of death, to the express instigation
of the devil. Clement of Alexandria has preserved the
tradition that St. Paul advised Christians to study them.
The Emperor Constantine quoted them in a solemn
oration before the Council of Nice, and both he and
Lactantius reproach the Pagans—not unjustly perhaps—
with dishonesty in seeking to discredit testimonies so
cogent against themselves. The adoption of the fish as

a sacred symbol was derived from the acrostic already mentioned, and the opening stanza of one of the grandest of the old Latin hymns almost ranks the Sibylline oracles with the inspired prophecies of the Psalter, in the famous third line of the *Dies Iræ*, still retained in the Roman missal, though altered in some later versions into *Crucis expandens vexilla*. The first eight books were collected and published at Basle by Vossius in 1545, and Castellio about the same time pointed out that they contained many passages which must be spurious. In the next century a Jesuit, Possevin, observed that there were many passages purporting to be written before the time of Moses, which must therefore have been interpolated, as the Sibyls were known to have flourished at a later date ; but he attributed these interpolations to the malice of Satan, who desired thereby to discredit the rest of the work. At last, in 1649, a French Protestant preacher, Blondel by name, ventured, for the first time among Christians, to denounce the entire compilation as a tissue of clumsy and deliberate forgeries. And later criticism has established the substantial correctness of his view. It does not of course at all follow, nor is there any reason for supposing, that the early Christian fathers and controversialists did not appeal to them in good faith. It was an uncritical age, and the Sibylline forgeries formed part of a whole literature of the same ambiguous kind, portions of which still remain to us in the apocryphal adjuncts to both Old and New Testament—*e. g.* the *Preaching of Noah*, the *Book of Enoch*, the *Epistle of Barnabas*, the Apocryphal Gospels, the *Clementine Recognitions*, and the like, all equally spurious, though not always of fraudulent origin.

Nor has the fount of prophecy, as was observed before, by any means run dry in the middle ages or even down to our own day, and these popular predictions often deal with secular as well as religious and ecclesiastical matters. There is, for instance, a whole series of them connected with English history, ascribed to the mythical Merlin, which Galfridus has put on record. It is not to be wondered at that some of these predictions—like those of St. Bridget and St. Hildegarde, which pointed to the Reformation — should have been remarkably fulfilled. There are many, no doubt, in the present day besides Mr. Kent—and not exclusively Roman Catholics—who attach a more or less definite credence to this Prophecy of St. Malachy, and whose belief would not be disturbed, were it conclusively proved to have originated with those who first published it to the world, at the close of the sixteenth century. They would argue, plausibly enough, that if the Papal mottoes of the first four centuries and a half were mere ingenious historical applications—many of them indeed, as Mr. Hemans has pointed out, hardly rising above the dignity of puns in their obvious derivation from the family names, names of birthplaces, or heraldic devices of pontiffs—it does not follow that the rest have no predictive value. And they would point triumphantly to such startling congruities as those to which Mr. Kent refers in the description of some recent popes. But the circumstance that for modern readers this prophetic catalogue carries with it, by necessary implication, an announcement of the approaching end of the world would alone give it a peculiar, if somewhat sombre, interest to many minds; and believers in Dr. Cumming at all events cannot blame them. Leo XIII. is to have only nine successors, whose character or destiny is thus mysteriously adumbrated :—*Ignis ardens, Religio depopulata, Fides intrepida, Pastor Angelicus, Pastor et Nauta, Flos florum, De medietate lunæ, De labore solis, Gloria olivæ.* Then comes the end. "In the last persecution of the holy Roman Church the chair shall· be filled by Peter, a Roman (or the Roman Peter), who shall feed the flock amidst ¦many tribulations, which being accomplished, the Seven-hilled City shall be destroyed, and the tremendous Judge shall judge the people." As the average reign of a Pope lasts seven years only, this method of reckoning would fix the final persecution of the Church and the consummation of all things somewhere about the middle of the next century. And that, we may fairly suspect, is the true explanation of this sudden revival, after two centuries of oblivion, of a critical and devotional interest in the so-called Prophecy of St. Malachy, which is no doubt strengthened by the curious felicity of the designations severally assigned to the late and the present Pope.

XV.

SOCIAL INFLUENCE OF CHRISTIANITY.

THE *Bibliothèque Universelle et Revue Suisse*, which frequently contains articles of interest on various subjects, is hardly as well known in this country as it deserves to be. In 1876 it contained a very remarkable posthumous paper of Montalembert's—originally written for the *Correspondant*, but declined by it, and published in accordance with directions given by the author after his death.[1] Two years later appeared a paper by M. Ernest Naville, on the " Social Influence of Christianity," which does not perhaps say anything very new in substance—for it would be difficult to be original without being paradoxical on so well worn a theme—but does bring out very forcibly and simply certain facts which, however undeniable, are apt in the present day to be forgotten.[2] Whatever may be the writer's theological views, his historical estimate is one well entitled to command the assent of heterodox and orthodox alike, based as it is, not on any doctrinal assumption even of the truth of Christianity, but on a review of the course of Christian history. He takes as his text the concluding

[1] See *Bibliothèque Universelle* for January, February, March, April, and May, 1876, " L'Espagne et la Liberté."
[2] *Ibid.*, August, 1878.

sentence of a paper read by M. Troplong in 1842 before the Institute of France :—"The Christian philosophy is the foundation of our social life. It lies at the root of our principles of right ; and, though the fact is not universally recognised, we live much more by it than by the ideas which have survived from the ruin of the Greek and Roman world." This is the more remarkable, as the reviewer justly observes, when we recollect that Christ neither claimed nor exercised any political power, and refused to be made a King. And moreover for the first three centuries this was strictly the condition of His Church. Yet what is the result ? We must distinguish the Christian faith as a religious system—which is not here in question—from the principles bearing on social and civil life to which it has given rise. It is quite true, as Newman points out in one of the most striking and characteristic of his Oxford Sermons,[1] that the latter kind of influence is not the direct and primary object of the Gospel, which addresses itself to the spiritual nature and needs of man. But it is also true that Christianity has always—ἐν παρέργῳ, to borrow an untranslatable phrase— done far more in the world than fulfil its immediate ends. As M. Naville expresses it with grave, but hardly un- deserved sarcasm, " Abstracting from faith and worship, there are Christian nations." Such language sounds almost satirical as applied to the character of individuals and the policy of States, but it has a very real sense nevertheless. It designates the broad and radical distinc- tion of Christian nations from, *e.g.*, Buddhist or Mahometan

[1] See *Parochial Sermons*, vol. iv., "The Visible Church for the Sake of the Elect."

nations. How is this distinction to be explained? Christ, as we have seen, disclaimed all temporal power. He bade His disciples "render to Cæsar the things that were Cæsar's, and to God the things that were God's." Yet in this very disclaimer is contained the secret of the great social and political revolution which the Christian religion was destined to accomplish in the world. In every ancient State the temporal and spiritual were inextricably confounded, whether the State ruled religion, or priests ruled the State. The words of Christ for ever separated the temporal and spiritual order. And hence followed at once two eventful consequences, on which our whole system of civilisation in great measure depends—the emancipation of the religious conscience, and the emancipation of civil society. By virtue of the first "the word of Christ abides as the imperishable seed of liberty"; by the second all civil constraint exercised in the name of religion is excluded. The influence of Christ and of His Church on society was therefore to be "purely moral." But this moral influence has produced the most momentous effects on national as well as individual life. In what does it consist?

If we come to analyse the great law of love to God and our neighbour, which Christ laid down as the compendium of the whole duty of man, we find in it three main elements of obligation; those which concern the dignity of man, as distinct from the lower animals, those of justice, and those of beneficence. Among the copious illustrations which suggest themselves of the social action of Christianity under these three heads, M. Naville selects three typical examples, and it may be doubted if any

better selection could have been made.   Taking first,
what lies most obviously on the surface, the beneficent
aspects of Christianity, we have a striking confession cited
from the works of Julian the Apostate, whose life was
absorbed in the abortive endeavour to put new wine into
old bottles and galvanize a decaying superstition by the
engrafted virtue of the forces which had destroyed its
life.   He complained that "the negligence of our (heathen)
priests about the poor has suggested to the impious
Galileans the notion of benevolence towards them," and he
desired to recover for Paganism the advantages which this
active beneficence had gained "for the progress of im-
piety," that is of the Gospel.   Of course he failed.   Paganism had no pity for the unhappy, the suffering, the feeble,
the sick, and "him that hath no helper."   There were no
hospitals in ante-Christian times.   Lives that were useless
to the State were not worth preserving.   The Gospel, as
M. Naville observes, has even been blamed for its care
for preserving the lives of feeble children and worn out
old men.   We have lately heard ominous suggestions of
a return to the more drastic methods of treatment in
fashion among the nations of antiquity, under the pretty
sobriquet of "euthanasia."   It is curious to observe how
there is hardly a touch in classical poetry of that love for
childhood, and tender reminiscence of their own childish
days, which hardly a single Christian poet fails to exhibit.
The reviewer quotes an interesting passage from Gratry's
works, in which he tells us that he has often advised
unbelieving or sceptical young men who consulted him
to take charge of some poor family, and that they have
always come to the same conclusion; "no progressive

prosperity without moral progress, no moral progress without religious progress." This charitable influence of the Gospel then has passed into the manners and even the legislation of all Christian States.

But there is something which comes before charity, and that is justice. Justice was recognised as a cardinal virtue by Pagan philosophy, but it was grossly outraged in the institutions of every Pagan State. Take one critical example, the system of slavery. How did the Church deal with it? She could not suppress it, for she neither possessed nor claimed any temporal power, and it was against Christian ethics to preach revolt. Spartacus not long before had headed a revolt of seventy thousand slaves, and the result was to make their condition worse than before. But Christianity enforced principles which sapped the foundation of the whole system of slavery. It proclaimed, for the first time in history, the responsibility and therefore the true dignity of man; it taught that slaves are men, and all men are brothers. The sacredness of human personality must have come almost as a new revelation on the first Christian converts. Nor did the Church merely proclaim an abstract principle. She bound on her own members the obligation of carrying out that principle to its legitimate results. The master who seduced a slave was obliged to marry her, and the master who ill-treated a slave was excommunicated. Slaves were forbidden to obey their masters in disobedience to the law of God. Christian slaves received the Eucharist, while their masters, if penitents or catechumens, were excluded. A slave could be ordained, and he thereby became the superior of his master in the Church. The emancipation

of slaves was encouraged and largely practised.   And thus
gradually, as the Christian spirit produced its natural fruits,
slavery was softened, modified, and transformed, till it had
almost disappeared from Western Europe.   There is indeed
a darker side to the picture to be seen in the revival of
slavery in the fifteenth century, first among the Portuguese
and then among the other nations of Europe.   Hardly a
century ago negroes were publicly sold in Paris.   But as
the Mahometans had first suggested this infamous traffic
to the Portuguese, so it was the revolt of the Christian
conscience which eventually put it down.   In America and
in Russia that work has been accomplished under our own
eyes.   In America the protest came from the Quakers.
In England at an earlier date the work was done by
"positive Christians" like Wilberforce and Buxton.   And
the Russian imperial manifesto of February 1861 closes
with an exhortation to "the pious and faithful people to
sign their brows with the cross, and join their prayers with
ours to call down the blessing of the Most High on their
first free labour."   If it is objected that the eighteenth
century took part in the work, and that there is a decree
of the Convention liberating slaves, the answer is not
far to seek.   "The Christian tradition had formed the
eighteenth century," and in labouring for the emancipation of slaves its philosophers were serving the cause of
Christianity.   And, while abolished throughout Christian
nations, slavery still survives in all its horrors among
Mahometans.   Persians, Arabians, and Turks require
slaves for their hard work and their harems.   They are
captured in Africa, and, according to Livingstone, for
every one who arrives at the slave market four or five at

least die on the road ; they are mutilated, and often killed in the process. A Society has been formed under the auspices of the King of the Belgians to put an end to these horrors, which owes its origin to the vigorous exertions and appeals of the Christian missionary, Livingstone. On this M. Naville justly remarks :—

Livingstone was an English Protestant missionary. Let us seize the opportunity of signalizing the accord of the two great branches of Western Christianity on the question of slavery. On August 1, 1838, by virtue of an Act of the British Parliament, the sun in rising on the English Antilles shone only on freemen. On November 3, 1839, a Bull of Pope Gregory XVI., recalling the efforts of his predecessors in favour of the slaves, confirmed and completed their decisions by pronouncing in a definitive and solemn manner the absolute condemnation of slavery in all its forms.

From justice let us pass to the third great principle enunciated by Christianity, the rights of the individual conscience and true dignity of man. It may be illustrated under one aspect, by contrasting the moral action of the old Attic drama and of Shakespeare, though both alike, but in a manner wholly diverse, maintain the great principle of retribution ($\delta\rho\acute{a}\sigma a\nu\tau\iota\ \pi a\vartheta\epsilon\hat{\iota}\nu$). One crucial and familiar example may suffice to remind us how far this principle was appreciated in the ancient world. No visitor to Rome can forget what is perhaps its grandest and most striking monument—the Colosseum. And few can visit the Colosseum without thinking of the gladiators. But it is an effort to our imagination to realise at once the hideous atrocity and the unnatural popularity of those ghastly spectacles. Not content with witnessing them in life, wealthy Romans would leave large sums by will for

gladiatorial contests to honour their memory after death.
Schmidt records two cases of rich citizens who bequeathed,
one all the young men in his establishment, the other all
his beautiful slave girls, for these combats.   From Rome
the custom spread over Italy, and gladiatorial contests
were introduced between the courses of a banquet, like the
performance of a band, for the amusement of the guests.
And this, be it remembered, not among a barbarous, but a
highly civilised people, who could appreciate the poetry
of Virgil and Horace, who had brought the fine arts and
the tactics of military organization to a rare degree of
perfection, and from whom we have inherited the science of
law.   Yet delicate and high-born ladies vied with each
other in their frantic enjoyment of these hideous exhi-
bitions of "the gladiator pale for their pleasure", writhing
in his last agonies of groans and blood.   Not only would
a worthless wretch like the Emperor Commodus himself
descend into the arena, but "the good Titus" reserved his
Jewish captives for the same horrible pastime.   There is a
startling passage in the Confessions of St. Augustine
which shows the hold it had on the Roman imagination.
He tells us how his friend Alypius, who had a horror of
the circus, and had resolved never to approach it, was one
day almost forced by his companions to accompany them
to a gladiatorial show, and at first kept his eyes obstinately
shut, but at last the shouts from 80,000 spectators so
excited him that he could no longer contain himself, and,
as he gazed, he became intoxicated with the sanguinary
delight, in spite of himself.   He shouted, he raved, he
retired at last burning with a mad desire to come again.
And how was this abomination finally put down?

Christian Emperors had vainly forbidden it, and nearly a century after the conversion of Constantine the Colosseum still reeked with gladiators' blood. But on the first of January, 404, a young monk named Telemachus, at the critical moment, flung himself into the arena to separate the combatants. He was instantly hacked to pieces amid the howls of the furious spectators balked of their entertainment, but he had done his work ; his blood was the last that stained the sands of the amphitheatre.

These examples are enough to establish the moral influence of Christianity. Nor is it any reply to point to the shortcomings or sins of individual Christians. Their condemnation is just, but its very severity renders homage to the sanctity of the doctrine they are felt to have so grievously dishonoured in their lives. And the same may be said of the persecutions which stain the annals of the Christian Church. They are in direct violation of the spirit of Christianity, and recall the old Pagan confusion between the things of Cæsar and the things of God, which the Founder of Christianity so emphatically condemned. The Massacre of St. Bartholomew, the dragonnades of Louis XIV., and the Republican *noyades*, all alike illustrate the saying of Christ that " those who take the sword shall perish by the sword." And the more completely the true spirit of Christianity penetrates the institutions and customs of Christian nations, the more entirely such contradictions will disappear. The worst foes of the Church have been those of her own household, who sought to serve her cause by the weapons their Master forbade them to borrow from her assailants. In many points, and especially in his exposition of the new teaching of Christianity as to the dignity and responsibility of man —which would of course bear a much fuller and more detailed treatment—M. Naville has closely, though apparently without knowing it, followed the line taken by Dr. Döllinger in his work on the Apostolic Age. His article incidentally throws a good deal of light on a question often raised in the present day, as to the bearing of Christian belief on morality, but that is too wide a question to enter upon here. It must suffice for the present to remark that *non sua poma* is the proper description of many excellences which are sometimes attributed to a non-Christian or even to an anti-Christian source. The effects of Christianity are not to be looked for always or exclusively in its nominal professors, while their antecedents cannot fail more or less closely to adhere, whether they will or no, to those who have renounced it.

XVI

PENAL LAWS AGAINST HERESY.

ONE of the many collateral questions growing out of the controversy stirred by Mr. Gladstone some years ago about the Vatican Decrees concerns the history of persecution, or of penal legislation against heresy, during the Christian era. Dr. Newman has shown conclusively—and indeed, as an *argumentum ad hominem*, it is one of the most telling points in his *Letter to the Duke of Norfolk*—that, if "the traditions of the old Empire" in religious matters are preserved in the Encyclical and Syllabus of Pius IX. they have also been preserved in the general system of European civilisation, and in particular among ourselves. The Puritans and Scotch Presbyterians, as Mr. Buckle testifies, held these principles quite as firmly as the school of Laud, and they have survived in Blackstone, and in the theory if not the practice of English jurisprudence down to our own day. Christianity is still officially declared to be the law of the land, and within living memory the phrase had a very practical meaning. Those who are shocked at the enunciation of the principle in Papal manifestoes are shocked at witnessing "the words, ways, and works of their grandfathers." Dr. Newman gives various illustrations of the actual recognition of this system in England down to quite recent times, and a writer so little in harmony with

him as Sir Fitzjames Stephen admits that he is quite right
in his facts. In some shape or other, though in very various methods and degrees, the punishment of heresy has
existed in Europe for fifteen hundred years—ever since,
that is, the Empire became Christian. At the same time
it is also true that, in some sense, the Church has always
disclaimed the responsibility of persecution. *Ecclesia ab-
horret a sanguine* is a maxim of the canon law, and in the
Roman Pontifical, a work of the very highest authority,
the Bishop, in delivering over a condemned heretic to the
secular judge, is directed *efficaciter et ex corde et omni in-
stantiâ* to intercede that he may not be punished with
death or mutilation, in the following prescribed form :—

Domine Judex, rogamus vos cum omni affectu, quo pos-
sumus, ut amore Dei, pietatis et misericordiæ intuitu, et
nostrorum interventu precaminum, miserrimo huic nullum
mortis vel mutilationis periculum inferatis.

It is often said—but, as will presently appear, with very imperfect accuracy—that this only makes matters worse by
adding hypocrisy to cruelty, and that the severities which
the Church thus affects to deprecate were in reality her
own work, and at a word from her, which was never spoken,
would have disappeared. And no doubt the principle of
persecution is clearly enough laid down in the Bull *Unam
Sanctam*, which some modern Ultramontanes regard as •
infallible, though the late Bishop Doyle denied in his
letter to Lord Liverpool that it had any force at all,
inasmuch as, "so far from being received by the Church,
it was violently opposed." For it is there expressly laid
down that there are two swords in the power of the Church,
the spiritual and material, the one to be used *by* the

K 2

Church, the other *for* the Church, *sed ad nutum et patientiam sacerdotis.* And the sword must imply the power of life and death. Indeed Boniface VIII., the author of the Bull, ruled that Bishops might surrender criminals to the secular arm, knowing that the intercession for mercy would not be attended to ; and this ruling was quite in harmony with the general opinion of the fourteenth century. Nor would it be fair to judge the sentiment of that age by the habits and circumstances of our own. Heresy was then to the full as much an outrage on the acknowledged standard of right and wrong as Atheism or blasphemy among ourselves, both of which are still punishable by English law, or Mormonism in the United States. The Lollards in England and the Albigenses on the Continent were looked on with the sort of feeling now entertained in respectable and religious society towards Mr. Bradlaugh and his allies; with this difference, that in those "ages of faith" a denial of the received belief was far more keenly resented as a crime of the deepest dye than in days when the strictest religionists feel obliged to make some allowance for the chances of involuntary error or ignorance. Innocent VIII. in 1484 went so far as to excommunicate all magistrates who delayed more than six days to carry out the capital sentence of the Inquisitors, who nevertheless were still obliged to use the form of intercession prescribed in the Pontifical. But it would be a great mistake to suppose that the forcible suppression of heresy had been from the first a recognised principle in the Catholic Church, or that the practice was suffered to take root without protest from the most orthodox and influential quarters. The language of the Roman Pontifical represents a genuine tradition, though it had for centuries fallen into desuetude. A glance at the original introduction of capital punishment for heresy will serve to illustrate this.

Sir Fitzjames Stephen asserts that penal laws against heretics followed close on the conversion of the Empire, and to a certain extent this is true. But so far as the secular power went beyond giving civil effect to the spiritual sentences of Councils, in the deposition of Bishops and the like, its action was for some time of a very uncertain and spasmodic kind, and was exerted, to say the least, quite as much in the interests of heresy as of Catholicism. The almost lifelong persecution of Athanasius at the hands of Arianizing Emperors is a case in point. The first example of the execution of heretics is in every way so noteworthy that it may be worth while to dwell for a moment upon the circumstances. Two chief pleas are commonly put forward by those who shrink alike from defending persecution in the abstract and from condemning the conduct of ecclesiastical authority in former ages; it is urged that either the civil power was alone responsible for the procedure, or that—as is sometimes alleged in excuse of Elizabeth's wholesale torturing and hanging of Roman Catholics—heresy was merely the cloak or the accompaniment of treason or some other heinous crime. The doctrines of Wicliffe and Huss, for instance, were notoriously dangerous to the State, and Dr. Maitland has shown that a similar excuse may be pleaded for the Albigensian crusade. Now both these explanations may be alleged, the former with unquestionable justice, in the case of the Priscillianists, who were the first to suffer death for heterodoxy. The facts are briefly these :—In 380 the Synod of

Saragossa condemned and excommunicated Priscillian and his adherents, who taught a kind of Gnosticism, and the Bishops Idacius and Ithacius procured an Imperial rescript for their banishment from Spain, which however they contrived, by bribing the Court officials, to get rescinded. Upon this Ithacius betook himself to the Emperor Maximus, who had just usurped the supreme power, and established himself at Trèves, and Priscillian was summoned to answer before a new Synod at Bordeaux. He came, but forestalled his sentence by an appeal to the Emperor, and this appeal to the secular power—contrary to all ecclesiastical precedent in questions of faith or internal discipline—was allowed by Ithacius, who himself became his accuser before the Imperial tribunal. But here St. Martin of Tours, one of the saintliest and most influential men of his age, appeared upon the scene, protesting first indeed against the gross and unprecedented breach of ecclesiastical discipline, but also vehemently deprecating the infliction of civil punishment on the heretics. He at length obtained a promise from Maximus to spare their lives; but as soon as he had left Trèves the persecuting Bishops renewed their importunities, and the Emperor had Priscillian and several of his adherents beheaded. But it is to be observed that he took pains to explain, in writing to Pope Siricius on the subject, that these "Manichæans" were not put to death simply for heresy, but for the practice and encouragement of the most hideous impurities, of which they had been convicted—perhaps under torture—on their own confession. The explanation was not deemed satisfactory, for a solemn protest against the whole proceedings was entered by Siricius, St. Ambrose, and two Italian Councils. Ithacius, a man of luxurious habits and insolent temper, was deposed and excommunicated, and when St. Ambrose afterwards came to Trèves, he refused to hold communion with Maximus. Martin himself, on his return to Trèves in order to intercede with the Emperor for some political offenders, would not hold communion with the persecuting Bishops, and only yielded this point at last, as the condition of inducing him to recall the military officers whom he had sent into Spain with a commission to put all heretics to death—a sufficiently alarming measure, as a pale face and peculiar dress were the tests of heresy adopted by the soldiers. To Martin also Maximus had represented the executions as inflicted for crimes within the cognisance of the civil courts. Fifty years later Leo the Great refers in an apologetic tone to this earliest sanguinary persecution, still however on the assumption that the doctrines of the Priscillianists were as utterly subversive of morality as had been alleged ; and it is worth noting that they were commonly reported to be a Manichæan sect. For the Manichæans " had a singular power of exciting animosity," as Sir Fitzjames Stephen justly observes, though he omits to give the reason, which is however pretty clearly indicated in one of his extracts from the Code of Justinian, where they are described as men " qui ad imam scelerum nequitiam pervenerint." We may infer from St. Augustine's Confessions that the charges against them were not altogether without foundation.

It was towards the end of the fourteenth century, in the period intervening between the persecuting enactments of Boniface VIII. and Innocent VIII. referred to just now that a regular system of penal legislation against heresy began in England, with the Act of 5 Richard II. for the arrest of heretical preachers, which was followed up in 1400 by the famous statute of 2 Henry IV. *de hæretico somburendo*, confirmed by 2 Henry V. in 1414, which authorized justices of the peace to inquire into heresies and commit heretics. These Acts remained in full force up to the time of the Reformation. Sir Fitzjames Stephen, after stating that they were repealed by Edward VI., and, after a short revival during the reign of Mary,[1] were again finally repealed by Elizabeth, adds that the burning of two Arians under James I. was therefore illegal; and he has since explained that the same remark applies to the burnings for heresy which unquestionably took place in the reigns of Edward VI. and Elizabeth also—one being the famous case of Joan Bocher, in which Cranmer played so discreditable a part—although these executions are not generally supposed to have been illegal. Serjeant Stephen indeed expressly affirms that the writ *de hæretico combu-rendo* was still in force in James I.'s reign, and Mr. Lecky fixes its repeal in 1677. To which it must be added that witches were burnt much later than that; in England the last execution took place in 1712, in Scotland ten or fifteen years afterwards. And witchcraft was closely akin to heresy, for—whether or not the elaborate dæmonology of

---

[1] The Marian persecution, cruel and impolitic as it was, demonstrably emanated from the Government, not the Church; it was neither inspired nor encouraged, but—so far as their power went—moderated by the ecclesiastical authorities. Something will be said on this point in the essay on Gardiner. No doubt Mary's personal, and very intelligible, dislike of Cranmer and his associates had a good deal to do with it.

the middle ages, with its evil hierarchy of *incubi* and *succubi*, was accepted entire—witches were always punished for the crime of a compact with the devil. But the Act of Charles II. abolishing capital punishment for heresy leaves untouched the power of the Ecclesiastical Courts to inflict, not only spiritual censures, but other punishments, "not extending to death," for "atheism, blasphemy, heresy, or schism, and other damnable doctrines and opinions." And this power they still retain, though it has of course long since become a dead letter except as applied to clerical delinquents. But to the end of Charles I.'s reign it was a very serious reality, being in fact a kind of modified Inquisition.   There are also certain provisions of the common and statute law against heresy, blasphemy, and Atheism still in force, to which Dr. Newman refers, in the passage on the Encyclical in his Letter, as having been acted upon within his own memory and giving a tone to society and to the publications representing public opinion.

There is a curious coincidence in the view taken by two writers of such widely opposite opinions as Dr. Newman and Sir Fitzjames Stephen, not only of the facts but of the moral deducible from them. The latter sets out by disclaiming any abstract theory about persecution, and considers it perfectly natural that sincere believers in Christianity should desire to make the confession of anti-Christian opinions penal, and only proper that sincere disbelievers should either remain silent or be ready to take the consequences of avowing their dissent. But he holds it to be impossible, in view of "several broad, patent, notorious facts" of the present day, to carry out with any consistency or success the system of repression still existing in the

theory of the law, and thinks therefore that it had better
be frankly and formally abandoned.   And he concludes by
sketching out a short Act for the purpose.   Dr. Newman
avows himself in the abstract "an admirer of the principles
now superseded"—meaning apparently such limited enforcement of respect for orthodoxy as was till lately a recognised principle of the English law courts and of public
opinion.   But he admits it to be impossible to maintain
such a system in the present intellectual condition of the
world.   No Government could be formed on the principle
of religious unanimity, and "as a necessary consequence
the whole theory of Toryism, hitherto acted upon, came to
pieces and went the way of all flesh."   And he only hopes
that in centuries to come some way may be found of
uniting the freedom of the new system of society with the
authority of the old without any base compromise.   There
can hardly be two opinions among thinking men as to
the practical conclusion arrived at on independent grounds
by these two diverse authorities.   No reasonable man, for
instance, could desire the "unequal justice" of prosecutions
for coarse and vulgar blasphemy, as such, while the subtler,
but for that reason far more effective, ridicule of refined
and educated sceptics must inevitably go unpunished ; but
of course a further question is involved, when the religious
sentiment of the great body of citizens is outraged, and
blasphemy becomes a public nuisance, as was alleged, *e. g.*,
in the recent prosecution of the *Freethinker*.   The altered
condition of things may be frankly accepted even by those
who regret the change, and it need not in any case involve
an unqualified condemnation of those who upheld a policy
which   may   naturally   have   been   thought   tolerable   or

expedient under very different circumstances. There will probably be many, even among the sincerest believers in a dogmatic creed, ready heartily to welcome the change, in view of the atrocities, the hypocrisies, and the manifold moral and intellectual evils generated by the old system, which never lost the original sin of its parentage from a profligate prelate and an usurping Emperor.[1] Professor Murray of Maynooth, in his written evidence delivered to the Parliamentary Commissioners in 1854, after examining at some length the opinions of distinguished authorities, both Roman Catholic and Protestant, on religious persecution, sums up with the avowal of his own judgment that "the punishment of heresy, *as heresy*, does not fall within the province of the civil magistrate." His concluding words may be profitably commended to the notice of theologians both of his own and other communions :—

I wish that all parties, Catholics and Protestants, would agree together that heretics should be coerced only by the force of argument, burned only in the fire of charity, cut off only with the sword of prayer and all good works ; that not only temporal punishments and civil disabilities, except for civil crimes, should be abandoned, but all angry revilings and recriminations—unchristian passions under the mask of Christian zeal. . . . For my own part "I have faith in my faith," and I believe that if we tried only the weapons which the Divine Founder of Christianity has put into our hands, we would come nearer to a united decision on that great controversy which can never be decided by the arms of worldly warfare.

[1] It may be as well to explain that this paper was in type before the appearance of Sir Fitzjames Stephen's article on Blasphemy and Blasphemous Libel," in the *Fortnightly Review* for March 1884, which, however, only confirms his previous argument.

XVII.

TOLERATION AND INDIFFERENTISM.

It is frequently affirmed or assumed that toleration and indifferentism are synonymous, or at least correlative, terms; or, in other words, that those whose faith is unhesitating are sure to persecute—if they have the means, while toleration, if it arises from anything but weakness, is an infallible sign of real, though possibly unconscious, doubt. Mr. Lecky, for instance, is constantly harping on this theme in his *History of Rationalism*, and it crops up again and again, though in a somewhat different connexion, in the works of Mr. Froude. Some modern writers, who are thorough-going advocates of toleration in general, have even gone so far as to say that no "exclusive" religion, such as the Roman Catholic, ought to be tolerated, because it is bound, in common consistency, to suppress all dissent whenever it has the power. Those who speak in this way do not usually care to argue about a point which strikes them as self-evident; or, if any argument is required, they think it enough to appeal to what they would call the broad facts of history, and observe that the ages of faith were the ages of persecution, and that toleration was the result of the Reformation. And it may be allowed that, on a mere *primâ facie* view, the testimony of history does

seem so far to be in their favour. Yet we shall venture to
maintain, at the risk of what may look like a paradox, that
the half-truth they have seized upon is not even half the
truth, and that it would be less inaccurate to say, though
it would be an exaggeration, that doubt is the foster-
mother of persecution, and faith of tolerance. It is not
true in fact that the most rigorous persecutions have been
based on religious principles, any more than that they
have served the cause of religion; neither is it by any
means true that those religions which are commonly
regarded as the most dogmatic and exclusive have always
been the most persecuting in principle or in practice.
Here, however, it is necessary to draw a distinction, or
rather to guard against a very common confusion of
language. Of course, if to tolerate all religions means to
regard them as all about equally true, to say that toleration
is synonymous with indifferentism, is much the same thing
as saying that a spade is a spade. But then that is not
the proper meaning of the word. And yet this confusion
runs through a great deal of the popular nonsense that is
talked on the subject. Thus, for instance, we saw it stated
the other day that it is absurd and intolerant to deny the
orthodoxy of Churches which have no episcopate; which
can only mean that it is absurd and intolerant to maintain
the High Church doctrines of apostolic succession and
sacramental grace, for it follows of necessity from those
doctrines that Churches which have no succession are, so
far at least, heterodox; but it does not at all follow that
they ought not to be tolerated, any more than that Jews are
not to be tolerated, though the broadest of Broad Churchmen
might hesitate to admit a Rabbi to his pulpit. Yet there

was a great deal of angry complaint not long ago about the frustration of an attempt made by some few Anglican clergymen to establish an interchange of pulpits with Dissenting preachers, and we were loudly assured that the great principle of toleration was at stake. But the real question at issue was something totally different—namely, whether there are any differences worth considering between the Church of England and the Nonconformist bodies which have separated from her communion. To tolerate a religion does not mean to treat it' as true, or even as free from the most serious errors, but simply as having a fair claim to exist and enjoy civil rights. With the improper and purely arbitrary sense often attached to the word we are not now concerned, and it may be dismissed for the present, with the obvious remark that it is simply inconceivable that all religions, or all varieties compre-hended under the common designation of Christianity, should be equally true, though it is of course conceivable that they all might be equally false.

Taking toleration then in its proper sense, is there any ground either of abstract reasoning or historical evidence for alleging that it is incompatible with genuine religious belief? None whatever. There are a hundred reasons why men may persecute besides the conviction that all heretics will be damned—for that, to put it plainly, is the principle assumed in the argument we are dealing with— just as there are a hundred reasons, besides mere want of power, why they may tolerate religions which they firmly believe to be false. Toleration may spring from a sense of superiority so strong that it despises all dissidents, and thus Mahometans are sometimes said to be tolerant from their scorn of "infidel dogs." But this is hardly a case in point, for Mahometans have little opportunity of persecuting in the present day, and intolerance is certainly a principle of their creed, which was originally propagated, as Christianity never was, by the sword, and that by the express directions of its founder. Still it remains true that a profound conviction of their own faith would naturally incline believers to trust to its inherent strength, and that the bitterest religious persecutors have for the most part been men whose sincerity was questionable. There is something in persecution analogous to the hard and confident professions by which waverers sometimes endeavour to disguise from themselves and others an uneasy suspicion that they may be wrong. To confine ourselves here to the case of Christians, it is surely no proof of latent scepticism to believe that all forcible methods of propagating truth are directly condemned by the letter or spirit of the Gospel. This was unquestionably the belief of the great body of the early Fathers, who yet never hesitated to sacrifice their own lives for their faith, as was conspicuously illustrated in the dispute between St. Martin and certain Spanish bishops about the Priscillianists at the end of the fourth century. St. Augustine may indeed be cited on the other side ; but as he was one of the most voluminous of writers, and almost always wrote *pro re natâ* to meet some immediate call, he is by no means always consistent with himself, and the general tenor of his writings points the other way. It was not till the middle ages that persecution became a recognised system, and that, as we shall see presently, on grounds more secular than religious. Some, again, advocate toleration neither from religious principle nor religious indifference, but on what may be called in this country the traditional Whig theory, that an opposite system serves to concentrate and sharpen the religious element in society, which it is the wisdom of statesmen to keep as much as possible in abeyance. This is one reason why so many Englishmen heartily disliked Prince Bismark's ecclesiastical policy in the *Kulturkampf*, though there were of course many also who sincerely condemned it as unjust. It is obvious again, that no persecution is likely to alter the inner belief of its victims, except by intensifying it, though it may sometimes be possible, by a sufficiently thorough process, to stamp out a weak or nascent sect altogether. And an earnest believer would feel the religious force of this objection the most keenly, while it would not affect the argument from political expediency. He would also be likely to remember that even a persecution which is successful for the moment is pretty sure in the long run to injure any cause with whose religious interests it is supposed to be identified. Thus, to take an obvious example, English Roman Catholics are suffering to this day for the disastrous policy of the last few years of Catholic ascendency in England under Mary and Philip. But, in fact, all the chief persecutions recorded in history have sprung much more from social and political than from religious motives. This will at once be admitted as to the persecution of Christians during the first three centuries of our era, which was carried on under some of the best as well as some of the worst of the Roman Emperors, and had from their point of view a good deal to say for itself. It was only to show his contempt for the religion he had abandoned that Julian the Apostate did not choose to dignify it by a revival of their ineffectual severities, and, had he lived longer, it is more than probable that he would have changed his mind.

What is not so generally understood is, that the same principle lay at the root of the mediæval treatment of heresy. No doubt a theological theory was framed to justify it, which eventually found its way into the canon law, but the theory grew out of the practical necessity, real or supposed, not *vice versâ*. Thus, to take a critical example, the extermination of the Albigenses was considered, and there were plausible grounds for considering it, essential for the preservation of Christian society, and that not simply on account of their immoralities, but of the social and political principles of the sect, which was moulded on a radically different ethical standard. It was regarded by contemporary public opinion much as we should regard a community of Thugs, or, to take a modern parallel, as the Salt Lake settlement is coming to be regarded in the United States. And the same idea was acted upon in cases to which its application is less obvious. It was thought dangerous to admit any new religion into a State organized on the basis of religious uniformity. Now there are obvious advantages in religious uniformity from a purely political point of view—witness "the religious difficulty," in educational and other matters, which is so perplexing to modern statesmen—and it may even be argued that it is necessary at a certain stage of political development. In the youth of States, when they are maturing their system of law and imbibing that religious spirit which lies at the basis of all law, and again in their weakness, so long as they cannot stand without the

L

support of an ecclesiastical organization and the sanction
of definite religious ideas, this uniformity may be said to
be necessary to them.   Some States again are more fragile
than others, and more sensitive to religious dissent.   This
at all events is the historical explanation of mediæval
intolerance, but it came inevitably in course of time to
be justified by simpler and less tenable arguments, and
then to be continued when it had already become an
anachronism.   It is always a temptation to men to gener-
alise from their immediate experience, and to imagine that
what is right or expedient or excusable in a given case
holds good as a universal law.   Thus the Southern States
of the American Union held a theory of slavery, and the
Northern States held a theory of abolition, equally absolute and equally unreasonable.   Mediæval, and indeed
Catholic persecution generally, was in reality, like that
carried on by the Roman Empire against the Christians,
more political than theological, and defensive rather than
aggressive, the great exception to this rule being found in
the cruel and senseless religious policy of Louis XIV.
But the practice, which had been formulated into a system
by theologians and canonists, survived when its original
grounds had passed away, and we look with natural horror
at the most glaring instance of it in the Spanish Inquisition, which may properly be regarded in the light of a
gigantic anachronism ; partly explicable, however, by the
peculiar circumstances of early Spanish history, which had
identified Catholic with national sentiment, much as in the
sixteenth century Protestantism became identified with
national sentiment in England.   It was to the last a
political rather than an ecclesiastical institution, and dealt

with sundry offences of a wholly secular kind, such as selling horses across the Pyrenees. After making all deductions for current exaggerations—and Llorente's figures are successfully demolished by Hefele in his *Life of Ximenes*— it was bad enough in all conscience, but it is worth observing that it does not seem to have done such fatal injury to literature as is often represented, and as we might *à priori* have expected. From 1500 to 1670 Spanish literature was at its zenith, and Spanish theologians took the lead at the Council of Trent. Cervantes died in the same year as Shakspeare, Lopez and Calderon much later. Mariana, who has been called "the only Jesuit that ever saw and spoke the truth in Church and State," and who was perhaps the ablest writer that powerful Order ever produced, lived and wrote and published in Spain under the Inquisition. Historical science, as distinct from the history of their own country, and physical science, have never flourished among the Spaniards, but that seems to be due rather to their national character than to the Inquisition, for national history and theology are more provocative of censorship, and Spain has done no more for science since the tribunal was abolished than before. But this by the way. It is not of course meant as an apology for the Spanish Inquisition, but merely as noting some points, apt to be overlooked, which may contribute to a more accurate appreciation of its historical position. Shocking as were the cruelties perpetrated, it still represented, like the Albigensian crusade and other mediæval severities, though under altered circumstances and with far less excuse, the political and defensive rather than the aggressive and theological principle of intolerance.

L 2

We have seen that the principal persecutions, Christian as well as Pagan, were justified, or capable of being plausibly justified, on other than doctrinal grounds, according to the circumstances of the case. But the practice gradually generated a theory, which came in time to be authoritatively sanctioned. Not to go further back, Leo X. condemned Luther's statement that to burn heretics is *contra caritatem Spiritûs;* Benedict XIV., the most tolerant of Popes, is hardly less explicit in a Brief of 1748, and Pius VI. in a Brief of 1791. At the same time it is true, and could easily be shown by copious references to their writings, that the speculative and purely theological principle of intolerance is far more universally and emphatically taught by the early Protestant divines than had ever been the case previously. All the leading Reformers of the sixteenth century, without a single exception, are most emphatic on this point, and they insist on it strictly as a religious duty, and for aggressive quite as much as for defensive purposes. Nor did they shrink, when they had the power, from translating their theory into practice. This arose partly no doubt from the Calvinist doctrine, which has always shown an affinity with persecution, partly from a literal application of Old Testament precedents, partly and in great measure from the belief—by no means extinct yet—that the Pope is Anti-Christ, and his adherents not heretics simply, but idolaters. Of the fact at all events there can be no shadow of doubt. Cranmer was zealous in burning Anabaptists; and Calvin won the warm approval of all the Protestant leaders in Germany when he sent Servetus to the stake. The gentle Osiander wished both Papists and Anabaptists to be suppressed. Luther, in spite

of the thesis condemned by Leo X., proclaimed the duty
of the State to put down "abominations," and he expressly
reckoned among them a denial of his dogma of justification
by faith ; no Government could tolerate heresy without
being responsible for the souls it destroyed, and the Mass
must be suppressed as the worst kind of idolatry.   Even
Melancthon insisted that new opinions should be punished
with death, and highly applauded the burning of Servetus
as "a pious and memorable example for posterity."   Bucer
and Zwinglius maintained the same view, and Bullinger
boasted that "by the grace of God we have always punished
heresy with fire."   Beza wrote an elaborate treatise in
defence of the same thesis.   John Knox, as is well known,
called toleration "opening the floodgates of heresy," and
objected to the Queen being allowed to have "the idol
of the Mass" in her private chapel.   Nor can it be fairly
said that the Reformers merely inherited these views from
their Popish ancestors.   For we have seen already that
the latter had usually based their persecutions on grounds
of ecclesiastical or civil policy, while the Protestant authorities, almost without exception, laid down the "principle"
that religious error, as such, deserved the severest punishment.   In the next century the same abstract principle of
intolerance is laid down by two writers so widely differing
from the early Reformers and from each other as Archbishop Laud and Milton.   But it must suffice to have
called attention to this important fact ; there is no need
to pursue the subject further here.   One other point
requires to be noticed in conclusion.   Whatever may be
pleaded in defence or in excuse of intolerance, under given
circumstances, on grounds independent of religious doctrine,

can hardly apply to the infliction of civil disabilities on the adherents of any particular religion, which do not preserve uniformity but supremacy, and are shown by experience to be a great political evil. It is easier, for instance, to justify the expulsion of the Moors from Spain, or the attempted suppression of Christianity in the Roman Empire, than the humiliating and unprofitable restrictions imposed on Roman Catholics in England before 1829, and on Protestants in Austria before 1859. To sum up what has been said ; so far from intolerance being a religious duty, as all the Reformers and several Popes have taught, the principle of toleration comes to us commended by all the best as well as the earliest traditions of the Christian Church. It is a principle, however, which has frequently been held liable to exception from ethical, social, and political considerations, on which it is enough to observe here that the necessity for making an exception requires at all events to be in each case distinctly proved.

XVIII

"BLACK AND BLOODY GARDINER."

IF there is any truth in the proverb, " Throw plenty of mud, and some will stick," it no doubt applies especially to cases where the *odium theologicum* comes in to clench the charge. There are no lies that die so hard as lies that have a controversial importance. The whole history of " the B. Reformation," from whatever side it is told, is a conspicuous illustration of this; but it is only with the English Reformation, and with one distinguished personage whose name is mixed up in the contest, that we are immediately concerned here. Everybody of course is familiar with the name of " Bonner, whom all generations shall call bloody," or, as Foxe, with characteristic coarseness, meant for humour, delights to call him, " that bloody bitesheep." But it was something new to find the " fixed epithet " which Fuller and Foxe have succeeded in attaching to Bonner, like Homer's " rosy-fingered morn," quietly extended, with hardly a word of explanation or evidence— in a speech of Sir William Harcourt's ten years ago on the Public Worship Bill—to "the black and bloody Gardiner." There may be some *primâ facie* ground—though it is really nothing more — for speaking of "the bloody Bonner"; but there is not even any plausible pretext for affixing such an epithet to Gardiner. That he has been denounced by historians like Hume, and in our days by Mr. Froude, as a persecutor is true enough; with what amount of reason will appear presently. But to justify such a description as "black and bloody," something more is required than to show that a high official took the part required by his office in the legal punishment of heretics, in an age when the very notion of toleration was scouted on all sides alike, certainly not least by the Protestant leaders. That there are persecutors of the sixteenth century fairly open to the charge of cruelty is true; no impartial student of history can doubt that neither Gardiner nor even Bonner is among them. And it is only fair to remember that Gardiner, unlike some of his contemporaries, did not seek to impose upon others a faith to which he was himself indifferent, or for which he had not, during the six years of Protestant ascendency under Edward, been content to suffer with patience and dignity. His position was rather a peculiar one, and Mr. Froude, who has a keen eye for theological distinctions, is not altogether wrong in calling him the "inventor of Anglicanism." He was firmly attached to those Catholic doctrines which continued to form part of the established religion to the close of Henry's reign, both before and after the breach with Rome, and he suffered imprisonment throughout the reign of his successor rather than abandon them. But while he consistently adhered from first to last to the whole cycle of beliefs which it is the modern fashion to stigmatize under the name of "sacerdotalism" —and that may perhaps help to explain Sir W. Harcourt's and Mr. Froude's peculiar bitterness against him — he cannot without a great abuse of terms be called a Romanizer or Romanist, hardly even, strictly speaking, a Roman Catholic. The Papal Supremacy he seems to have regarded as a matter of indifference in itself, though, after six years' experience of Edward's Protestant headship, he may naturally have thought the Royal Supremacy a worse than questionable substitute.[1] But this was seldom or never the critical question in the Marian persecutions. Of the three hundred or so of victims—the precise number appears to be 277—put to death for heresy during her reign, scarcely any suffered for rejecting the Pope's supremacy. Their trial almost always turned on the denial of doctrines about which—unlike Cranmer, who burnt Zwinglians, while he shared their opinions—neither Bonner nor Gardiner had ever wavered, most often on the Real Presence. There is no evidence whatever that either of these prelates was harsh or bloodthirsty in enforcing the law on that matter, and there is much evidence to the contrary; and this is especially true of Gardiner.

Let us first take the testimony of an impartial historian of the last generation, whose sympathies are strongly Protestant, and who had not the means which now exist of correcting popular misconceptions of history. To the common assumption, repeated by Sir W. Harcourt—on which a word shall be said presently—that Gardiner had a

[1] He had written in the reign of Henry VIII. in defence of the Royal Supremacy, in his book *De Vera Obedientia*, to which Bonner contributed a preface. But in a sermon at St. Paul's Cross, preached the Sunday after the public reconciliation of the realm by Cardinal Pole, he made a general retractation of the errors he had fallen into under Henry VIII. He preached before Edward VI. against the Papal Supremacy, but in defence of the Real Presence and Sacrifice of the Mass, for which he was sent to prison.

hand in the " Six Bloody Articles," or was their main
author, Sir James Mackintosh does not even allude. He
does indeed assert that Gardiner was "at least in the
beginning" a chief author of the Marian persecution, but
only on the wholly inadequate ground that his great
abilities, commanding character, and high station do not
allow us to doubt it; but he adds that the Chancellor
probably did not intend the persecution to extend beyond
the Protestant ringleaders, and that, when disappointed by
their resistance, he "withdrew from a share in vain bloodshed." That Gardiner did his best to confine the executions for heresy within these limits is perfectly true, and
we may gather even from Foxe's one-sided narrative a
similar inference as to Bonner. If there was to be persecution at all—and that neither of them could have
prevented, had he desired it—this was obviously the wisest
as well as the most merciful policy. Sir James Mackintosh
goes on to say—what has since been proved in detail by
Dr. Maitland—that many of the prelates are recorded
by Protestant writers to have exercised an effectual
and perhaps hazardous humanity, and that their violent
language was often a cloak for more effectually screening
the accused. He observes that of fourteen dioceses they
altogether prevented bloodshed in nine, and reduced it
within limits in the remaining five; "justice to Gardiner
requires it to be mentioned that his diocese was of the
bloodless class." And although he quotes with approval
Fuller's libellous description of Bonner—Dr. Maitland had
not then exposed its absurdity—he feels bound to point
out that Fuller's charge against the Bishop of London of
burning about one-half the martyrs in the kingdom really

proves nothing, inasmuch as they were sent to the capital from all parts of England for the purpose. We may add that many of Foxe's most ill-natured stories, when they come to be sifted, prove just as little, even assuming their accuracy to be beyond dispute, and that is not often the case. Thus, for instance, the well-known story—illustrated by a large woodcut in the old editions of Foxe's Martyrology—of Bonner's holding the hand of Thomas Tomkins, the weaver, over a lighted taper "to try his constancy," after exhausting all his powers of persuasion to induce him to recant, simply proves, if true, his persistent desire to save the prisoner from a punishment which it was not within his discretion to remit. As Maitland justly remarks, "Whether it was wisely done, people may dispute; but that it was kindly meant no person of common sense can doubt." And it is worth noting that in all similar tales about Bonner's cruelty, he is never alleged to have done these things in order to extort confession of guilt or names of accomplices by torture, but always with a view of inducing convicted heretics to adopt the only available means of saving themselves from further punishment. And he often, on Foxe's own showing, kept them in confinement for weeks or months, notwithstanding their refusal to listen to his persuasions, in the hope of their eventual submission. This hardly corresponds with the language of Foxe's elegant couplet :—

> This cannibal, in three years' space, three hundred martyrs slew,
> They were his food; he loved so blood; he spared none he knew.

But it would be mere waste of time to follow Foxe through the details of his nauseous indictment; Maitland's Essays may be consulted for a minute exposure of his wholesale mendacity.

If we turn back from Mackintosh to Hume, we shall find him taking the ordinary Protestant view of Gardiner's character, and implicitly crediting him with the Act of the Six Articles, but without alleging any evidence whatever for this charge, or for saddling him with the graver responsibility of the Marian persecution, while he mentions one fact which looks entirely the other way. After Mary's accession, Peter Martyr, anticipating trouble, was anxious to leave the country, but some zealous Catholics moved for his commitment to prison. Gardiner not only opposed this, urging that he had come over by invitation of the Government, but supplied him with the means for his journey home. Mr. Froude, as might be expected, is both more explicit and much more bitter than Hume. His way of dealing with the case is highly characteristic. He tells us in his third volume that the cruel nature of the Act of Six Articles was attributed "by sound authority" to the influence of Gardiner, but the only authority he gives, besides Foxe's—which he admits not to be worth much—is a phrase in a letter of Melanchthon's to Henry VIII., "Oh cursed bishops! oh wicked Winchester!" which is certainly worth no more.[1] When, however, he comes in the sixth volume to sum up Gardiner's character on his death, the indictment opens with "He passed the Six Articles Bill," as though it were one of the most

---

[1] Dixon, who gives the letter in full (*Hist. Church of England*, vol. ii. pp. 159, 160), observes, with obvious justice, that the writer is evidently hitting at the King in hitting the bishops, the supposed advisers of the King. What he dared not say of the King he said of them.

notorious facts of history, instead of resting at best on
mere gratuitous conjecture. His other allegations of
cruelty against Gardiner are based on much the same kind
of evidence. As to his high abilities and services to the
State, Mr. Froude of course finds himself obliged to speak
with decent respect of a man who was conspicuously
among the foremost statesmen and ecclesiastics of his age.
But when he calls him "vindictive, ruthless, and treacherous," and "the incarnate expression of the fury of the
ecclesiastical faction," he simply describes his character
and career by contraries; and when he winds up with
the dogmatic assertion—veiled under the thin disguise of
a Latin extract—that after his death Gardiner "went
down to hell," his authority may fairly be questioned for
interpolating this new article into the Protestant creed.
Lingard may perhaps be put aside as a prejudiced
witness, yet his History is generally colourless enough,
and he had no particular reason for admiring a prelate
who, if in one sense a staunch Catholic, was very vacillating
in his allegiance to Rome. He mentions Gardiner's being
on one of the two Committees named for drawing up the
Act of Six Articles—as was also Cranmer—but mentions
further that, as there is extant a Bill nearly similar
in Henry's own handwriting, there is good reason for
believing the King himself to be its real author. Blunt
states absolutely that it was so. Cranmer as well as
Gardiner voted for the Bill. Lingard emphatically denies
that there is any authentic document to support the
charge made against Gardiner by Reformed writers of
being responsible for the Marian persecution, while the
whole tenor of his conduct contradicts it. It was Gardiner,

as he points out, who saved Elizabeth and Courtenay not without considerable risk to his own reputation with the Queen, from the penalties of treason to which their share in Wyatt's rebellion had exposed them ; and he further records how, when the epithet . " bloody " was first applied to him by Francis Hastings, Parsons indignantly replied that " any good-natured Protestant that lived in Queen Mary's time, and hath both wit to judge and indifference to speak the truth without passion, will confess that no one great man in that government was further off from blood and bloodiness, or from cruelty and revenge, than Bishop Gardiner, who was known to be a most tender-hearted and mild man in that behalf."

To come down to contemporary writers, the estimate of Gardiner's character and conduct given in Dixon's *History of the Church of England*—far the fullest and most impartial work on the English Reformation published in our own day—accords entirely with that of Lingard and Maitland. The work has not as yet advanced beyond the second year of Edward VI., but the author acquits Gardiner of any but a purely official and formal share in the passing or enforcement of the Act of Six Articles, and points out, in opposition to Foxe, how his influence as well as Bonner's was habitually employed to mitigate rather than to fan the flame of persecution. The testimony of Mr. Blunt, another learned Anglican writer, in his *Reformation of the Church of England*, is still more explicit. After citing the savage indictment of Foxe and Fuller, he observes : " The charge against Bishop Gardiner may be soon dismissed. So long as his influence lasted "—*i. e.* till the Queen's marriage—" *no person was executed on the ground of heresy.*"

During the year he lived after that time he sat on one
trial of heretics only, upon a Commission over which he
had to preside as Lord Chancellor, and here it fell to his
duty to pronounce formal sentence of excommunication;
but "no persons in his diocese were burnt for heresy until
a year and a half after his death." And in the case of
this solitary trial, he used his utmost endeavours to provide
a way of escape for Hooper, Rogers, and the rest of the
accused, as he also did his best to procure the pardon of
Cranmer, whom he had every personal reason for disliking
and distrusting, and who had shown him no mercy or
justice in Edward's reign. Such was the man described
by the infamous Poynet—a favourite of Cranmer's intruded
into his see under Edward, and who lived there in
adultery with a butcher's wife of Nottingham—in language
worth putting on record, as an illustration of the traditional
Protestant fable about Gardiner, the more so as it is
endorsed, with some slight reserve, by the veracious Foxe,
though contradicted by the testimony alike of Holbein's
portrait, of the monumental effigy at Winchester, and of
Gardiner's own writings, which "give abundant evidence
that he was a man of solid learning." Poynet says : "This
doctor hath a swart colour. He hath a hanging look,
frowning brown eyes an inch within his head, a nose
hooked like a buzzard's, nostrils like a horse, ever snuffing
in the wind, a sparrow mouth, and great paws like the devil,
talons on his feet like a gripe, two inches longer than the
natural toes, and so tied to with sinews that he cannot
abide to be touched, nor scarce suffer them to touch the
stones." [1] As to this last detail of the " monstrous making

---

[1] Poynet elsewhere calls him "the great devil and cut-throat of
England, the Papists' God."

and misshaped fashion of his feet and toes," Foxe says it
"hath been constantly reported" to him, but retains just
enough self-respect to decline positively to commit himself. After dismissing Gardiner, Mr. Blunt proceeds to
Bonner, who, according to Cowper's familiar couplet, based
on Foxe,

> "blithe as shepherd at a wake,
> Enjoyed the show, and danced about the stake,"

though in fact he was never present at the stake at all.   It
is shown at length that he also did no more than discharge
his office as ecclesiastical judge, which he "had no more
power or authority to refuse to exercise, as the law then
stood, than a judge of assize has to refuse to try the
prisoners brought before him at a gaol delivery"; and it is
further shown that in the discharge of his office he exhibited
the utmost gentleness and forbearance, so much so indeed,
that he was publicly reprimanded for his leniency by the
Crown.   Of him, as of Gardiner, the great Foxian tradition,
on which writers like Strype and Burnet have implicitly
relied, is not only a baseless myth, but a myth founded on
a categorical contradiction of the facts.

As regards the Six Articles Act, however, there is a
word more to be said.   Lingard naturally enough calls it
"a severe and barbarous statute," and so it was, judged by
any modern standard of toleration.   But the Act was
framed in a severe and barbarous age, and the offences
against which it was in fact mainly directed were of a
nature that would not now be tolerated in any civilised
society.   Subsequent events show that it was intended
to frighten people rather than to hurt them, and was never

---

[1] Blunt's *Reformation,* vol. ii. pp. 229 *sqq.,* 282 *sqq.,* pp. 124 *sq.*

meant to be executed according to the letter. It caused several of the more violent partisans of the Reformation to quit the country, and made those who stayed at home more quiet and peaceable. At the outside, according to Foxe's list, which is not likely to be defective, only twenty-eight persons suffered death under the Act during the eight years it continued in force. But the sort of "ribalds" against whom it was chiefly put in use were for the time effectually suppressed. It may sound strange to our ears to hear of persons being arraigned and punished for "reading the Bible in Paul's", or "depraving the Sacrament"; but when we find that the first charge meant collecting a multitude of people and making a tumult in the Cathedral, while the second includes such practises as maintaining boys to sing songs against the Sacrament of the Altar in public, and interrupting the solemnities of Divine service with studied mockery of what was still, be it remembered, the religious belief of the immense majority of the nation, we can hardly wonder that the Government should have thought it time to interfere. Nor is there any proof that the Bishops carried out the Act in a violent manner, but the reverse. Of all the prosecutions that took place under it, Dixon observes: "These were lay prosecutions, not clerical; they were neither instigated by the clergy nor in the main conducted by them." On one occasion, for instance, when two hundred persons had been presented to Gardiner for tumultuous proceedings of this kind, he was "content that one should be bound for another," and on this easy bail they were all discharged. There is, however, as was said before, no reason to believe that Gardiner had any hand in originating the Act, and of the first four

M

persons condemned to death under its provisions one was begged off by him. And his dealings with those brought before his Court as Lord Chancellor for sedition or heresy in Mary's reign were quite of a piece with this conduct, although, like Lawrence Saunders, who "gave a privy nip to Winchester," as Foxe expresses it, they often publicly and grossly insulted him to his face. It would be easy of course, if space permitted, to go more fully into detail, but enough has now been said to show what sort of reliance can be placed on writers like Fuller and Foxe, or even on Strype and Burnet, who, like some later writers, are their servile copyists in describing the bishops of the Marian period generally as a whole forest of wild beasts raging among a flock of defenceless sheep, and Bonner in particular as an ogre whose fury no sex, quality, or age could escape. If their language about "wily Winchester," who is now held up to odium as "black and bloody Gardiner," is a trifle less grotesquely virulent, it is still not one whit more consonant with the truth of history.

XIX.

ICONOCLASM.

THE first impression made on most readers of the telegram announcing the destruction of the Vendôme column, in May 1871, was one of regret that the Versailles Government had not shown sufficient promptitude in mastering Paris to anticipate this act of wanton Vandalism. Many and bitter were the reproaches levelled at the Philistine brutality of Red Republicanism, and for the next four years, till in 1875 it was restored, English visitors took up their parable about the curse of mob rule, as they turned from the vacant site of what had been for sixty years one of the most conspicuous ornaments of the French capital. Nor can it be said that such reproaches were unreasonable. The love of destruction for its own sake, and especially destruction of anything that may be considered a badge of superior authority, is a passion strongly developed in the manly bosoms of those who delight to call themselves "the People;" and we may well believe that the men of Paris gazed on the downfall of the column in the Place Vendôme with much the same feeling of coarse satisfaction which inspired "the men of London", as they witnessed or helped to effect some few years before the smashing of the Hyde Park railings. Only

M 2

their satisfaction would be so far more intense, as the column was not only a symbol of sovereignty, but a very beautiful and costly work of art. Most of us are not disposed to think very highly of the culture of the Commune, notwithstanding Mr. Bridges' favourable estimate of it as compared with the results of an Oxford education; and the indignant censors of the iconoclastic tendencies of Republicanism might point their moral by reminding us that the Parisian democrats of to-day are but treading in the footsteps of their ancestors in the first Revolution, who destroyed the statue of Louis XIV. on the very spot afterwards selected by Napoleon I. for the monument to commemorate his victories. Nor is the analogy merely one of outward form. Neither Louis XIV. nor Napoleon was a model of exalted virtue, and history has a heavy indictment to bring against the principles and policy of their administration. But that they were two of the greatest rulers who ever swayed the destinies of France, and that they raised her to a height of material splendour unequalled at any other periods of her history, is beyond question. Their rule may not unfairly be characterized as an immoral despotism; but Frenchmen might be expected to treat with some decent respect the memory of despots whose faults represented and flattered the national character, and who contributed so much to the realisation of its ideal of national greatness. The *sans culottes* of the '89 Revolution, like the Commune of 1871, were otherwise minded. No sense of historic continuity or æsthetic grace could avail to stay their hand in defacing the beautiful records of a magnificent but monarchical past. They quite deserve all the hard words that are said of them. But it would be a mistake to regard iconoclasm as a mere incident of republican excess. It is one of those natural instincts, partly good, partly evil, which have played an important part in the history of the world.

We are reminded of the passion of destruction for its own sake among the uneducated masses. Perhaps Mr. Darwin would tell us that it is a relic of that earlier stage of development when we were gradually fighting our way to full humanity by the process of natural selection, and with the aid of those destructive organs which have gradually disappeared since the struggle for existence ceased. At all events it is a fact. The pleasure felt by a baby in smashing a toy is very much akin to the pleasure felt by a boor in smashing a work of art. Probably in both cases it consists partly in a sort of rude sense of power, or " consciousness of the *ego*," which finds its intellectual expression in the *man fühlt sich* of the German student who is breaking loose from the trammels of hereditary belief. It is the same sort of feeling that leads a savage to value himself on the number of men he has killed in battle. To make is of course a much higher test of power than to unmake, but it is also much more difficult, and children and savages naturally catch at that exercise of independent action which comes readiest to their hand. And men who have little or no education remain in many respects grown-up children all their lives. This goes far to account for the— often quite purposeless—mischief of a mob who are set free for the time from all restraints of custom or police. There is a story in the life of John Wesley of a lawless rabble who surrounded the house where he was staying, somewhere in the North of England, and spent half the night in carrying him about from one place to another, with occasional threats of ducking or more serious outrage, and then took him home again. Yet they had no particular spite against him, and cheered lustily when he addressed them. It was simply a stupid and brutal frolic, which the local magistrates were too orthodox or too inert to interfere with. The midnight revellers who destroyed the Hermes busts at Athens were probably of a very different class, but probably also they were drunk; and the characteristic "insolence" of Alcibiades made him act more like an overgrown schoolboy than a man of genius and high culture. But his iconoclasm was not the mere instinct of mischief, still less the boorish pleasure in defacing what one cannot appreciate. The Hermes busts, like most popular idols, are said to have been exceedingly ugly, but they were the object of profound if not very intelligent veneration, and to deface them was to inflict one of the keenest possible insults on the national religion. It gratified the sense of power, not so much by an act of wanton destruction as because it was an outrage on public decency, which, if suffered to go unpunished, would show that the perpetrators could hold themselves superior to the laws by which the rest of their countrymen were bound. And thus it was a more refined, but not one whit a nobler, form of iconoclasm than the vulgar pleasure of a Parisian mob in pulling down Imperial statues, or of a Protestant mob at the Reformation in tossing elaborate missals and vestments into a bonfire, and dancing to the music of an ecclesiastical chant round the burning pile.

It must not, however, be supposed that the iconoclastic instinct is never anything more than the aimless passion

for destroying, with a consciousness more or less realised
of the exercise of power in the act. In coarser natures
such a sentiment is almost sure to be present, even when
it does not predominate. The reformer who breaks with
axes and hammers the carved work which his ancestors
had reverently laboured at, is apt to be quite as much
influenced by love of mischief as by hatred of idolatry;
but the latter motive has dominated some of the strongest,
if not the largest, minds among those which have shaped
the course of history. Iconoclasm, when it rises above
mere wanton destructiveness, expresses abhorrence either
for the thing destroyed or for the ideas it is supposed or
intended to convey. The distinction is necessary to be
borne in mind. The column in the Place Vendôme was
designed to commemorate Napoleon's German victories;
but the more rational agents in the piece of Vandalism
perpetrated there in May 1871 meant to signalize their
hatred, not of French victory, but of Imperialism. So
again, the Puritan zealots, who smashed crucifixes and
images of the saints, did not, we must presume, wish to
assail the sacred personages represented—at all events
as regards the crucifix—but what they considered an
objectionable method of honouring them. But iconoclasm
implies feelings and tends to produce results very much
beyond what the iconoclasts themselves are thinking of.
This may be illustrated by two comments which have
been made, from very opposite points of view, on the
great iconoclastic controversy of the eighth and ninth
centuries, which ended in the use of images, as distinct from
pictures—we need not trouble ourselves here with the
point of this somewhat fanciful contrast—being proscribed

in the Eastern Church, and authoritatively sanctioned in
the West. The bitterness of feeling which it evoked may
be judged from the opprobrious sobriquet of Copronymus,
bestowed on the Greek Emperor who had made himself
most notorious as a leader of the iconoclast party. Yet
why should the question between images and "icons," as
the Greeks called their pictures, so violently embitter those
who had no disagreement in their belief about what either
symbol equally represented? It was hinted at the time,
and has often been said since by Latin writers, that the
doctrine of the Incarnation was at stake, and that the
dislike to images of Christ was prompted by a repulsion of
the subtle Greek intellect from the anthropomorphic side
of Christianity. There is certainly some force in the
criticism, but the Easterns as certainly had no conscious
intention of disparaging the Incarnation, and the first
decree against images was immediately prompted by the
reproaches of the Mahometans against the idolatry of the
Christian Church. On the other hand, modern writers, like
Dean Stanley, have spoken, not without reason, of the
Greek Church rejecting in her prohibition of images the
influences of Christian art and civilisation, and have contrasted her conduct with that of Rome in accepting the
Renaissance. And it is quite true that the close of the
iconoclastic controversy marks the period of the decadence
of all religious and intellectual energy in the East. We
need not adopt Mr. Froude's extreme, not to say extrava-
gant, view that the Eastern Christians stood on an immea-
surably lower level than their Mahometan assailants, but
there can be no doubt that Eastern Christianity, for the
last thousand years, has presented very much the appear-

ance of a sterile petrifaction of its former self. Yet it would be absurd to suppose that the iconoclastic Emperors and Synods of the eighth century had any conscious intention of repudiating art, and the civilising influences which it indicates or effects. But the iconoclastic instinct, though it has its nobler side, and has not unfrequently been the vehicle of righteous indignation against falsehood and oppression, is in itself essentially narrow and debasing. It belongs to the lower, not the higher part of our nature, and inclines us directly not so much to reject the evil as to refuse to recognise what is good.

The religious narrowness of iconoclasm was illustrated at the Reformation in the reckless demolition of all outward adjuncts of devotion, because some of them had been perverted to idle or superstitious uses. Its political narrowness is not the exclusive badge of any one party, though, for reasons already referred to, it has a natural affinity with the violence of democratic agitators. Napoleon I., whose statue was demolished in Paris, displayed an almost puerile littleness in his anxiety to efface every visible memorial of the ancient monarchy of France. The statue of Louis XIV. had indeed fallen already, but his stringent orders to obliterate the *fleurs de lis*, wherever found, were hardly less absurd than the attempt to expunge from French literature all mention of the former state of things, as though he really thought it would be possible to make Frenchmen forget that they had any history before the 18 Brumaire. This is no doubt an extreme, but it is also a highly characteristic, instance of the genuine spirit of iconoclasm. As there can be no image worship without images, so there can be no iconoclasm without images to break. It is essentially a protest against what has hitherto been held in honour, and its radical vice is the resolve to break with the past, because in the past there have been errors and abuses, as though forsooth the present or the future were at all more likely to be free from them. Far truer and nobler is Mr. Ruskin's eloquent tribute to the memory of those great mediæval church builders, whose faith he does not share: "Of them, and their life and toil upon the earth, one reward, one evidence, is left to us in those grey heaps of deep-wrought stone. They have taken with them to the grave their powers, their honours, and their errors; but they have left us their adoration." No doubt there are some idols which deserve to be utterly abolished, but it is not often that the outward symbol even of a rejected creed or a justly dispossessed sovereignty has no historic or artistic interest which gives it a claim to live. The most ardent Christian would hardly think it a discredit to the Popes that they have done their best to preserve the relics of Pagan and Imperial Rome, although the Paganism had become in its dotage a coarse and heartless superstition, and the Empire a gigantic system of tyranny and corruption. To make a clean sweep of the past is an unhopeful augury for the future. The life of nations as of individuals is made up of their accumulated experiences, and France can as little divest herself of the traditions of the monarchy or of the Empire as England can ignore the elements of national life which the Stuart reigns or the Commonwealth have bequeathed to her. We should have more faith in the stability of some future Government in France, if she had shown less eagerness in effacing all traces of those which are passed away.

XX

CHRISTIAN TEACHING ON THE RIGHT OF REBELLION.

IN a Papal Encyclical, issued about five years ago, occurred a passage which was criticized at the time in some quarters as teaching that "a government, *however bad, is not to be resisted,* except it require from its subjects that which is rebellion against God, but that in that case God is to be obeyed rather than man." It was observed that this theory, unless very freely interpreted, " would hardly cover the ground of most Catholic rebellions." But the words in the original Latin are patient, not to say suggestive, of a different construction. The passage runs as follows :—"Si tamen quandoque contingat temere et ultra modum publicam a principibus potestatem exerceri, Catholicæ Ecclesiæ doctrina in eos insurgere *proprio Marte* non sinit, ne ordinis tranquillitas magis magisque turbetur, *neve societas majus exinde detrimentum capiat.*" The phrase " proprio Marte," especially when coupled with the reason added for this prohibition, seems to point to violent and seditious actions on the part of individuals, who have not the general body of the nation at their back. And as the Pope does not profess to be laying down any new doctrine of his own, but only recording " the teaching of the Catholic Church," it may be worth while to inquire what that teaching is, as a matter of history, which is in itself a question of considerable interest. There is not indeed any formal dogma or definition either of the ancient or mediæval Church on the subject, and the "Catholic doctrine," if there be any, must therefore be gathered from the general Christian tradition and the teaching of accredited divines. And if we go back to the Fathers, it cannot be denied that the most stringent interpretation of the Pope's language would be supported and even demanded by the almost unanimous tenor of their teaching on the absolute duty of submission. The very few apparent exceptions occasionally quoted only serve to prove the rule, as, *e.g.*, when St. Gregory Nazianzen and St. Cyril inveigh against the memory of Julian the Apostate, after his death, and St. Hilary denounces the Arian Emperor Constantius as a precursor of Antichrist and the like, when he may be supposed to have already been virtually deposed for his heresy. As a rule, the early Fathers seem to have taken St. Paul's admonition to obey the powers that be in its most rigorous sense, and would admit no right of rebellion against a Nero or a Caligula, though Nero was by many of them regarded as the personal Antichrist. De Maistre stands almost alone among modern Catholic writers in maintaining this view. He declares it to be a maxim of the Catholic religion "that against our legitimate Sovereign, though he be a Nero, we have no other right than respectfully to tell him the truth, and let him cut off our heads for doing so."[1] That the maintenance of this principle, which was not only taught but consistently acted upon by the early

---

[1] *Correspondance Diplom.*, II. 132.

Christians throughout the ages of persecution—and where-by, as a modern writer expresses it, they constituted themselves the champions of legality in an age of turbulence and disorder, when the rival forces of civilisation and barbarism were engaged in an internecine strife—was salutary in its results, may be readily admitted. It would have introduced fresh and disastrous complications if the Christians, when they became strong enough, had assumed the position of insurgents against the persecuting Empire. They acted on a true and generous instinct, but their theory was certainly an excessive one, and this became manifest when it was reproduced under altered circumstances in the English Church of the sixteenth and seventeenth centuries, where the doctrine which has been ascribed, on very insufficient grounds, to Leo XIII. was persistently inculcated in all its fulness.

We need not endorse the characteristic maledictions of Macaulay against the Church he so little loved, which "continued to be for one hundred and fifty years the servile handmaid of monarchy, the steady enemy of public liberty," and "once, and but once—for a moment, and but for a moment—when her own dignity and property was touched, forgot to practise the submission she had taught." But he has not misrepresented what may be called the *consensus* of the great Anglican divines on the duty of passive obedience. Their teaching is summed up with unmistakable emphasis and precision in the authorised Homilies on *Obedience* and on *Wilful Rebellion*, forming part of the First Book, published by Cranmer under Edward VI., in 1547, but the Homily against Rebellion was enlarged in 1573 under Elizabeth. We are there

taught that "eternal damnation is prepared for all impeni-
tent rebels in hell, with Satan, the first founder of rebellion,"
while "heaven is the place of good obedient subjects, and
hell the prison and dungeon of rebels against God and their
prince." Nor does the badness of the government make
any difference in the paramount obligation of obedience,
for "a rebel is worse than the worst prince, and rebellion
worse than the worst government of the worst prince hath
hitherto been." Bad government is indeed to be accepted
as a righteous punishment, not made an occasion of fresh
sin. "God placeth as well evil princes as good," and it
follows that "for subjects to deserve through their sins to
have an evil prince, and then to rebel against him, were
double and treble evil by provoking God more to plague
them." And the example of the Jews submitting to
Nebuchadnezzar, and St. Paul to Nero, are cited in
evidence of this view. Jeremy Taylor, in the chief Anglican work on Moral Theology, the *Ductor Dubitantium*,
lays down the same doctrine, declaring it to be so plainly
set forth in Scripture as hardly to need the comment
supplied in the teaching and practice of the Church, which
is however equally unmistakable. Hooker, whose moral
and philosophical teachings are much more shaped on
scholastic than patristic models, though he does not always
acknowledge his obligations, takes a different line, but he
stands almost alone. And even he, though he lays down
principles very like those of Suarez—of whom something
will be said presently—hesitates to draw the natural conclusion. He considers the royal power to be derived from
the people, and subject to the law ; and yet when he
comes to inquire whether "the body politic" may with-

draw the authority it has delegated, when it is misused, he only ventures to reply that "it must be presumed that supreme governors will not in such cases oppose themselves and be stiff in detaining that the use whereof is with public detriment ; but surely without their consent I see not how the body should be able by any fresh means to help itself, saving when dominion doth escheat."[1] There is no need to follow the course of this absolutist teaching in secular and even sceptical English writers of later date, like Barclay, Filmer, Hobbes, Bolingbroke, Hume, and others, as we are at present concerned with the theological aspect of the question, as it has in successive ages presented itself to the mind of the Church. We have seen that the great Anglican divines reproduced on this matter the stringent teaching of the Fathers, without making any allowance for the altered social and political conditions of their own day. But they certainly did not inherit that teaching by un-broken succession from the earliest ages to their own, as Taylor's language would imply, when he says that the doctrine of the Church is " without any variety, dissent, or interruption, universally agreed upon, universally practised and taught, that, let the powers set over us be what they will, we must suffer it and never right ourselves."

Two distinct and in some sense opposite tendencies of mediæval thought conspired to induce a gradual modifica-tion of the patristic doctrine of passive obedience. On the one hand, the growth of the Papal power, with its steadily ascending claim of supreme jurisdiction over all temporal governments, introduced a new element into the discus-sion. In deposing tyrannical and heretical sovereigns,

[1] *Eccl. Pol.*, VIII. ii. 10.

who, unlike the Pagan Emperors of a former day, had become by baptism her own children and subjects, the Church professed to act, and often did act, as the organ and executor of the moral sense of the Christian community, and thus the idea was at once suggested, under whatever limitations and control, of the nation having rights as against its rulers. On the other hand, the rise of the scholastic philosophy marked a great upheaval of thought, struggling to emancipate itself from the fetters of a mere dead traditionalism. It has been called, and in one sense not unjustly, a rationalistic movement, for it aimed at bringing all questions within the sphere of its cognisance under the domain of reason, though it accepted as ultimate premisses and starting points of inquiry revealed as well as scientific truths assumed to be certainly and finally fixed. Archbishop Trench speaks of the Schoolmen as seeking " to inaugurate a supernatural rationalism in the Church." Thomas Aquinas, the greatest of them, was probably influenced by both religious and rational considerations when he argued that the duty of obedience to secular princes is only obligatory *in quantum ordo justitiæ requirit*, and is therefore forfeited by an unjust or usurping ruler. It was the general teaching of the Schoolmen that the power of Kings is derived mediately, not immediately, from God, and directly from the people. And this doctrine was reasserted and developed by Bellarmine, Suarez, and other great Jesuit theologians of the Reformation period, mainly of course, but by no means exclusively, in the interests of Papal supremacy over civil governments, and in opposition to Protestant princes. The Gallican divines naturally took a different line, harmonizing much more closely with that of the Caroline school in England, and Bossuet quietly observes that the Schoolmen, who for some centuries after St. Thomas were nearly unanimous in maintaining the view he opposes, are manifestly mistaken. The works both of Bellarmine and Suarez were publicly burnt by order of the Parliament of Paris. The work of Suarez—which was, by the way, written in reply to one bearing the name of James I. of England—distinctly subordinates the rights of the sovereign to those of the nation, even independently of the interposition of the Pope, or the lapse of the sovereign into heresy, which *ipso facto* annulled his right to the throne, though in that case it was better to await a definitive sentence of deprivation from the Pope; nor does he shrink from maintaining, as indeed Aquinas had done before him, that in extreme cases the sovereign may be put to death.

But the most remarkable work on the subject is that by the Spanish Jesuit Mariana—who was at once one of the ablest and the most honest and independent writers of his order—*De Rege et Regis Institutione*, which elaborately vindicates the doctrine of tyrannicide, and pronounces a warm eulogium on those who have had the courage to practise it, from Harmodius and Aristogeiton and Brutus to the young Dominican Clement, "the eternal glory of France," who killed Henry III. And it is carefully explained that a tyrant does not mean only a ruler who had originally no right to his throne, but a sovereign who by governing on selfish principles, instead of for the interests of his people, has forfeited his right to govern them. Of course this extreme remedy of assassination was only to be resorted to in extreme cases, and when all

N

constitutional methods of putting down the tyrant had failed or had been rendered unavailable, but Mariana evidently supposes such cases not to be so very uncommon. The same doctrine of tyrannicide was defended by other Jesuit writers, though it had been expressly condemned by a decree of the Council of Constance, occasioned by Jean Petit's advocacy of it at Paris. This decree Mariana rejects altogether, as not being confirmed by the Pope, while Suarez, who admits its authority, explains it as only applying to a legitimate sovereign. Many Protestant writers of the Reformation period advocated the same principle, which was acted upon in the assassination of the Duke of Guise and of Cardinal Beaton. But its systematic elaboration and defence was the special work of the Jesuits. It would of course be most untrue to say that the Church of Rome is in any way committed to the doctrine of tyrannicide, though canonized Saints and Popes, like St. Pius V. and St. Charles Borromeo, as well as Protestants like Buchanan and unbelievers like Sarpi, have deliberately maintained it. But it would be equally untrue to say that the duty of passive obedience, as taught by the Caroline divines, is a "Catholic doctrine" in any intelligible sense of the word. It was an ethical principle generally asserted and acted upon by the early Christians, but never thrown into a formal or dogmatic shape; and when questions of this kind came to be handled as matters of philosophical discussion, which was not the case in the early ages, it was at once challenged and very generally repudiated. De Maistre has already been referred to. He insists that the absolute despotism, and in fact virtual infallibility, of the civil ruler is the proper corollary of the absolute infallibility of the Pope, and that both are alike essential for the preservation respectively of Church and State.[1] In practice, both Catholics and Protestants in periods of fierce religious conflict have been too apt to bend their theories into conformity with the immediate exigencies and interests of their respective causes; but a close similarity may be traced between the abstract theories of Ultramontane and Puritan divines as to the proper method of dealing with "heretical" or "idolatrous" sovereigns. John Knox's *First Blast of the Trumpet against the monstrous Regimen of Women*, issued at Geneva in Queen Mary's reign, is an example in point. But, putting aside the extreme theory of tyrannicide, which is condemned, to say the least, by the verdict of enlightened experience, the doctrine of Mariana, that nations have an ultimate right of resisting an unjust ruler, whether his original title be legitimate or not, has never been either formally or practically rejected by the Church, and most persons in our own day would probably agree with him in thinking that it is supported by "the voice of nature and the common sense of mankind."

[1] "Il ne peut y avoir de société humaine sans gouvernement, ni de gouvernement sans souveraineté, *ni de souveraineté sans infaillibilité;* et ce dernier privilége est si absolument nécessaire qu'on est forcé de supposer l'infaillibilité *même dans les souverainetés temporelles* (ou elle n'est pas) sans peine de voir l'association se dissoudre. *L'Eglise ne demande rien de plus que les autres souverainetés."—Du Pape,* p. 147. Lamennais at the time expressed his full agreement with this view.

XXI

DIVINE RIGHT OF KINGS.

THE Prussian royal rescript which took Europe by surprise two years ago, whatever may be thought of it from a constitutional or practical point of view, did not profess to claim for the Prussian dynasty an indefeasible hereditary right to the throne. Nor do the claims it put forward go far, if at all, beyond those habitually asserted and to a large extent successfully enforced by George III. in this country less than a century ago. The doctrine of the Divine right of kings, satirized by Pope, and in our own day by Macaulay, as "the right Divine of kings to govern wrong," meant a good deal more. It is rightly called a "doctrine," for the theory of royal prerogative once maintained in this country by a powerful school both of jurists and divines was for about a century regarded and taught almost as a thirteenth article of the Apostles' Creed. It will perhaps surprise some readers, who may have been accustomed to laugh at the belief as an exploded mediæval superstition, to be told that it only originated at the close of the sixteenth or opening of the seventeenth century, and was in fact coeval in its origin and its decay with the succession of the Stuart line in England, including the reign of Queen Anne, if we choose to treat the Sacheverell affair as a kind of posthumous survival or recrudescence of the principle virtually expelled with James II. No doubt, both in England and in Christendom generally, there had been in earlier days a reverent appreciation of the Divinity which doth hedge about a king. But the highest expression and representation of monarchical supremacy in Europe throughout the middle ages was "the Holy Roman Empire," so called, as Mr. Bryce points out, as being nothing less than the visible Church or Christian society organized on its secular side under a form Divinely appointed. Yet the Empire was avowedly not hereditary but elective, nor was the elected Emperor authorised by custom or public opinion to assume his supreme title till he had received coronation at Rome from the hands of the Pope. Divine right indeed, if the powers that be are ordained of God, every legitimate Government, whether monarchical or not, must in one sense possess, or it would have no right to exist at all; and so far the phrase, at least in the mouth of a theist, is a mere innocuous truism. But what is meant by the doctrine known to history under that name is an indefeasible hereditary right to the succession by Divine ordinance. And that in this sense the doctrine was as little known in England as elsewhere before the reign of James I. is matter of history. England, like the Holy Roman Empire, though the fact may not be so readily acknowledged, was at first an elective monarchy. Our Saxon and Norman sovereigns did not succeed by simple right of inheritance, though a high regard was paid—partly perhaps on the *fortes creantur fortibus et bonis* principle—to the claim of lineal descent, and thus Henry IV. sought to justify his

usurpation by showing that he had a better hereditary
right than Richard II., which was not the case. Still the
modern rule, which we have inherited from the days of
James I., that "the King never dies," was as yet unknown.
There was sometimes a long interregnum, nor was it
always closed by the election of the next of kin ; and the
elected Sovereign, like the Roman Emperor, did not
venture to assume his title till it had been sealed by the
sacred unction of Coronation. That is perhaps one reason
of the anxiety Queen Mary is said to have betrayed about
the due consecration of the oil to be used at her coronation. Saxon kings were formally elected by the Witan,
and the very form of Coronation, both in Saxon and
Norman times, included an appeal to popular acceptance.
Some of our kings, like Henry VIII. afterwards, assumed
the right of bequeathing the crown by will, and the Conqueror based his claims on the will of Edward the Confessor.
Several of them, including five out of the eight Henrys,
reigned in defiance of the strict rule of descent. Stephen
was chosen in order to exclude a female sovereign, and
John because his nephew Arthur was still a boy. Henry
VIII. himself, who had the blood both of York and
Lancaster in his veins, could put in an undisputed claim,
but its security was again imperilled by his matrimonial
eccentricities, and so little respect did he show for the
hereditary principle that he had an Act of Parliament
passed to enable him to bequeath the throne by will, and
he actually made a will, afterwards confirmed afresh by
an Act of Elizabeth's reign, excluding from the succession
the very family who immediately succeeded her. Edward
VI. was induced by Cranmer, without any Parliamentary

authority, to make a will excluding his sister Mary. Both
Mary and Elizabeth reigned only by Parliamentary right,
for it was impossible that both of them could be legitimate,
and the highest authority in the realm had pronounced
both to be illegitimate. Elizabeth went further than
Henry, and got an Act of Parliament passed making it
high treason to dispute her right to leave the crown by
will. Yet within a few hours of her death, James I., who
was doubly excluded by law from the succession, but was
the heir by lineal descent, was proclaimed King amid the
universal acclamations of the people. The nation had
settled the matter for itself as though by instinct, and
when the line of Henry VIII. had failed, fell back on the
lineal representative of Henry VII. With James I. the
principle of Divine right mounted the throne of England,
and with James II. it was banished.

It is a further question, of course, how this was brought
about, and what endeavours were made after the fact to
bring theory and practice into accord. But meanwhile it
is important to emphasize the fact that James I., first of
our English Sovereigns, did reign by virtue of Divine
right, if he reigned by any right at all. He not only
had no Parliamentary claim, but he was expressly excluded
by the will of one Sovereign made under Parliamentary
sanction, and endorsed by a second Act of Parliament
passed in another reign. It is true, indeed, that on his
accession Parliament hastened to acknowledge him, but in
the very act of doing so it virtually admitted his right to
be not Parliamentary, but Divine. The first Act passed in
his reign declared "that immediately on the decease of
Elizabeth, late Queen of England, the imperial Crown of

the realm of England, and of all the kingdoms, dominions, and rights belonging to the same, did, *by inherent birthright and lawful and undoubted succession*, descend and come to your Most Excellent Majesty, as being lineally, justly, and lawfully next and sole heir of the blood royal of this realm." This was almost to assert *totidem verbis* the principle of hereditary Divine right, hitherto unknown to English law or history, and, so far as the immediate succession of the next heir to the throne on the death of his predecessor, without waiting for any formal ratification of Parliament or for coronation, is concerned, it has held good ever since. But how came it to be so universally and peacefully recognised ? No doubt the way had been prepared for it by the troubles about the succession since the death of Henry VIII. and the pressure of dangers from opposite quarters to which the country was believed to be exposed. Elizabeth, on whatever basis her rights reposed, clung tenaciously, and with the general assent of the nation, to her supremacy. And that supremacy was assailed, from points of view more or less cognate, by two very opposite parties called respectively Papists and Puritans, who were accordingly denounced as the two great enemies of the State. Both alike denied her religious authority, and not only held her to be liable to ecclesiastical censure and excommunication in the abstract, but held also that, unless she would consent to reform the national Church on their own principles, she actually deserved or had incurred it. Moreover, the scholastic divines generally, and the Jesuits especially, had always maintained a theory of popular as opposed to Divine right, and argued that a power which the people had originally given they might again in certain contingencies resume ; and the question was further complicated by the dispute about the deposing power of the Pope.   Moreover the famous Jesuit, Father Parsons, had published, towards the close of Elizabeth's reign, a treatise elaborately discussing the rival pretensions of five different families and twelve possible claimants, who after her death might plausibly dispute the succession.   This may help to explain why, immediately upon her decease, the Earl of Northumberland wrote to inform James that the eyes of the whole nation were fixed on him, while nobody gave a thought to any of his competitors.

Thus then the way had been paved for James's peaceful succession to the throne ; but some theoretical justification was also required, and this it became the business of theologians and jurists to supply.   We have seen that the schoolmen, and the Jesuits after them, maintained a popular theory of the right of government.   Suarez indeed, one of the most distinguished theologians the Order has produced, wrote a work against the Divine right of Kings, in reply to James I., but dealing chiefly with the right of the Pope over heretical sovereigns.   It would be a mistake, however, as Mr. Lecky justly observes, to suppose that the Jesuit divines advocated popular principles of government only on theological grounds, or as applied to Protestant countries.   Mariana, *e. g.*—perhaps the greatest and certainly the most impartial writer they can boast— has discussed the whole question of tyrannicide from an entirely independent point of view, nor does he admit the distinction usually drawn between a tyrant *in regimine* (*i. e.* a lawful King who governs tyrannically) and a tyrant *in*

titulo, i. e. a usurper ; or at least he insists that a tyrant
who governs in his own selfish interests, and not in the
interests of his people, however legitimate his hereditary
pretensions, is no better than a usurper, and may be
deposed, or if necessary killed. It is curious to notice
how Hooker, who had studied the schoolmen carefully,
modified their theories on this matter, though he does not
go the whole length of the Divine right doctrine afterwards developed by Filmer and the Caroline divines.
And it must be remembered that the Eighth Book of the
Ecclesiastical Polity, in which he discusses it, was written
towards the close of his own life and of Elizabeth's reign,
though not published till fifty years afterwards. He
begins by laying down the obviously reasonable principle
that "on whom [supreme power] is bestowed even at men's
discretion, they likewise do hold it by Divine right," and
therefore "unto kings by human right honour by Divine
right is due"; but this power is not unlimited, for "the
king is *major singulis, universis minor."* Hooker allows
then with the old Latin divines that royal power comes
originally from the people, but he deserts them and favours
the new theory just then coming into vogue in maintaining
that, once given, it becomes hereditary, and cannot be
recalled. He expressly rejects, as "strange, untrue, and
unnatural conceits," the opinion that no man's birth can
make him a king, or that succession, in a family once
established on the throne, depends on the acceptance or
election of the incoming heir ; whereas, on the contrary,
"in kingdoms hereditary birth giveth right unto sovereign
dominion, and the death of the predecessor putteth the
successor by blood in seisin." The question then arises

whether the body politic may, for sufficient cause, with-draw from the dynasty or the individual sovereign the power once bestowed. Hooker thinks "it must be presumed" that, when "grave inconvenience doth grow thereby," they will be willing to resign it—a presumption hardly borne out by history—but denies that it can be taken from them "without their consent." This reads very like the doctrine of "non-resistance" afterwards so hotly contested, but we may perhaps infer from the context that Hooker would have allowed some modifica-tions of it in practice, and we must at all events bear in mind that the last three books of the *Ecclesiastical Polity* were not published in the author's lifetime, and may not have received his final touches, though there is no just ground for the doubts sometimes cast on their authenticity.

This then was the state of the controversy at the accession of James I., when divines and lawyers lost no time in taking up the question. Convocation prepared a draft of canons condemning all resistance to sovereign authority in terms sufficiently sweeping, but, as they did not very clearly distinguish between kings *de jure* and *de facto*, James only snubbed them for their pains. Then the Professor of Civil Law at Cambridge, Dr. Cowell, published a dictionary which defined the royal prerogative to be above all positive enactments, and "though it be a merciful policy, and also a politic mercy" for the king to make laws only by consent of Parlia-ment, he neither is bound to ask their consent, nor bound by the laws when they are made. The House of Commons not unnaturally protested against this work, and James discreetly suppressed it, acknowledging—what however, as we have seen, was certainly not the fact—that he was indebted to the law for his crown. But then again the Papal controversy came in, and one Talbot, "a Popish recusant," who had refused to repudiate the deposing power, was prosecuted by Bacon, as Attorney-General, before the Star Chamber, and this helped on the growing tendency to assert, at least in words, an indefeasible and absolute right of the hereditary sovereign. It was strengthened no doubt by that passionate personal devotion which the Stuarts, however we may choose to explain the fact, had an almost unique gift of evoking, and consecrated in many minds by the aureole of martyrdom which wreathed the brows of "the Blessed King Charles the First," and was for two centuries enshrined in the Anglican Prayer Book. With the Stuarts the power of touching for "the King's Evil" went out. But the great exponent of the theory of Divine right, who has therefore been the favourite butt for the bitterest ridicule of later Liberal assailants from the time of Bishop Burnet, though Locke did not disdain to answer him, was Sir Robert Filmer, a zealous royalist whose house in Kent was ten times plundered during the civil wars in the reign of Charles I. His *Patriarcha*, said to have been written in 1642, was not published till nearly forty years afterwards when he had long been dead, but other publications of his had appeared during his lifetime, which are pronounced by a very competent critic to be remarkable not merely for sagacity but for shrewd common sense. The argument of the *Patriarcha* is briefly this. He began by denying the scholastic theory, affirmed alike by "Calvinists and Jesuits," and, we may add, by Hooker, that sovereign power was originally bestowed at the will of the multitude, from which radical sophism they inferred consistently enough that the multitude might for any lawful cause—of which they were themselves to be the judges—withdraw or change the powers they had conferred. Filmer insisted, on the contrary, that all men were not equal by nature, but from the first Adam, and then the Patriarchs, had by Divine institution power over their children, and after the flood and subsequent dispersion of the descendants of Noah "we find the establishment of regal power throughout the kingdoms of the world." From this he inferred that, however this or that particular dynasty might have originated—by election, usurpation, or otherwise—the "natural right of a supreme father over every multitude" remained an established principle, and therefore the actual king must always enjoy a Divine right over his subjects. God may suffer him to be removed by the instrumentality of men, but their action in displacing him is not the less sinful and damnable. In the case of there being no legitimate heir to the throne, the sovereign power "escheated," not to the multitude, but "to the prime and independent heads of families," as a kind of natural aristocracy, and on them devolved the duty of conferring the crown afresh on whom they pleased. "And he that is so elected claims not his power as a donative from the people, but as being substituted properly by God, from whom he receives his royal charter of a universal father, though testified by the ministry of the heads of the people." The theory thus stated is not otherwise than plausible in itself; the real difficulty lay in its application, as expounded by Caroline and Jacobite divines, into whose treatment of the question it would take too long to enter here. But it may fairly be asked whether Filmer's principle is any less defensible than the modern popular dogma, as repeated and interpreted *usque ad nauseam* from a thousand platforms, that all power comes from the people. ·For politicians like Gambetta or Victor Hugo the Divine right of the Republic is as absolute a truth as ever was the Divine right of Kings for Strafford or Laud. Bishop Sanderson, one of the very few casuists the Church of England has produced, maintains a view not greatly differing from Filmer's in his *De Obligatione Legum*, where he lays down, first, " præsidendi in republicâ potestatem . . ab ipso Deo esse, solo et immediaté, *nullatenus autem a populo* "; secondly, " dominationem politicam ab initio non nisi patriæ potestatis propaginem fuisse," which implies the rule of a single monarch ; and hence, finally, " in conferendâ regiâ potestate nullos fuisse, nec quidem esse potuisse, populi partes, certo certîus est." Royalty therefore is the Divinely ordained form of government, and the sovereign or dynasty actually in power, " quocunque modo ad eam perveniatur," holds its power from God. Burke at a later day declined to discuss the abstract question of " the sovereignty of the people ", but to the practical question, whether anything can justify their resuming the sovereignty, whose seat has once been fixed, he replied as peremptorily as Hooker : " I am satisfied that no occasion would justify such a resumption, which would not equally authorise a dispensation with any other moral duty, perhaps with all of them together." But Burke wrote with all the horrors of the first French Revolution fresh before his eyes.

XXII

FESTIVAL OF CHRISTMAS.

CHRISTMAS has, at least in this country, a double significance; it is both a secular and a religious festival. It is indeed rather curious that, even in its ecclesiastical character, it should hold a more prominent place in England than anywhere else. Not only in Presbyterian Scotland, which is intelligible enough, but in Catholic France, it is virtually superseded or overshadowed by the great secular anniversary of the New Year in the following week. That does not mean of course that it is not solemnly observed in church in all Roman Catholic countries, where it still retains the singular and appropriate distinction— abolished strangely enough of late years among English Catholics—of the Midnight Mass, on which a word shall be said presently. But still, although it holds confessedly the third place in the Christian calendar, yielding only to Easter and Pentecost, it is certainly not made so much of among any other people as with ourselves. The Yule-log, the boars'-head, the plum-pudding, the mince-pies, the waits, and the mummers, as well as the "roast beef of old England," are specialities of our Christmas, partly of Scandinavian origin. An ingenious reason has been suggested for the precedence which its domestic observance has established over Easter in the fact that roast beef is more easily and widely procurable than the lamb of the Paschal feast.   Another incident of its domestic observance which appears to be peculiarly Teutonic—as Santa "Klaus" and the Christmas-trees of Germany may remind us—was probably borrowed from the old Pagan festivals which Christmas superseded in the early Church.   The *Saturnalia* among the Romans, representing the golden age and abolishing for a while the distinction of ranks, had been associated with the custom of making presents (*strenæ*), and as early as the second century Tertullian reproached Christians for following this ancient practice.   And the *Saturnalia* closed with the festival of infants—the *Sigillaria* —when children were presented with little images (*oscillis fictilibus*), as Macrobius tells us, coinciding more or less closely with the Feast of the Holy Innocents.   Then again the Roman festival of the shortest day of the winter solstice (*dies invicti Solis*), designed to celebrate the birthday of the new sun, was of course directly suggestive of the Christian celebration of the birthday of the True Sun of Righteousness.   And hence Faustus, the Manichean, charged the Catholics of his own day with observing the Pagan *solstitia*.   But it does not at all follow, as Neander points out, that the date of the Christmas festival was actually suggested by these older observances.   On the contrary, there can be little doubt that it arose out of a very ancient tradition, for which Benedict XIV. cites various early authorities, that the Nativity really took place at this season of the year.   In aftertimes the words of a hymn of Prudentius came to be literally accepted, and it was thought that at the first and each recurring Christmas, "the cry of the Holy Child imparted to the earth a verdant spring." The words of Isaiah (i. 3) were interpreted to signify, not only the presence of the ox and ass in the stable of Bethlehem, but that the cattle knelt down year by year at the Christmas midnight. A Cornish peasant told Mr. Brand, in 1790, that he had himself on Christmas Eve seen the two oldest oxen in their stalls fall on their knees at midnight, and "make a moan like Christian creatures." In the words of the old hymn,

> " Cognovit bos et asinus
> Quod Puer erat Dominus."

Several other touching traditions of this kind—it sounds hard to call them superstitions—formerly existed, and some still survive, both in our own country and other parts of Europe, such as are noticed by the poet in a familiar passage of *Hamlet:*

> " Some say, that ever 'gainst that season comes
> Wherein our Saviour's birth is celebrated,
> The bird of dawning singeth all night long :
> And then, they say, no spirit dares stir abroad ;
> The nights are wholesome; then no planets strike,
> No fairy takes, nor witch hath power to charm,
> So hallow'd and so gracious is the time."

But best of all is the time-honoured traditional usage—enshrined of old in one of the capitularies of Charlemagne, and to this day nowhere more religiously observed than in England—of making Christmas the special season for those varied ministries of human kindliness and beneficence, which are our response to the Divine message of " peace on earth " proclaimed in the angels' midnight song at Bethlehem.

It is clear from Church history that St. Paul's warning

O

against the Jewish observance of "days and months, and times and years" was never understood, as some Protestants have imagined, to preclude or discourage the setting apart of special seasons for religious worship and commemoration. There is evidence indeed in the New Testament of Sunday being kept as the weekly feast of the Resurrection, and the appropriation of Wednesday and Friday—named *stationes* by a military metaphor—to commemorate the Betrayal and Death of Christ followed very soon after. The yearly anniversary of the Resurrection had already become an established and highly prized institution in the second century, as we know from the long and angry disputes as to the proper method of fixing the day. Christmas was added rather later, but certainly not later than the fourth century, and was closely connected with the proximate feast of the Epiphany, instituted mainly to commemorate the Baptism of Christ. But whereas the Epiphany originated in the East, Christmas first came to be observed in the Western Church, and in some places, as at Antioch, its introduction into the East met with considerable opposition. The Donatists, on the other hand, "refused to communicate with the Eastern Church, where that star appeared," as St. Augustine tells us, because of its keeping the Epiphany, which they condemned as an innovation. The Gnostics seem, from what Clement of Alexandria says, to have been particularly zealous in observing the Epiphany, to which they gave an interpretation of their own, but it is absurd to suppose that the observance was their own invention. The Catholic Church would certainly not have chosen to borrow it of them. It is not impossible however, as Neander suggests, that the Epiphany, representing the unction of the Messiah by the Holy Spirit for His earthly work, may have originated with the Jewish Christians, while Christmas, which presents Him "as the God-man, the Word made flesh, whose humanity was from the first filled with the Divine Essence," undoubtedly had a Western origin.

Be that as it may, these two great festivals of the Birth and Baptism of Christ, though existing in germ from very early times, first came into general use in the fourth century, when indeed the public worship and ritual of the Church were for the first time able to develop themselves freely, as the pressure of persecution was withdrawn. St. Chrysostom speaks, in a sermon preached at Antioch, of the Epiphany as one of the ancient and principal feasts of the Asiatic Church, and the only one having reference to the appearance of the Lord among men. By 361 it had penetrated into some regions of the West at all events, for Marcellinus records how the Emperor Julian kept it that year at Vienna. But in passing westwards it acquired a new meaning, and, without dropping the reference to the Baptism of Christ, the Latin service for the festival dwells mainly on his manifestation to the Gentiles, symbolized by the visit of the Magi to Bethlehem. And thus in its Western form it was closely associated in idea, as well as in the time of its celebration, with the greater festival of the Nativity. It was also taken to commemorate the "beginning of miracles" in the Public Ministry by the conversion of water into wine at Cana of Galilee, whereby Christ "manifested forth his glory" to the Gentiles. This triple significance of the day is expressly noted in the ritual, "Tribus miraculis ornatum diem sanctum colimus;

hodie stella Magos duxit ad præsepium ; hodie vinum ex
aquâ factum est ad nuptias; hodie in Jordane a Joanne
Christus baptizari voluit ut salvaret nos." Nor is it unlikely
that the importance attached in the Latin Church to the
festival of Christmas may have been connected with the
prominent place assigned in Latin theology to the doctrine
of original sin, from which all men born into the world
required to be cleansed ; this also accounts for the practice
of infant baptism first coming into general use in the West,
whence it spread to the Eastern Church. Certain it is
that in the time of Pope Liberius the Christmas festival
had become an established usage throughout Western
Christendom. Some thirty years later St. Chrysostom
preaching again at Antioch, on Christmas day, speaks of
the feast having been recently introduced there, but dwells
on its rapid and general reception, calling it "the mother
(μητρόπολις) of all the festivals, since from it Epiphany,
Easter, Ascension, and Pentecost derived their origin and
meaning." In some Eastern Churches, as at Jerusalem and
Alexandria, the commemoration of the Nativity was for a
time united in a common festival with the celebration of
the Epiphany or " Theophany " of Christ, which could of
course be explained as another name for the Incarnation.
And the simultaneous observance of the two festivals was
further justified, according to Cosmas Indicopleustes, by a
strange inference from Luke iii. 23 that the Baptism of
Christ took place on the day of his Birth.

One of the most ancient and characteristic distinctions of
the festival in the West was the treble celebration of mass,
the first taking place at midnight in memory of the time of
the Nativity, which is found in the Sacramentary of Gelasius

in the fifth century. The Pope used to celebrate the first mass in the Liberian basilica, the second, at daybreak, in the church of St. Anastasia, the third in the Vatican ; and hence the custom grew up of every priest saying three masses on Christmas day. Gregory the Great speaks of these three masses, of which various explanations are given by liturgical writers ; but that of Aquinas is most commonly adopted, that by the first at midnight is signified the Everlasting Generation of Christ from the Father, concealed from human gaze ; by the second at daybreak, His temporal birth of the Virgin Mary ; and by the third His spiritual nativity by grace in the hearts of the faithful. There was formerly a midnight mass at Easter also, traces of which still survive in the forms of the Latin ritual, and perhaps at some other festivals, but the Christmas celebration, which has of late years been popularised in many Anglican churches, and originated the now universal custom of ringing the church bells on Christmas night, has alone held its place. The custom of carol-singing on Christmas night is another very old-established and popular speciality of the festival, and the wording of many of our English carols reaches far back into the middle ages. It is curious, as Milman observes, how many of the quaint traditions — sometimes very touching, sometimes more strange than reverential — enshrined in the Apocryphal Gospels have thus been preserved and handed down to our own day. But this transmission is also due in part to the mediæval miracle plays, some idea of which may be gained from the Play of the Nativity in Longfellow's *Golden Legend ;* and with the Christmas miracle plays were associated the more questionable and boisterous burlesques of the Boy Bishop, the Abbot of Misrule, and the like, which must have ministered to merriment rather than to edification, and must too often have degenerated into such coarse profanities as Scott has depicted at St. Mary's Kennaquhair in the *Abbot*. It was remarked some years ago on a Christmas sermon of Dean Stanley's at Westminster Abbey, about the coronation of William the Conqueror, which took place there on that festival, that "he seemed unaware of the day having been rendered memorable by any previous event." He might, however, have recalled one still earlier historical event of an equally secular, but wider and more pregnant significance, which had marked the recurrence of the same festival more than two centuries before the Norman Conquest. On the Christmas day of 800, during High Mass at St. Peter's, Leo III. placed the Crown on the head of Charlemagne, and thus consecrated the revival or inception, as we may choose to view it, of the Holy Roman Empire. There is a sense therefore in which Christmas, while it has become from immemorial usage our great domestic festival, may be also regarded as the birthday of the Christian State, as well as of the Church.

XXIII

MIRACLE PLAYS.

IT has come to pass from various causes, during the last twenty or thirty years, that the *Passionsspiel* at Ober-Ammergau, formerly known only as a local religious solemnity, has risen into a centre of interest and attraction, not only for England, but for the·whole Christian world.[1] And this naturally suggests some inquiry into the origin and history of those Mysteries or Miracle Plays once so common throughout Europe, but of which this decennial celebration in an obscure Tyrolese valley is now the almost solitary memento; for we cannot reckon in the same

[1] The performance of 1850 was described by the Baroness Tautphæus in a novel entitled *Quits*, which first drew attention to the subject in England. In 1860 there were several English visitors, and among them Dean Stanley and Dean Milman. The former recorded his experiences in an article in *Macmillan's Magazine*, the latter in a note to the third edition of *Latin Christianity* (vol. ix. p. 180), where he relates, with an enthusiasm unusual in his pages, how he had "never witnessed a performance more striking for its scenic effect," or "passed a day in more absorbed and unwearied attention." After this there was naturally a rush of visitors from England, as well as elsewhere, to the next decennial celebration in 1870, which moreover was interrupted by the outbreak of the Franco-Prussian war at the end of July, and had therefore to be continued in the August and September of 1871. My own *Recollections of Ober-Ammergau* in 1871 (Rivingtons), describes a visit paid in the August of that year.

category the grotesque, not to say profane, representations
of sacred subjects occasionally interpolated into the dramatic
programme at some Spanish theatres. The Ammergau
Passion Play is not indeed itself a mediæval institution, but
it can only be rightly understood in connexion with those
popular "Mysteries" and "Moralities" of the middle ages,
and they again must be traced back to a more remote
antiquity and to earlier forms of faith. The drama, as has
been justly said, is based on a principle inherent in human
nature—that instinct of imitation which is not peculiar
to any age or people. And hence there is evidence of its
early existence among the most diverse and even the rudest
nations. Not only was it in high repute at the same time
in Greece and in Hindostan, but even the Chinese have
from time immemorial possessed a regular theatre, and the
ancient Peruvians had both tragedies and comedies. And
they must in each case have invented the drama for themselves. But there is a further point in common among all
the earliest dramatic performances of which we have any
record, though it is most conspicuously brought out in the
case of the Greek drama, which is the best known to us.
They seem, like ancient art generally, to have always had
a religious origin and significance. Mythology supplied
the materials alike for the Comic and the Tragic Muse,
and the frequently recurring festivals of local or national
deities afforded the occasion for public representations.
Music and poetry, wherever they exist, are sure to be
enlisted in the service of religion, and with an agricultural
population like that of early Greece, Dionysos, the god of
the vineyard, held necessarily a prominent place in the
national worship. The hymns sung round the festal altar,

whether solemn or jocose, gradually developed into all the artistic splendours of the drama; the stately dithyrambic ode, with the Satyric chorus, became the basis of Greek tragedy, and the Phallic song was expanded into the comedy of Aristophanes. We know of but two historical tragedies by Greek poets, which therefore have not a mythological origin; the *Capture of Miletus* by Phrynichus, and the *Persians* of Æschylus. And the exception proves the rule. Phrynichus was fined by the Athenians for harrowing their feelings by the representation of contemporary misfortunes. It must be remembered too that the Eleusinian and other Mysteries of ancient Greece, to which the initiated alone were admitted, consisted, as far as anything can be ascertained about them, mainly of symbolical and dramatic representations. And here we touch on the connecting link between the classical and Christian drama.

The early Fathers of the Church, whether with or without sufficient information it may be difficult to determine, invariably denounce the Greek Mysteries in the strongest terms as hotbeds of the grossest obscenity. Even St. Clement of Alexandria, with all his admiration of Greek philosophy, is no exception. And for many centuries no Christian could be present at the theatre without forfeiting his religious position and privileges, and no actor could be baptized without first renouncing his profession. But if the authorities of the Church were unsparing in their denunciation alike of the Mysteries and of the Stage, they were too wise to ignore the human instincts to which the drama appeals. They put forward Mysteries of their own as a counter-attraction to these old heathen rites, and thus the Christian drama grew up by degrees on the ruins of the

Greek theatre. During the ages of persecution there was comparatively little scope for such a process of development; yet even then a considerable dramatic element may be traced in the earliest Christian liturgies, and the modes of celebrating the greater Church festivals. And no sooner did the Church emerge from the Catacombs than we find not only a rapid elaboration of ceremonial splendour in worship, but also direct attempts to compete with the Greek tragedians on their own ground. An early instance of this is given in the " Dying Christ " of St. Chrysostom, which was acted in church at Constantinople, partly in *tableaux vivants* and partly by dialogue. St. Gregory Nazianzen was another sacred dramatist. A solemn dance is still performed at Easter before the high altar of the cathedral at Seville, which is said to recall the movements of a Greek chorus. It was thus in the East that these religious plays originated, and they were only imported at a later date, probably by the Crusaders, into Western Europe. There are, however, records of convent plays in Germany as early as the time of Charlemagne, though the earliest specimen of such compositions still extant is a manuscript of twelve dramas written in Terentian Latin by Hrotsvitha, abbess of Gandersheim in the tenth century, and performed in her convent, as we are told, " to the delight and edification of the nuns." Such representations soon became popular all over Europe, and nowhere more so than in England. It may be interesting to notice more particularly the " Mysteries " performed in our own country and in Germany. Strictly speaking, it should be said, that " Miracle " or " Mystery Play " designates a representation based on the Lives of the Saints, as distinguished from the "Passion Play," which represented the sufferings of Christ; but the distinction of terms is not always adhered to.

Matthew Paris tells us that the story of St. Catharine was dramatized by one Geoffrey, master of a school at Dunstable, afterwards Abbot of St. Albans, and acted by his boys early in the twelfth century. But the earliest play which has come down to us is the *Harrowing of Hell*, composed in Latin two centuries later, in which the principal *dramatis personæ* are our Lord, Satan, Adam, and Eve. The so-called "Chester Mysteries," of about a century later again, are the best known of the English Miracle Plays. They include both a tragic and comic element, and in fact these performances seem always to have had a tendency, especially in England, to degenerate into such coarse buffoonery as Longfellow has sought to reproduce in the "Gaudiolum of Monks" in the *Golden Legend*. This was no doubt one element of their popularity, but it also led to their often being placed under the ban of ecclesiastical authority. Bishop Grandison, of Exeter, expressly forbade them as early as 1360. But they were too popular both with the Court and the masses to be easily put down. Edward III. was passionately addicted to such spectacles, and appears to have himself taken part in them, if we may judge from an inventory of articles used in a play acted at Guildford at Christmas 1347, which includes mention of "a harness of white buckram, inlaid with silver—namely, a tunic and shield, with the King's motto, 'Hay, hay, the Wythe Swan, by God's soul I am thy man,' *for the use of the King himself*." To the Miracle Plays succeeded "Moralities," in which abstract qualities—Justice, Mercy, and the like—were personified, and these in turn led to the representation of real persons on the stage. In the fierce contests of the Reformation, the drama, like the pulpit, was eagerly appropriated by both sides for purposes of mutual attack. The marriage of Luther with a nun was satirized in a Latin Morality at Gray's Inn in 1529. So profane and indecent were some of the controversial plays of the Reforming party that they were forbidden by the Privy Council, not only under Henry VIII. and Mary, but even under the fiercely Protestant sway of the " B. Edward VI.," on pain of imprisonment. But they held their ground nevertheless down to the time of Charles I. There are old men still living who can remember seeing something like a Miracle Play in their childhood in remote country districts of England, as for instance in Cornwall ; and a performance of the kind was reported not many years ago in a Dissenting Chapel in Wales. We have seen that these Miracle Plays were at first always in Latin. They came, however, before long to be translated into the vernacular both in England and Germany. One of the earliest of the German Mysteries is the *Lament of the Virgin*, which was acted in church on Good Friday, and to this succeeded afterwards the " Passion Plays," representing the death and resurrection of Christ. In the fourteenth century the performances were transferred from the church to the street and market-place, and the number of actors largely increased. There is a curious history attached to one of the most famous of these early German plays, the *Tragedy of the Ten Virgins*, which was performed at Eisenach in 1332, to celebrate the restoration of peace. The Landgrave Frederic, named the Joyful, was present, and was terribly alarmed and angered by the close of the drama, where the Foolish Virgins are represented as appealing in vain to the intercession of the Blessed Virgin, and finally thrust down into hell, notwithstanding her entreaties to her Son to pardon them. "What means this, if God will not pity us even when Mary and the Saints intercede?" he exclaimed. His fright and indignation threw him into a fit of apoplexy, from which he never recovered till his death two years afterwards. So painfully realistic did these Passion Plays become in Germany, that in one acted at Metz in 1437 the priest who took the principal part nearly died of exhaustion on the cross, and another priest, who represented Judas, narrowly escaped hanging himself. The Crucifixion scene is still found very trying to the principal performer at Ammergau, who has to remain some twenty minutes on the cross, and a younger actor had to be substituted in consequence in 1870 for the person who had taken that part in the three previous celebrations of the decennial solemnity.

It is remarkable that this one remaining memorial of the old Miracle Plays is of comparatively recent origin. In 1633 a deadly plague raged in the Ammerthal, and within three weeks eighty-four of the small community were corpses. The inhabitants then made a solemn vow that, if God would hear their prayer and remove the pestilence, they would every tenth year, in thankfulness for His mercies, represent the Passion of the Redeemer. It is said that not a single death occurred after this vow was made, and it has been religiously observed ever since. The King of Bavaria has to give his sanction every time for the performance, and in 1810 an attempt was made to put it down by a general prohibition of all Miracle Plays. The inhabitants sent a deputation to Munich to plead their cause before King Louis, but in vain; he was, however, induced to relent by the intervention of his chaplain, and no difficulty has since occurred to disturb the periodical recurrence of the solemnity. It usually lasts from Whitsuntide till the end of September, being repeated on most of the intervening Sundays. On one previous occasion it was interrupted, as in 1870, by the performers being summoned to join the army, and the omitted representations were then also supplied in the following summer. It is a remarkable circumstance that of some sixty actors who were called away, to take part in the Franco-Prussian war, only seven were killed, and none of those taking any important part were included among the slain. This is not the place to discuss at length the obvious objections raised against dramatizing the Passion altogether, as derogatory to the sacredness of the subject. Nor does the precedent, often noticed, of the dramatic character of the Holy Week offices of the Latin ritual offer a more than partial reply. That such representations become at once profane and injurious to those concerned if witnessed or enacted in any other than a religious spirit is self-evident. And it may not unnaturally be feared that, in an age like ours, the growing popularity of the Ammergau *Passionsspiel* will eventually prove fatal to its permanence; but few who have ever witnessed it could fail to regard such a contingency, if it occurs, as matter of very serious regret. To the simple and devout denizens of that secluded mountain village the decennial solemnity as yet manifestly continues to be, what it has ever been, not an occasion of histrionic display

or pecuniary profit, but—in the words of the pious editor
of one of the local text-books—"a religious duty, from
which they neither can be nor wish to be dispensed by any
earthly authority." Their most general ordinary occupation as wood-carvers, chiefly of devotional objects, helps of
course to develop both their artistic and religious instincts,
and thus the study of the great religious painters, which is
enjoined on those selected for the principal parts in the
Play, especially for the highest, comes natural to them as a
labour of love. And we may well hope that the writer
already quoted is also at least substantially correct in the
expression of his charitable belief, that "all who have
hitherto been spectators of the *Passionsspiel* have returned
home nobler and better men." It may safely be asserted
that the fault, where it is not so, is their own, and that none
can fail to be both edified and benefited who are content
to witness the drama in the spirit of those who enact it.

XXIV.

ORIGIN AND GROWTH OF UNIVERSITIES.

THE festival observed at Munich, in August 1872, with every circumstance of royal and popular solemnity, to celebrate the four hundredth anniversary of the foundation of the University, was naturally regarded in Germany as an event of national interest. The University, originally founded at Ingoldstadt by Duke Albert in 1472, transferred in the beginning of the present century to Landshut, and then, twenty-six years later, to Munich, by King Louis, is one of the oldest and still one of the most important of the German Universities—the most important probably of those in Southern and Catholic Germany. And although the festival was of a strictly academical and not ecclesiastical character, it no doubt derived some additional significance from the fact of Bavaria being just then the centre of the Old Catholic movement, and from the venerable Dr. Döllinger having been called by an almost unanimous vote of his colleagues to fill the office of *Rector Magnificus* on the occasion. His speech, which was received with continuous and enthusiastic applause from all his hearers, young and old alike, has a permanent interest. It was of course to be expected that he would say something of the antecedents and distinctions of the

University which he was there to represent, and of which he has for so many years been a conspicuous ornament. But he did more than this. He took the opportunity to give what in less experienced hands might have been a mere superficial sketch, while in reality it contains a vivid and critical appreciation of the origin and growth of University education in Europe. That is a subject on which few men are so well qualified to speak, and he handled it with that depth and accuracy of learning, that intellectual grasp and breadth of moral sympathy, and that ardent but intelligent patriotism, which will at once be recognised as characteristic of the speaker by all who are familiar with him personally or through his writings. It is worth while to put on record here the salient points of a discourse which occupied nearly two hours in delivery, and which well deserves to be read in full by those who are in a position to study it for themselves.[1]

Dr. Döllinger begins by referring to the first consolidation of national unity a thousand years ago under Louis the German, and its revival in 1871 in the new German Empire. Since then the University of Munich has been the first to celebrate its anniversary, which thus attains a sort of national importance, and the more so as the different German Universities are closely united, and there is a frequent interchange of professors and students among them. The corporate idea which was so powerful in the middle ages, but was wholly wanting under the old governments,

---

[1] This discourse of Dr. Döllinger's has been collated, for the present purpose, with an earlier one of his on the same subject, delivered before the University of Munich in 1867, when also he held the office of Rector.

whether democratic or Imperial, of Greece and Rome, could alone make possible the foundation of Universities as independent communities, with their own rights and privileges, bound together by a community of interests between teachers and taught. Among such institutions the University of Paris, dating from early in the thirteenth century, for a long time stood supreme, and Paris became, far more than Rome, the intellectual metropolis of Western Europe. It was a common saying that, as Italy had the *sacerdotium*, and Germany the *imperium*, France had the *studium*. Far different in character were the Italian Universities, which began to be founded in the twelfth century, but never approached the theological and literary eminence of Paris and Oxford, and made no claim to the universality of teaching now associated with the name ; they were schools of one or two sciences only, the first established, at Salerno, being a school of medicine only ; their aim was practical, and the studies principally culti-vated were jurisprudence and canon law. Their origin and system were of a casual and purely democratic kind, without any recognised authority and position in Church or State. Two or three professors of canon and civil law and medicine combined to form a University, and students gradually gathered round them, but its prosperity was at best fluctuating and uncertain. Leo X. founded the Sapi-enza with eighty-eight professors, but a few years later Clement VII. diverted the endowments to other objects, and its days of prosperity were gone for ever. The teachers at these Universities had no corporate *status* or dignity, and were looked on simply as paid agents for the supply of a marketable commodity ; there was no *genius loci*, as at Oxford, no sense of pride in belonging to a great institution either among the teachers or the taught. Bologna, however, has an historical importance as the birthplace and chief home of the allied sciences of Roman civil law and canon law, which exercised so large an influence on the development of the Papal autocracy; in 1262 there were 20,000 students of law there. Alexander III., Innocent III., and Innocent IV., the great founders of the system, had taught or studied there; there, too, the German Emperors learnt lessons of absolutism derived from the maxims of the old Roman Empire which they were supposed to inherit, and openly proclaimed their superiority to law. Paris, however, exerted a more direct influence than the Italian Universities on the national life of Germany, through the crowds of students who flocked thither, having as yet no Universities of their own, and who brought back with them the French spirit and language on their return; many men spent fifteen or sixteen years there in the study of theology. Even so late as the end of the sixteenth century the Venetian Ambassador says it had 30,000 students. Yet even Paris till latterly had no Faculty of Law. But everywhere the curriculum was a very narrow one, and the entire absence of any historical and critical sense left unbounded room for the dominance of fiction and forgeries. Two men, in Germany and England, made the first attempt to break the ice; Albert the Great, who has been not inaptly called the Humboldt of his age, and Roger Bacon, both of whom laboured to introduce the study of natural science, while Roger Bacon also paved the way for the cultivation of Greek literature.

And now the time was come for Germany to take her

part in the academical life of Europe. The ancient Universities of Paris, Oxford, Cambridge, and Bologna own no founder and no cognisable date of institution—"they were a natural growth."[1] But it was the princes, secular and spiritual, who in the middle of the fourteenth century began to establish Universities in Germany, and the municipal authorities afterwards followed their example. The first was founded at Prague in 1348 by Charles IV., and is said to have numbered 40,000 students by the end of the century; but the quarrels between the Czech and German students, which have lasted down to our own day, soon made an end of its prosperity. In the same century were founded the Universities of Vienna, Heidelberg, Cologne, and Erfurt, all of which were originally to a great degree ecclesiastical institutions, and supported by the revenues of Church benefices. They often had no fewer than six professors of canon law. But the great schism of the anti-Popes evoked a spirit of reform throughout the Church, and the German Universities, following in the wake of Paris, threw themselves into the movement of which Gerson and D'Ailly were the acknowledged leaders, and all united in proclaiming the superiority of Councils to Popes. But all hope of an effective reform was shattered by the transition of Frederick III. to the Papal party, and he forced the University of Vienna, by the threat of withdrawing its

---

[1] The foundation of University College by a bequest of William of Durham, who died in 1249, marks the real beginning of the *University* of Oxford as such, about half a century after the first formal recognition of the University of Paris in the diploma of Philip Augustus, though there had been *schools* at Oxford for many centuries before. And there is good reason for believing that the original statutes were borrowed almost wholesale from Paris.

endowments, to renounce the Council of Basle. Meanwhile a distinct but cognate movement had been originated at Oxford by Wycliff, and was taken up at Prague by Huss with greater immediate success, while a third University, that of Wittenberg, eventually gave it the form in which it has exercised so momentous an influence on the subsequent history of the Church. The Universities, too, in Germany rather than in Italy, became the nurseries of that revival of classical literature which, however little such an alliance was intended or acknowledged on either side, materially aided the progress of the Reformation. Three more German Universities, at Greifswald, Freiburg, and Basle, were founded shortly before Ingoldstadt (in 1472), and Tübingen a little later. Paris was the common mother of them all, and Ingoldstadt borrowed its statutes from Vienna, which had received them from Paris. It was a dark period in the political life of Germany; but for a time, from 1494 to 1518, Ingoldstadt gained celebrity for its classical teaching under Conrad Celtes, Locher, and Reuchlin, and the historian Aventin was its most distinguished ornament. The number of students, however, was not large. It may be said that the history of these mediæval universities illustrates the distinctive national character of England, France, and Germany. England, which abjured centralisation, and has ever pursued a twofold aim, of practical utility and political freedom, has naturally had two Universities, correcting and supplementing each other, which retain to this day their independent constitution, and represent respectively "the two leading tendencies of the English mind, the ecclesiastical and the mathematical." On the other hand, the centralising tendencies of the nation, which make Paris the only place where an educated Frenchman cares to live, found expression in its one University seated in the metropolis. In Germany the decentralising tendencies (*particularismus*), which gradually dissolved the unity both of the Empire and the Church, led to the separate foundation of a number of small Universities in various cities.

Then came the Reformation, of which Wittenberg was the centre, and the new Universities of Marburg, Königsthum, Jena, Altdorf, and Helmstadt were founded for its promotion, while Leipsic, Rostock, Greifswald, and Heidelberg joined the movement. Prague and Vienna, which adhered to the old faith, were almost deserted, and Ingoldstadt became, and continued for two centuries, one of the chief strongholds of Catholicism; there, as at all the German Universities, Catholic or Protestant, theology overshadowed every other Faculty. With the Reformation had in fact sprung up a new order of things, and the German Universities became "the arsenals where the weapons of war were forged, and often the battle-fields where the victory or defeat of the rival doctrines was decided." The German princes accordingly, who always assumed the right to fix the faith of their subjects, used them—as the Jesuits of the period used the confessional, and Lutheran preachers the pulpit—as *instrumenta dominationis*, keeping in their own hands the appointment to professorial chairs, especially those of theology. All that can be said of the seventeenth century is that the German Universities survived "that darkest period of German history," and the Thirty Years' War; but the Catholic Universities scarcely deserved the name, while the Protestant were completely subordinated to theological interests and antipathies, and their history is the history of the conflict between Lutheran orthodoxy, on the one hand, and Calvinism, Syncretism, and Pietism on the other.   Up to the beginning of the eighteenth century all lectures were delivered in Latin, which was fatal to any real originality and comprehensiveness of teaching.   In the last century Kant made Königsberg famous, and Jena in the hands of Fichte and Schelling became the theatre of a great philosophical movement.   In 1810 the King of Prussia founded at Berlin the first German University since the Reformation which had no confessional character or object, and among its earliest professors were included men like Humboldt, Wolff, Fichte, Schleiermaeker, and Savigny ; it now numbers over 2000 students.   With the eighteenth century the German Universities had received a new lease of life, which culminated in the foundations of Berlin and Bonn.   It is curious that, at a period of such intense theological energy throughout Europe, Paris, which had long been "the Queen in that region to whose decisions every one submitted," entered on her period of decline. But the causes of decay were external, and are not difficult to explain.   The place itself, which was now the constant scene of civil strife and bloodshed, was most unfavourable for learning.   But, more than that, the immediate neighbourhood of a Court which claimed supreme control over the minds and consciences, as well as the lives, of its subjects, made all freedom of writing and teaching impossible.   Thus in 1624 a Royal decree forbade on pain of death any divergence from Aristotelian doctrines on physical and metaphysical subjects, and Louis XIV. would have instantly lodged in the Bastille any professor who contradicted his opinions. It is not wonderful then that during the seventeenth century Paris lost nine out of her forty colleges, or that, while two-thirds of the most distinguished German writers belong to the Universities, scarcely a single name eminent in French literature since 1660 is connected with the Parisian or any other French University. Enforced subscription to arbitrary professions of faith completed the work of degradation, and when at last the University fell with the destruction of her property, the event was hardly noticed, nor has any French Government since the Revolution thought of restoring it— *etiam periere ruinæ*. Louvain, which had long been a flourishing University almost fit to compete with Paris, was strangled under a similar system of coercion, and her one great scholar in the last century, Van Espen, had to fly for his life when an old man of eighty-two. Leyden, on the other hand, founded by the Prince of Orange, and with far smaller resources, has produced a long line of illustrious scholars, and known no period of decay ; while the Spanish and Portuguese Universities, which once stood so high, have suffered a total and tragical eclipse. The Scotch Universities are very inferior to the English, and the North American, which are simply institutions for conferring degrees in law and theology, do not deserve the name. Nor can any very high praise be accorded to those of Denmark, Holland, Belgium, or Sweden. In Russia they are as yet a mere exotic, imported from Germany.

There is no need here to follow Dr. Döllinger through the long catalogue of illustrious philosophers, linguists, historians, and divines who have adorned his own *alma mater*, and who naturally found honourableand appreciative mention on such an occasion.   It includes Schelling, Baader, Savigny, Feuerbach, Stahl, Windischmann, Sailer, Möhler, and many other memorable, though less widely celebrated, names.   When he comes in conclusion to dwell on the present and future of his country, he points, as might be expected, with pardonable pride to the bright prospect opened before her through the restoration of political unity, and to the mission assigned by general consent to the Germans of enriching other nations out of the fulness of their scientific and literary wealth ; though it must be remembered that in former ages they have learnt much successively from Italy, from France, and from England. He trusts that the single-minded and unwearied pursuit of truth for its own sake will always continue to be a distinction of Germany, and that she will avoid that vicious centralisation which, in intellectual culture as in other matters, has proved the ruin of France.   On one important point—too much forgotten in some recent schemes of academical reform at Oxford and Cambridge—he earnestly commends the example of the English Universities to the imitation of his own, where he thinks that the College system, unknown except partially at Tübingen, would supply a manifest and serious defect.   And no less earnest is his caution against the danger of sensualism and materialism incident to a widespread cultivation of the natural sciences, especially among the half-educated, which would inevitably prove the harbinger of national decay. Against that danger the Universities, if only they are true to their high position and duties, will provide a sure defence.   "Let us then," are the concluding words of this most instructive and eloquent discourse, "continue to labour indefatigably, in a pure scientific spirit, and with loyal self-devotion, to build up the one temple of truth. That will be an imperishable monument, surviving all changes of fortune, of the honour and greatness of Germany."

XXV

JEWISH PATRIOTISM.

A QUESTION was debated some years ago in the *Nineteenth Century*, which has an historical and practical interest beyond the particular occasion which suggested it. It opens out indeed an inquiry of such wide significance and bearings alike in a religious, a national, and an historical sense, that a very cursory treatment of its leading specialities can alone be attempted within our present limits. The point in dispute may be thus stated. It is maintained on one side that the Jews are simply a religious sect, standing in the same relation as any other religious sect— say Unitarians or Methodists—to their countrymen, having the same stake in the national welfare, and the same claim on the privileges and rights of citizens. The opponents of this view, as represented by Mr. Goldwin Smith, disclaim all desire to curtail the civil privileges of Jews. They "do not wish to repeal Jewish any more than Catholic Emancipation"; but just as they look suspiciously on that religious party who profess to be "Englishmen, if you please, but first Catholics," so they think there is something in the specific character of Judaism that requires its political action to be watched with a jealousy which there is no need to exercise over the political action of the

members of any other religious community, because
Judaism is not, like Methodism or Unitarianism, merely
a religious belief, but a distinction of race also. It does
not quite meet this difficulty to ask, with Dr. Adler, than
whom no more competent authority can be found on his
own side of the question, whether "the sacred books of the
Jewish religion fail to inculcate the virtue of patriotism"?
There can be no doubt whatever that patriotism is far
more strongly inculcated and illustrated in the Old Testament than in the New. But then it is the patriotism of
the Jewish nation, as such, which was then indissolubly
bound up with their religious belief. As Mr. Lecky puts
it, "In Judæa the spirit of patriotism and of sect were
united; each intensified the other, and the exclusive
intolerance which is the result of each existed with double
virulence." The grandest religious traditions of the Jews
were associated with their national triumphs, and the
Mosaic Law accepts and consecrates exclusive national
distinctions which are certainly abhorrent to modern ideas
of the universal brotherhood of man, as, *e. g.*, in the different
rules of dealing with strangers and with countrymen. This
fact is equally and inevitably admitted by those who
maintain and those who deny the Divine authorship of the
Mosaic dispensation; though the former reasonably insist
that it marks a temporary and necessary stage in the
gradual education of mankind, and they may justly point
in defence of this view to the clear superiority of the
Hebrew over contemporary heathen systems in the matter
of humane and equitable dealing. It is further argued by
Mr. Goldwin Smith, as evidencing the exclusively national
character of the Jewish religion, that Warburton is clearly

right in maintaining that there is no trace in the Old
Testament of the doctrine of a future life. There is no
doubt some ground for Warburton's contention, but his
statements in the *Divine Legation* are as grossly exaggerated as the ingenious paradox he built upon them is
eccentric. However, it may be admitted—whatever may
be the value of the admission—that temporal blessings are
the main inducements to righteousness held out under the
Old Law. The point is dwelt on, with his usual vigour
and subtlety of thought, by a writer as unlike Warburton
as the late Professor Mozley, in one of his posthumous
essays. So far then, while patriotism is unquestionably a
prominent characteristic of Judaism, it is a patriotism binding the Hebrew people in close bonds of religious and civil
relationship with each other, but would seem at first sight
likely rather to hinder than to help their fusion into one
homogeneous body with the various nations among whom
their lot may be cast in their present state of dispersion.
And when we speak to-day of the patriotism of the Jews,
we mean of course to inquire, not whether they were
patriotic when they dwelt as one nation under the shadow
of the Temple, of which there can be no sort of doubt, but
whether they are likely to be patriotic citizens now of
England or France or any other European country where
they have found a home.

If we look back on the history of the Jews since the
destruction of the Temple of Jerusalem, we shall find that
they were regarded in a peculiar light, quite differently
from any other class of religionists, first in the Roman
Empire, and then in the community of Christian States
which gradually took its place. Under the Empire they

were not subjected to such severe and persistent persecution as the Christians; and Mr. Lecky is probably right in thinking that this was mainly owing to the tribal and "inexpansive" nature of their religion, which gave them no desire to proselytise, and so far brought them into less direct and constant collision with Roman ideas and institutions. On the other hand, it is clear from the classical literature of the period that they had incurred the deepest hatred and contempt of their Roman masters; and this reacted on the popular estimate of the Christians, who were long regarded in the Empire as a Jewish sect, with the additional demerit of an obstinate passion for propagandism. To this it must be added that the early Christians, who generally viewed the Empire as a special embodiment of Antichrist, could not, in spite of their rigid view of the duty of absolute submission to authority, feel any very ardent sympathy for its welfare. When the civil and ecclesiastical organization of mediæval Europe had succeeded to the rule of Pagan Rome, we still find the Jews holding an exceptional position everywhere, which, however, exposed them now not only to bitterer obloquy but to sharper persecution than other dissentient sects. It is fair to remember that several Popes and Saints—as, *e. g.*, St. Bernard—creditably exerted themselves to screen the victims of so deep and universal an unpopularity, but, as a rule, Jews were looked upon with even a deeper detestation than the most detested heretical sects. Intermarriage with them was denounced as a horrible pollution, and in France and Spain any one taking a Jewish mistress was liable to be burnt to death. St. Thomas Aquinas maintained that their property might at any time be confiscated,

because it was gained by usury. Without of course for a
moment excusing the horrible cruelties to which they were
subjected, it is difficult to believe that there was nothing
in the character of the race to explain this universal
sentiment of distrust. And, apart from the charges of
usury, slave-holding, crucifixion of Christian children, and
the like, their isolation from all national aims and interests, to which Dean Merivale refers in his Roman History,
had certainly a good deal to do with it :—

> The Jew, with a spirit no less restless, with propensities
> no less migratory, neither conquered nor colonised nor
> civilised. He intruded himself silently and pertinaciously
> into every known corner of the globe ; and no one could
> say wherefore he came or what was the object of his
> sojourn. His presence in foreign lands was marked by no
> peculiar aim or mission. He cultivated neither literature
> nor art, nor even commerce on a great scale or as a national
> pursuit. He subsisted for the most part by the exercise of
> active industry in petty dealings, evaded as much as he
> could the public burdens of the nations among whom he
> dwelt, while their privileges he neither sought nor coveted,
> and distinguished himself alike in every quarter, under
> every form of government, and in the midst of every social
> system, by rigid adherence to the forms of an obscure and
> exclusive creed.

That something of the same feeling still survives on the
Christian side may be inferred from the fact that many
Liberals, while strongly opposed to the general principle of
religious disabilities, were found some years ago in alliance
with those who denounced "the unchristianizing of our
Legislature," in their opposition to the emancipation of
the Jews. On the other hand, if the intermarriage of Jews
and Christians was considered a pollution in mediæval
Europe, the *Jewish World* has quite lately deprecated it

on the very intelligible ground that it must eventually lead
to an absolute extinction of Judaism.

It does then seem obvious that Judaism differs from
Methodism or any other merely religious form of denomi-
nationalism in the circumstance that it denotes a "tribal"
as well as a theological distinction. The same might be
said, *mutatis mutandis,* of Mormonism, which also does not
constitute a purely theological platform, but aspires to the
formation, as Judaism implies the preservation, of a special
form of national life. But before this distinction is applied
for any practical purpose to the actual condition and
claims of the Jews in the States of modern Europe, one or
two important considerations have to be borne in mind.
In the first place, as indeed Mr. Goldwin Smith himself
admits, "before Christianity *all* religions were tribal," and
of these tribal religions Judaism was confessedly the
highest. And it is therefore natural to inquire whether it
may not be tending, under the intellectual and social
influences of the modern world, to become less exclusive
and more universal. And this leads us to notice the
significant fact that there are two parties, or rather two
sects, among the Jews of our own day, the one adhering
closely to their traditional creed, while the religion of the
other is hardly distinguishable from theism, and the latter
party are said to be rapidly gaining ground. Whether
this process of disintegration should be regarded with
satisfaction or the reverse from a strictly religious point of
view, is another question. But it is at all events clear that
there can be no more reason for questioning the patriotism
of the theistic, or, as they are sometimes called, rationalistic section of Jews, as such, than for questioning the

patriotism of, *e. g.*, Unitarians, as such. And at the same time it must be remembered that, if Judaism of the narrow and traditional type is held to be inimical to patriotism in a modern State, as hindering the genuine fusion of Jews with any nationality other than their own, there is also a point of view from which Christianity may be regarded as a counter influence to patriotism, and that precisely because it is not a tribal but a universal faith. The criticism has often been urged with exaggerated emphasis, and even pushed to paradoxical lengths by sceptical writers, but a moment's consideration will show that it has a certain weight. If there is any force in the argument noticed just now, that Judaism is proved to be an exclusively national faith from its appealing to temporal rewards and punishments only, the converse must hold true, that a religion based on supernatural sanctions, and which bids its votaries look for their recompense not in this world but in the next, has a tendency to denationalise them by withdrawing their minds from earthly and secular interests and concentrating them on the world unseen. And thus the early Christians were out of harmony with the social and political life of the Empire, not merely because the language of St. Paul and St. John had taught them to look on Rome as an Anti-christian power, but because there were laws and customs obligatory on all citizens to which they could not conform without violating their religious belief. It is another way of expressing this contrariety or divergence of character to say that the heroic and the saintly ideal, though not of course incompatible, do not exactly coincide. Saints, and especially martyrs, are sometimes loosely designated Christian heroes, and there may be some, like St. Louis of France, to whom the designation is peculiarly appropriate, but, broadly speaking, heroism and sanctity represent different though not inconsistent types of excellence. To put an extreme case, Harmodius and Aristogeiton were reverenced by the Athenians as national heroes, but it would be difficult from any point of view to regard them as saints. In other words, Christian piety is not identical with patriotism, and may even conceivably conflict with it, as was the case under the Roman Empire.

Moreover Christianity has from the first taken shape in some kind of visible organization claiming the religious allegiance of its members. This need not and ordinarily does not interfere with their civil duties, but it does—to recall a phrase very prominent in the controversy about "Vaticanism" some years ago — introduce "a divided allegiance," in so far as the Christian recognises his membership of a second society, having independent laws and interests of its own, and whose boundaries are not at all necessarily conterminous with those of the nation. Hence the frequent rivalries of Church and State, which were unknown under the Jewish and Pagan systems of government, where Church and State were one. It may happen here and there that religious and patriotic zeal run, so to speak, in the same groove, and thus the course of history served at one time to identify Catholicism with the national character of Spain, and Protestantism with the national character of England. But that is an accident. As a rule, the Christian and the national sentiment are distinct, and may therefore become divergent or even antagonistic forces. And thus if the patriotism of Jews may be plausibly disputed, the patriotism of Christians may be, and has been, for plausible but in one sense very opposite reasons, disputed also. The loyalty of English Catholics, for instance, was distrusted—as a rule quite unjustly—in the reign of Elizabeth, and the Huguenots were notoriously out of harmony with national sentiment in France. The result seems to be that in the abstract a Jew who is heart-whole in his loyalty to traditional Judaism cannot at the same time be heart-whole in his loyalty to a modern, and especially a Christian State, because his own nation, though at present dispersed and with no visible prospect of restoration, has a prior and paramount claim upon him. On the other hand, an Englishman or Frenchman, of whatever religious persuasion, remains simply an Englishman or Frenchman, and can have no temptation to prefer the interests of any other nation to those of England or France. But ecclesiastical may take precedence of national interests in his mind, as was objected to the Ultramontane advisers of Louis Napoleon who were said to have forced him into the Franco-Prussian war. From which quarter any practical danger to the State is most to be apprehended it seems hardly worth while to discuss, inasmuch as no one seriously proposes to deprive either Jews or Ultramontanes of equal civil rights.

XXVI

THE *JUDENHASS* IN HISTORY.

IT is a curious and at first sight perplexing fact that there has always been something strained and abnormal in the relations of Christianity and Judaism. There is a kind of historical symbolism in the story of the drunken sailor who thrashed a Jew on Good Friday, because he had just heard of the Crucifixion. Christians have acted again and again for centuries as if they had only just heard of the offences of the Jews in days long past, and did not care to draw nice distinctions between the sins of the fathers and the children; while the Jews, if any credit is to be attached to mediæval chroniclers, have retaliated savagely enough when they happened to have an opportunity. It looks as if an armed neutrality were the nearest approach to peace that could be established between the rival creeds. For some apparently inscrutable reason no considerable body of Christians seems to have been able to regard the Jews with that feeling of mere indifference or compassion which is entertained by the most orthodox believers, except under circumstances of temporary and special provocation, towards other forms of religion, such as Mahometanism or Buddhism, diverging yet more widely from their own. When the Jews have not been hated with a passionate and fanatical hatred, as has been too commonly the case, they have—at least in modern times—been loved with an equally strange and uncritical though comparatively innocuous affection. And thus in our own day a vast periodical literature has grown up on what is called the Anglo-Israel movement, which counts its circulation by hundreds of thousands, and includes a bishop and a retired Indian judge among its contributors, while an organized society, with all the machinery of newspapers, public meetings, and the like, has been formed for the purpose of maintaining that the Lost Tribes have found their home in England, and that the Jew is our brother in blood, if unhappily an alien in creed, and should be restored by English arms or diplomacy to the sacred soil which is his own.[1] Such silly crazes, however ridiculous, may be left to find their own level. But they serve to illustrate from another side the curious phenomenon already mentioned of some occult tension in the relations of Jews and Christians, which is apt to take the shape of paradoxical

[1] It may serve to modify our contemptuous ridicule of mediæval follies and fanaticisms to remember that, towards the close of the nineteenth century, a body of ostensibly educated Englishmen, considerable in point of numbers, has deliberately set itself to propagate what is in fact a new religion, having for one of its not least credible articles of faith;—that the Coronation Stone at Westminster Abbey is that on which Jacob's head rested at Bethel, which Jeremiah and Baruch, after the Captivity, conveyed to Ireland, being wrecked by the way on the Spanish coast, where it fell into the hands of the "King of Spain," whoever he may have been, and was rescued from him by its prophetic bearers, who eventually deposited it at the Irish village of Tara, so named from *Thora* (the Jewish Law), with various other equally remarkable—Taradiddles. The strangest legends in the lives of the saints are a trifle after this marvellous specimen of Protestant mythology.

sympathy when it does not break out into a storm of fanatical antipathy.

This chronic feud, which is shown by recent experience still to retain a perilous vitality, is of course no growth of yesterday. It is as old as the Christian era, and was already at work long before the conversion of the Empire. At first indeed the Roman Emperors looked on the Christians as a mere sect of Jews, and were disposed rather to despise than to persecute them as such. For the Jews on the whole, in spite of their numbers and influence at Rome, escaped persecution. Augustus issued a rescript in their favour, which was confirmed by two later edicts of the proconsuls, Agrippa and Julius Antonius. Suetonius indeed tells us how Domitian imposed on them a severe and special taxation, but this appears to have been more with the object of replenishing an exhausted exchequer than from any general motive of policy. The Emperor Julian naturally petted them, desiring for ends of his own to re-build the Temple. And yet Jews were perhaps the most hated, from various causes, of all Roman subjects; they were held notorious, as we learn from Cicero, Juvenal, and other writers of the day, as the most sordid, most turbulent, and most unsocial of mankind. But the exclusively national and therefore unaggressive character of their religion pre-served them from the overt hostility provoked by Christian proselytism. They were hated and despised, but they were not feared. No doubt they had spread in Rome; even the Empress Poppæa was said to be a convert, and it is surmised by Gibbon that through her influence the Jews escaped proscription under Nero; Juvenal tells us of the passion for Jewish rites among Roman ladies, and Josephus

has an extraordinary story of an exorcism performed in
the reign of Vespasian by a Jew named Eleazar, which he
himself witnessed, when the demon was visibly drawn out
through the nostrils of the person possessed. But on the
whole Judaism, unlike Christianity, was an essentially
unexpansive creed ; the Jews simply held aloof from other
religionists in silent disdain, and neither denounced nor
attempted to convert them. And thus, in spite of their
hatred of the Gentile world and their frequent and bloody
rebellions against their Roman masters, they were for the
most part let alone ; they were not worth attacking.
But they detested the Christians, whom they regarded as
renegades from the Law, with a peculiar detestation, and,
as Justin Martyr informs us, did their utmost to foment the
calumnies and passions of the Pagan populace against
them. In Milman's words, " the Jew, who had lost the
power of persecuting, lent himself as a willing instrument
to the heathen persecutor against those whom he considered
apostates." They took a more prominent part than the
heathen in the martyrdom of St. Polycarp. The Christians, on the other hand, exulted over the downfall of
Jerusalem and the dispersion of its citizens, as a signal
fulfilment of prophecy and triumph of the Gospel. And
thus already, during the ages of persecution and while both
alike were pressed down under the iron heel of Rome, the
seeds of a bitter antipathy were sown between them.
The Gnostics, the most widely-spread sect of early heretics,
even went so far as to treat the Jewish religion as the work
of the Demiurgos, an inferior deity, or of the Principle of
Evil—a view which is obliquely censured in the Seventh of
the Thirty-Nine Articles.

This pre-existing antagonism was not likely to be diminished when at length after three centuries of trial and suffering the Christians, through the conversion of Constantine, got the upper hand. Moreover the rise of some Judaizing sects within the Christian body, and several cases of actual apostasy, had served just then to accentuate the prevalent feeling against the obnoxious race. The Jews were accused of stoning converts from their own faith to Christianity, and of other enormities. Constantine accordingly made a law sentencing those who so acted to be burnt, and also punishing with confiscation of their property any Christians who apostatized. But in the persecution of Jews, as of heretics, it was the heretics themselves who took the lead. The Arian Constantius dealt more severely with them than Constantine, and the Visigoths at a later day showed themselves more intolerant than either. Theodosius, on the other hand, when a Christian mob had wrecked a Jewish synagogue, commanded it to be rebuilt at their expense. The earliest alleged case of their crucifying a Christian boy—a crime so frequently charged on them in the middle ages—is related by Socrates (*Eccl. Hist.*, vii. 16) as having taken place at Inmestar, a place between Chalcis and Antioch in Syria. He records it as a fact, without the slightest intimation of any doubt, and says that the perpetrators were searched out and punished. As we come down to the middle ages there were various influences at work to sustain or intensify this anti-Jewish sentiment, some due to their own conduct, some to causes beyond their control. Among the last may be reckoned the crusading movement, which, however, as will appear presently, in other ways indirectly benefited them. Already at the beginning of the eleventh century, when the prevalent idea that the Second Coming of our Lord was at hand had led to a great outburst of penitence and devotion, which found one expression in crowded pilgrimages to the Holy Land, Hakim, the Sultan of Egypt, organized a fierce persecution of the Christians of Palestine, and had the Church of the Holy Sepulchre and other Christian buildings in Jerusalem razed to the ground. It was currently rumoured, whether with or without grounds, that the Jews of Orleans had instigated him, and a savage persecution of Jews in France was the result. When at the close of the century the preaching of Peter the Hermit had roused all Europe to undertake the first crusade, it seemed to the ardent enthusiasm of the newly-enlisted soldiers of the Cross needless, if not presumptuous, to distinguish between one class of misbelievers and another, and there ensued a terrible massacre of Jews in the flourishing cities of Germany and the Rhineland. At a later period St. Bernard used the whole of his enormous influence—and it required even in him no slight display of energy and courage—to press on them the obvious distinction between the armed Saracen and the defenceless Jew. There had again been a frightful outbreak in the German cities, incited by a monk named Rudolph. Bernard confronted him in all the dignity of Christian heroism, and denounced the outrage in the severest terms; "it was not for men to punish by murder those whom God had punished by their dispersion." Meanwhile the Emperor Henry IV. had done his best to protect the Jews, not perhaps from motives of unmixed benevolence, for while he ordered a strict restitution to be made to all who had been plundered of their wealth, he decreed that the property of those who had been put to death had escheated to the imperial treasury. In France more than a century afterwards Philip the Fair plundered impartially his Jewish and Christian subjects, but the enormous wealth of the former was a tempting bait, and twice during his reign they were expelled from the country and their whole property confiscated. In the next reign they had again become numerous and prosperous, and this time they tempted the cupidity not of the monarch but of the mob ; throughout the south of France, in town and country alike, they were mercilessly massacred and pillaged, and the royal officers refused to protect them. At the end of the fourteenth century they were expelled from France altogether under Charles VI.

The vast wealth amassed by the Jews explains one main cause of their unpopularity, which was further aggravated by the way in which they had obtained it. Usury had all along been strongly condemned by the patristic and mediæval Church, and as it was forbidden to Christians by laws both of Church and State, the usurers in the early middle ages were almost exclusively Jews, who adopted the profession partly as being one of the very few open to them, partly for the huge profits it secured them. Some notion may be formed of the rate of interest they were in the habit of charging from an edict of Philip Augustus of France limiting them to 48 per cent. The crusades, however, led to a revival of commercial enterprise, and this brought orthodox Catholics into amicable relations with both Jews and Mahometans, and tended to soften the prejudice against them. It is only fair also to remember that many of the Popes, and some other leading ecclesiastics—as the Jewish historian Bedarride has acknowledged — made strenuous, though not always successful efforts to arrest the violence of their assailants; even Alexander VI., of whom there is not too much good to be recorded, distinguished himself by his generosity to the Jews, and did all in his power to alleviate their sufferings. But the general sentiment ran entirely the other way, and it found utterance both in the canon and the civil law. They were compelled to live in separate quarters and wear a distinctive dress; Christians might not eat, or bathe, or enter into partnership, still less intermarry with them; by the laws both of France and Spain a Christian who took a Jewish mistress was to be burnt alive; till the fourteenth century a Jewish criminal was hung head downwards between two dogs. At the beginning of the sixteenth century it was proposed by the theologians of Germany and France, backed by the University of Paris, to destroy the whole literature of the Jews, with the exception of the Old Testament, and it required all the influence of Reuchlin to avert this wholesale proscription. They were burnt of course in large numbers, like heretics, by the Spanish Inquisition before their final expulsion from Spain in 1495 by Ferdinand and Isabella; but the exceptional atrocity of the Spanish persecutions is in either case to be explained mainly by the peculiar conditions of the national history and character, on which it would be out of place to enlarge here. In the Italian republics, where they had succeeded in making themselves indispensable to the Christian community, they were tolerated and protected in their rights, and were allowed to practise as physicians, which was elsewhere forbidden. But they were tolerated because they were needed, not because they were loved or repected. Besides the reproach of usury, the stigma of slaveholding had from a very early period attached to them, and one of the first and most frequent, as well as most legitimate, measures directed against them by imperial legislators was the manumission of their Christian slaves. The number of the Christian slaves bought up by them was among the complaints of Agobard in the ninth century. Christians, on the other hand, had not much scruple about enslaving Jews.

There was usually less of fanaticism and more of self-interest in the policy of Christian governments towards them than in the popular sentiment, and it must be remembered that, having no civil rights or status, they were normally beyond the protection of the law. King John threw all the Jews in England into prison, and exacted 66,000 marks for their ransom; on another occasion he extorted 70,000 marks from a single Jew of Bristol, by ordering one of his teeth to be drawn every day till he complied. In 1241 Henry III. exacted 20,000 marks of them, and again, in 1255, 8000 under threat of hanging them if they refused compliance. In the same reign Dispenser, the justiciary, imprisoned 500 Jews in order to extort a large ransom from the wealthier of them, and then abandoned the rest to the fury of the populace, who massacred them all, men, women, and children. In 1255 eighteen Jews were hanged, and their goods confiscated to the royal exchequer, on the charge, recorded by Matthew Paris and Chaucer, of crucifying a

Christian boy, known afterwards as St. Hugh of Lincoln.[1] Du Cange mentions a French law forbidding the conversion of Jews to Christianity, under pain of forfeiture of goods and chattels to the king, as the convert would no longer have the opportunity of amassing usurious wealth which Christian sovereigns could plunder; it must be hoped the law is apocryphal. Edward I. was sterner and less politic than his predecessors in his dealings with the Jews. In his first year they were forbidden to lend money on interest, which was to deprive them at once of their occupation and their principal means of livelihood. They took, therefore, to clipping and adulterating the coin, a fraud not so easily detected at a time when the silver penny was allowed to be divided into halves and quarters. No less than 280 of them were hanged for this offence in London only in one year, and in 1287 all the Jews in England were thrown into prison, and a fine of 12,000 marks extorted from them. In 1290 they were finally expelled from the country, under pain of death if they remained or returned, and Hume observes that "very few of that nation have lived in England since." We have seen already that within the next two centuries they were banished from France and Spain.

It will be clear from this brief sketch that, for one cause

---

[1] The best-known example of these mediæval stories of crucifixion, for some of which there may possibly have existed a basis in fact, is that of St. Werner, whose ruined chapel at Bacharach on the Rhine— whither his body is said to have miraculously floated up stream from Oberwesel, where he was martyred — will be familiar to English tourists. There are many more alleged cases of these boy-martyrs, as, *e. g.*, St. William of Norwich in 1144; St. Robert of Bury St. Edmunds in 1181; St. Rudolf of Berne in 1287; a boy murdered at Trent in Holy Week 1475; and St. Robert of Poland in 1598.

or another, there has been a chronic antipathy between
Jew and Christian, sometimes smouldering, sometimes
bursting into flame, from the time when St. Paul turned
his back on "the unbelieving Jews," who on their part
stirred up the Gentiles against him. It has been already
observed that even in this country, the natural home of
religious toleration, Jewish Emancipation did not follow
till above a quarter of a century after the emancipation of
Dissenters and Roman Catholics, and not then till after
a protracted struggle, in which professed Liberals were
ranged on opposite sides. There were many like the late
Dr. Arnold, including some of Jewish descent though no
longer of the Jewish faith, who were eager to merge or
ignore, for political or even ecclesiastical purposes, all
differences however wide among professing Christians,
while they argued that aliens not in creed but in race had
no part or lot in the administration of a Christian commonwealth. There is no need to reopen that discussion
here. It must suffice to have traced the broad outlines of
the history of that *Judenhass*, which in these closing years
of the nineteenth century still shows itself strong enough
to foment bitter antipathy and even provoke deadly feuds
in more than one country of Europe.

XXVII

REVIVAL OF GOTHIC ARCHITECTURE.

ON the Sunday after Sir Gilbert Scott's death, Dean Stanley preached a sermon which was published under the title of "The Religious Aspect of Gothic Architecture." It contains, as might be expected, a good deal that is true, though not particularly new, but it is by no means free from the inveterate passion for paradox characteristic of its versatile author. The revival of Gothic architecture, which is closely and notoriously connected with the great religious revival of the present century, is the main subject of the discourse. That style has been generally considered to be, what Mr. Ruskin calls it, the one specifically "Christian" style of architecture. Dr. Stanley is therefore careful to begin by observing that it "was altogether unknown to Pagan *or Christian* antiquity." He adds that after flourishing for four centuries—no explanation being suggested of how it arose—it died as completely as if it had never existed, being "repudiated alike by Catholic and Protestant." Of course this is true in a sense, but it is just one of those statements which go far to explain, if not to justify, the seeming paradox that nothing is so delusive as facts. The Gothic style was undoubtedly unknown to the early Christians, for sufficiently obvious reasons ; and

it was rejected throughout Europe, at the period of the
Renaissance, in Catholic and Protestant countries alike, for
reasons not less easy of apprehension.   But to infer from
this with the preacher that Gothic architecture does not
possess any peculiarly Christian and indeed peculiarly
Catholic significance, but has nearer affinities with Protestantism, and was therefore first restored "among the
Protestant churches of England, rather than in the
Catholic churches of the Continent," is to betray as
complete a misapprehension of all the deeper bearings
of the question as could well be conceived.   Let us look
a little more closely into the matter.

The early Christians did not build Gothic churches,
first because they did not, and could not, build churches
at all.   Lord Shaftesbury had probably forgotten this
when he once said, on a memorable occasion, that " he had
rather worship with Lydia on the river's side than with
hundreds of surpliced priests in the temple of St. Barnabas"; but a professed scholar and historian might have
been expected to remember it.   And when the age of
persecution had passed away and Christians began to erect
temples for their worship, they naturally adopted the style
they found prevailing around them ;   in certain cases
indeed they adopted the actual buildings, and thus
basilicas were turned from courts of justice into Christian
churches.   The next four centuries were occupied with
theological controversy and the gradual construction of the
edifice of Catholic dogma, and then followed the dark
period of " Europe's middle night," only broken by the
great religious reformation of the second half of the
eleventh century.   In the twelfth century Gothic archi-

tecture arose. Christianity, as Mr. Lecky puts it, has
created three things which have been recognised as special
types and expressions of its religious sentiment, "the
church bell, the organ, and the Gothic cathedral." The
first is attributed to Paulinus, bishop of Nola, early in the
fifth century; the second took its origin in the East, and
was imported into Western Christendom about the seventh
century; the third, like the revival of painting which soon
followed, was due to the reawakening sense of beauty
interpreted by the Christian instinct of the twelfth century.
It became the channel of the religious enthusiasm and the
purest expression of the religious feeling of the age, and
gave abundant scope for the display of the "lamp of sacrifice."   There is, to cite Mr. Ruskin's words, "an essential
baseness in the Renaissance, and an essential nobleness in
the Gothic, consisting simply in the pride of the one and
the humility of the other." Mr. Lecky, who approaches the
subject from a somewhat different point of view, coincides
entirely in Mr. Ruskin's estimate of the specifically Christian character of Gothic architecture.   He observes that no
other building that the world has seen can rival a Gothic
cathedral in producing a sensation of blended awe and
tranquillity, harmonizing or assuaging passion, lulling to
rest the rebellion of the intellect, and creating that unworldly but most impressive atmosphere befitting a
"Church which acts on the imagination by obscurity and
terrorism, and by images of solemn and entrancing beauty."
He adds very justly that, in proportion as these modes of
feeling have prevailed or fallen into disrepute, Gothic
architecture has been rapturously admired, or has sunk
into disfavour and neglect.   It was natural therefore that

R

a form of architecture which was distinctively Christian, and "in which the highest sense of beauty was subordinated to the religious sentiment," should have arisen at a time when the dense ignorance that had overspread Europe during the ninth and tenth centuries was yielding to a great revival of moral and intellectual energy under the control of the Church. It was equally natural that, when "the moral and intellectual chaos that preceded the Reformation" was universal, when painting had been secularised, and had passed entirely into the worship of sensuous beauty, the Gothic style should be everywhere superseded by one which some persons may consider more beautiful, but which is universally admitted to be wholly devoid of a religious character.   The dominant feeling throughout Europe produced by the Renaissance, which in some countries issued in Protestantism, in others in a kind of diluted and rationalistic Catholicism, was a passionate recoil from mediæval Christianity to classical antiquity, which might be summed up fairly enough in Mr. Swinburne's "Hymn to Proserpine":—

O lips that the live blood faints in, the leavings of racks and rods !
O ghastly glories of Saints, dead limbs of gibbeted Gods !
Though all men abase them before you in spirit, and all knees bend,
I kneel not, neither adore you, but standing, look to the end.

It was not an age to appreciate the great works of those who have only "left us their adoration."   A certain analogy may indeed be traced between the contrast of Gothic and classical styles of architecture and the contrast of Christian and classical modes of appreciating natural scenery, which is illustrated—as Humboldt points out in his *Kosmos*—by the entire absence of descriptive poetry among the Greeks and Romans, whereas "Christianity expanded the views of men in their communion with nature." He cites in proof of this a striking letter (in the middle of the fourth century) of St. Basil's to his friend St. Gregory Nazianzen—which is also quoted in a different connection in Newman's *Historical Sketches*—describing his retreat on the banks of the Iris in Pontus, and observes upon it very justly: " In this simple description of scenery and forest life feelings are expressed, which are more intimately in unison with those of modern times than anything that has been transmitted to us from Greek or Roman antiquity." [1]   And the last century, which decried Gothic as a barbarous monstrosity, could see nothing in a Swiss mountain but an object of shuddering disgust, and would have found Coleridge's magnificent " Hymn before Sunrise in the Vale of Chamouni" as unmeaning and unmusical as a Gregorian chant.

It is quite true then that Gothic architecture was repudiated, as Dean Stanley says, "by Catholic and Protestant alike" in the sixteenth century; but they repudiated it in virtue of an influence, by which both alike were at that time dominated, entirely alien to the spirit of historical Christianity.   And, as always happens in such cases, the false taste once formed survived and outran the direct operation of the causes which had first produced it. In the sixteenth century our greatest writers, like Spenser and Shakspeare, have no word of sympathy, appreciation, or regret for Gothic architecture.. A curious work was published not many years ago by a French priest, the Abbé Corblet, on the *Architecture of the Middle Ages*

[1] *Kosmos*, vol. ii. p. 394. Bohn's edition.

judged by the Writers of the Eighteenth Century, and among those who spoke of it, not only without appreciation, but with mere unqualified contempt, appear the names—strangely combined in any common sentiment—of Fénelon, Bossuet, Molière, Fleury, Rollin, Montesquieu La Bruyère, Helvetius, Rousseau, Mengs, and Voltaire. Some reached the height of grotesque absurdity in their depreciatory assumptions. Thus Dupuis thought the zodiacs on cathedrals were a remnant of the worship of Mithra; Montluisant explained the sculptures on the façade of Notre Dame by the science of the philosopher's stone; a third critic traced the shape of the ogive to the eggs of Isis. If we turn to English writers of the same period, Smollet gravely declares, speaking of York Minster, "that the external appearance of an old cathedral will be displeasing to the eye of every man who has any idea of propriety and proportion"; while he describes Durham cathedral as "a huge gloomy pile"—somewhat as Archbishop Whately called Milan cathedral "a big idolatrous temple"—and could associate no better idea with a church spire than that of a man impaled. Hutcheson, in an able work on the Philosophy of the Beautiful, thought it necessary to enter into an elaborate argument in order to show that the ancient preference of Gothic to classical architecture need not disprove the universality of the sense of beauty, but was an accidental aberration due to historical associations. At such a time it was natural that Cologne, the latest and one of the most splendid of mediæval cathedrals, which Wordsworth invoked "the help of angels to complete," should be left unfinished, while the energies of Europe were concentrated on St.

Peter's.   The "aspiring heat" had failed.   And, to cite Mr. Lecky's testimony once more, it is unquestionably " to the Catholic revival of the present century that we mainly owe its revival."

To say that this revival took place among the Protestant churches of England rather than the Roman Catholic churches of the Continent, is only partially true in fact, and wholly misleading is the inference intended to be conveyed. One of the earliest Gothic restorations was of St. Germain des Près at Paris, about the time of the commencement of the Tractarian movement which so much contributed to the architectural revival in England.   And "the splendid if eccentric genius," as Dr. Stanley himself calls him, who took the lead in that revival began as an Anglican High Churchman, and, while to the last he retained strong affinities with Anglicanism, became a Roman Catholic many years before his death.   By "the Protestant churches of England" must be meant of course principally and directly those belonging to the Church of England, for the extension of " ecclesiological " taste to Nonconformist places of worship is only a very recent afterthought, when the turn in the tide had become too strong to be resisted. But it was precisely to the renewed impulse given, not to the Protestant but to the Catholic side of Anglicanism, as Mr. Lecky has quite correctly apprehended, that the architectural revival must be ascribed, which has covered the land with some thousands of new Gothic churches, and restored the greater number of the English cathedrals to much of their pristine grandeur.   It is not very clear what is meant by saying that the religious power of our cathedrals has gained " in proportion as our worship has become more

solemn, more simple, more reverential, *more comprehensive,*"
nor does the passage referred to in Milman's *Latin Christianity* throw much light on the matter. Milman points
out—what is obvious at a glance—that the Gothic cathedral was "the consummation and completion of (what he
calls) mediæval hierarchical Christianity," and was necessary to the full majesty and impressiveness of the mediæval
ritual, with its "remote central ceremonial," its solemn
music, its "curling incense," and its long processions.
That the religious power of our old cathedrals is not
discredited by the Anglican ritual is true, so far as it is
true, because of the likeness, not the unlikeness, of that
ritual to the forms originally observed in them, from which
it is mainly derived, as any one may easily satisfy himself
by observing how it fares with those Scotch and foreign
cathedrals—say at Basle, or Geneva, or Glasgow—where
Protestant "simplicity" is completely emancipated from
that "cloud of superstition which has settled down over a
large part of the ecclesiastical world."

It is indeed remarkable that a paper on Cologne cathedral, contributed some forty years ago to the *Quarterly
Review*, as was reported at the time, by no less distinguished and staunch an Anglican than the late Judge
Coleridge, should open with this melancholy confession :
"It is a painful reflection, and one that conjures up a
multitude of others, that a great cathedral can never again
be built in this country. It is perhaps as painful to reflect
on the utter disproportion of scale to use in those which
still remain to us, but to this habit has familiarised us.
We are accustomed to hear the glorious echoes of their
nave and aisles awakened at best to the footsteps of a

small congregation—for the most part only to those of the solitary verger. We are accustomed to see their grand quadrangular cloisters treated merely as covered passages to prebendal back-doors; their beautiful chapels, those greatest imaginable luxuries of former wealthy piety, used only, if used at all, as waste places for mouldering rubbish. . . . We have forbidden the pilgrimage, levelled the altar, smashed the image, and extinguished the candle." No doubt there is a visible change since then. Much has been done in England in the way of restoring old cathedrals, and some attempt has been made at building new ones; "the echoes of nave and aisles" have once more been awakened to the tread of a procession, occasionally even the defiled and desecrated "chapels" have been again turned to account, "the altar" replaced, and "the extinguished candle" lit. But this has only become possible by applying a principle exactly the reverse of that recommended by Dean Stanley, and seeking by such means as were available to emulate or revive the old solemnities of Catholic devotion. A Gothic Cathedral derives its supreme value and significance from the conviction which prompted the original builders, and can alone insure the permanence of their work—that it is *not* only or chiefly a "magnificent architectural monument," but the fitting instrument and expression of the highest ideal of Christian worship. It is precisely because "they dreamt not of a perishable home," who reared those glorious piles, and desired to bequeath to posterity "their adoration," not their handicraft, that both alike still survive.

XXVIII

INTOLERANCE OF SCOTCH CALVINISM.

IT appears to be pretty generally agreed that there is a great break-up going on of the old dogmatic temper once so characteristic of Scotch Calvinism, though there may be differences of opinion as to the precise extent or the probable consequences of the change. No traveller can fail to be struck with visible signs of a decrease of the rigid Sabbatarianism once held sacred, and it is already becoming difficult to realise the period, not so very far distant, when a Free Kirk minister was warned by his host not to scandalize the congregation by appearing in the pulpit on Sunday morning with a shaven chin. Ministers, both Free and Established—the latter especially—are said to sit loosely to the Westminster Confession now, and Dr. Macleod Campbell, who was excommunicated for heresy about fifty years ago, received a doctor's degree from the University of Glasgow before his death. Thomas Erskine of Linlathen, whose theology was of a still broader and more eclectic, not to say nebulous, type, was a layman, but he seems to have been popularly accepted almost as a prophet by his fellow-countrymen. Dean Stanley was always readily welcomed in Presbyterian pulpits. And the synods of more than one of the three disunited but doc-

trinally concordant Churches which accept the formularies
of John Knox have been exercised by the open or implicit
disavowal on the part of influential preachers and professors, like Dr. Robertson Smith, of the authority of the
Longer and Shorter Catechism and the Confession of Faith.
It has even been rumoured that, in the event of disestablishment, a large section of the ministers of the Kirk would
pass over to the Episcopal Church and bring their flocks
with them, not indeed from any abstract preference for
episcopacy, but in pursuit of a wider freedom than the
Presbyterian platform seems likely to afford them. Be
that as it may—and we need not here concern ourselves
with future possibilities—the change of feeling which has
recently taken place, if it is not greatly exaggerated, is a
sufficiently remarkable phenomenon, and can hardly imply
less than a serious change, whether for better or for worse, of
national character. Most of us are familiar with Mr. Buckle's
elaborate comparison of Scotch and Spanish bigotry ; he
even identifies the two countries as the most "priest-
ridden " in Europe. The word no doubt requires explanation, when so applied, but the meaning is obvious enough.
And it may be worth while to show by a brief review of the
facts, that there was in the temper of Scotch religionism an
element of dogmatism, or bigotry, or intolerance, or whatever we may please to call it, distinguishing it alike from
that of England and of most nations of the Continent.

It has been observed by a modern writer that there was
one country where the Puritan ministers succeeded in
moulding alike the character and the habits of the nation,
and that, while England was breaking loose from old superstitions and advancing along the paths of knowledge,

"Scotland still cowered in helpless subjection before her clergy." And one way in which this clerical influence was kept up was by fostering the belief in a continual succession of miracles, sometimes wrought for the protection or greater honour of the clergy themselves, but in most cases miracles of terror. Disease, tempest, famine, and other calamities were attributed to the direct intervention of evil spirits, who were supposed frequently to appear in bodily shape. Sir Walter Scott has pointed out in his *Letters on Demonology* that the Calvinists were of all sects the most suspicious of sorcery, and the most eager to punish it as a heinous crime. Hence in a country where almost every kind of amusement was suppressed or tabooed, and men's thoughts were concentrated with peculiar energy on theological ideas, the dread of witchcraft was all but universal. It was not, as elsewhere, a superstition diluted by imposture; Mr. Buckle has called attention to the remarkable circumstance that among all the terribly numerous witch trials in Scotland, not a single instance of imposture is recorded. These trials were almost entirely conducted by the clergy, but "the secular arm" was placed ungrudgingly at their service for execution of the sentence. On the hideous tortures employed to extract confessions, and the punishments eventually inflicted, it is unnecessary to dwell here. Suffice it to observe how one traveller casually mentions having seen nine women burning together at Leith in 1664, and how in 1674 nine others were condemned to be burnt in a single day. James VI.—our James I.—was peculiarly sensitive in the matter of witchcraft, and had this bond of hearty union with the ministers of the Kirk, whom otherwise he so little liked. And it is noticeable, considering what is said of mediæval ignorance and superstition, that the first law against witchcraft in Scotland was passed in 1563, and it was not till thirty years later that it began to be systematically carried out. The persecution was therefore in a very special sense the work of the Presbyterian ministry, or rather of their creed, which, partly from political causes, connected with the history of the Scotch Reformation, was shaped more directly on the lines of the Old than of the New Testament. These executions for witchcraft came to an end about 1730, but not apparently by the good will of the Presbytery, who passed·a resolution fifty years afterwards deploring the prevalent scepticism on the subject.

It must not, however, for a moment be imagined that the dogmatism and intolerance of the Scottish Kirk showed itself only or chiefly in the matter of witchcraft.   There was no less zeal displayed in persecuting Papists and other misbelievers when opportunity for it occurred.   One of the first results of the final triumph of the Reformation in Scotland was a law prohibiting any priest from celebrating, or worshipper from hearing mass, under pain of confiscation of his goods for the first offence, exile for the second, and death for the third.   John Knox, " the ruffian of the Reformation," who, according to Mr. Froude's characteristic paradox, " was no narrow fanatic who, in a world *in which God's grace was equally visible in a thousand creeds* (he would have burnt any one for saying so), could see truth and goodness nowhere but in his own formula," is described with perfect accuracy by Dr. Johnson as "the most intolerant of an intolerant creed and an intolerant country."   Mr. Froude forgets to remind his readers of Knox's angry denunciation of permitting

the "idolatry" of the mass, even in the single case of
the Queen's private chapel at Holyrood, seeing that "one
mass was more fearful to him than if 10,000 armed enemies
were landed in any part of the realm." Nor does he tell
them how Knox in his *Appellation* teaches that "none provoking the people to idolatry ought to be exempted from
the punishment of death," while the charge of idolatry is
carefully explained to include "the whole rabble of the
Papistical clergy." At the time of the Commonwealth the
Presbyterians did their utmost to thwart the more liberal
policy of the Protector, who was willing to tolerate all
forms of Christianity, with the significant exceptions of
"Popery and Prelacy." They wished those only to be
tolerated who accepted the "fundamentals" of Christianity,
and the list of fundamentals was so drawn as to exclude
not only Socinians, who were to be punished with death,
but Papists, Arminians, Antinomians, Baptists, and Quakers,
who were to be imprisoned for life. In 1645 the Scotch
Parliament solemnly protested against "the toleration of
any sects or schisms contrary to our Solemn League and
Covenant." And the Puritans carried with them across
the Atlantic to the new world the intolerance they had
practised at home. Maryland in the hands of its Catholic
founders had been—much to their credit—the solitary
refuge of oppressed sectaries of every kind, but when the
Puritans gained the upper hand there, they at once sub-
verted the existing rule, and enacted the whole penal code
against those who had so generously received them. So
again the Pilgrim Fathers revived in Massachusetts the
Puritan panic about witchcraft, which was dying out in
England though still dominant in Scotland. Multitudes

were scourged, tortured, and imprisoned on this charge, and many were put to death.

The New England colony indeed, during the quarter of a century or so that it had its swing, represented with a perfection unattainable elsewhere the Puritan ideal of toleration, which is the more remarkable considering that the settlers had fled from the ecclesiastical tyranny of Archbishop Laud and the Star Chamber, expressly and avowedly in order " to enjoy the blessing of a pure Gospel." It was not perhaps unnatural that they should be somewhat exercised by the vagaries of a certain Anne Hutchinson, a " preacheress " two centuries and a half before her age in resolving to flout the authority of St. Paul, though the result certainly justified the wisdom of the apostolic veto. Not content with assailing the regular Puritan ministers as " Baal's priests, Popish factors, Scribes, Pharisees, and opposers of Christ," she went on to propound a miscellaneous assortment of heresies, including *inter alia* a denial of the Personality of the Holy Ghost, of heaven and hell, and of what she termed "the deadly doctrine of the covenant of works." This was too much for the ruling authorities, who had already decided that " it is impious ignorance to say "—what they denounced Laud for disputing—" that men ought to have liberty of conscience," inasmuch as " religion admits of no eccentric notions,"—*i. e.* none differing from their own,—and therefore " for the security of the flock we pen up the wolf." The lupine Mrs. Hutchinson, however, was not " penned," but excommunicated and banished, and she afterwards came to a miserable end at Long Island in a massacre of the colonists by the Indians, to the undisguised satisfaction of her former judges at Massachusetts.

The Rev. Thomas Welde, who had taken a prominent part in her condemnation, lost no time in proclaiming from the pulpit that, as no such outrage had hitherto been committed by the Indians, " therefore God's hand is the more apparently seen herein, to pick out this woeful woman, and make her and those belonging to her an unheard-of heavy example of their cruelty above all others." But this was not the worst. Sir Harry Vane, who sincerely disapproved of persecution on all sides, had returned to England, where, however, he was himself shamefully persecuted by Cromwell, as a consistent opponent of every form of arbitrary government. Meanwhile in New England proscription, fine, banishment, and capital punishment became the order of the day for Anglicans, Quakers, Anabaptists, Adamites, and other such "unhappy sectaries and energumens." Not only did the " Blue Code "—so named apparently as seeming to be written in blood—strictly forbid "reading the Common Prayer, keeping Christmas Day or Saints' days, making mince-pies, or playing on any instrument except the drum, the trumpet, and the Jews' harp," which were supposed to have a kind of Biblical flavour about them ; it also forbade mothers to kiss their babies on the Sabbath day, and enjoined that no one " should run or walk in his garden, or elsewhere, except reverently to and from meeting." Readers of *The Scarlet Letter* will readily understand the moral results of this sort of legislation. As to religious toleration, " If," says one of their leading writers of that day, "after men continue in obstinate rebellion against the light, the civil magistrate shall still walk towards them in soft and gentle commiseration, his softness and gentleness is excessive large to foxes and

wolves, but his bowels are miserably straitened and hard-
ened against the poor sheep and lambs of Christ.   Nor is
it frustrating the end of Christ's coming, but a direct
advancing it, to destroy the bodies of those wolves who
seek to destroy the souls of those for whom Christ died."
It is a curious satire on human weakness and inconsistency,
that the hideous system of persecution enjoined in New
England by the very men who had fled, as they elegantly
expressed it, from "those proud Anakimes, the tiranous
bishops, and their proud and profane supporters and cruel
defenders" under Charles I., was at last brought to an end
after the Restoration by a peremptory order from Charles
II.   There are no crimes like those that are wrought in the
name of liberty.

In Scotland the interference of the Kirk Sessions with
every department not only of public but private life was no
less inquisitorial and vexatious.   Resistance was punished
by fines, whipping, branding with red-hot iron, and public
penances of the most humiliating kind.   And the sins
which incurred those penalties, and many of which have
till very recently lain under the ban of public opinion in
Scotland, were of the most various and most fanciful kind.
For an innkeeper to admit a Catholic to his house, or for a
town to hold a market on Saturday or Monday, as being
too near the Sabbath, were sins.   It was a sin to visit a
friend, to water your garden, to shave, to ride, to walk, or
to whistle on the Sabbath.   To bathe was a deadly sin on
Sunday, and of very questionable lawfulness at any time ;
a boy had once been miraculously struck dead while
indulging in that carnal amusement, and the Glasgow
Kirk Sess'on in 1691 invoked the aid of the civil power to

prevent boys from swimming altogether. As Chambers puts it in his Annals of Scotland, "to the Puritan Kirk of the sixteenth and seventeenth centuries every outward demonstration of natural good spirits was a sort of sin, to be as far as possible suppressed," and thus "the whole sunshine of life was, as it were, squeezed out of the community." The standard of a religious nation was the prevalence of universal gloom.

That this scheme of life is the consistent and logical outcome of the Calvinistic theology is true enough. And we cannot wonder that the Scotch, who are a logical people, should have thus exemplified in practice the faith which had been so deeply ingrained into their national character. Still less need we be surprised to learn that the outward change, which has of late years attracted the notice even of casual observers, does not stand alone. It is obvious that the Westminster Confession must have been subjected to a "verifying faculty" of divines, and the Longer and Shorter Catechism have lost their hold over the popular mind, before the tone of ordinary preaching and practice could undergo any material alteration. What may be the moral or religious results of this change in the long run is a question on which it would be premature as yet to hazard any confident opinion. A narrow or prejudiced creed may often be better than none, and the collapse of a firmly compacted dogmatic system, whether true or false, not unfrequently brings with it, at least for the time, a dissolution of all religious belief; if not also of all moral restraints. Thus, as Macaulay observes, Catholic countries have become infidel and again reverted to Catholicism, but have never since the sixteenth century become Protestant.

On the other hand, it must be remembered that the profession, however sincere, of a rigidly ascetic code of religious obligation has by no means always proved a sure guarantee for even an average observance of morality.   Nature will have her revenges, and when the most ordinary and harmless recreations are forbidden as sinful, is apt to seek compensation in indulgences which no moralist would be willing to condone.   The charges brought against Novatians and Manicheans in the early ages of the Church have been brought with equal plausibility against Puritans in our own day.   One vice at all events, which Christians of every school, as well as non-Christian moralists, are agreed in condemning, is reputed to be a special opprobrium of Scotland, and the strictest observance of all those minute and oppressive Sabbatarian regulations, to which reference was made just now, has been found compatible with consecrating the day of rest to a quiet but unlimited assimilation of the liquid which inebriates but does not cheer.   And under the old *régime* to be drunk in private, though of course not sanctioned as allowable, would have been accounted a far less heinous outrage on the dignity of the "honourable Sabbath" than to whistle in the public street.   On its theological side Calvinism has in all continental countries shown a tendency to develop into Socinianism, which the early Calvinists, after the example of their founder, who burnt Servetus, never hesitated to treat as a capital crime, and it will be curious to watch whether a relaxation of the old orthodox strictness in Scotland tends in the same direction.   Swedenborg, we may remember, insisted on connecting the Nicene doctrine with Calvinism, and therefore repudiated both together.   At present perhaps the

S

prevailing disposition among the Broad school of Scotch Presbyterian divines is to reject dogmatic restrictions of all kinds, whether orthodox or the reverse. But it is needless to speculate on future contingencies ; let us be content for the present to take note of existing facts. For the last three centuries the traditional Calvinism of Scotland has shown a stern and vigorous tenacity of life, which has no parallel in any of the Reformed Churches elsewhere. It has now, for the first time since the Reformation, entered on a state of transition of which as yet we see only the beginning, but which cannot fail, whatever may be its ultimate term, to have an important bearing not only on ecclesiastical matters, but on the habits and character of the people.

XXIX

FORCE OF INDIVIDUALISM IN RELIGIOUS MOVEMENTS.

THERE are some passages in Mr. Gladstone's very interesting and suggestive paper on the Evangelical Movement in the *British Quarterly Review* for July 1879, which open out a wider question than that with which the writer is immediately concerned. And it will therefore be suitable to introduce the present subject by a reference to one particular portion of his argument. After pointing out that the Evangelical movement, influential as it was, never attained, even at the close of the last and the beginning of the present century, anything like predominance in the Church of England—that it remained to the last more or less under the ban of authority, and was viewed with distrust or aversion by the great majority of the clergy—Mr. Gladstone proceeds to explain how, as it appears to him, it has left its mark generally and permanently on the English Church. The explanation may sound at first paradoxical or far-fetched, but there can be little doubt that it is substantially correct. He considers that the Evangelical movement was, not simply in order of time or by process of reaction, but in some degree by direct causation, the parent of the Tractarian movement which

S 2

followed it. And he holds that it is through this latter movement, especially in the later offshoot from it called Ritualism, that the Evangelical revival has so largely affected the tone of Anglican preaching and religious life. There is a great deal to be said for this view of the matter, but we may confine ourselves for the present to one argument on which Mr. Gladstone lays, and justly lays, special stress. He recalls to our memory what is indeed well known, but is apt to be forgotten or ignored, how nearly all the great leaders of the specific Oxford movement—notably the greatest of them all—began their course as Evangelicals, and, what might seem still stranger, how all the most conspicuous men among the Tractarian converts to Rome also belonged originally to the same school. It was not divines trained in high Anglican principles, like Keble, Isaac Williams, and Hook, or— to add another illustrious name—Hugh James Rose, so much as "the Newmans, the Wilberforces, and the Mannings," whose antecedents were very different, who gave its shape and direction to the movement. And the latter class also supplied the most distinguished converts to the Church of Rome, such as the two Cardinals, who may be called respectively the moral and the official heads of that Church in England, the Wilberforces, Mr. Sibthorpe, and, as the writer might have added, the late Dr. Faber, whose early Evangelicalism was perhaps more pronounced than that of any of his fellows, and certainly exercised a more perceptible influence on his religious tone and teaching to the last, in spite of his fervid Ultramontanism. On the other hand, Mr. Gladstone is surely mistaken in speaking of Mr. Manning as a Tract-writer. For some time after his abandonment of the Evangelical party he sided with the pronounced Anglicanism of Hook and his school. It is forgotten perhaps that, on the collapse of the *British Critic*, the High Church party was represented by two quarterly reviews—the *Christian Remembrancer*, which took a broader line under the editorship of the late Professor Mozley and the late Mr. Scott of Hoxton, in which Dean Church wrote most of the papers afterwards published as *Essays and Reviews;* and the *English Review*, the representative of the most rigid Anglicanism. Archdeacon Manning was a contributor to the latter periodical.

So far we are concerned with facts which can hardly be disputed ; and now for the explanation. Mr. Gladstone indicates his belief that the extreme individualism which was a weakness of the Evangelical movement, and which neither the Roman Church nor the Nonconformist bodies would have tolerated, acted throughout as a drawback on the work of these men as Anglicans, and finally drove them out of the Anglican pale altogether. The correctness of this assumption turns on what may be termed a chronological question. Did the " Tractarian " seceders precede, coincide with, or follow a remarkable change in this respect in the temper of the Church of England ? Individualism of doctrine is no doubt at present virtually tolerated in the Church of England to an extent which neither the Church of Rome nor, probably, any of the Dissenting communities would endure. It is obvious that such toleration must have its limits from the nature of the case, for a clergy of whom it could justly be said *quot homines tot sententiæ* would be fatal to the coherence, and therefore eventually to the existence, of any religious body. And it may be

true enough, as the writer hints, that these limits have
been nearly reached in the Church of England, and that
there is a risk of divergence increasing till it lets in the
peril of disestablishment. Be that as it may, it remains
none the less true that, in spite of this wide *doctrinal*
variety, which is in its present extreme form a thing of
very recent growth, and partly in consequence of it, the
Church of England has not usually shown herself very
tolerant of any other kind of individualism among her
clergy, and that she has suffered from want of doing so.
On the other hand, it is surely quite clear that there has
been not less but more scope given for this diversity of
vocation, certainly in the Roman Catholic Church, and
in some at least of the Nonconformist bodies. There
is evidently much force in Macaulay's famous contrast
between the position of John Wesley and that of Ignatius
Loyola; the Church of Rome utilised Ignatius, while the
Church of England drove Wesley into revolt. Whether a
different policy on the part of her rulers would have availed
to retain Mr. Newman permanently within the Anglican
pale, is a question which it would be scarcely possible,
perhaps even for himself, to answer confidently now, and
is hardly fitting for others to discuss ; that the policy they
actually did pursue materially helped to drive him out of
it, he has expressly told us. And there can be no doubt
at all that a different treatment would have turned Wesley
into one of its most effective bulwarks, instead of the
founder of a sect which has proved its most determined
and powerful rival. It is remarkable that Mr. Newman
himself should have taken as the theme of one of his
earliest University sermons, preached the year before the

beginning of the Oxford movement (January 1832), " Personal Influence the Means of propagating the Truth." There are passages in it which he might not be disposed to endorse now as they stand—though he has not qualified them by any annotations in the new edition — for the visible Church is almost put aside as a teacher, and everything is ascribed to the moral influence of gifted persons, who are represented as the sole " legitimate interpreters " of Scripture. But there is no reason for assuming that the main drift of the discourse would be out of harmony with his present opinions, and it is illustrated by his whole career, since the day when he sat " sobbing bitterly " on his bed in an inn at Castro Giovanni, and replied to the startled inquiries of his servant, " I have a work to do in England." The same idea is worked out in the lines on " The Course of Truth" written at Malta in the previous December ; while another of his poems in the *Lyra Apostolica* ends with the significant query, whether in the " dim future " we shall " NEED (*sic*) a prophet for Truth's Creed." And he reaffirms it in more prosaic form in the *Apologia*, where he observes that " living movements do not come of Committees," but rather from " the force of personal influence and congeniality of thought."

Nor can it be said that there is anything peculiar to Cardinal Newman in this insistence on the importance of individual action and influence, in the promotion of religious truth, though it is of course a conviction likely to come home with special force to men of exceptional genius and intensity of character. But the fact itself is one which lies on the surface of all ecclesiastical history, not to say of the history of all religions. But, as the subject is a wide one,

we had better here confine ourselves to Christian history.
In the Sermon already mentioned Mr. Newman gives a
single example only of the principle, when he says that
"before now even one man has impressed an image on the
Church which, through God's mercy, shall not be effaced
while time lasts"; and this is explained in a note to refer
to Athanasius, on whose works he was at the time engaged.
The example is a critical one. Athanasius in the East and
Augustine in the West have undoubtedly left their impress
from that day to this on the doctrine of the Church, the
one, as might be expected, in its theological, the other in
its anthropological aspect. But this is not the ordinary
way in which individualism has taken effect. When we
speak of *Athanasius contra mundum*, we mean that
Athanasius in his day supported, or seemed to support,
alone the burden of orthodox belief, on a point vital
to the whole structure of Christian doctrine, against an
heterodox world. But such a doctrinal crisis as that of
the Arian controversy is not common in Church history,
nor has it generally been met by the energy of a single
individual. The elaboration of dogma is mostly carried
on by theological experts and through the corporate
action of the Church. It is rather in the conversion of
worldlings or unbelievers, the enforcement or application
of great principles, and the development of the moral or
spiritual life of the age, than in the abstract enunciation or
vindication of dogmatic truths, that personal influence has
played so prominent a part. It would be obvious to refer
to the case of the Apostles, but it might be replied—
though the reply would be only partially relevant—that
the gift of inspiration and of miracles differentiates them

from ordinary teachers. Take, however, the gradual construction of the splendid edifice of the mediæval Papacy ;
for a splendid edifice it was, whether we admire it or not.
Viewed on its theological side, it may be regarded by one
party as a creation of Divine Providence, and by another
as the masterpiece of Satan ; but viewed on its human side,
it was chiefly the work of some half-dozen great pontiffs
in successive periods, who had grasped at once the significance of their own position and its relations to the
social and religious needs of the age. If we subtract from
the catalogue of Popes such names as Leo I., Gregory I.,
Nicholas I., Hildebrand, and the third and fourth Innocents, it is difficult to see, humanly speaking, how the
result could have been achieved. And what these master
spirits did for building up the external polity, men like
Benedict, Dominic, Francis of Assisi, and Ignatius Loyola
did, in very different ways and at different periods, for
moulding or reforming the internal life of the Church.
It must be clear, for instance, even to those whose information is confined to Sir James Stephen's charming but
discursive and sketchy biography, how thoroughly indi-
vidualistic, if we may use the term, was the Franciscan
revival of the thirteenth century. And the same may be
said of the origin and idea of the widely diverse, and in
its final result rigidly regimental, system introduced three
centuries later by Ignatius Loyola. It was his individual
influence more than anything else that stemmed the
advancing tide of the Protestant Reformation. Nor was
the success of the attack less due to the personal energy of
Luther than the successful resistance to Ignatius. And in
both cases alike the determining force lay far more in the

vigorous personality of the men than in theological argument. Luther, as a theologian, is not to be named in the same day with Calvin, but his influence was infinitely greater; his peculiar scheme of theology had a moral and personal rather than an intellectual basis, and it may well be questioned whether it would ever have taken the shape it ultimately assumed, had a Pope otherwise minded than Leo X. understood how to appropriate his reforming zeal, as Innocent III. had appropriated the devotion of Francis. But the Papacy of the Renaissance had lost its cunning, and Luther was rudely repelled, like Wesley afterwards, with not very dissimilar results.

If we turn back to England, the same phenomenon again presents itself. The English Reformation is an exception which helps to prove the rule. It was, properly speaking, not a religious or theological, but a political movement; there was not, as Döllinger has pointed out, a single man of first-rate eminence, either for character or capacity, among the English Reformers; too many of them sank in both respects below the level of respectability. Unlike the Scotch and Continental movement, it emanated from the Government, not from the people, and the Puritan revolt which grew out of it was closely connected with the advance of the democratic spirit. But the Caroline reaction of the next century, which has left its permanent mark on the Established Church, owes its origin and success mainly to the individual energy of men like Laud, and the individual piety of men like Andrewes and Ken; and when the awakening came from the long spiritual slumber of the eighteenth century, it was again through the personal influence of a few gifted and devoted men that the work was wrought. Wesley himself never willingly departed from the lines of the received orthodoxy, and was so far from sympathising with the Calvinism of Whitefield that he said he could sooner be a Turk, or a deist, or even an atheist, than believe a doctrine which made God an almighty tyrant. And Whitefield's electric power over the masses gathered on the bleak hill-side to listen to him did not arise from the peculiar doctrine, or even exactly from the eloquence, of his sermons—for they are commonplace enough to read—but from the marvellous force of individual earnestness he put into them; it was the contact of soul with soul that gave reality to his message, when the tears streamed down the grimy faces of the rough Cornish miners, who had known little before of the love of God or man. In the Church of England the Evangelical movement owed whatever success it had at the time to the personal zeal and weight of men like Simeon and Wilberforce and Fletcher of Madeley. And if Mr. Gladstone's estimate of the net result of the movement be correct, as there is good reason to think it is, that is a still more striking testimony to the true secret of its power. For, so far as it has acted on the country through the medium of Tractarianism, the process was effected by individual agency alone, not only without the aid of authority, but in the teeth of its most strenuous and persistent opposition. The Tractarian leaders, as has been pointed out, were most of them trained in the Evangelical School, and the new revival was carried on by the same means of direct individual action as the old one, but with far more commanding attributes of moral and intellectual power. It was a true instinct which told

Dr. Newman he had "a work to do in England"; the movement which never bore his name, and from which he retired at an early stage of its progress, is hardly conceivable without him. "A prophet" is in one sense constantly needed "for truth's creed." The purest system of doctrine, the most perfect organization, will not hold its own without the individual energy which can alone breathe into the dry bones the breath of life. Systems grow out of individual exertions, and require to be sustained or renewed by them. And hence Churches which repress that energy, and in proportion as they repress it, must be regarded as in a state of partial or incipient decadence. The Catholic Church was at its lowest ebb at the beginning of the sixteenth century, and the Church of England at the close of the eighteenth. Heresy signifies in etymological strictness the obstinate preference of individual opinion, and the best security against its triumph is found in giving free scope in the service of orthodoxy to individual zeal. To use Scriptural language, unity of spirit can only be preserved by a generous recognition of the diversity of gifts.

XXX

PREACHING ANCIENT AND MODERN.

A WELL-KNOWN Oxford tutor of a former generation, when asked why he preferred long walks on Sunday to attendance at St. Mary's, replied that he preferred sermons from stones to sermons from sticks. It is presumably a similar preference or a similar dread which has inspired so many discussions on preaching of late years. There have been articles in reviews, and a book by Mr. Mahaffy, better known for his classical publications, and "Conferences on Pew and Pulpit" at the City Temple, and an address by Mr. Walter in the Chapter House of St. Paul's, both critical and suggestive. It may, however, be doubted whether he attached its due weight to a preliminary distinction, which he mentioned, but scarcely appeared to have thought out in all its bearings. He observed that oratory is far less cultivated now than in ancient Greece and Rome, where public speaking monopolized that control of public opinion which it has come to share with the press. But it necessarily follows from this that preaching, and still more the public reading of the Bible, to which a large portion of his discourse was devoted, cannot hold the same position in the Church of our own day as in days before printing was invented, or even before "the schoolmaster was abroad."

It is in fact very difficult for us to realise to its full extent the distinction between a hearing and a reading age. It has justly been observed that, if society had never known any but a reading age, the history of the world would have lost one cf its most brilliant scenes, and oratory its greatest recorded triumph. When Demosthenes persuaded the Thebans, while the Macedonian army was already hovering on their frontiers, to join the alliance of Athens, his eloquence wrought a wonder second only to that ascribed by poetry to Amphion's lyre, when the walls of that same city of Thebes rose obedient to its call. But the most eloquent speech of Demosthenes delivered in the present House of Commons might hardly influence half-a-dozen votes. The ablest speeches in the present day are made rather to be read than to be listened to, and this holds good also of many contemporary sermons. It may indeed be truly said that the whole character of modern as distinguished from ancient literature is affected by this fundamental change. Socrates taught his philosophy not by writing but by word of mouth; the "erotetic," or, as he himself called it, obstetric method was of its very essence. Herodotus recited his history at the Olympic games, where, we are told, it drew tears from the sterner eyes of Thucydides. The poems of Homer, if our modern critics will allow them to be so named, were chanted by the Rhapsodists. The same distinction has left its mark on our theology. As a well-known writer puts it, " the hymns of Luther and the sermons at St. Paul's Cross may find their parallel in the first age of Christianity, not in the confession of Augsburg or the decrees of Trent." The greatest Fathers of the Church, like St. Chrysostom, St. Ambrose

St. Augustine, and St. Leo, were also among the greatest
preachers of their day. For all practical purposes the
centre of influence has been completely shifted by the
printing press. Thus, to take a very different illustration,
Demosthenes has left us (in the *De Coronâ*) a graphic
picture of the arrival at Athens of the messenger announcing
Philip's seizure of Elateia, and how all the citizens, from
the prytanes downwards, thronged to the market-place
to hear the news. But when tidings arrived in London
of the battles of Waterloo, Inkermann, or Sedan, the centre
of attraction was the post or telegraph office. And so even
in ordinary times the Roman or Athenian idler, whose
object in life was to hear or tell something new, loitered,
not in the Club or Coffee-house, but in the barber's shop.
It was there the fatal news of the destruction of the
Athenian army in Sicily was first made known, and a
barber was actually put to the torture for spreading the
report. To come to later times, when Richard III. wished
to secure his own succession to the English Crown by
discrediting the legitimacy of his unhappy nephews in
public opinion, his first care was, not to send an inspired
article to a political organ, but to cause Shaw, a noted
preacher of the day, to deliver a sermon to that effect at
Paul's Cross.

To return to our immediate subject, we may readily
conceive with what keen and breathless interest the public
reading of a manuscript Gospel or Epistle would be
listened to by an infant Christian community of the
apostolic age. And for some centuries afterwards the
reading of Scripture continued to form an integral portion
of the worship of the Church, as before of the Jewish

Synagogue ; and it was usually followed, as in the Synagogue, by what Justin Martyr calls "a word of exhortation," which gradually developed, especially among the Greeks, into a regular sermon by the bishop or some priest appointed by him. The selection of Scripture lessons, as we should call them, was at first left to the discretion of each bishop, but in course of time a systematic arrangement was adopted with reference to the various seasons and solemnities of the Christian year. St. Chrysostom, himself the most eloquent preacher of his age, frequently complains of the prevalent habit of attaching an exaggerated importance to the sermon, to the disparagement of public prayer, and the evil consequences, shown on the one hand in the growth of a too theatrical and declamatory style of preaching, and on the other in the custom of noisily applauding impressive passages of popular preachers. "This," he told his hearers on one occasion, "is no theatre, nor are you sitting here as spectators of a tragedy." It is, indeed, curious to observe how close is the similarity, in points of detail, between ancient and modern preaching, though the stricter decorum of our own day has banished, at least in the Church of England, all outward demonstrations of approval from the sacred walls. Then, as now, the sermon was sometimes delivered from the altar steps, sometimes from the βῆμα or pulpit; then, as now, shorthand writers eagerly employed themselves in taking down notes of the discourses of famous preachers, so that St. Gregory of Nazianzus especially addresses them in his farewell sermon at Constantinople, and at a later date Gaudentius of Brescia complained of their transcribing him inaccurately. Then too, as now, sermons were sometimes, though rarely, read off entirely from notes or manuscript, as is so common in England, or committed to memory, like those of Bourdaloue, Massillon, and the great French preachers generally; sometimes delivered partly extempore, according to a plan previously prepared; and sometimes altogether extempore. Thus St. Augustine tells us that his choice of subjects was occasionally suggested by the passage of Scripture which the *lector* had been reading, and St. Chrysostom speaks of something he witnessed on the way to church, or which occurred during divine service, suggesting the theme of his discourse, as when the lighting of lamps during his sermon had drawn off the attention of his audience. Very likely we might be able to trace an analogy in another respect also, if our means of information about those remote ages were as full as those supplied by the more various and voluminous literature of the present day. But, as a matter of fact, only the discourses of really distinguished writers have come down to us, and there are no journals or biographies, or serials and newspapers, of the patristic era to enlighten us on the popular taste in the matter. But we know that even apostles anticipated the snare of " itching ears," and it is more than probable that popular preachers often won as cheap a reputation among the early Christians as among their descendants.

By degrees, however, preaching died out altogether in the East, and in the middle ages it had from various causes sunk to a low ebb in the Latin. Church. It was still supposed to be the special function of the episcopate, but the statesman or warrior prelates of mediæval Europe lacked alike time, inclination, and aptitude for discharging it, and thus again the Anglican prelates at

T

a later date were stigmatized by their Puritan assailants as "dumb dogs that cannot bark." And hence it naturally became, as Milman observes, "the strength of all the heresiarchs of all the sects," till St. Dominic in the thirteenth century founded the Order of Friar Preachers, in order to meet them with their own weapons. The Reformation, it need hardly be added, gave a fresh impetus to preaching both among the assailants and the defenders of the old faith, though the pulpit was then already beginning to share its influence on public opinion with the press. And we must remember, after making all allowance for change of circumstances, that oratory will ever be a power among men, while human nature remains what it is, and especially that sacred oratory can never fail to hold an important place in the prophetic ministry of the Church. It is of course quite true, as has often been pointed out, that "preaching the Gospel" does not mean in the New Testament only or even chiefly what we call sermons,—still less of the kind so lovingly commended by the Methodist old woman in *Loss and Gain*, "Dear Mr. Spoutaway, he goes to my heart, he goes through me,"—and that the ritual and ordinances of the Church are, and were intended to be, in a very real sense a proclamation or setting forth of Christ. But it is also true that from the first, preaching, as we now understand the term, was a distinctive and almost unique peculiarity of Christian worship. It formed no part of the official duties of the Pagan, or even of the Mosaic priesthood, though it had latterly been introduced into the service of the Synagogue. Mr. Lecky speaks of "a system of popular preaching" being created and diffused by the Stoics of the later Empire; and he instances the

Cynics, who may be compared to the Mendicant Orders
of the Church, and the Rhetoricians, who were a kind of
itinerant lecturers. But he admits that the analogy in
the latter case is a faint one, neither the talents nor the
character of these Rhetoricians, any more than of the
Sophists of a previous age, being usually such as to command respect. And as regards both classes, it may be
doubted whether their "system of popular preaching," so
far as it existed at all, was not consciously or unconsciously
borrowed from the contemporary usage of the Christian
Church, as was certainly the case with the Emperor
Julian's not very successful attempt to import it into his
unreal and semi-Christianized revival of the Pagan cult.

There can be no question then that the object of raising
the standard of preaching is one of high practical importance. As to public reading, there can perhaps little more
be done than to take all available precautions against
slovenliness or irreverence. The well-known example, to
which Mr. Walter and others have referred from their own
recollection, of the marvellous effect produced by Mr.
Newman's reading of the lessons at St. Mary's, Oxford,
at once sympathetic and suggestive yet perfectly simple,
is one which ordinary men must be content to admire
rather than to imitate. If careless reading is to be condemned, there is also an opposite and by no means purely
hypothetical danger of affectation arising from overmuch
care. The case is not singular of an Evangelical divine
of the last generation, who had taken lessons in reading
the service from Mrs. Siddons, and the result, though he
was himself not otherwise than devout, was decidedly more
striking than devotional. But with preaching it is different.

T 2

Orators indeed, like poets, are born and not made, but still a good deal may be done by judicious training, and even born orators cannot with impunity neglect it. No doubt, as has been often said, " the secret of good preaching must be learnt on the knees," but that is no excuse for ignoring the more human elements of success. A great barrister is reported to have expressed his surprise that the clergy did not make better use of their quite unique opportunities :— " A whole week," he exclaimed, " to get up the case, and no reply!" But the requirements alike of conscience and of public opinion would leave a parish priest of the present day a very limited fraction of the " whole week" for composing his Sunday sermon, or possibly his two sermons, and the absence of " reply" is by no means an unmixed benefit to the preacher, or at least to his discourse. That he is never under the fire of contradiction may tempt him to be shallow or supercilious, and is a good reason why some such purifying process of criticism should be supplied in the education of preachers. And it does seem strange that what is practised almost everywhere else should be omitted in the ordinary course of training for the Anglican ministry. The composition and delivery of sermons form part of the regular training of candidates for orders among the Presbyterians and Protestant Nonconformists, as also in Catholic seminaries.[1] And without some such prepara-

---

[1] Some such plan is said to have been adopted by the late primate, when Bishop of London, and an amusing story is told about it. He had set a candidate for deacon's orders to preach in the private chapel at London House before himself and his Examining Chaplain, the late Dr. Stanley. The young preacher, whose conception of the duties of his office was a very definite and somewhat narrow one, began by dividing his hearers into "the converted and the unconverted." The

tory discipline we cannot fairly expect those who are not endowed with exceptional gifts, or even wish them, to preach without book. Reading sermons is a peculiarity, and a comparatively modern peculiarity, of the Church of England; it is almost unknown, and would scarcely be tolerated, in other communions, Catholic or Protestant, as neither would it be tolerated in Parliament, or at a public meeting, or in a law court. It does not of course at all follow that sermons any more than speeches should not be carefully prepared. The great French preachers used to write and learn their sermons by heart, like the Greek orators of old, and one at least of the most eloquent extempore preachers in the Church of England at the present day is said to do the same. Others might find the preparation of notes sufficient, perhaps committing to memory certain critical passages, as is the habit of some of our greatest Parliamentary orators; not but that there is a danger in trusting too much to *purpurei panni*. Every one has heard the story of an ambitious young preacher, who had been discoursing before Rowland Hill, and who afterwards pressed the great man to tell him which passage in his sermon had struck him most. "Sir," was the prompt reply, "what pleased me most was your passage from the pulpit to the vestry." Mr. Walter, by the way, brought a charge against "our pulpits themselves", which he had heard an American preacher describe as "an invention of the Devil." And it is true enough that "to be cabined, cribbed, confined in a wooden or stone box a few feet above the ground, with a brass

Bishop at once interposed: "Stop there, Sir; in which class do you place *me?*"

bookstand in front, and a pair of candlesticks on each side, is not the most favourable position for giving full expression to the impulses of the soul." In the early Church, as we have seen, the sermon was sometimes preached from the *ambo*—which, however, was probably more spacious than a modern pulpit—and sometimes from the chancel steps, and there is no reason why the latter practice should not be followed now, as indeed it often is, where the size and arrangements of the building admit of it. Or the Italian plan might be adopted of making the pulpit a sort of open gallery running round a pillar, which would equally meet the requirement that the whole person of the preacher should be visible, and would also leave room for freedom of action and movement. But these are matters of detail which may safely be left to find their natural adjustment.

A more important suggestion has been urged both by Mr. Mahaffy and Mr. Walter. They are agreed in desiring that the Church of England should follow Catholic precedent in establishing an "Order of preachers" to supplement the work of the parochial clergy, many of whom, however admirably fitted for their ordinary duties, are quite unequal to the task of preparing a fresh sermon of any value every week, not to say two or three, which is often demanded of them. Mr. Mahaffy is careful to add—and such a recommendation comes of course with peculiar significance from an Irish Protestant clergyman—"an Order of *celibate* preachers in the Reformed Churches"; he gives his reasons for emphasising this condition, which are very sensible ones. But if that suggestion be thought impracticable—and one can imagine the wry faces the new Irish "Synod" would make over it—he pleads at least for "an

Order of *itinerant* preachers," who, though having wives, to their occasional and scattered audiences, removed from all knowledge of their personal foibles and domestic *désagréments*, may be as though they had none. And here no doubt he has abundant Nonconformist precedent, Wesleyan and other, on his side. A distinguished Canon and Professor, whose leanings are decidedly Protestant, was once heard to say that the first time he mounted the pulpit, after his marriage, he could not help feeling that half his authority had gone from him. Apart from criticism of graver deficiencies, the faults of style most commonly charged on modern preachers may be summed up under the two heads of priggishness and over familiarity. The former temper was exemplified by the lady who was taken by a friend to hear a famous Jesuit preacher, and came away much shocked, complaining that "she could hardly help laughing in church." Her friend's reply shocked her still more : "Well, my dear, why didn't you ? that is just what he meant you to do." The same confusion of thought between reverence and priggishness was differently illustrated by the preacher, at the time of the Irish famine, who spoke of the potato— a word offensive to pious ears—as " that esculent succulent, the loss of which has deprived so many hungry sinners of their daily sustenance," and by another who called it " that root on which so many thousands depended for support, and which in the inscrutable wisdom of Divine Providence has for a time ceased to flourish." But an opposite fault, apart from doctrinal questions, may fairly be charged on the Calvinistic minister, mentioned in *Macmillan*, who never preached without referring to " the back settlements of eternity," wherein the predestination of the elect had been irrevocably fixed before the foundation of the world. It must be remembered, however, that the critical faculty, when employed upon sermons, is peculiarly liable to be distorted or obscured by personal or party bias, as when the Evangelical spinster, who had listened in rapt attention to what she fondly imagined to be a most edifying discourse, exclaimed in anguish, as the preacher turned to the altar at its close, "Alas! I thought he had the gift of the Spirit, but he has only the gift of the gab." Originality of thought and genuine power of speech are of course essential ingredients of all true eloquence. But we cannot expect every preacher to be eloquent; and after all, the main distinction between a good preacher and a bad one, is the difference between the man who has to say something and the man who has something to say.

XXXI.

HUGO GROTIUS.

THE observance last year at Delft of the tercentenary of Hugo Grotius—to give him the name by which he is known to the world—or, as he was called by his own countrymen, Huig van Groot, serves at once to remind us of a great memory and of the truth that prophets are so little apt to be honoured in their own country, during life, that it is usually left for the children to build the sepulchres of those whom their fathers have destroyed. Grotius was not indeed slain, but he was sentenced to perpetual imprisonment by his native Government, and only escaped the full endurance of the penalty through the courage and ingenuity of his wife. And three centuries had been suffered to elapse before the commemorative ceremony at Delft, when the Prince of Orange attended to lay a wreath on his grave, and a subscription was organized for erecting a monument to him, marked the first tardy instalment of respect or reparation paid by Holland to her greatest jurist, if not her greatest citizen. However, if he has suffered the usual fate of a great prophet at home, he has enjoyed from his own day to ours an European celebrity. In spite of the marvellous criticism hazarded by De Quincey, whose pen was too apt to run away with him, on the principal work of Grotius, as a medley of " empty truisms and

time-serving Dutch falsehoods" combined in equal quanti-
ties, the general verdict of posterity was pretty fairly
summed up in a remark of the *Times*, that the author of
De Jure Belli et Pacis had done more than any writer
except Adam Smith to establish the working principles of
modern society.   His *Mare Liberum* may even be said to
contain in germ at least the doctrine of Free Trade.   Like
many other great men, Grotius was a prodigy of precocious
genius, though infant prodigies by no means always verify
the promise of their youth.   At eight years old he composed good Latin verses ; at twelve he entered on his
University course at Leyden, where he came under the
guidance of Scaliger ; at fifteen he published an edition of
Martianus Capella ; at seventeen he edited the remains of
Aratus, and took his degree of doctor of law, and began
practice as an advocate.   He had meanwhile published
three Latin dramas on Scriptural themes, one of which,
Adamus Exul, is said to have supplied hints to the author
of *Paradise Lost.*   At the age of twenty he was appointed
historiographer to the United Provinces, and a year later
he composed a treatise *De Jure Prædæ*, which was never
published till 1868, but which in fact contains the ground
plan of his best-known work, the treatise *De Jure Belli
et Pacis*, published twenty years later, in 1626.   The *Mare
Liberum*, printed without his sanction in 1609, and answered
by Selden in his *Mare Clausum*, formed a chapter of the
unpublished treatise *De Jure Prædæ.*   In 1613, at the early
age of thirty, Grotius succeeded Elias Oldenbarnevelt as
Pensionary of the city of Rotterdam—an office he was not
long allowed to retain—and the same year he came to
England with a deputation sent from Holland to adjust

the rising differences between the two maritime States, and was received with distinguished courtesy by James I., as afterwards at the Court of Louis XIII. But his visit to England also influenced him in another direction, and of this a word may now be said.

We have seen already that, in spite of his eminence as a jurist, Grotius was a man of very varied interests and acquirements, and was far from restricting himself to the study of the law. History, theology, politics, classics, even poetry, found a place, as well as jurisprudence, in his studies and his writings. And his chief interest, which led in fact to the great misfortune of his life, and may be said indirectly to have shaped his subsequent career, was theology. He had previously indeed given evidence of this, but his visit to England helped both to confirm and define it. He cultivated while in this country the society of leading ecclesiastics of the nascent High Church school, like Overall and Andrewes, and became intimate with Isaac Casaubon, who warmly commends the piety, probity, and profound learning of this "wonderful man," and "the rare excellence of his divine genius." The principles then implanted or fostered in his mind by the influence of the Caroline school of divines adhered to him through life. On his return to Holland he found the strife raging hotly between the Arminians and the Gomarists, or Anti-Remonstrants, as they were then designated (the Supralapsarian Calvinists), and took part very decidedly with the former. But Prince Maurice of Nassau dreaded the influence of Oldenbarnevelt, the Grand Pensionary, who was an Arminian, and determined therefore to support the so-called "orthodox," or extreme Calvinist party; in 1617

Oldenbarnevelt was condemned to death, and Grotius to
confiscation of goods and imprisonment for life. He was
accordingly, on June 6, 1619, shut up in the fortress of
Loevestein, and there he remained for nearly two years,
during which period he wrote his famous treatise *De
Veritate Religionis Christianæ.* His wife was allowed to
share his imprisonment, and in April 1621 she contrived
his deliverance by placing him in a chest, supposed only
to contain books and dirty linen. The soldiers employed
to carry it complained of the weight, and observed that
"there must be an Arminian inside." His wife replied
that there were Arminian books in it. He made his escape
to Paris, where Louis XIII. received him graciously, and
promised him an annual pension of 3000 livres, which, like
other French pensions of that day, was never paid, and he
was reduced to great poverty. At this time he composed
the work on which his reputation chiefly rests, *De Jure
Belli et Pacis,* based, however, in large measure, as has been
before observed, on his earlier unpublished treatise *De Jure
Prædæ.* He was prompted to write it by the same sort of
feeling which inspired another important work of a religious
nature to be noticed presently, his love of peace. It dis-
tressed him to witness the spectacle presented throughout
Christendom of "war waged with a licence even barbarous
nations might be ashamed of, for trivial reasons or for no
reason at all"; he was writing amid all the horrors of the
Thirty Years' War. The title of the work, which has been
translated into every European language, gives a very
inadequate conception of its real scope. It is in truth a
treatise on moral, social, and international law, and may be
said to exhibit the first serious attempt to establish on

independent grounds a principle of right and basis for society and government. Hallam has drawn out a careful abstract of it, and Mackintosh pronounced it to be "perhaps the most complete that the world has yet owed, at so early a stage in the progress of any science, to the genius and learning of one man." That the superadded knowledge and experience of two centuries and a half show his theory to be in some respects defective, is no disparagement to the high merits of the work.

Nor were his theological writings less remarkable in their way. The earliest and perhaps best known of them, the treatise, already mentioned, *De Veritate Religionis Christianæ*, became a classical manual of Christian Apologetics, and was translated not only into most European, but several Oriental languages. Another considerable work was his Commentary on Holy Scripture. But he is more likely to be remembered for two theological treatises on what were then burning questions of the day. One is the *Defence of the Catholic Faith on the Satisfaction of Christ*, written in vindication of the doctrine of the Atonement against Socinianism, which, however, advocates a modification of the Lutheran rather than the Catholic view of the subject. The *Via et Votum ad Pacem Ecclesiasticam*, published only three years before his death, may be said to have given the first powerful impetus from the Protestant side to the Reunion movement of the seventeenth century, taken up so warmly on the same side by Calixtus among his contemporaries, and afterwards by Molanus' and Leibnitz, and which met with a cordial response later in the same century from men like Royas de Spinola, Cardinal and Bishop of Neustadt, who acted with the full sanction and encouragement of Pope Innocent XI., and latterly by Bossuet. Mr. Mark Pattison, who compares Grotius to Erasmus, in the *Encyclopædia Britannica*, says that both of them, though for very different reasons, felt the same "indifference to dogma," which Erasmus put aside with the superior contempt of a scholar for monkish wrangles, while Grotius wished to get rid of it as an impediment to religious unity and concord ; and Hallam evidently inclines to the same view. That, however, is hardly an accurate way of stating the case. Grotius betrays in his treatise on the Atonement a very keen eye—one might say the keen insight of a jurist—for theological subtleties. But he had an overpowering conviction of the supreme importance of unity and authority, and was willing to go a long way to meet the Catholic party in order to secure these great religious sanctions. On the necessity, for instance, of a centre of unity he spoke very decidedly, and hence he was ready to concede to the Papacy quite as much as the Gallican school of that day would have cared to claim ; he defended many Tridentine doctrines in detail, and thought the schism of the Reformation had done more harm than good. It is quite intelligible that an Amsterdam preacher should have denounced him as "*papizans*," and that reports of his conversion to Rome should have been rife in many quarters. Hallam, who thinks he had "a bias towards Popery," expresses his conviction that, had Grotius lived a little longer, he certainly "would have taken the easy leap that still remained "; and he is probably right. It may be true, as Mr. Pattison insists, that he looked at the matter rather from the standpoint of a statesman than of a divine, from his intense appreciation of the need of ecclesiastical

organization and unity, but he had also a very deep sentiment of piety, and his religious leanings—vivified perhaps
by the Calvinist intolerance to which he had himself been
subjected—pointed in a Catholic rather than a Protestant
direction.   He avowedly much preferred the Anglican
Church to continental Protestantism.

His historical works, among which the chief place must
be assigned to the *Annals of the Low Countries* published
after his death, are of less permanent interest than his
theological and juridical treatises.   But the many-sidedness
of his mind, his vast erudition, his wide range both of
thought and sympathy, and his curious anticipation in
many respects of principles repudiated or ignored at the
time, but which have since then passed into general acceptance, constitute his characteristic excellence, and his claim
to rank among the foremost pioneers of human progress.
The bent of his genius was speculative rather than practical, and in diplomatic life he attained to no great success.
His mission was to lay down principles, which it was left
to others to develop and apply.   Like Erasmus he was a
born man of letters, but unlike Erasmus he felt a keen and
absorbing interest in the moral and religious welfare of
mankind.   His great political treatise was prompted by
a genuine desire to promote the good government and
harmony of Christian nations, and to abate the horrors of
war.   His great ecclesiastical treatise was designed, not to
minimise the importance of Christian dogma, but to enforce
the paramount obligations of Christian unity, and exhibit
what appeared to him the grave religious evils and dangers
of a state of schism.   Whatever abstract preference he
might entertain for particular Protestant doctrines, he not

only did not love but intensely loathed "the dissidence of Dissent and the Protestantism of the Protestant religion." Such a man was scarcely intelligible to the Protestants of his own day in France and Holland, with whom he remained in outward communion, while his nominal Protestantism was a scandal and perplexity to contemporary Catholics. The man who most thoroughly appreciated—one might indeed say shared—his religious position was Casaubon. "Their aim," as Mr. Pattison says, "was the same, the reunion of Christendom." Döllinger observes that he "insisted far more strongly than Calixtus on the profound and extreme divergence of Protestantism from the Church of the early centuries, and the necessity of either seeking reunion with the ancient Church, or at least restoring much which had been rejected." But whatever might have occurred, as Hallam not unreasonably conjectures, if his life had been prolonged, he did not in fact see his way to a change of communion when it was urged on him by his Gallican friends during his residence in France. His health had never been robust, and the end came rather suddenly at last, after a brief visit to the Court of Queen Christina of Sweden, where he was cordially welcomed, but did not find himself at home. He died in 1645 at the age of sixty-two. It is truly remarkable that, in a life of less than average length and more than average trouble and vicissitude, he should have accomplished so much as he did. In an age of multiplied discoveries and feverish competition such many-sidedness as his becomes almost or altogether impossible. But it would be difficult to name another in his own or perhaps in any age who has earned a high and permanent, if not equal, celebrity, at once as a scholar, a jurist, an historian, and a divine.

XXXII

'SWEDENBORG AND SWEDENBORGIANISM.

THERE are not probably a very large number of people in England who either know or care much about that most mystical and eccentric of theologians and heresiarchs, Emanuel Swedenborg, nor has the sect he founded ever had any large following in this country. It appears, however, to be entering on a phase of special activity in the United States, where a recent writer in the *North American Review* informs us that strenuous efforts are being made by disciples of the Swedish reformer to spread his opinions. And he adds with regret that "they naturally lay chief stress on his religious opinions," whereas it would be much better to approach him "from the scientific side," where "his base is secure." Possibly, but religionists are apt to lay the chief stress on the religious opinions of their founder. There is, however, an enlightened minority of American Sweden-borgians, 94 in number, "receivers of the heavenly doctrines in this country," who three years ago presented a memorial to the "General Convention"—which is apparently the ruling authority in their communion—asking in courteous terms, and with citations from Swedenborg's writings, that "the attitude of the organized New Church may no longer continue to be one of seeming antagonism or conscious

U

superiority to other religious bodies, but rather one of modest self-appreciation, and kindly, fraternal recognition of other Christians." This looks rather like asking their Church, which holds doctrines widely different from those of most "other Christians," to efface itself. One can hardly wonder that, after being unfavourably noticed by the *New Jerusalem Magazine*, the memorial was quietly dismissed, nor is it easy to dispute the inference that "the controlling powers in the New Church cling to the exclusive system, perhaps fearing lest a removal of barriers might cause their alleged peculiarity to disappear." Still less can it be reasonably denied that the controlling powers are wise in their generation ; we all know how much the growing disuse even of a distinctive dress has tended to weaken the force of Quakerism as a religious sect. The reviewer's belief is that "Swedenborgianism, as a form of religious institution, has outlived its excuse for being," which is likely enough, but he can hardly expect that view to be shared by the authorities of the Swedenborgian Church. What does appear strange, not to say paradoxical, in his contention is, not the belief that Swedenborgianism—like Fourierism, the Individualism of Emerson, and other forms of thought which were closely associated with it in America forty years ago —has outlived whatever *raison d'être* it may once have had, but the bold suggestion that Swedenborg's followers have all along mistaken the true meaning of their master's teaching, when they turned a great philosopher into a seer and the founder of a sect. "The claim to 'angelic' authentication"—which Swedenborg certainly made—" is really a drag on the doctrine ;" and the writer proceeds to sum up the doctrine in a series of "truths" or "divine commonplaces," some of which are commonplace enough, while others, if true, are so far from being either indisputable or undisputed that they are repudiated by the immense majority of Christians of every communion.   And he thinks that Swedenborg was led to adopt them from observing the utterly corrupt state of all existing Christian organizations, in support of which he quotes from one of the prophet's works a long story of what "the bishop, looking at me, said," which is both so silly and so profane that one cannot help suspecting the episcopal interlocutor looked at Swedenborg in vision, and not in the flesh.   Be that as it may, it is rather perplexing to be told that the doctrines of Swedenborg have in our own age become religious truisms, which form the burden of popular preaching and are enunciated from all more or less liberal pulpits.

It may be worth while, in view of this marvellous assertion, briefly to recall what the principal doctrines of his religious system really are.   Emanuel Swedenborg, the son of a Swedish Lutheran bishop, was born at Stockholm in 1688, and began, according to his own account, to receive spiritual manifestations about 1745.   His theological inspirations undoubtedly originated in a violent recoil from the current Protestant doctrine of justification, which he regarded—not without good reason—as subversive of morality; but in rejecting Lutheran doctrine he rejected with it the great body of the traditional belief of the Church.   His teaching on the Trinity is not easily distinguishable from Sabellianism, and in order to cut up by the roots the Lutheran scheme of justification, he denied original sin altogether.   The reviewer says that

U 2

he "abolished the devil," but that is not by any means equally clear ; his whole teaching on the future life, and on future states of reward and punishment, is clothed in obscure and mystical language, though it includes very precise statements about the condition in the next world of the leading Reformers—Luther, Calvin, and others— who were doomed to expiate hereafter the immoral theories of justification by faith only which they had inculcated here. One part of Swedenborg's system, to which he attached a high importance, and which had indeed long before been a favourite idea with both Jewish commentators and early Christian Fathers, though their application of it differed of course widely from his own, was "the doctrine of correspondencies." It meant that over and above the literal and direct sense of Scripture, which can be ascertained by the ordinary methods of exegesis, there is an occult and spiritual sense only to be discerned by the eye of faith. And thus, while the historian is apparently relating a very simple narrative of facts, it may be the primary object, if not of the writer, at any rate of the writing, composed under Divine guidance, to convey some deep Christian mystery. All patristic students know what extensive use Origen among others has made of this allegorical method of interpretation. It is one which naturally commends itself to men of a devout and somewhat visionary habit of mind, and Sweden- borg, strange as were his views, and in spite of a keen intellectual penetration, was an enthusiast, if there ever was one, and a devout enthusiast. "Piety," he observed himself, and he was no doubt describing his practice, as well as his theory, "consists in thinking and speaking piously, spending much time in prayer, behaving humbly at that time, frequenting churches, and attending devoutly to the preaching there, often receiving the Sacrament of the Supper every year, and performing the other parts of worship according to Church ordinances." Into his interpretation of particular passages of Scripture, and other details of his doctrinal system, there is no need to enter here. Enough has been said already to show that it is a very peculiar one, and certainly does not consist so exclusively of "the cardinal doctrine of love to the Lord and charity to the neighbour," as to deprive Swedenborgians of any plausible pretext for continuing to maintain a separate religious organization of their own, as is contended by the reviewer; who, it must be added, is certainly well qualified in one respect to be the exponent of Swedenborg, if obscurity of style be a qualification for interpreting a writer who is himself obscure. It must be allowed that Swedenborg was a far more vigorous and hardly more heterodox thinker than an earlier (German) " theosophist," whose " incoherencies of madness " are noted by Hallam, and who is best known in England from the circumstance that unhappily the wild mysticism of "the blessed Böhmen"—which he learnt in his later years virtually to prefer to the teaching of either Scripture or the Church—served to cloud the keen and masculine intellect of no less eminent a divine than William Law, author of the *Serious Call,* and to convert his once robust theology into a strange farrago of maundering imbecilities.

The reviewer seems to consider the real essence of Swedenborgian doctrine to correspond pretty much with the so-called rationalistic or very " Broad Church " teaching

of the present day, and thus "the age has overtaken
Swedenborg, who anticipated its drift, interpreted its secret,
and was for a few years in advance of its course." It
follows that, "as all churches are fast becoming liberal,"
the New Jerusalem Church, as a separate society, is
doomed to inevitable extinction. He further appears to
consider that Swedenborg was really much more of a
philosopher than a theologian —"a scientific prodigy, a
combination of Euclid, Copernicus, Laplace, Vesalius,
Galen, Boerhaave, Harvey, Oken, Göthe, and whomsoever
(*sic*) else may have been distinguished among explorers,
discoverers, inventors"—and that the false position into
which the perverse reverence of his religious disciples
intruded him has prevented his scientific eminence being
as yet adequately recognised. It is impossible to agree
with this estimate on either point. Swedenborg was confessedly a man of considerable scientific attainments, but
his chief claim to posthumous celebrity, *valeat quantum*,
will always be based on the peculiar form of religious
enthusiasm which he exemplified and in a measure com-
municated to his followers. Nor is it at all correct to
represent his teaching, in its idea and intention, as a mere
anticipation of modern "liberal" theology, though it is
more than doubtful whether any single article of the
Apostles' Creed except the first can survive the application
of so subtle and powerful a solvent. It is therefore
perfectly true that "Swedenborg's ideas are quite unortho-
dox"; but heterodoxy is one thing, and modern religious
liberalism—which affects a sublime indifference to all
"doxies"—is quite another. That Swedenborg's principles
logically carried out would result in an "extremely radical"

form of heterodoxy, "from which [most] religionists instinctively recoil," is unquestionably true; but a form of heterodoxy it would be after all, and not a mere negative "anti-preternaturalism," to adopt the reviewer's somewhat cumbrous phrase.   Still less can his suggestion be admitted—but here he becomes rather hopelessly obscure —that Swedenborg's ideal of a regenerated humanity points not at all to a future life, but to a perfected society on earth ; that he was, in short, endeavouring to substitute for what his critic calls preternaturalism a kind of glorified secularism.   "To contemplate this," he says, "almost takes one's breath away, for it forces one to imagine the entire power of the so-called religious world diverted from its present employment and devoted to social· ends."   A delightful prospect, no doubt, but this interpretation of the Divine revelations, in which he unfeignedly and passionately believed, would not almost but altogether have taken Swedenborg's breath away, who was much addicted, as we saw just now, to church-going, prayer, and "receiving the Sacrament of the Supper."   It may be an ingenious gloss on his teaching, but only in the same sense as Euemerus put an ingenious gloss on the old Greek myths. Even the reviewer shrinks from insisting "that Swedenborg *fully* entertained the views outlined above."   He might not, perhaps, have anathematized them, for he was not given to anathemas, but he would assuredly have consigned their teachers, had he known of them, to some such uncomfortable purgatory, or still worse position, as the Protestant Reformers, who propounded immoral theories of justification, occupied in his visionary world. The reviewer "rejoices in the existence of a Swedenborg

Publication Society," which may serve to diffuse the works of the great philosopher of the future, but " cannot rejoice in the existence of a New Jerusalem Church," which only serves to smother his philosophical light under the bushel of an effete theology. " If indeed the New Church would establish itself on this rock "—of the secularist and social schemes indicated just now—"there would be no complaint of its decadence." There would surely, however, be no adequate reason, or ground of hope, for its continuance. If secularism cannot hold its own without the help of some " Church," new or old, " preternaturalism " has no cause to be alarmed at the future aggressions of its rival ; least of all can secularism expect to gain a fresh lease of life by the hypocritical *tour de force* of thrusting itself under the incongruous patronage of the most eccentric, most devout, and most incomprehensible of modern religious enthusiasts. Meanwhile the American reviewer has simply reproduced, in a cruder form, the transparent fallacy of his French Protestant biographer some twenty years ago, M. Matter, who argued that Swedenborg was a rationalist, and therefore not a mystic ; like Böhmen, a century earlier, he was really both.

XXXIII.

STRAUSS.

THE death ten years ago of David Frederick Strauss
was a notable event in Germany and the theological world
generally, and could hardly pass unnoticed by those who
were neither Germans nor divines. To Englishmen even
who took no interest in theology, or who looked on German
speculation—as it has been somewhere expressed—as "a
vast Hercynian forest, out of which Bunsens and other
monsters occasionally emerge," his name at least was
familiar. He had long been dreaded or admired as the
chief living representative of the rationalist or sceptical
school of theology, and in this sense his latest work, *Der
Alte und der Neue Glaube*, was made the text of an address
delivered the year before his death by Mr. Gladstone at
Liverpool College, which provoked a good deal of comment at the time. Nor was such an estimate of his
position altogether an unreasonable one. Other writers
of kindred tendencies may have shown, like Baur, a more
balanced judgment and a firmer argumentative grasp of
their subject, or, like Renan, may have attracted, even in
Germany, a wider circle of readers than Strauss. But the
phrase so often applied as a mere idle conventionalism has

its full meaning here. It is perfectly true to say that the appearance of the first *Leben Jesu* in 1835, when the author was only twenty-seven years of age, "constituted an epoch" in theological literature and thought in Germany. His success as a writer was no doubt due in some measure to that transparent lucidity of style in which he contrasts so remarkably with the great majority of his countrymen, of whatever school, and which has been not inaptly compared to Döllinger's. But in the rival champions of faith and unbelief that very clearness of language is partly, if not mainly, due to the clearness of thought which distinguishes both of them from too many of their contemporaries; they know exactly what they mean, and therefore know how to say it. A similar remark might be applied to the late J. S. Mill, whose conclusions in religious matters did not perhaps materially differ from those of Strauss, though they were arrived at by a very different process. Before, however, we can adequately appreciate Strauss's place in the history of modern thought, it will be necessary to glance at the antecedent and contemporary state of theological speculation in Europe, and especially in his own country.

Meanwhile the main incidents of his uneventful life may be dismissed in a few words. Born in 1808 at Ludwigsburg, and educated for the Protestant ministry, he is described by Quinet as "a young man full of candour, sweetness, and modesty, of a spirit almost mystical, and saddened, as it were, by the disturbances which had been caused." After completing his university studies, he went in 1831 to Berlin to hear Schleiermacher lecture on the Life of Christ, and returned to Tübingen, where he had already become acquainted with Baur, as a *privatdocent* in the

Protestant Faculty of Theology. The appearance of the *Leben Jesu* led to his dismissal in 1835; but four years afterwards a theological chair was offered him by the Government at Zurich, from which he was driven by an armed insurrection of the orthodox Protestant party, and thenceforth he devoted himself to a literary career, hardly interrupted by his election in 1848 to a seat in the Diet of Würtemberg, which the unpopularity of his strong political · Conservatism led him soon afterwards to resign. It may be observed in passing, that this union of the most revolutionary theories in philosophy and theology with a rigid bureaucratic Toryism—reminding one in some ways of the ἀταραξία theory of the Stoics—is a very common phenomenon among advanced thinkers in Germany; it was disagreeably exemplified in the political pusillanimity and toadyism of Göthe. The *Leben Jesu* was followed in 1840 by a work on Christian Doctrine in relation to Modern Science, in which the pantheistic views which the author had learnt from Hegel are more fully developed. In 1847 appeared *Julian the Apostate*, and in 1858 a Life of Ulrich von Hutten, the well-known author of *Epistolæ Obscurorum Virorum*, which was republished in a somewhat altered form in 1871, both editions having avowedly something more than a purely literary or historical purpose, the first being directed against the Austrian Concordat, the second against the influence of " priestly obscurantists " in the restored German Empire. An English translation by Mrs. Sturge appeared shortly after the author's death, in 1874. These are minor works, but the second *Leben Jesu für das deutsche Volk bearbeitet*, published in 1864, and the *Der Alte und der Neue Glaube*, in

1872, complete the theological trilogy, so to call it, by which Strauss will be permanently remembered.

It is so much the fashion to regard Germany as the fountain-head of modern Rationalism that many persons may be surprised to learn, what is undoubtedly the fact, and is expressly acknowledged by Strauss in his latest work—that the sceptical movement really took its rise in England, and passed thence into France, and from England and France into Germany. "To England's share fell the first assault and the forging of the weapons, the work of the Freethinkers or Deists; Frenchmen brought these weapons across the Channel, and wielded them briskly and adroitly in constant light skirmishing; while in Germany one man chiefly undertook the regular invest-ment of the Zion of orthodoxy. Voltaire on one side, Reimarus on the other, typified the character of their respective nations." The English Deistic school, of which Lord Herbert of Cherbury and Hobbes may be called the founders, and which culminated in the teaching of Tindal and Chubb,—whose keynote may be said to be "Chris-tianity as old as the Creation,"—was coloured in its later development by the reflex influence of the French sceptical writers, who had received their first inspirations from this country; it became less serious and more aggressive, and the sneering tone of Voltaire and Diderot is reproduced in Gibbon and Tom Paine. Far different, as a rule, is the temper of German rationalism. But in the first half of the eighteenth century the philosophical speculations of Wolff combined with the introduction of English Deism, through translations of Tindal and other writers, and the influence of French infidel refugees at the

court of Frederick II.—himself disguising under the outward profession of Protestantism his cynical disbelief
both in morality and its Divine Author—to stir the slug-
gish waters of traditional Lutheran orthodoxy. Between
that time and 1835 we may trace first a destructive and
then a reconstructive period in German Protestant theology.
The destructive criticism was begun by Semler, a Professor
at Halle, who meant, however, to be an apologist, but
remodelled the Canon of Scripture on *a priori* grounds,
and first introduced the distinction, of which Baur and
others have so largely availed themselves since, between
St. Peter and St. Paul as leaders of two opposite parties in
the infant Church. Lessing, of whom Strauss is reported
to have left an unfinished biography, though perhaps
himself rather a doubter than a Deist, gave a powerful
impulse to the same movement by the publication of the
Wolffenbüttel Fragments of Reimarus. The rationalistic
criticism of Semler was continued by Eichorn and Paulus,
who eliminated the supernatural element from Scripture
altogether, while maintaining its historical accuracy. The
miraculous portions of the narrative were not so much
denied as explained away. Thus, *e.g.*, the healing of the
sick was effected by natural means or by a kind of
magnetic influence on their minds, the multiplication of
the loaves by a secret supply, walking on the water meant
walking on the bank beside it, and the Resurrection itself
was only a way of recording the fact that the Saviour had
never really died on the Cross. The critical and moral
difficulties of this method of interpretation have been by
no one more mercilessly exposed than by Strauss himself ;
but it was popular for a time, and was applied to Christian

doctrine by writers like Bretschneider, Röhr, and Weg-
scheider.   The philosophical teaching of Fichte, Schelling,
and Hegel tended of course in the same direction, though
they came into less immediate contact with the theological
controversies of the day.   It was only natural that a
reactionary movement should be provoked, and it was
equally natural in a country of mixed religions like
Germany that it should assume a double form.   On the
one hand, there commenced with the present century a
Catholic reaction, of which Count Stolberg, Frederick and
Augustus Schlegel, Tieck, and Novalis are leading representatives, though only the first two actually joined the
Roman Catholic Church.   On the other hand, Schleiermacher, who was, as we have seen, one of Strauss's earliest
teachers, attempted in his *Glaubenslehre* to find a basis for
orthodox belief, or rather orthodox sentiment, by founding
it on the collective Christian consciousness, emulating to a
certain extent the "pietism" of Spener a century before;
but in fact, as Strauss has pointed out, he gave up the
genuineness of the Gospels, the divinity of Christ, and the
reality of prayer, which for him had a purely subjective
value.   His treatment of the New Testament miracles
differs in form rather than in substance from that of
Paulus.   Religion became in his hands a matter of devout
emotion, independent of history and dogma, and he
created a spirit rather than founded a school.   De Wette
and Ewald, and still more of course Neander—whose *Life
of Christ* was expressly designed as an answer to Strauss—
returned more nearly to the Evangelical standard of orthodoxy; while the advanced Lutheran school, represented by
Hengstenberg, Hävernick, and Stahl—which was partly a .

reaction from the enforced fusion of the Lutheran and Calvinist Churches by Frederick William III. of Prussia, in 1817—may even be said to have some analogy to the Tractarian movement in England. Thus we are brought to the appearance in 1835 of the first *Leben Jesu*, which was a protest, addressed, as the author was careful to explain, not to the general public but to scholars, at once against the rationalism of Paulus and the mysticism of Schleiermacher; not, however, a protest in the interests of orthodoxy. In 1846, when the work had reached its fourth edition in Germany, an English translation appeared from the pen of the writer, then unknown, who afterwards became famous under the *sobriquet* of George Eliot.

The *Leben Jesu* may be divided into three parts, the first giving an introductory sketch of previous systems of Biblical criticism and the formation of the mythical theory, the second examining the Gospel narrative in detail, the third and concluding portion discussing its doctrinal significance. Towards the end, in a section on the " Christology of the Orthodox system," which is shown to have its roots in the New Testament, the author describes in a strain of almost rapturous eloquence the idea of Christ, " so full of blessing and elevation, encouragement and comfort," which prevailed in the early Church. There were abundant materials, he adds, in the New Testament for constructing the rule of faith eventually formulated in the so-called Apostles' Creed ; and the condemnation, as they arose, of the successive heresies, from the Ebionite to the Monothelite, which contradicted that faith, was fully justified.[1]

---

[1] A fuller analysis of this section, comparing it with the preface of the second *Leben Jesu*, is given in Excursus VI. of my *Catholic Doctrine of the Atonement.*

Nearly thirty years elapsed before the author published in 1864 his second *Leben Jesu*, addressed this time not to a learned but to a popular audience, as he rather oddly phrases it, "as Paul turned to the Gentiles, when the Jews rejected his Gospel." But the two works differ in form, not in principle, and the preface to the latter contains a distinct affirmation of their essential identity. The "Christology of the Church" is still represented as the product of several "groups of myths," of which twelve are enumerated ; but the word must not be understood in the sense which Comparative Mythology, as treated by Professor Max Müller and Sir G. W. Cox, has attached to it. The Gospel myths are not a poetical presentation of sunrise and sunset or other natural phenomena, but have grown up round a nucleus of historic fact. The personal existence of Christ, which was left uncertain in the earlier work, is now expressly affirmed—and here we trace the influence of the Tübingen school, which practically means of Baur, on the mind of Strauss ; but he insists that there are few great men of whom so little is known, and that the religion which bears His name was created by St. Paul rather than by Himself. "Little of His real history can now be certainly ascertained ; what is certain is, that the supernatural acts and events on which the faith of the Church has chiefly fastened never occurred at all." It is true, however, that the Divine wisdom was remarkably (*in ausgezeichneter Weise*) manifested in Christ, but His example can only be regarded as a partial and onesided one, for, as it is elsewhere stated with much force against Keim —perhaps also with a view to Schleiermacher—so long as He is regarded as a mere man, He cannot be said to represent the perfect ideal of humanity. The same argument has been urged in this country, by writers like Professor F. Newman on one side, and Dr. Liddon on the other, against the Unitarian compromise. These views about the life and character of our Lord are repeated and dwelt upon in Strauss's last work. The distinction between the old orthodox Christianity — which is again declared to have been the belief, and the natural belief, of the early Church—and the religion of the future is drawn out at length in the preface to the second *Leben Jesu*, and resolves itself into the substitution of a purely rationalistic and intellectual system for a faith resting on a professed revelation. And therefore the Church, whether Catholic or Protestant, must be superseded, for a supernatural religion with sacraments and means of grace necessarily implies a sacerdotal hierarchy, and the first step towards getting rid of the priesthood is to eliminate the supernatural element from religion. The author, while differing in important points, as well as in general tone, from the *Vie de Jésus*, which had an enormous circulation in Germany through translations, hails Renan as a fellow-labourer in the same cause. His book opens with a long dedication to the memory of his brother, who died within a few months of its publication, and who is congratulated on his manly endurance of a long and painful illness without the fictitious aids of a supernatural belief.

If there is little difference of view between the earlier and later versions of the *Leben Jesu*, the closing work of the series, which followed after an interval of eight years, does but sum up and expand, in what is meant for a sort of literary testament, the conclusions previously worked out.

X

It is mainly an answer to two questions, "Are we still Christians?" and "Have we still a Religion?" And it is characteristic of the straightforward honesty and clearness of thought, which those who differ from him most widely cannot fail to respect, that the author replies to his first question with an emphatic negative. There are those who talk of a Christianity purged of all Christian dogma, a Christianity, in short, which is sufficiently enlightened to dispense with Christ. But Strauss says in effect, what an admirer of his system has lately repeated in this country, "To proclaim an undogmatic Christianity, is to proclaim that Christianity is dead." As he himself puts it, "Christianity is a definite form of religion; it is possible to relinquish it and still to be religious, but not still to be Christians." And accordingly, speaking for himself and those who agree with him, "If we would speak as honest upright men, we must acknowledge that we are no longer Christians." He will have nothing to do with the ingenious devices of a subtle rationalism or a vague and inconsequent pietism, by which so many of his predecessors and contemporaries have sought to deceive both their followers and themselves, but says plainly that Christian theology must be replaced by "the modern kosmic conception educed painfully from scientific and historical research." There is a quiet humour in the passage where he draws out in detail the supposed teaching of a Protestant pastor, who has found himself obliged to explode one by one each successive article of the Apostles' Creed, the first not excepted. For it is in fact a "mere Hebrew prejudice" to suppose that monotheism is necessarily superior to polytheism; both were but temporary stages in the gradual advance to a higher truth. The ideas of a personal God and a future life are now shown to be untenable, but we need not therefore acquiesce in the pessimism of Schopenhauer, which is "blasphemous, arrogant, and profane," or admit that we have no religion. On the contrary, "we claim the same piety for our Kosmos which the devout of old claimed for his God." But of course the notion of religion acquires, on this hypothesis, a wholly new meaning. It will no longer produce or justify a worship, though it will not fail, the author thinks, to exert a moral influence—an assumption which, except in the case of very peculiarly constituted natures, may well be questioned. It is to consist in dependence on the Kosmos, in other words, on the laws of the material universe ; and that, we are bidden to believe, is a far truer and nobler conception than the "low anthropopathism" of dependence on God.

This is not the place to enter into a detailed examination of the merits, religious or historical, of Strauss's theological system, if a system which ends in pure materialism is to be called by such a name. The praise of a fearless and consistent thinker, and a luminous expositor of the views he had deliberately adopted and held unflinchingly to the last, he may fairly claim. There is no reason to doubt the sincerity of his almost dying assertion, made, as he assures us, under a solemn sense of the duty of giving an account of his stewardship, that he fought through life for that which appeared to him as truth, and against what appeared to him as untruth, while he disclaims all desire to shake the faith of those who have not already lost it. Strauss's originality of genius, one cannot but think, has sometimes been overrated. Apart from his negative criticism there is very little really new in the theories he advocates. He began and ended as a disciple of Hegel, though Hegelianism has no doubt been very variously interpreted ; and it is not necessary here to inquire whether his interpretation of his master is the most correct, as it is certainly a very common one. His intellect was clear and critical rather than creative, and in historical grasp he was certainly inferior to Baur, to whom indeed he owed a good deal. But he has left his mark, whether for good or evil, on German theology ; and for one important service at least all serious believers are indebted to him, however little they may sympathize with his barren and unhopeful creed. He has unmasked a host of shams, if he has put nothing better in their place, and has made the elaborate, however unconscious, subterfuges of such teachers as Semler, Schleiermacher, and Paulus for ever impossible in the future. In him, whatever be his faults, the advocates of revelation need fear no treacherous ally ; he meets them with the downright challenge of an able, an honest, and an open foe. He does not, like some writers whose names are familiar to us, insult the faith it was his misfortune to abandon by professing Christianity, while he repudiates the teaching and the mission of Christ.

XXXIV

JOHN BERNARD DALGAIRNS.

THE announcement in April 1876 of the death of "the Rev. John Bernard Dalgairns, priest of the London Oratory," could not fail, over and above its necessary interest for his own co-religionists, to recall to others also who remember the Oxford of some forty years ago many cherished recollections and associations of the past. Mr. Dalgairns took his degree in 1839, when his name appears in the same class-list with Professor Jowett, Bishop Fraser of Manchester, Dr. Kay, and Dr. Anderdon, a nephew of Cardinal Manning's, who has since become a Jesuit; and he was one of the first batch of Tractarian converts who followed their great leader in 1845 across the Rubicon. Oxford has passed since then through at least three stages of religious transition. When the advance of the Tractarian revival was arrested for the time by the loss of its chief author and apologist, there set in a period of theological stagnation, which may be said to have lasted till about 1851. The backwater of this great movement, which Dr. Whately had characteristically christened "Newmania," was still felt, but its first force was spent, and in the turn of the tide "the Oxford of the *Lyra Apostolica*," as it has been observed with considerable truth, "was slowly giving way to the Oxford whose spirit is best reflected by the poems of Clough and Matthew Arnold." Some exception might perhaps be taken to the coupling of two such incongruous names, though both represent a spirit the reverse of Tractarian; but the statement of fact is substantially accurate. With the second half of the century there began at Oxford what may be considered a reaction against the movement of 1833, which culminated in 1860 with the publication of *Essays and Reviews*, emanating from seven writers—gibbeted at the time by an Oxford tutor, who has since become a bishop, as the *Septem contra Christum*—of whom five either had been or still were residents and office-bearers in the University. One conspicuous effect of the change, however little intended by those who were instrumental in introducing it, was a sensible diminution in the supply of Oxford graduates, and especially of classmen, for the ministry of the Anglican Church. The party for the time in the ascendant, though far from deficient in men of high ability, can hardly be said to have had a leader in the sense in which Mr. Newman had been the leader of that which it had superseded. Mr. Jowett was for the time its hero, on account of the long quarrel about the endowment of the Greek professorship; but neither he nor Dr. Stanley, who then held the chair of Ecclesiastical History at Oxford, and whose social capabilities added much to his influence, was exactly fitted to wear the mantle while the author of Tract XC. had dropped. On the Broad Church reaction supervened a revival, not exactly of Tractarianism—for the Tracts had become things of the past—while the clumsy *sobriquet* of "Ritualism" is at all events singularly inappropriate in describing its academical phase. A High Church revival, however, there was, by whatever name it may be best designated, the force of which is by no means spent. Mr. Pattison, some years ago, in an article in *Mind*, contrasted it, not without bitterness, with the original movement of 1833, as substituting for intellect and learning the domination of an "ecclesiastical ring"; and so far, of course, he was right, that no second leader had inherited the transcendent gifts of Mr. Newman. At present the rival schools of Catholic tradition and of Rationalism are engaged hand to hand in sharp conflict at Oxford, as in the Church of England generally. But it must suffice to have thus briefly sketched the successive waves of religious thought which have passed over the life of Oxford, since Mr. Dalgairns was a member of Exeter College, and one of the most promising among the younger disciples of the Tractarian movement.

When the crash came in 1841, and Mr. Newman bowed before the storm of academical and ecclesiastical censure, he did not, as is well known, resolve at once on his final step, but retired for awhile to Littlemore, with a band of chosen friends and followers, several of whom did, while some did not, eventually accompany him in his secession. Conspicuous among these "monks," as they were sometimes rather absurdly called, were Mr. Dalgairns and Mr. Anthony Froude, both of whom took part in the Littlemore series of *Lives of the English Saints*, to which Dean Milman refers in his *Latin Christianity* as admirable for their "research and exquisite charm of style," though he complains of their unhistorical character. It is certainly not very easy at first sight to recognise the future author of

the *English History* in the biographer of St. Neot, though
Dean Milman's charge will by many critics be held equally
applicable to both works. By general consent, however,
one of the most popular of these biographies was the first,
to which Dean Milman more especially refers, the *Life of
St. Stephen Harding*, written by Mr. Dalgairns, who had
already challenged attention by his article on Ozanam's
Dante in the *British Critic*. His style, as was natural
under the circumstances, bore evident marks of Mr. Newman's influence, though he could not be said to equal that
great master of pure English ; while, on the other hand, he
had too much originality to be merely an even unconscious
copyist. In 1845 Mr. Newman finally quitted Oxford and
the Church of England, and of those who went with him
the two best known, and best deserving to be known, at
the time and since, were Faber and Dalgairns. Faber
passed away in 1863, after a long and painful illness ; and
the grave has since closed over his intimate friend and
associate for many years, who succeeded him in the headship of the London Oratory. In some respects the two
men were very unlike each other. Faber was by nature
a poet and an orator, and his impassioned delivery of
"Roll on, thou deep and dark blue Ocean, roll," in the
Harrow Speech-room, was remembered long afterwards
by his schoolfellows ; there is nothing to show that Mr.
Dalgairns ever wrote a line of poetry in his life. As a
preacher he lacked the persuasive eloquence and musical
intonation of voice which would have made Faber a
favourite anywhere, and which helped to account for
the large gathering of Protestants, as well as of his own
congregation, round the pulpit of the London Oratory,

whenever he was announced to preach; but in power of thought his sermons were hardly inferior to Faber's, while in philosophical and historical knowledge he surpassed him.

There is little of interest to record in Mr. Dalgairns's life after his conversion. He spent some years abroad in studying theology, and was ordained in France. On his return to England he again joined his old master, who was then founding the Oratory at Birmingham; and he was subsequently allied with Faber in the establishment of a branch of the same institution in London, of which he remained a member to the last, though for some years before his death failing health, induced by overwork of the brain, had unfitted him for active work. To the outer world he was chiefly known as an able and acute, though not prolific, author. Besides occasional contributions on philosophical questions to the *Contemporary Review*, the *Academy*, and other periodicals, he published two works displaying considerable historical as well as theological research, and an interesting Essay on "Tauler and the German Mystics," which originally appeared in the *Dublin Review*. His earliest Roman Catholic work, on the *Sacred Heart*, has all the charm of style which won Dean Milman's admiration in the *Life of St. Stephen Harding;* but the Introduction, on the history of Jansenism, able and interesting as it certainly is, shows rather the skill of a brilliant advocate than the judgment of a critical historian, though it does not deserve the very severe censure pronounced on it, in the preface to his *Jansenist Church of Holland,* by the late Dr. Neale, whose strong bias in favour of the Jansenists puts him also out of court as an impartial witness. Both writers require the correction of some really independent authority, such as Mr. Jervis's admirable *History of the Church of France.* The subject of Mr. Dalgairns's principal work, on the *Holy Communion,* offers less scope for religious partisanship, and it contains much of interest to students both of theology and ecclesiastical history, whether they happen to agree with all the writer's conclusions or not. His intellectual tastes seem through life to have lain chiefly in a metaphysical direction, and it is to be regretted that he had not fuller leisure and opportunity for utilising his familiarity with the general course of modern thought in this subject-matter, and especially his knowledge of the great German metaphysicians. Such acquirements are not too common even in the present day, and are essential for the discussion of many questions which, from different points of view, have a pressing claim on the attention alike of the philosopher and the Christian apologist. Among English Roman Catholics, Mr. Dalgairns, at the time, stood almost alone in these, his most characteristic aptitudes. To say this is no disparagement to Mr. Renouf, whose specialities are not exactly of the same kind; and unfortunately the absorbing duties of a School Inspector leave him little leisure for prosecuting them. It is certainly a noteworthy circumstance that, with the exception of Cardinal Wiseman, all the Roman Catholic writers in this country who have attained any celebrity during the last half-century have been converts; and— which is still more curious—this remark applies as much to theological as to general literature. The fact suggests one or two concluding reflections which can only be indicated here.

It has been observed that converts always bring to their adopted faith much more than they gain from it. The statement can at best only be received with considerable qualifications. There are converts and converts, as also there are very great differences between one religious system and another. If "the zeal of a renegade" is proverbial, it is often so entirely disproportionate to either his knowledge or discretion as to be a very questionable acquisition to the cause he has undertaken to support. On the other hand, some systems are so thoroughly rotten that no infusion of fresh blood can be of much service to them, while rival communions are not likely to gain much from the accession of any neophytes trained under them. The Eastern Church, for instance, is probably in want of a good deal of internal reform, but it could not expect much help for that purpose from a contingent of Turkish proselytes. In the particular case before us, the Tractarian converts, among whom Mr. Dalgairns held a prominent place, did unquestionably bring to their adopted Church an accession of moral and intellectual power out of all proportion to the mere increase of numerical strength. Fresh from the best culture Oxford had to bestow, and having many of them taken the fullest advantage of it, their enthusiasm, however vehement and one-sided, was backed by a solid reinforcement of learning and ability which could not fail to tell. It is actually the case that about forty years ago the English Roman Catholics had no single publisher of any standing. As it happened, two publishers of established repute were among the earliest converts, and in every form of religious literature, from the slender novelette "with a purpose," which ladies delight to write as well as read, to the grave theological treatise, convert authors supplied the wares for their customers. And very soon too, again with the solitary exception of Cardinal Wiseman, the leading Catholic preachers came to be exclusively converts, and Protestants who would never before have dreamed of entering a "Romish" place of worship—unless it were to hear what Pugin used to call "the shilling opera"—came in large numbers to listen to them. There is of course another side to the picture, which is naturally suggested by every fresh announcement of the removal of a leading author or preacher of the convert body from the scene. The immediate gain to the cause of Catholicism in England has been manifest enough ; but now for several years past there have been comparatively few accessions to its ranks of any great importance, if recruits are to be weighed as well as counted. It becomes therefore a question of some interest what will be the net result of the change which has passed over it, when the original generation of converts shall have died out. Within a week of the death of Dalgairns, news arrived from Rome of the departure of another of the early Tractarian contingent, Mr. Simpson, author of the *Life of Campion*, whose literary powers were of no mean order, while his sincere devotion to the faith he had embraced was not darkened by the slightest shade of theological bitterness, and his genial kindliness of disposition and social gifts endeared him to all who knew him. Of both men indeed it may be said that they had, as they deserved to have, many friends, and never made a personal enemy. But who will fill their place in the future ? Cardinal Newman indeed remains, and he is a host in himself. But to no cause and no communion is such a gift vouchsafed twice in the same century. To many, who still listen with eager reverence for every utterance from his lips, his own old question may perhaps even now recur with a fresh significance: "Dim Future! shall we *need* a prophet for Truth's Creed?"

XXXV

BISHOP DUPANLOUP.

THE late M. Veuillot of the *Univers* composed a highly characteristic epitaph on Bishop Dupanloup, whom he described as a questionable theologian and an equally questionable politician, emphatically denied to be "a model Bishop," and finally dismissed, in terms far more applicable to himself, as *un de ces passants remarquables qui n'arrivent pas*. The description was characteristic, because neither good taste nor discretion ever restrains Ultramontane organs of that type from throwing plenty of dirt, in the hope that some will stick, at the greatest men of their own Church, whether living or dead, who are suspected—as such men are sure to be suspected—of any taint of Liberalism. The gross insults heaped on the memory of Montalembert will not easily be forgotten. Archbishop Darboy's heroic, not to say martyr, death did not shield his great name from something more than studied obloquy and neglect. Lacordaire, like a yet greater man among ourselves, was distrusted and snubbed during life by the same "insolent and aggressive faction," who have shown little disposition since his death to remember his splendid services to Catholicism. Horrible beyond all expression—a kind of ghastly parody of "the Curse" in Southey's *Kehama*, translated into a jargon of Christian, or rather unchristian, Billingsgate—was the elaborate imprecation hurled by M. Veuillot in his *Parfum de Rome* at Passaglia, far the greatest Jesuit theologian of his day, and the compiler of the Bull *Ineffabilis*, and of a learned treatise in defence of it, when he dared to pronounce against the temporal power. Dupanloup could expect no better treatment at such hands. If he was not in all respects a man of the same calibre as those already named, he was eminent alike as a preacher, a speaker, a writer, a politician, and a prelate. To say that "he was a failure" is true of course in a sense, but only in a sense which applies with at least equal force to the leaders of the party that his critics delight to honour. He failed no doubt to realise his ideal of Church and State, and it was inevitable, in the existing condition of the world, that he should fail. It is still less conceivable that Ultramontanes of M. Veuillot's school should succeed in making their own programme a reality. But in the ordinary sense of the word, and as regards his own personal influence, Dupanloup was anything but a failure. He certainly did not become a Cardinal, though it is very likely, had he lived a year or two longer, that he might under the present pontificate have attained to that dignity; but he was not, as was once observed of a still more eminent personage, who is now in the Sacred College, "the stuff Cardinals are made of," under the sort of *régime* which then prevailed. Even then, however, his opinion on French ecclesiastical matters counted for something at Rome, little as he was loved there, because he was well known to be the most active and influential member of the national episcopate. By the present Pope he appears to have been unreservedly trusted and consulted, and His Holiness was reported, no doubt correctly, to be deeply afflicted at his death. No French Cardinal for many a long year has wielded half the influence of the late Bishop of Orleans over his countrymen. But the reasons why the *Univers* refused to recognise that fact are not far to seek.

It was the lot of Dupanloup through life to be assailed by Ultramontanes as a Liberal, and by Liberals as an Ultramontane, and both classes of assailants had something to say for themselves. Not that the Bishop was ever, at least consciously, insincere, though he was far from being always consistent. He had strong Liberal sympathies and strong Catholic sympathies, but his Liberalism always succumbed to his Catholicism when the two came into conflict, and Catholicism, for a French Bishop in the reign of Pius IX., could hardly, in extreme cases, mean anything short of Ultramontanism. A century ago, when Gallicanism was still a power, he would have been a leading Gallican. There was much about him to recall not only the eloquence but the personality of Bossuet, though of course the two are not for a moment to be compared. He had inherited, to a great extent, the dignified presence as well as the doctrinal traditions of the old Gallican episcopate. He was in heart a monarchist no less than a prelatist, and a national Church, subordinate of course to Rome, as the centre of unity, but independent in its local self-government, was the object of his aspirations, if not of his practical aims. In his sternness, his pugnacity, and something of personal hauteur—which prevented his becoming popular among his clergy—he reproduced characteristic traits of the famous Bishop of Meaux. He had in him, however, as is clear from M. Renan's *Souvenirs*, a vein of chivalry and tenderness which evoked the passionate devotion of youth. But above all things he was to the backbone a Frenchman, and a French ecclesiastic; and that may account for many of his seeming inconsistencies. If M. Thiers, who was a layman and a statesman, could say, as he is reported to have said, in reference to the Roman question, "je ne suis pas Chrétien, mais je suis papiste," it is not wonderful that Dupanloup, who was very emphatically a Christian and a Catholic, as well as a Frenchman, should have been "a Papist," as regards the temporal power and some other points too. The whole course of French history since the Revolution of '89 has tended to alienate the Church from the Government, and thereby inevitably to throw it into the arms of Rome. Yet in theological matters, so far as he dared to trust his own feelings and convictions, Dupanloup was not "a Papist"; and hence the Ultramontane antipathy to him. The *Univers* complained that "his submission to the Vatican Council was tardy." That is true, but it is not the whole truth. Before going to Rome for the Council, the Bishop published a Pastoral professedly discussing the "opportuneness" of the proposed dogma, but most of the arguments urged against the expediency of defining it turned really on the evidence for it, as his opponents were not slow to discover and indignantly to proclaim. And during the sitting of the Council the most vigorous Opposition pamphlets emanated from his pen. That was a fatal offence, which no "tardy submission," no zeal for the Church, or even for the temporal power, could condone in Ultramontane eyes. And moreover it was not what is, or used in our schoolboy days to be called, "a first fault," which might exempt the culprit from a flogging.

Y

Bishop Dupanloup had not been a good boy, in the Ultra-montane sense, before that. In one notable instance he had shown—what is by no means an invariable charac-teristic even of gifted Frenchmen, especially of French ecclesiastics—his possession of strong common sense. Some years ago it pleased the Abbé Gaume and certain other obscurantist wiseacres of his school in France to get up a crusade against the use of the Greek and Latin, or as they preferred to phrase it the "Pagan," classics in the education of youth. Dupanloup, backed by the immemorial tradition of the Church both in France and elsewhere, and relying on his own educational experience, threw the whole weight of his not inconsiderable influence into the opposite scale. The scheme of teaching the Greek and Latin languages from the writings of the Christian Fathers was certainly an original one, but it was warmly espoused at the time by the Ultramontane zealots, who even perpetrated the absurdity of drawing up a series of school books modelled on this programme, but it eventually collapsed. The scheme was of course ardently supported by M. Veuillot, whose contempt for classical learning was only equalled by his ignorance of it ; and the Bishop of Orleans, who had not unjustly taunted him with making calumny the chief weapon of religious journalism, was not readily forgiven for his powerful opposition to it. Moreover, he had forbidden his clergy to read the *Univers*.

But if Dupanloup defended—as any educated man, who is not a fanatic or a fool, would be sure to defend—the study of "the Pagan classics," it was assuredly from no tenderness for atheism or unbelief. One of the first acts for which he is remembered as a priest had been to receive the dying abjuration and confession of Talleyrand, and among his earliest achievements was a lecture against Voltaire, delivered before the students of the Sorbonne—which cost him his profes-sorship, owing to the tumult it produced—while his latest literary efforts were directed against the recent Voltaire cen-tenary. His detestation of Voltaire, as an infidel and licen-tious writer, was intensified by a kind of chivalrous devotion to the Maid of Orleans—the heroine of his episcopal city—whose canonization he exerted himself to procure, and he could not pardon the gross outrage perpetrated on her memory by the foul-mouthed author of *La Pucelle*. His in-fluence availed for many years to keep M. Littré out of the Forty of the French Academy, and when the Positivist—whose deathbed conversion was not then foreseen—had at last effected an entrance in spite of him, he shook off the dust from his feet, and himself retired from the mystic circle whose sanctity had been profaned, though his resignation of his chair was not accepted by his colleagues. But within the limits of orthodoxy his sympathies were gener-ous and comprehensive, and leaned always to the liberal side. He used every effort, through the medium of Mont-alembert, to whom he was warmly attached, to induce Dr. Döllinger to attend the Vatican Council—to which, how-ever, he had not been invited—in order to join in opposing " the base acts " he thought only too likely to be attempted there ; Dr. Newman he invited and urged to attend the Council, as his " theologian." It was natural enough then that, while the *Univers* refused him the praise of a model bishop, the *Débats*, premising that he had always been its political opponent, should offer a high tribute to " the generosity, frankness, and true nobility of his nature," and

Y 2

declare him to be "one of the glories, or rather the glory, of the French episcopate, whose place will not easily be supplied." This is perfectly true, and not the less true because his influence, like that of Bishop Wilberforce in England, was of a kind to be felt at the time rather than to be perpetuated. He was a copious as well as a brilliant writer, but more of a pamphleteer than an author; in this respect a thorough Frenchman, though not, like Renan, whom he sharply attacked, a master of French style. He wrote endless pamphlets on theological, ecclesiastical, social, educational, and political questions of the day, calculated to make a telling impression for the moment, but had not leisure or patience for the composition of what the Germans call *ewige Werke*, and here he differed widely from Bossuet. He cannot in fact be said to have made any permanent contribution to theology or literature, and it must be regarded as more than questionable whether his works will live, though his name is not likely to be forgotten. His career was a long and honourable one, and he carried with him to the grave the respect of his countrymen of all shades of opinion, with one conspicuous and not very creditable exception. Yet he can hardly be called *felix opportunitate mortis*, for while he outlived by a few months the pontiff who, devout and single-minded as he was, could not appreciate and would never have rewarded his distinguished services to the Church, his death followed too closely on that of Pius IX. to give him the opportunity of profiting by the tardy but sincere appreciation of the Holy See in the person of his successor. He has left behind him no prelate of equal or nearly equal mark on the roll of the French episcopate.

XXXVI

CANON OAKELEY.

ON January 29, 1880, another of the oldest and most distinguished of the early Tractarian converts passed away. Frederick Oakeley, formerly known as Fellow and Tutor of Balliol, and afterwards as Minister of Margaret Chapel, but for the last thirty years Missionary Rector of St. John's Roman Catholic Church, Duncan Terrace, Islington, and Canon of Westminster, died in his seventy-eighth year, leaving behind him many kindly memories, both in the Church of his birth and of his adoption, and probably no ill will anywhere. Mr. Oakeley was a man of powers decidedly above the average, and, had he been of a less retiring disposition and his conscientious convictions less decided than they were, he might fairly have expected to rise to high distinction in the Church of England. The youngest son of Sir Charles Oakeley, formerly Governor of Madras, he was born in 1802, and began, like Mozart, at four years old to give evidence of his musical taste—which lasted through life—being able at that early age to reproduce on the pianoforte simple airs which had taken his fancy; and at the age of eight the organist of Lichfield Cathedral (his family were then living in the episcopal Palace there) used to let him play the chants on week days. When he was fifteen he was sent as a private pupil to Mr.

Charles Sumner, afterwards Bishop of Winchester, for whom, in spite of all differences of opinion, he retained a warm affection through life; and a long letter of his appears at the close of the Bishop's Life by his son, where it is amusing to find him recounting how on one occasion, in his undergraduate days, the Bishop, with whom he was breakfasting, rebuked him gently, but very justly, for his sweeping abuse of Roman Catholics, of whom he was obliged to admit that he had no personal knowledge whatever. He went up to Christ Church in 1821, and obtained a second class three years later; in 1825 he gained the Chancellor's prize for a Latin Essay "On the Power of the Tribunes among the Romans," and in 1827 the prize for an English Essay "On the Influence of the Crusades on the Art and Literature of Europe," and also the Ellerton Theological Prize. In 1827 he was also elected Fellow and three years afterwards appointed Tutor of Balliol, where he had among his colleagues Mr. Tait, afterwards primate, and the present Bishop of Salisbury. His friendly relations with Dr. Tait were never interrupted, and we find his name in the Memoir of Catherine and Crawfurd Tait among those who were foremost to testify their sympathy with the Archbishop in his heavy bereavement. He held the offices of Public Examiner and Select Preacher at Oxford, and was appointed in 1837 by Bishop Blomfield one of the Preachers at Whitehall. It was in the preface to a volume of Sermons preached there that he first indicated his sympathy with the Tractarian movement, having previously been, like nearly all the leading Tractarians, a decided Low Churchman. In 1839 he gave practical testimony to his new views, when he left Oxford to take the incumbency of the Proprietary Chapel in Margaret Street, of which Henry Drummond was lessee, and which had been previously held by the late Mr. Dodsworth—who himself joined the Church of Rome some years after Mr. Oakeley—and had before belonged to the Unitarians. It is here that his theological career may be said to have begun.

Mr. Gladstone spoke of Mr. Oakeley some ten years ago, in an article in the *Contemporary Review*, as one "who united to a fine musical ear a much finer and much rarer gift in discerning and expressing the harmony between the inward purposes of Christian work and its outward investiture, and who had gathered round him [at Margaret Chapel] a congregation the most devout and hearty that I, for one, have ever seen in any community of the Christian world." In that congregation Mr. Gladstone himself and the late Mr. Hope Scott were constant worshippers, while many others who had little sympathy with Tractarian views, such as Bishop Thirlwall, were attracted by Mr. Oakeley's thoughtful and weighty sermons, which dealt mainly with the ethical aspects of religious truth. But it was the specialty of Margaret Chapel in those days to be the pioneer of what is now called "Ritualism" in the Established Church, though scarcely any of the distinctive details associated with the term were to be found there or would then have been tolerated. Mr. Oakeley's fondness for ritual, which he carried with him into his new communion, probably received its first impulse from his boyish delight in the services of Lichfield Cathedral, where, as we have already seen, he used to play the organ on week days. But choral services and surpliced choristers were then considered a startling innovation anywhere out of a cathedral, and the "eastward position" must have looked still more unusual; of vestments, or even of lighted candles—except, as he afterwards explained, "on foggy mornings"—there was no thought; while the plain wooden altar cross was considered quite alarming. It is curious to find a letter in Bishop (then Archdeacon) Wilberforce's Life expressing his disgust after going to Margaret Street at the oddness and Romanizing character of what would now be thought very moderate ceremonial, hardly above the average of many "Evangelical" churches, and his consequent determination never to go there again. But it is not too much to say that to Mr. Oakeley's ministry at Margaret Chapel, more than to any other single instrumentality, is due that marked restoration of musical and ritual solemnity which has triumphed over the parson-and-clerk duet constituting the almost solitary ideal of Anglican worship in the days of our grandfathers, though it has now almost faded into a dim tradition of the past. It may be difficult for those of a later generation to understand how, in 1844 (which falls within the period of Mr. Oakeley's incumbency), the *Times* was fiercely asserting "the repugnance of the laity to the introduction of these obnoxious novelties," which involved "a contest not about words but about principles," and their indignant demand "to be allowed to worship as their fathers worshipped, and to observe the same ritual they had been accustomed to from infancy"; and how mobs of thousands of persons would wait for hours in pouring rain to hoot and yell at the clergyman who introduced these "obnoxious novelties," the whole dispute being about the wearing of a surplice in the pulpit. It is still harder perhaps for us to realise how a year later

a huge vestry meeting was gathered in London to complain
that "a parish containing upwards of 43,000 souls (of whom
it may be doubted if 43 had been in the habit of attending
the parish church) was disturbed to its centre at the will
of one individual, who at his mere pleasure disturbed and
deranged *the beautiful and solemn ceremonial of Church
service* which had been handed down to us unchanged for
more than two centuries," *i. e.* the parson-and-clerk duet.
At last the matter found its way to the House of Lords,
and the Bishop of Exeter (Phillpotts)—who had been
sharply admonished by the *Times* "as a conscientious man
to retire from the bench, and let the people of England
have the sacred service of the Church as their sires and
grandsires had it "—ventured to ask Earl Fortescue " what
these obsolete forms and usages were " which he had denounced, and which, as was asserted, "forced the son to
pass the grave of his father, the widower of his wife, the
mother of her child, to seek in some remote and unaccus-
tomed house of worship that spiritual sustenance which the
novel practices at their own church had rendered unacceptable ?" Lord Fortescue, being thus brought to book, had
to reply that "the innovations complained of, and which
had caused all the mischief, were three in number—namely,
preaching in the surplice, the sentences in the Offertory,
and the collection after service." It is likely enough that
these extracts may raise a smile of incredulity; but it is
necessary to bear the actual state of things in mind in
estimating the nature and extent of the ritual reform, as
most Anglicans of every school would now agree to call it,
first inaugurated at the obscure little chapel which has
since grown into one of the stateliest churches of London.

It was while Mr. Oakeley was still at Margaret Street that the disturbance arose at Oxford about his friend and brother fellow Mr. Ward, whose *Ideal of a Christian Church* led to his being deprived of his M.A. degree by a decree of Convocation of very questionable legality. Mr. Oakeley, who had nothing to do with the book, chivalrously placed himself by his friend's side, declaring that he also "claimed the right to hold, though not to teach, all Roman doctrine"; and this avowal led to one of the earliest of those ecclesiastical *causes célèbres* in the Arches Court which afterwards became so frequent, and have at last brought the whole machinery of the Anglican Church Courts under the hammer of a Royal Commission. But the defendant did not care to await its termination. Within a few months his great leader Mr. Newman had decided on leaving the Church of England, and Mr. Oakeley almost immediately followed him. After going through a theological course at St. Edmund's College, Ware, and serving for a short time at St. George's Cathedral, Southwark, he was in 1850 appointed to the charge of St. John's, Duncan Terrace, and was two years afterwards made a Canon of Westminster, and he retained both offices till his death. At Islington, as before at Margaret Street, Mr. Oakeley paid great attention to musical and ceremonial arrangements, and he may be said to have effected no inconsiderable reform in these respects in his new as well as in his old communion. Discarding the services of the "shrieking sisterhood" of female professionals, then almost universally in vogue in Roman Catholic places of worship in England—though expressly forbidden by the Roman ritual—he entrusted the singing to a well-trained choir of men and boys, and had soon established for his church the reputation of one of the best musical services in London. But it would be a great mistake to imagine that, either there or at Margaret Street, his attention was absorbed by externals, however important. Both in his Anglican and his later ministry he always showed himself an indefatigable parish priest, and his church was thronged by a multitude of devout worshippers. It may perhaps be regretted that the career of active usefulness which he had deliberately marked out for himself since he gave up residence at Oxford left him so little time for literary work. Some volumes of sermons and devotional treatises, and several pamphlets and review articles, he has left behind him, which go far to show that under different circumstances he might have made a name in literature. One of the most popular of the Littlemore Series of *Lives of the English Saints* was from his pen, the Life of St. Augustine of Canterbury. His style was evidently, though perhaps unconsciously, modelled on Cardinal Newman's, and has much of the grace, though it lacks the concentrated force, of that great master of English. It should be added that his controversial writings, if such they can be called, are free, as he was himself, from any taint of bitterness. Nothing could be more out of harmony with his refined taste and with his whole tone of mind than, *e.g.*, to designate the Church of which he was once a minister, as another clerical convert did not long ago, "a monarch's cast-off mistress, now in her dishonourable age vainly striving to cover her nakedness with the gifts which purchased her seduction "—rather an unintelligible sarcasm, as the Church was not enriched but greatly impoverished at the Reformation—or to describe English

Protestantism generally as an "offensive centipede." He kept up through life, as was observed before, habits of friendly intercourse with his old associates, and six years before his death he might have been seen at the Union Jubilee dinner at Oxford, sitting by the side of Mr. Matthew Arnold, who was an undergraduate at Balliol when he was a Fellow there. One can hardly help wondering, as the Oxford converts of that generation are passing away one by one—there are few of the more eminent left now besides the two Cardinals—how far their departure may affect that better understanding between members of the rival communions on which Cardinal Newman discoursed some years ago. There can be no doubt that the influence of their antecedents and personal character has done much indirectly in many ways to bridge over what once seemed an impassable chasm, the more so as many of them, like Mr. Oakeley himself, had shared to the full in their earlier days that hatred of the Pope and all his works which Dr. Hook's biographer tells us he used once to consider the essential duty and characteristic of an Englishman. And Cardinal Manning has thus been enabled, in his present position, to do much to raise the dignity and social status of the Archiepiscopal See of Westminster, as well as its directly spiritual influence. It would be another point well worth inquiring into, but is far too wide a question to discuss here, what kind and amount of permanent impression the Tractarian converts have made on their adopted communion. There is certainly a conspicuous difference, which can hardly fail to strike outsiders, between the general tone not only of Roman Catholic society in England, but of Roman Catholic worship and preaching, as it is now and as it was thirty or forty years ago.

XXXVII.

DR. CUMMING.

THE news of Dr. Cumming's death would have created a much greater sensation than it did, had it occurred a dozen years earlier, when the Prophet of Crown Court was still in all his glory, or when at all events the perennial stream of unfulfilled prophecy had not yet run dry. For two or three years before his death he had retired from public view, and for some time previously the public had been retiring from his pulpit. Those who were suddenly reminded of his old reputation by learning, in July 1881, that he had passed away, were probably surprised to find that he was only seventy-two years old. The fact is that Dr. Cumming began to preach, which meant with him to prophesy, at a very early age, and occupied his familiar tripod in Crown Court for nearly half a century. That he should have managed during most of that period to retain his hold over a numerically not inconsiderable section of the religious world—including at one time Duchesses and other such notabilities—may seem startling at first sight, but it may be said without disrespect to that eminent poet that Dr. Cumming was the Martin Tupper of theology. And if it be true that Martin Tupper has his tens of thousands of readers, especially of the fair sex, where

Tennyson has his thousands, we need not marvel that multitudes who turned away from Newma or Westcott or even from Dean Stanley, as from a sealed book, should have eagerly imbibed the fiery contents of the *Seventh Vial*, and listened with awful suspense to the trumpet tone which announced — though it announced in vain — the imminent approach of the *Battle of Armageddon*. There was indeed one little drawback, for the predictions confidently repeated year by year, and usually about twice a year, somehow never came true, and the fateful dates had to be again and again reconstructed. The *Sounding of the Last Trumpet* was found to give a very " uncertain sound," and the *Last Warning Cry* was uttered, not indeed exactly to heedless ears, but to ears too likely to be rendered heedless for the future by disappointment of the expected result. But these little incongruities never ruffled for a moment the self-complacency or the self-confidence of the prophet himself. He always had some excellent explanation ready, as to why the prediction had not been fulfilled at the precise time or in the precise way anticipated, or some ingenious way of showing that in fact it really had been fulfilled, though nobody but he who had dreamed the dream had the gift of discerning the interpretation thereof. We all know how the *Times*, though it often changes, is always consistent, and never lacks an opportune quotation to prove that it has been always right. Dr. Cumming, though he traced his inspirations to a higher source, was equally consistent, and always " knew he was right." And, what is more, he always got a great many people—" mostly fools," perhaps, in the Carlylese sense—to believe him. Nor is this altogether inexplicable. In the first place, it is

only fair to admit that he had the courage of his halluci-
nations. His literary conscience, as will appear presently,
was almost as queer as his literary taste ; but there can be
no doubt that he really believed in the main what he said.
The Pope was to him as real an object of mingled terror
and detestation as to Bunyan's " Pilgrim," only a much
more formidable one, and his final doom was a constant
theme of Divine prediction from Genesis to the Apocalypse.
The Doctor gave indeed in his latter days a strong proof
of the sincerity of his sentiments on this point, if it be true
that he made a pilgrimage to Exeter with his family on
the Fifth of November, and took lodgings in the Cathedral
Yard, in order to witness the huge bonfire whereby it
pleases " Young Exeter" year by year to testify its
Protestant zeal—or presumably its rowdyism—in defiance
of official warnings, cordons of police, and the angry
reclamations of the inhabitants of that " ancient and loyal
city," especially those living in the precincts, who are in
dread as each November comes round of their Cathedral
and themselves being involved in a common conflagration.
Then again Dr. Cumming was not only manifestly sincere
in his strange vagaries, but he had a pleasing presence, an
unfailing supply of the kind of eloquence which the British
Philistine can appreciate, and a geniality of temper—not
perhaps quite in harmony with his awful denunciations—
which made him personally popular. And if each new
composition that appeared, under whatever variety of title
—*Babylon, Armageddon, The Last Woe, The Great Tribula-
tion*, &c.—was little else than a new setting of the last, so
that one might almost literally say *Ex uno disce omnes*, still
fresh events were constantly happening which could be

somehow or other dovetailed into the general plan, and fresh articles and books were being published, which could be quoted at any indefinite length, whether for approval or censure, though neither events nor extracts were always very much to the purpose. To use a favourite but some-what unintelligible quotation of his own, he got *rem quomodo rem*.

Dr. Cumming will live, if he lives at all, by his works, and ill-natured critics may possibly suggest that he has built himself a monument *ære perennius*, in more senses than one. Nobody can wish to be unkind to his memory, but it is simply impossible to accept him for what to the last he claimed to be, a great teacher and prophet of the highest truth. Whether his theology was right or wrong in the abstract, need not be discussed here, but his ignor-ance was as unbounded as his confidence; and the plain fact is that he had a habit all his life, which grew into a second nature, of talking nonsense without knowing it. A brief glance at two or three of his later works will sufficiently illustrate the point of this criticism.

In 1867 the Ritualistic movement, as it has come to be called, was beginning to attract attention, and it occurred to Dr. Cumming that a new variation of the old Babylonish melody would be appropriate. He accordingly seized his opportunity, and at once preached and published twelve lectures under the fascinating title, *Ritualism the Highway to Rome*. The date given for the destruction of the world had already been fixed—not indeed for the first time—and was then definitively settled for 1868. What occurred in the short interval might therefore have been supposed to be not very important. But in the preface to this new

work the author professed himself " deeply persuaded that
never was our country in greater peril in its highest and
holiest interests." A leading Roman Catholic newspaper
—which must have borrowed for once something of Dr.
Cumming's prophetic tone—had avowed its belief that the
time was coming " when High Mass will once more be
sung in Westminster Abbey," and the prediction bore to
his mind an almost Apocalyptic significance. On the
other hand, a serial called the *Protestant Churchman* had
shown by " tabular statistics " the fearful growth of Romish
priests, chapels, convents, and colleges, since the fatal year
1829 ; and this increase was mainly due, he thought, to
Ritualism or its Tractarian parent. Moreover, Dr. Cumming had just discovered that " vast masses of the poor—
especially Irish poor—are already Roman Catholics," and
the context implied, what it might surprise themselves to
learn, that " Ritualist ceremonial " had made them such.
Then, again, the *Directorium Anglicanum* — a Ritualist
work—was somehow responsible for the mischievous Act
which allowed Romish priests to officiate in gaols, and
even " to be paid out of the rates, according to their work,"
and to have an altar, sacrificial vestments, and " a Virgin
Mary " supplied in aid of their ministrations. And there
were actually men eating the bread of our Protestant
Establishment, who dared to call themselves—what their
own Prayer Book calls them—"priests," and took every
means, by the use of candles and rich dresses, " which,
whether at the ball, or the opera, or a Ritualistic church,
are no doubt very attractive," to inculcate Romish dogmas.
Here was a sufficiently alarming basis of fact to go upon,
and an elaborate argument follows—borrowed wholesale,

Z

by the way, from Tillotson—against the Real Presence, capped by a somewhat obscure inference from what is *not* contained in a long passage of Justin Martyr, "who probably saw the Apostle John"—if he ever did, it must have been as a baby—to the effect that in his day there was neither liturgy, priesthood, nor sacrifice in the Christian Church. And there is another still more obscure argumentation against the Ritualistic and Popish figment of the apostolic succession. But the learned Doctor also adds *more suo* some touching little anecdotes. He tells us *e. g.* how he once met "in that exquisite Corinthian structure, La Madeleine," a venerable French priest, who was already "a real Christian," and had thoughts of coming to London to attend the May Meetings. On another occasion, however, at Bruges his landlord assured him that "his life would not be safe," if he attempted to preach Christ in that priest-ridden city, but he would be listened to with enthusiasm, if he liked to preach the Virgin Mary, "even in very bad French." We are left to infer that under the circumstances he wisely preferred to remain silent.

Three years later—that is, two years after what should have been the final catastrophe—came the Vatican Council, and here of course was another great opportunity for Dr. Cumming. He had offered, indeed, to attend that venerable assembly in person, if the Pope would allow him full freedom of speech when he got there; but a somewhat curt and almost sarcastic message conveyed to "Dr. Cumming of Scotland," through Archbishop Manning, intimated that his offer could not be entertained; so he took his repulse like a man, and put into print those views on *The Fall of*

Babylon Foreshadowed in Her Teaching, in History, and in Prophecy, which he had once hoped to utter in the Council Chamber. One can hardly help regretting that Pius IX., who had a considerable sense of humour, did not give him the opportunity of discharging his "olive branch out of a catapult", at the heads of the assembled fathers. In this work, which covers nearly 500 pages, the date of the Battle of Armageddon is once more rearranged, and placed this time "*about* 1870"; but there is not very much else in it new. We are told that the Romish religion is "supernatural," which evidently means infra-natural, for the writer immediately adds that it is too impious to come from above, and too artful to be the work of man; in short, it is "the masterpiece of the Devil." There have been, however, some few good Christians in the Church of Rome—of whom three are named—but then they were good "in spite of their creed." At the same time, so far from being a corruption of Protestantism, we are assured that Popery is nearly as old as the creation of man. It is "coëval in principle with the Fall. Adam was a Papist before he became a Protestant." And unfortunately Adam's first-born followed his parent in his original error, and not in his subsequent conversion. "Cain was, in principle, the first Roman Catholic priest," for he offered "an unbloody sacrifice, exactly typical of the Mass." So, by the by, did Melchisedech. And the same evil "principle" appears to have survived in the chosen people up to the time of their final rejection, for we are asked, "What land, *from the sacred heights of Calvary* to the pinnacles of the Alps, has not been drenched with the blood of martyrs, who have been slain by her" (Rome)? It was the year of the

Vatican Council, so we have of course a chapter to prove
the fallibility of Ecumenical Councils, which is demonstrated by the fact that "in the fourth century *nineteen
Councils of the Church were orthodox and nineteen heretical.*"
The italics are the author's, but he omits to add that only
two of these thirty-eight Councils were reputed Ecumenical, both of which he classifies as orthodox. There are
some odd historical puzzles about "the canonization of
Teresias," apparently meaning St. Teresa, the revolting
immoralities of Pope Alexander VI. and of Borgia, who
are treated as two different persons, and the proceedings
of "Gregory" and "Nyssen," whose personality is bifur-
cated in the same uncomfortable fashion. But on this
and some other very strange historical complications we
need not linger here. We have seen already that the date
of the end of the world is fixed in this volume for "about
1870," but this is based on a calculation that the world
was to last 6000 years, and had then reached the year
6002, which might seem to show not that "the sands of
our present mundane economy are nearly run out," but that
they had run out two years before. The prophet, however,
cautiously adds, mindful perhaps of former disappointments, "I give dates. I refuse to decide." In another
book, issued some months later, he denied that there was
"one solution published in previous works that demands
reversal or recasting," and thinks the battle of Armageddon may "with no great difficulty" be identified with
Sebastopol.

This second work of 1870, entitled the *Seventh Vial*—in
the rhythmical and euphonious diction of the Revised
Version it becomes the "Seventh Bowl"—appeared after

the prorogation of the Vatican Council, when "this unclean spirit from the Pope had inspired 533 prelates to proclaim an aged priest infallible"; and we hear a good deal about "the false prophet," and "the croaking frogs," and "the lie," and how "Rome, filthy, bigoted, and cruel, is the nursery of brigands, the nest of priests, and the throne of beggars"; with much more to the same effect. This, by the way, was published just after Victor Emmanuel had entered Rome. One peculiarity of Dr. Cumming's style, which is signally exemplified in this and his next volume of the following year, is what might in a less devout and unworldly kind of literature be designated bookmaking. The simple fact is that at least half the volume is made up of extracts from the newspapers and serials of the day, the *Times*, the *Standard*, the *Westminster Review*—euphemistically described as "making no pretension to be a religious organ"—and the *Saturday Review* being heavily taxed for the purpose. Then again, à propos of "the Great Earthquake," we have nearly seventy pages of extracts on the natural history of earthquakes, and several more about "tidal waves," to illustrate "the Sea and the Waves roaring"; while the "signs in the sun and moon and stars" are illustrated by a further series of extracts about "spots in the sun." The work on the *Cities of the Nations*, which appeared in the following year, reads very like a sequel to the *Seventh Vial*, and is also largely made up of cuttings from the daily papers and other publications of the day, together with long extracts from "Alison, the historian," who was a great favourite of Dr. Cumming's. In this work the author was able to exult over "the light" that had broken on Rome, and the substitution of "an

enlightened civil law" for the "sanguinary canon law";
but he had to mourn over the sceptical teaching of Dr.
Colenso and his allies—for Dr. Cumming kept an eye on
the sceptics as well as on the Pope—and he urged some
very odd arguments, partly based on personal experiences
of his own, in reply to them. But one cannot help suspecting that this modern and mundane element in his
books—the gossiping stories and still more the gossiping
extracts they are so full of—constituted one of their principal charms. There are religious people who object to
reading newspapers or novels, and especially object to
them on Sundays. To such persons it must have been
quite a godsend to meet with an indubitably pious and
"Sunday book," which was nevertheless choke full of
cuttings from the periodical press. They not only found
pleasure and piety combined ; their curiosity was gratified
in a manner not simply innocent, but positively devotional.
If on the other hand we inquire why the popularity Dr.
Cumming had enjoyed so long began to wane at last,
the explanation is hardly far to seek. Even the religious
world will grow weary in the end of the dull monotony of
perpetual repetitions and predictions constantly falsified by
the event ; but there was a further cause also. When Dr.
Cumming began to preach, the latent Protestantism of the
country had been recently lashed into fury by the Catholic
Emancipation Act of 1829 ; and the Tractarian movement,
with its direct and incidental consequences, kept the "No
Popery" passion at fever heat for many years afterwards.
But times had changed before the close of his ministry ;
new storms were breaking over the theological horizon, and
the old watchwords offered no guidance or protection amid

dangers a former age had not experienced or foreseen. In spite of the inspiration he almost claimed, the Protestant Prophet had no chart to steer by in these untried seas. A generation had grown up which knew not Joseph, and Dr. Cumming found his occupation gone from him. If we could hope his career might act as a warning to others against a course of unconscious, but not wholly innocuous, charlatanism, it would be true to say that he did not live in vain. But it is difficult to point the moral without seeming to suggest an imputation he was too transparently credulous to deserve.

XXXVIII.

DEAN STANLEY.

THE death of the late Dean of Westminster after only a few days' illness, at no very advanced age and in the full vigour of his powers, removed with startling abruptness a conspicuous figure from the scene. There are very few persons not occupying a still higher position, in Church or State, who have attracted of late years so much of public attention, or whose death would have called forth so universal a chorus of lamentation, comment, and eulogy. And even for those who find it impossible to join unreservedly in the effusive laudations so copiously showered on his memory, one thing at least is attested by the very prominence of the place he had made for himself in the world's estimation from the first. For it may fairly be said that, from the day when Stanley and Vaughan, then Dr. Arnold's two most promising and devoted pupils, were "bracketed even," as Bishop Wordsworth, who examined them, has since reminded us, in the Sixth Form examination at Rugby, he always held his own. The fact is, that he possessed in a remarkable measure what is alleged to be, under the conditions of modern society, becoming less and less possible, the gift of individuality, or, as Mr. Matthew Arnold would say, "distinction." In his whole character, attitude, and tone of mind, as in his person, there was an unmistakable idiosyncrasy. You could generally be pretty sure beforehand what line he would take on any given subject, and that it would be like himself and unlike everybody else. One of his panegyrists has observed that the Dean "never twaddled, or declaimed, *or repeated himself.*" Certainly he did not twaddle, nor was declamation much in his line, for that implies real or simulated passion, and he was not a religious enthusiast, still less an actor, but as to his never repeating himself, it would be more accurate to say that he repeated himself in every volume or article he published, almost in every sermon he preached. To say this does not, of course, mean that he repeated himself in the way, for instance, that Dr. Cumming did, but that one leading idea, which was apt to become somewhat tedious from constant iteration, formed the keynote of his teaching as of his life. He was always harping on one string, and whether history, or theology, or ecclesiastical discipline was the professed subject of discussion, the supreme excellence of liberalism or "latitudinarianism"—the term in his mouth was one not of reproach but of honour—would invariably turn out to be the moral of the tale. This has indeed been made by his admirers their special theme of commendation, but neither in an intellectual nor a moral sense can the praise be accepted without reserve. In one respect, however, it is pleasant to be able to put on record the unanimous agreement of all, however widely differing in principle, who came into contact with him. In his personal conduct and demeanour his liberality was alike graceful and genuine, and knew no distinctions of opinion, school, or creed; after the fiercest wranglings in the Jerusalem

Chamber the Dean and Archdeacon Denison, who seized
the first opportunity of paying a warm tribute to his
memory in Convocation, might be seen seated side by side
in friendly converse in the hospitable refuge of the Deanery
drawing-room.   He was, in short, a thoroughly amiable,
kind-hearted, and generous man in all the relations of
private life, and the various positions he successively occupied, especially during his later years at Westminster, gave
him abundant opportunities of exhibiting those estimable
qualities, of which he was never slow to avail himself.   It
has been said, probably with truth, that he never had a
personal enemy ; and to this kindliness of heart was added
the rare charm of conversational powers which made his
presence an acquisition to every company he entered.
There is the more reason for rendering this just tribute,
because, as will presently appear, there are decisive objections against unreservedly endorsing all the commendations
bestowed on the impartial breadth of his liberality in a
wider sphere.   But that inquiry runs up into a general
estimate of his position as a writer, a theologian, and a
dignified and influential Churchman.

Lord Beaconsfield exemplified his wonted felicity of
phrase when he selected " picturesque sensibility " as the
special characteristic of Dean Stanley's mind.   He was not
a deep or philosophical thinker, and therefore was never
likely to wield such influence as *e. g.* Cardinal Newman has
exercised on one side, or, to name divines more nearly
allied to him, Professor Jowett or the late Mr. Maurice
on the other.   The marvellous effect attributed to Dr.
Newman's sermons at Oxford, which has been described
with thrilling force by the most unsympathetic hearers,

could never be produced by any discourse of Dean Stanley's, who was a graceful and picturesque rather than a touching or eloquent preacher, and whose voice was the reverse of musical. For theology properly so called, that is for the abstract discussion of doctrine, he had a positive inaptitude and distaste, though he was constantly writing about it. It was not so much that he disliked this or that particular tenet, as that he disliked and failed to grasp the idea of doctrine or dogma altogether, and his liberality on its intellectual side was largely based on his inability to appreciate distinctions which to him were empty forms. His paradoxical and morbid passion for tracing impossible analogies was matched by an equal incapacity for discerning distinctions plain as the sun at noonday to every eye but his. He had an instinctive aversion to definite statements on abstract subjects, not because they were false, but because they were definite, and one could as little conceive his being martyred for a specific heresy as for an article of the Creed. Had he lived in the fourth century, he would have fully shared Gibbon's unphilosophical contempt for a Christendom divided about "the difference of a single diphthong," and would have been as little willing to subscribe or to condemn the Arian confessions as the Nicene Creed. One could almost imagine his sharing the fate of the unhappy victim of Turkish red-tapism, who is said to have been executed at Constantinople, not for being a Mahometan or a Christian—for he was free to profess either religion—but because he could not decide, or at least could not intelligibly explain, to which of the rival creeds he adhered. In a lecture to working men some years ago. Dean Stanley ridiculed the notion of psychology or theology being at all concerned in the problems raised by the Darwinian theory of the origin of species. He referred, in an Oxford University Sermon, to Renan's *Vic de Jésus*, with its profane and loathsome ravings about "Galilean idyls," pastoral loves, *et id genus omne*, as "homage offered to Christ from an unexpected quarter." He told the students of St. Andrew's, on another occasion, that "the faith of each successive epoch of Christendom has varied enormously from the faith of its predecessors" —which only shows his strange incapacity for distinguishing fixed doctrines from passing phases of opinion—and that "the true faith" has been to no one more largely indebted than to "the excommunicated Spinoza," who is regarded by all competent interpreters as having been either an Atheist or at best a Pantheist, but to whom, the Dean thought, "was vouchsafed the clearest glimpse into the nature of the Deity." In a paper on the three Creeds, published only a year before his death, while dismissing, as no better than "algebraic symbols" and "arithmetical enigmas," the doctrines they are commonly supposed to contain, he seeks to elicit from them some broader and loftier, but scarcely intelligible, conception of "Christianity, as it has appeared to Voltaire, Rousseau, Göthe, Mill, Renan." He would not have said in so many words, with Strauss in the *Leben Jesu*, that "the moral contents of Christianity" are alone valuable, for, unlike Strauss, he recoiled from all definite statements; but from first to last, whenever he spoke—as in his latest and not least typical work on *Christian Institutions*, and in the highly characteristic posthumous paper "On the Revised Version of the New Testament", published in the

Times—of "the great doctrines which all Christians alike
hold," he invariably and exclusively referred to the moral,
as distinct from the doctrinal, teaching of the Gospel. It
is difficult to understand how such vague and colourless
exhortations can, as Archbishop Tait declared after his
death in Convocation, have "confirmed in the faith vast
numbers whose temptations lay entirely in the direction of
scepticism"; for, if anything beyond faith in moral goodness is intended, the question must at once arise, in what
faith were they to be confirmed ? But the Archbishop's
loyalty to his friends was stronger than his critical acumen.

To say with one of his eulogists that the Dean was less
a theologian than an ecclesiastical historian is greatly to
understate the case. He was not and never could have
become a theologian at all, and unfortunately his theological or anti-theological peculiarities, combined with the
inveterate passion for paradox which grew out of them,
materially affected his character as an historian also. The
same vagueness of mind which led him rather to adumbrate
than to define his theological views reappeared in his treatment both of Jewish and Christian history. As a writer
he was versatile rather than accurate, brilliant rather than
profound, and was always happier in illustrating his subject
than in explaining it. And hence in truth those works,
like *Sinai and Palestine*, and the interesting *Memorials of
Canterbury* and *of Westminster*, which gave the amplest
scope for pictorial illustration and the least for theological
or ecclesiastical disquisition, were at once the most pleasing
and most instructive of his writings ; the *Life of Dr. Arnold*,
which first brought him into public notice, stands in a
category by itself, from the singular charm as well of the

subject as of the treatment.   In his *Lectures on the Eastern Church*, his description of the Council of Nice throws far greater light on the details of the national costume and temperament of the assembled prelates than on the momentous, but to his mind comparatively trivial, question they met together to decide for all future ages of the Church ; while elsewhere he dismisses the whole series of General Councils as of no practical value, because they failed to accomplish, what of course they never attempted or from the nature of the case could possibly have achieved, and did not create the art, the science, the literature, the poetry, the philanthropy, or even the theology of Christendom.   It did not occur to him that the same line of argument would equally prove the Roman Senate or the English Parliament to be shams.   All competent judges again will agree with Mr. Lecky that Christianity has created three things generally recognised as special types and expressions of its religious sentiment, "the church bell, the organ, and the Gothic Cathedral."   But Dean Stanley's paradoxical temper led him to argue in *Good Words*, in defiance of all historical evidence, that there is nothing distinctively Christian, still less distinctively Catholic, in Gothic architecture, and that, in fact, it has closer affinities with Protestantism than with Catholicism.   But there is no need to go further into detail on a familiar theme.   Those who are acquainted with his writings will be aware that Dr. Stanley was hardly more reliable as an historian than as a divine ; and it was a peculiarity of his mind that, while he was constantly making mistakes, which were at once detected and exposed by his critics, he could never be persuaded to admit them himself.

It remains to say something of the Dean's career as a Churchman, "the successor," as he was fond of styling himself, "of the Abbots of Westminster." And considering the singularity of his own views and policy in Church matters, there was a curious, though probably accidental, fitness in his occupying the one post of eminence in the English Church independent of all episcopal control. The mitred Abbots of Westminster were exempt from all superior jurisdiction save that of the Roman Pontiff, and when the Abbey was suppressed by Henry VIII. the same immunity passed on to the Deans, subject only to the supreme authority of the new Head of the Church, which for centuries past has meant that for practical purposes they can do as they please. This exceptional immunity of the Abbey Church enabled Dean Stanley to try experiments there which could have been tried nowhere else. On one occasion he induced a layman to preach in the nave, and more than once he invited suspended clergymen or Nonconformist ministers to occupy the pulpit—an offer they had what most people considered the good taste to decline. That however was only one illustration of the ecclesiastical liberalism which shaped the Dean's peculiar view of the relations of Church and State. He is credited with being fearless and impartial in the breadth of his toleration, and always ready to defend the unpopular side. In one sense this is true, but not in another. It need hardly be said that in the present day the liberal or latitudinarian is really the popular side, and few men enjoyed a wider popularity in the outer world than the Dean of Westminster. But it is true that he braved, one might almost say scorned, ecclesiastical public opinion, and among

his own order and in the Church of England generally he
was an object of suspicion. But for a man holding a
dignified and independent position, with a powerful public
opinion and very high authorities both civil and ecclesiastical at his back, it did not perhaps require any very
exceptional courage to face a clerical opposition which at
worst could only denounce him, and which, with all his
personal forbearance to individual opponents, he never
hesitated to denounce and satirize, not without some
asperity, in return. One can hardly help indeed being a
little reminded by his lofty scorn of " sacerdotal " pretensions of the old story of Diogenes " trampling on the pride
of Plato," as Plato quietly remarked, " with a greater pride
of his own." On the other hand his liberality, however
wide, was most readily and freely extended to the left
wing of his own party. We never heard for instance of his
voice being raised against the worrying Ritualist prosecutions or the harsh penalties which in some cases followed
them. Yet, even assuming all the Privy Council judgments
to be sound in law, and the Ritualist contention in every
respect mistaken — which is a strong assumption — the
victims had surely as much claim for toleration as Mr.
Gorham, or Dr. Colenso, or the writers of *Essays and
Reviews*—of whom it was said at the time that "they
escaped by the skin of their teeth"—or Mr. Voysey, who
did not escape, or Mr. Stopford Brooke, who did not
indeed incur legal censure, but felt bound in honour to
retire from an untenable position; and for all these Dr.
Stanley manifested an active sympathy. It may be replied
that every one, however comprehensive his toleration, is
most keenly alive to the wrongs of his own party, and, of

course, that is perfectly true; only something must in fairness be discounted from the impartial largeness of a tolerance, which is chiefly exhibited towards partisans whose extreme opinions incline to the extremity most closely in harmony with one's own. And the public protests twice raised against himself by Churchmen of markedly moderate and conservative temper—one by Bishop Wordsworth, then Canon of Westminster, against his installation in the Deanery, the next some few years later by the Dean of Norwich, against his appointment as Select Preacher at Oxford—suffice to prove that Dr. Stanley needed for himself a full measure of the toleration he claimed for others. It was characteristic of his one-sided liberalism in historical questions that, while he fiercely denounced "the atrocious Act of 1662," which imposed subscription to the Prayer-Book, and led to the ejection of two thousand Nonconformist ministers from the livings into which they had been illegally thrust, he had no word of censure for the far more arbitrary and sweeping ejection of some 7000 episcopal clergy under the Commonwealth, whose places these intruders had usurped. In practical matters, his eagerness to secure for the Abbey the remains of the Socinian author of *Pickwick*, at the cost of forcing the hand of his family and contravening his own express directions, contrasted oddly with the omission to offer a resting-place in the same hallowed precincts to the author of the *Christian Year*.

And now for a word in conclusion on the peculiar theory of the relations of Church and State, which held a prominent place in the Dean's entire teaching and policy. He never, of course, precisely defined it, any more than he

A A

defined his theological views, but it would probably have
coincided pretty closely in practical result with the scheme
propounded by his old master, Dr. Arnold, that all sects
except Jews and Roman Catholics should be united, by
Act of Parliament, in one national communion.   Their
differences of belief or worship would have appeared to
him of infinitesimal importance, or, rather, one main
advantage of a Church Establishment was to hold such
differences in check.   At a great meeting convened in St.
James's Hall, under the presidency of Archbishop Longley,
to protest against the disestablishment of the Irish Church,
he commenced a speech, which the frantic howls of his
fervently Tory audience would not allow him to finish, by
declaring that he was " a Whig of the Whigs and a Liberal
of the Liberals," and intended to support the motion on
Liberal principles.   He would no doubt have explained at
length, had he been suffered to proceed, what he took
occasion to set forth in print more fully elsewhere, that the
essence of an Established Church is " to be under the
supremacy of the Crown, that is, of the law," and that
Joseph II. of Austria—" my brother the Sacristan," as
Frederick II. aptly named the meddlesome lay-pope—
was his model of a liberal monarch.   He was careful to
add that the possession of endowments, and still more of
any exclusive system of doctrine or polity, or any separate
clerical order, is not of the essence of the Church ; that
it should be made as comprehensive as the nation, all
theological tests being abolished, " except, perhaps, the
Apostles' Creed "— this doubtful exception disappears
from some later writings on the subject—and that " every
man capable of rendering good service to the community

be recognised as a minister." The advantages of this arrangement are further explained to be that it secures to the Church the supremacy of just and good laws—though one hardly sees why all Church laws should be necessarily bad, and all State laws necessarily good—that it gives scope for the growth of various diversities of opinion ; and that it protects "humble and devout souls from being borne down by the current of local and transitory clamour," which was supposed to refer to Bishop Colenso, whose quarrel with the South African bishops was then at its height, and whose pertinacity in maintaining it was more conspicuous than his humility to ordinary observers. In a lecture he delivered some years afterwards in Scotland the Dean pronounced a still more emphatic eulogium on "the principle of a national Establishment," not indeed that the State gains anything from union with the Church, but, on the contrary, "the Church is elevated and enlarged by contact, however slight, with so magnificent and divine an ordinance as the national commonwealth." It was in strict accordance with these views that, when in Scotland, he habitually worshipped and preached in the Established Presbyterian Kirk, and held aloof entirely from the unestablished Episcopal Communion. The simple fact of establishment was to him a far more fundamental "note of the Church" than any specialty of doctrine, discipline, or ritual. This is not the place to discuss whether such an establishment as he adumbrated and desired could ever become a practical reality, or how far, if *per impossibile* it came to be realised, it would differ from what Mr. Goldwin Smith once called "an established chaos." To call such views Erastian would be an obvious misnomer.

Erastianism subordinates the Church to the State ; the Stan-
leyan hypothesis reduces it to an impalpable abstraction,
which cannot even be conceived of except as a variable
accident of the civil administration, having no independent
officers, principles, doctrines, or ordinances of its own.
The wildest heresies which disturbed the early or mediæval
Church were less utterly alien to the whole temper and
teaching of historical Christianity than such an estimate of
religious obligations. Had the early Christians shared it,
the "ten persecutions" would have been diminished at
least by nine, for the first would have secured and justified
their submission to "so magnificent and divine an ordinance as" the Imperial polity of Rome—incomparably the
grandest polity the world has ever seen. But it must
suffice to have indicated the true nature of the ideal of
"toleration, charity, and comprehensiveness"—as an ardent
panegyrist has worded it—which Dean Stanley made it the
aim of his life to promote, and which he appears to the
last to have expected or hoped might some day be translated into fact. Its very vagueness and impracticability
give a sort of nebulous grandeur to the ideal, but it is not
wonderful that the man who desperately clung to it, and
never tired of preaching it, in season and out of season, as
the last word of religious truth and wisdom, should have
found himself out of harmony with almost every section
of his clerical brethren.

It was a curious coincidence that within the same week
with Dr. Stanley there passed away another representative
dignitary, differing widely in many ways from him—an
old-fashioned high-churchman, a Conservative, a man of shy
and retiring nature, and a bookworm, but also a man of

deep learning, great kindliness of disposition, and munificent liberality, to whom more than to any other individual is owing the splendid restoration of Exeter Cathedral — Chancellor Harington, who was loved by all who knew him, and reverenced, one might almost say, throughout the whole West of England. No two men could be more utterly unlike in their opinions, habits, and the entire course of their lives, than these cathedral dignitaries, who in the time of their death were not divided. Meanwhile, if for Westminster Abbey, viewed as a centre of spiritual influence, Dean Stanley was not exactly the ideal head, it might have been difficult to find any one better qualified to do justice in its secular aspects to a position of unique historical, social, and national interest.

XXXIX

WILLIAM GEORGE WARD.

IN a sketch of Cardinal Newman originally published in the *Century*, Mr. Kegan Paul refers to the curious fact that Mr. Ward's name is not once mentioned in the *Apologia*, and infers from it, justly enough, "how little he (the Cardinal) considered Mr. Ward an exponent of his own views." At the same time there are few of the old Tractarian party who took a more prominent part in the Oxford movement than the able writer and metaphysician who, after a brief and painful illness, passed from among us in July 1882, at the age of seventy. His popular sobriquet of "Ideal Ward," which could not fail to bring a smile to the faces of all who knew anything of his outer man, was derived from a work which at the time produced an immense sensation ; and Mr. Mozley has reminded us that he was, in more senses than one, "the *largest* contributor to the *British Critic*," the recognised organ of the school. Mr. Ward was indeed a man whose personality, both physical and mental, it was impossible to overlook or ignore. Of his achievements at Winchester there is little to record ; but even as an undergraduate he had distinguished himself as a frequent and telling speaker at the Oxford Union, and from the time he gained his double second in 1834, and

was soon afterwards elected, together with Archbishop
Tait, a Fellow of Balliol, his name rapidly grew famous
in the University and in the Church. Though not a
Rugbean, but a Wykehamist, he fell early under Dr.
Arnold's influence, and represented at Oxford, as Mr.
Mozley puts it, "the intellectual force, the irrefragable logic,
the absolute self-confidence, and the headlong impetuosity
of the Rugby school." There is a story of his once paying
a visit to Rugby to consult Dr. Arnold on his intellectual
difficulties, when he plied his teacher so unsparingly with
questions and arguments that on his departure the indomit-
able Doctor was fain to confess himself utterly exhausted,
and to retire at once to bed. But his allegiance was soon
to be transferred to a yet more illustrious master. There
was a tradition current at Oxford that he was instantane-
ously converted to Tractarianism by a single line in the
preface to the third volume of Newman's *Parochial Sermons*—published in 1836—to the effect that "Ultra-Pro-
testantism could never have been silently corrupted into
Popery." Converted at all events he was, very speedily
and very completely, from Arnoldian to Anglo-Catholic
ideas, and his great literary powers were at once devoted
to the service of the rising school. As a writer he was
both startling and irrepressible ; "Ward alone was enough
to fill the world with alarms." The "doctrine of reserve,"
which was elaborately and somewhat ponderously preached
by Mr. Isaac Williams in one of the later *Tracts*, and for
which the writer was mercilessly castigated by indignant
Protestant critics as "a Jesuit," was not at all in his line.
He not only knew what he meant, but said it with what in
modern phrase would be called "a brutal frankness." And

hence the enemies of the movement denounced him as at
once impudent and treacherous, impudent for his avowed
design of "un-Protestantizing the Church of England,"
treacherous for remaining to " eat the bread of the Cuhrch ".
while he carried on this work, though in fact he never
held any ecclesiastical preferment. The writer of a long-
forgotten pasquinade, once widely circulated under the title
of the *Oxford Argo*, thus gibbeted him, in what unfortunately was by no means the most offensive of his stanzas, in
point either of reverence or good taste :—

> There's Balliol's honest knave,
>   Non-natural but real,
> To waft them o'er the wave
>   Winding a blast ideal.

And if Mr. Ward's lucubrations acted on opponents like
a red rag on a bull, they were in other ways hardly less
irritating to his friends. For one thing, he was terribly
voluminous. His *Few More Words* in defence of Tract
XC. covered 90 pages. The length of his contributions to
the *British Critic* so overpowered the much-enduring
editor that " for many years his idea of Ward was of a huge
young cuckoo, growing bigger and bigger, elbowing the
legitimate progeny over the side of the little nest." Nor
was this the only grievance. From the first Ward's chief
interest was philosophical, and the editor, who did not
profess to be a philosopher, records pathetically how, if " I
did but touch a filament or two in one of his monstrous
cobwebs, off ran he instantly to Newman to complain of
my gratuitous impertinence," so that he not only thought
of him as of a huge young cuckoo, but also as of " a plump
little Cupid flying to his mother to show a wasp sting he

had just received." And "as for cutting short (his articles), where was one to commence that operation when they were already without beginning or end?" Graces of style indeed Ward had less than none, differing therein widely from his friend Oakeley, who to the last remained, as a writer, very much what Mr. Mozley describes him as being in his earlier Oxford days, "an *elegant* and rather dilettante scholar;" his English is always pleasant to read, and often felicitous, but is more remarkable for elegance than force. At the same time Mr. Mozley admits, what is not difficult to understand, that many readers of the *Critic* "looked to Ward's article as the gem of the number." But moreover the practical difficulties he threw in the way of editorial revision were vexatious enough; "his handwriting was minute and detestable; it defied correction. The MS. consisted of bundles of irregular scraps of paper, which I had to despatch to the printer crying out for copy." There was always indeed something of the humorous as well as the alarming associated with the name of Ward, by friend and foe alike. The crisis of his Anglican career was brought about, as is well known, by the publication of his *Ideal of a Christian Church* and the censure pronounced on the book and its author by the Oxford Convocation: and on that occasion he sat down in the middle of his great speech, to read—not his notes, as was supposed at the time—but a letter from the lady who afterwards became his wife. Of the book itself it is superfluous at this distance of time to say much. It was marked by the keen insight and logical acuteness which never deserted him, but he would probably have allowed himself in later days that, if he did not exaggerate the slavery of the Church "working in chains," which he had tried and found wanting, he had at least somewhat idealized the actual working of the Church which as yet he had only had the opportunity of observing from without. The story of the conflict at Oxford in 1845 and its issue has been told too often, and from almost every point of view, to need being told again. But it may be worth while to observe that "the very interesting and amusing account" of it by the late Dean Stanley in the *Edinburgh Review*, referred to by the writer of Mr. Ward's obituary in the *Times*, was chiefly amusing for its marvellous travesty of the facts. His own accuracy may be gauged by the novel information that "the votes *were taken*, and the majority was found to be for the censure [of Tract XC.], when the Senior Proctor, the present Dean of St. Paul's, pronounced the famous words, '*Nobis procuratoribus non placet*,' and the swarm dispersed." The proctors, it ought to be unnecessary to observe, have no such autocratic power of reversing a vote of Convocation once given ; the power they have, and exercised on that memorable occasion, is to prohibit a motion they deem objectionable being put to the vote at all. Mr. Ward was deprived of his degree by a sentence, the justice of which few adherents of any religious party would now care to vindicate, and the legality of which would have been challenged, probably with success, had he cared to retain his position at Oxford. But within a few months he had vacated his fellowship by marriage, and had been received into the Roman Communion.

His marriage of course precluded him from pursuing an ecclesiastical career, but the Pope recognised his intellectual distinction by conferring on him the degree of Doctor of

Philosophy, and Cardinal Wiseman appointed him to the Chair of Dogmatic Theology—not Moral Philosophy, as the *Times* stated—at the Seminary of St. Edmund's, Herts, which he held for several years, till he came, by the death of his uncle, into a considerable property in the Isle of Wight. In most respects he would have agreed with Sir George C. Lewis, that "life would be tolerable, but for its amusements." Of operatic music, however, he was passionately fond, but he used to stop his ears, when compelled to listen to Gregorian chanting, which, he said, "always reminded him of original sin." His literary activity was not checked either by his conversion or his succession to a fortune; it constituted, in fact, his ruling passion and his main interest in life. In 1860 he published an able treatise on *Nature and Grace*, and for fifteen years he held the editorship of the *Dublin Review*, to which, as before to the *British Critic*, he was himself a copious contributor. He had been, so to speak, an Ultramontane while still an Anglican, and his Ultramontanism naturally became more pronounced in his adopted Church. We have seen already that Dr. Newman never acknowledged him as an exponent of his own views at Oxford, and in his *Letter to Dr. Pusey on the Eirenicon*, published in 1866, while commending his "energy, acuteness, and theological reading," he peremptorily asserts him to be "in no sense a spokesman for English Catholics," of whom very few "go his lengths in their view of the Pope's infallibility." His extreme theological line and his vehemence, not to say arrogance, in his way of enforcing it, frequently brought him into collision with writers of his own communion, whose dissent he could least patiently endure, notably with

Father Ryder of the Birmingham Oratory, and some of the contributors to the *Rambler* and the *Home and Foreign Review*, and he had an unpleasant habit of intimating that those who differed from him on some detail of theological opinion, or ecclesiastical or educational discipline, ought in strict consistency to be sceptics or atheists. Of his sincerity there can be no shadow of doubt, nor did he ever intend to be unfair. But in dealing with a theological opponent, who had the misfortune to be one of his co-religionists, fairness was to him a psychological impossibility. Nobody ever exemplified more consistently Warburton's dictum that " orthodoxy is my doxy ;" it was inconceivable to him that a Catholic should not be heterodox, whose " doxy " differed from his own. He may be said in a sense to represent the same type of fierce and aggressive Ultramontanism which on the continent found a mouthpiece in the late M. Veuillot. But the comparison would be doubly unjust. Ward was a deep and powerful philosophical thinker ; Veuillot was at best no more than a racy and shallow pamphleteer. And if John Knox is rightly named " the ruffian of the Reformation," Veuillot was the ruffian of modern Ultramontanism, modified of course by this difference between the conditions of the sixteenth century and the nineteenth, that Knox had command of knives and bludgeons, whereas Veuillot had to content himself with stabbing reputations—of some of the noblest of his Catholic contemporaries—with a pen habitually dipped in the acidulated quintessence of vitriol. Of Ward, overbearing and arrogant as he was apt to be in theological controversy with his fellow Catholics, it would be untrue to say this. He was not personally venomous or vindictive.

The *Times* was quite right in intimating that it was partly, if not chiefly, Ward's opposition which some years ago wrecked the scheme of founding an Oratory— not " a Roman Catholic College "—at Oxford, as a religious centre for Roman Catholic undergraduates, for which Dr. Newman had already received generous promises of support and warm assurances of sympathy from a large body of his co-religionists. Great as was Ward's admiration both personal and intellectual for his old leader, there was from first to last a marked divergence of sentiment and opinion between them. But, in spite of his keen interest in religious controversy, and pugnacious advocacy of his own side, his real greatness was always rather as a speculative thinker than a theologian. He was most at home in the Metaphysical Society, which he helped to found, and where he met and argued on equal terms with some of the first thinkers of the day, and it is not his theological but his philosophical articles in the *British Critic* and *Dublin Review* which are the likeliest to survive. He republished during life one or two volumes of the former, but all who are familiar with his series of papers on the Intuitional and Free-will controversies, directed against the theories of J. S. Mill and Herbert Spencer, whether accepting his conclusions or not, must desire to see them collected and reprinted in a permanent form ; his leading opponents, like the late Mr. Mill, never hesitated themselves to acknowledge him as a foeman worthy of their steel.[1] It is fair to add that the many controversies in which he was

---

[1] While these sheets are passing through the press, two vols. are advertised of *Essays on the Philosophy of Theism* by the late W. G. Ward.

engaged through life seldom or never involved any interruption of personal friendships, though it has often been
observed that his relations were far more cordial with
Protestants, from whom he could afford to differ, than with
" Liberal Catholics," whom he could not easily bring himself to regard as any better than traitors in the camp. In
one respect he was honourably distinguished from some of
his clerical fellow-converts who, owing to their marriage or
other circumstances, were constrained like himself to retire
into lay communion, and have been reproached with sinking into a state of intellectual apathy. It was not in
Ward's nature to suffer the edge of his intellect to rust, or
even rest for a moment, nor would he willingly let any one
who came into contact with him escape "the keen en-
counter of their wits," which he was ever on the watch to
challenge or eager to accept.

XL

DR. PUSEY AND THE OXFORD MOVEMENT.

ON the 14th of July 1883 the Tractarian Movement became entitled to celebrate its jubilee. Mr. Keble's Assize Sermon at Oxford on Sunday, July 14, 1833, marks, as Cardinal Newman has told us, what must be considered the date of its commencement, though some years had yet to elapse before it could be said to be in full swing. Nor did anything so much contribute, as the same high authority has reminded us, to its consolidation and eventual success as the accession to its ranks of the learned and saintly divine who on Sept. 18, 1882, passed away, in a ripe and honoured old age, amid the regrets of thousands of friends and disciples, and with the universal respect of his countrymen of all shades of opinion. There is room of course for comment from many points of view on a life, singularly uneventful indeed in its outward circumstances, but of such large and manifold influence on the destinies of the Church of England, and the course of religious thought in this country, that to it the hackneyed epithet of "epoch-making" might not unfitly be applied. And we may confidently anticipate that full justice will be done to a theme of such wide and varied interest in the biography now in course of preparation by the writer of all others most competent to undertake the task, as well from his intimate personal knowledge of Dr. Pusey, as from his having so largely inherited both the convictions and the influence of the teacher he loved so well. Meanwhile a few general remarks are all that can be attempted here, on the significance of a career which will retain its permanent place in the annals both of Oxford and of the religious life of England.

For more than half a century the late Professor of Hebrew at Oxford held the post to which he was appointed, at an unusually early age, in 1828, and the long and yet imperfect list of his works, copied from *Crockford*, which filled more than half a column of the obituary notice in the *Guardian*, would alone suffice to prove his unwearied and lifelong assiduity. Nor was there to the last any sign of failing power. Clearness of style was never Dr. Pusey's strong point, and for this his Hebrew, patristic, and German studies might sufficiently account; but his latest work, published only two years before his death in reply to Dr. Farrar's *Eternal Hope*, is not only one of the most masterly and decisive, but perhaps the most tersely and clearly written, that ever emanated from him. Within a few days of his death he was engaged in preparing his Hebrew lectures for the next term, though for some years past he had been unequal to the task of himself delivering either lectures or sermons, which were read by others for him. But, while throughout his long life Dr. Pusey realised the ideal of a student, in a sense which we are wont to associate rather with German than with English professors or divines, he was never a mere book-worm. To call him a party leader would convey an incorrect impression, for no one

could have less of the ambition of leadership or the spirit
of a partisan ; yet it was at bottom as true an instinct as
that which almost invariably dictates schoolboy nicknames
that identified with his name the great religious revival
commenced at Oxford fifty years ago. Mr. Newman (as
he then was) was earlier in the field, and his is unquestionably a mind of more rare and commanding genius ; yet
the attempt, made at one time by the late Dr. Arnold, to
saddle the movement with the sarcastic sobriquet of " Newmania " from the first completely failed. Whether it would
ever have been begun, or would have attained the influential position in the University and the country which it
soon acquired, without the impetus derived from his devoted
energy and transcendent powers, may well be doubted ;
but, once fairly started on its course, it has owed more in
the long run, as Cardinal Newman has himself, with characteristic generosity, been forward to remind us, " to the great
learning, immense diligence, scholastic mind, and simple
devotion to the cause of religion " of his loved and distinguished colleague, whom he " used to call ὁ μέγας."
" There was henceforth," adds the author of the *Apologia*,
" a man who could be the head and centre of the zealous
people in every part of the country who were adopting the
new opinions ; and not only so, but there was one who
furnished the movement with a front to the world, and
gained for it a recognition from other parties in the University. . . . Dr. Pusey was, to use the common expression,
a host in himself; he was able to give a name, a form, and
a personality to what was without him a sort of mob. . . .
Such was the benefit he conferred on the Movement exter-
nally ; nor was the internal advantage at all inferior to it.

B B

He was a man of large designs; he had a hopeful, sanguine mind; he had no fear of others; he was haunted by no intellectual perplexities."

When Dr. Pusey was appointed at the age of twenty-nine to the chair of Hebrew at Oxford, and first occupied the canonry house at Christ Church which was ever afterwards his home, he had already spent a considerable time in studying successively at three German universities—Jena, Göttingen, and Bonn—and had published a work on German theology, long since out of print, which incurred the charge of rationalism, chiefly, no doubt, because anything coming out of Germany was then supposed to deserve the name. It was at all events the first and last time such a charge could with any semblance of plausibility be brought against him. It is somewhat curious to recollect that the book provoked two replies from Hugh James Rose, of Cambridge, who filled a conspicuous place in the Church movement of a few years later. As a Hebrew lecturer, a preacher, and a theologian, Dr. Pusey throughout a long and laborious life resolutely and consistently maintained the cause of Christian orthodoxy against all assailants. But while circumstances rather than choice often forced on him the office of a controversialist, and his own deepest convictions made him always an unflinching upholder of the dogmatic principle, there was ever about him a largeness of mind and a depth of Christian sympathy which rendered all bitterness of feeling or expression impossible. He was often bitterly attacked, and from opposite quarters, but while he felt it his duty, not so much for his own sake as in the interests of his Church, to defend himself against charges of disloyalty which involved an arraignment of his theological position, he never bitterly retaliated. The so-called Evangelical party for many years assailed him with unsparing virulence, but when the appearance of *Essays and Reviews* seemed to him to indicate a serious menace to truths held in common by all sincere believers in the Gospel, he did not hesitate to appeal to the readers of the *Record* for sympathy and support in resisting the common enemy. The secession in 1845 of his great friend and ally, with many of his followers, brought him of necessity into what was evidently to him a most unwelcome conflict, against claims he felt unable to admit, in defence of a position about which he had never entertained a doubt. But of controversial animus against the great Communion which had attracted so many of those on whose continued support he had once confidently reckoned, or against the seceders themselves, whose fidelity to conscience he respected while he dissented from their conclusions, there is no trace in his writings, as there was none in his heart. And when the growing pressure of the Rationalistic attacks, which had prompted his appeal to the Evangelicals, seemed to call for united action on the part of all who cherished their traditional faith in Divine Revelation, not only in England but throughout Europe, he put forth, under the winning title of *An Eirenicon*, a work which, however barren of any immediate practical result, will certainly live, as an abiding monument both of deep theological learning and of calm far-sighted Christian wisdom and charity. He was never wild, paradoxical, or, in the bad sense of the word, enthusiastic; no one, begging Dr. Arnold's pardon, could be less like Don Quixote. And if he sometimes lent his great name to phases of opinion or practice which were considered

"extreme," this arose from a fault, if fault it be, which leant
to virtue's side. So far from sharing that base disposition,
on which "safe men" are apt to pride themselves, to throw
over dangerous allies, his generosity of temper, as Cardinal
Newman has somewhere observed, always inclined him
rather to go beyond than to fall short of his own deliberate
convictions, in defending those with whom he substantially
agreed, though it were to his own hindrance. He disapproved, for instance, at the time of the publication of
Tract XC., though it contained nothing to which he did
not in principle assent. But when the author was assailed
with a storm of authoritative censure and popular abuse,
he at once came forward with an elaborate and unqualified
vindication of it. So, again, at a later period, when the
Oxford movement itself had won a recognised position, and
it had become the fashion to contrast "Ritualism" with
Tractarianism, as a new and parasitical excrescence, it
might have been supposed that Dr. Pusey, who knew little
and cared less about ceremonial details—so that it has
been not inaptly said, that "to the end he remained in
practice a Berkshire country clergyman"—would at least
stand aloof from this new development, if he did not openly
condemn it. On the contrary, while mingling words of
counsel and caution with his commendations, he did not
hesitate to throw his shield over those whom he believed
to be honestly carrying out in practice—whether judiciously
or not—the principles which he had devoted his life to
reaffirming and propagating ; the fact that in doing so they
had incurred an obloquy to which "the old Tractarians,"
as they were sometimes termed in contradistinction from
their later disciples, were no longer subjected, was to him

an additional reason not for disclaiming but for acknowledging them. When Sisterhoods were a new thing in the
English Church, and were almost as universally censured
or disparaged as they are now universally accepted and
encouraged, he was the first to come forward as the spokesman and champion of this salutary revival. He was not
indifferent to the force of public opinion—though no one
less sought or cared for mere personal popularity—and
never thought it beneath him to say or do what lay in his
power to disarm unreasonable prejudice and distrust; but
he would not consent to escape unmerited criticism by the
sacrifice of his friends, even when he might think that in
particular points they were indiscreet or mistaken.

The main interest of Dr. Pusey's life, as has been already
intimated, lies in its relations to religion and to the Church
of which he was so conspicuous an ornament. And the
wonderful change, which during the last fifty years has
passed over the worship, the teaching, and the general tone
of the Anglican Church, constitutes at once its explanation
and its crowning triumph. Those who agree and those
who disagree with him must alike confess that he has not
lived in vain. On the ultimate results of the movement,
which he did so much to promote, it would be premature
as yet to pronounce any comprehensive and final verdict;
to do so would be in effect to predict the future of the
National Church, and to some extent of Christianity
throughout Europe; for it was part in fact of the general
Catholic reaction which followed on the French Revolution. But it may safely be asserted that he has left his
mark on the Communion he served so faithfully and loved
so well, as few, if any, of her prelates or divines have done

since the Reformation. Such as he found it fifty years ago it can never again become; it will be for those who come after him to decide whether or not it shall decline from the higher standard which his teaching and example so largely contributed to establish. Of his private life this is hardly the place to speak. It was uniform and monotonous in its outward course, but not wanting in severe trials and sorrows. More than forty years ago he lost a wife to whom he was deeply attached, and soon afterwards his eldest daughter; between two and three years before his death his only son was suddenly taken from him, who, in spite of what to many would be crushing bodily infirmities, had been not only a comfort and support to his father in his advancing age, but a ready and invaluable assistant in his literary labours. His sufferings from the separation, and in some cases alienation, of friends, are too well known to need being dwelt upon. But through all trials he preserved the even tenor of his course; his spirit was not soured, and his energy never flagged. His life teaches many lessons of self-denial, charity, generosity, industry, and perseverance; but perhaps the most precious memorial he has bequeathed—not to his own disciples only, but to all who, in whatever ministry of action or of thought, would "serve their generation after the counsel of God"—is the example of that unselfish singleness of purpose, which is the surest secret of success.

XLI.

THE LATE PROVOST OF ORIEL.

IT cannot exactly be said that the death of the late venerable Provost of Oriel, at the advanced age of ninety-three, removed a prominent figure from Oxford life. In the first place, Dr. Hawkins had retired eight years before from residence at Oriel, and from all active discharge of his duties as head of the College, which devolved on the Vice-Provost, Mr. Monro, who has since succeeded him. His death threw open the office for the first time to lay competition, as the canonry which formed part of its endowment has now been annexed to the ill-endowed chair of Scripture Exegesis, which happened by a curious coincidence to be also vacant at the same moment through the resignation of Dr. Liddon. But neither can it be said that the late Provost, though so long a well-known and familiar figure at Oxford, ever exercised any commanding influence as a leader of thought in the University or the Church of England generally. His tone of mind was critical and cautious rather than original, and his characteristic attitude was not such as to conciliate disciples or kindle enthusiasm. He belonged to what may be called the broader section of the old High and Dry School, and disliked innovations either religious or academical beyond a very limited range, and hence he had little sympathy with either of the two great intellectual movements, the Tractarian and the Rationalistic, which passed successively over the Oxford world of his day. Cardinal Newman's account in the *Apologia* of his personal influence over himself remarkably illustrates this temper of mind :—" He was the first who taught me to weigh my words, and to be cautious in my statements. He led me to that mode of *limiting and clearing* my sense in discussion and in controversy, and of distinguishing between cognate ideas, and of obviating mistakes by anticipation. . . . He is a man of most *exact* mind himself, and he used to snub me severely on reading, as he was kind enough to do, the first Sermons that I wrote and other compositions that I was engaged upon." He did, however, though probably beyond his own knowledge or intention, influence Mr. Newman's mind at the time in a Catholicizing direction, as well by the books he lent him as by giving him a copy of his famous University Sermon on " Unauthoritative Tradition." But the special interest of Dr. Hawkins's life lies not so much in any paramount influence which he exerted over others, as in the exceptional prominence of the men and the events he was brought into contact with during his long University career, and the marvellous changes he lived to witness during the half-century of his provostship, as well in Oriel and Oxford as in the entire social, political, and religious condition of the age. Born in the very year of the outbreak of the French Revolution, and elected to his fellowship two years before the battle of Waterloo, and to the headship of his College the year before the Catholic Emancipation Act was passed, he seems, while many who knew him intimately, and many more to whom his erect form and sharp, clear-cut face with its wreath of snow-white hair remain among their most familiar recollections, are still actively engaged in the work of life, already to belong rather to history than to the living world. Nor can it be forgotten that in his person passes away, if not by any means the greatest, the last but one—a far greater than himself—of that historic group, including Keble, Whateley, and Arnold, who combined to make the name of Oriel illustrious.

It was in 1828, the same year when Dr. Arnold, partly through his own strong recommendation, was elected head-master of Rugby, that Hawkins succeeded to the provost-ship of Oriel, in place of Copleston, author of the *Prælec-tiones Academicæ*—considered at the time a model of. Ciceronian Latinity—who had been raised to the See of Llandaff. His election strangely enough was brought about through the influence of Mr. Newman, who there-upon, succeeded him as vicar of St. Mary's, the rival candidates being Tyler, a late Fellow of the College and then a London rector, and John Keble. The latter is said to have jokingly proposed that "the Fellows should divide the prize, giving Tyler the red gown, Hawkins the work, and himself the money." But the choice really lay between Hawkins and Keble. It is idle now to speculate on the reasons which may have induced Mr. Newman to throw his whole weight on the side of Hawkins; but it is impossible not to feel, in the light of subsequent events, how much really hinged on the decision, not only as regards the fortunes of Oriel, but of the English Church. The *Christian Year*, indeed, would not in any case have been lost to the world, for it had appeared the year before ; but the later studies and energies of its author must inevitably have been directed into a somewhat different channel if, instead of going down to a country living, where he had ample leisure to devote himself to the theological and ecclesiastical questions of the day, he had, during that busy and eventful period, occupied the headship of the most conspicuous College in Oxford. Still greater might have been the difference as regards Mr. Newman's career, and the whole history of the Tractarian movement, which so largely depended on him, if his activity had not been forcibly diverted from the tutorial work of his College, to which he had keenly addicted himself, and thus driven by no seeking of his own to find satisfaction in another and wider sphere. In 1828, to cite Mr. Mozley's words, "with a Provost who owed his election to him, himself tutor, and with two other tutors, Robert Wilberforce and Hurrell Froude, entirely devoted to him," he seemed to have the College at his feet. Within two years he and his friends had found themselves compelled by the action of the new Provost to resign their tutorships. They had desired to introduce some reforms—moderate enough when compared with subsequent changes — into the College system, such as the use of modern books to illustrate the ancient classics, paying an exacter regard to the character and special gifts of each undergraduate, and establishing a closer relation between tutor and pupil. Dr. Hawkins would not hear of it ; he thought the scheme revolutionary, and moreover a menace to his own supreme authority, and "his idea," says Mr. Mozley, "was the French king's, *L'état, c'est moi*." It would even then have been an almost unprecedented stretch of authority for the Head of a College to dismiss his tutors without some better reason than a mere difference of opinion, but the Provost did what came practically to just the same thing. He "announced that no more undergraduates would be entered to their names, so that in three years they would have no classes at all," and he anticipated their resignation, which speedily followed this announcement, by a far more revolutionary innovation on existing practice than any which they had advocated, when he called in Hampden, a former Fellow who was then married, and whose Bampton Lectures six years later gained for him such an equivocal notoriety, to give the College lectures in their place.

The truth is that while his power lasted—and heads of colleges were little less than autocrats before the first University Commission—Dr. Hawkins was always apt to be somewhat arbitrary in his exercise of it, and if he was respected, he was feared rather than liked, especially by his undergraduates, whom he was much in the habit of snubbing severely, as Dr. Newman words it. A circumstance, which occurred some ten years after this affair of the tutorships, may serve to exemplify his peremptory method of procedure. In a letter to Mr. Hope, dated Nov. 10, 1841, Mr. Newman says: "Our Provost has asked a man why he was not at Chapel on Nov. 5, and because he did not like the State Service has said he will not give him testimonials for orders."[1] To give a

[1] *Memoir of J. R. Hope Scott,* vol. i. p. 315. Those who have ever heard the 5 Nov. Service—with its reiterated denunciations, in prayer after prayer, of "the hellish malice of Popish conspirators," and "all such workers of iniquity as turn religion into rebellion and faith into faction"—read in church or chapel (as I often have myself)

fresh illustration of the same temper, which occurred some twelve years later[1]: a Scholar from another College, whom he had reason to suspect of belonging to the Irvingite Community, called on the Provost before the fellowship examinations to put down his name as a candidate. He proceeded at once to cross-question his visitor closely on his religious opinions, and in spite of his assurance that he was prepared *ex animo* to subscribe the 39 Articles, and was a regular attendant at the Chapel Services and Communions, he refused to allow him to stand. "You may believe all we do," he observed, "but you believe a good deal more, and that won't do." The Provost had the absolute power of refusing permission to stand, and he would of course have been authorized and even bound at that time to reject a candidate who declined to subscribe the Anglican formularies ; but it was a very arbitrary exercise of his official rights to go behind the declaration of one who professed himself ready to comply, and in fact did comply, with all the statutable requirements of the University in the matter. On another occasion he displayed the same animus in a characteristic but amusing manner towards a member of his own College, of excellent abilities but feeble health, who had therefore felt unable to go in for classical honours. The Provost knew this well, but did not choose to recognise the plea, and accordingly took occasion one day at his own dinner-table, after the schools were over, but—as he had forgotten—before the

---

will appreciate the justice and propriety of this refusal, even supposing the Provost to have been—as he probably was not—within his statutable rights.

[1] This circumstance came directly under my own cognisance, when at Balliol, the victim being a fellow-Scholar of mine.

result was announced, to ask the offender what class he
had taken. This time he found his match ; " The class
list is not yet out, sir," was the appropriate reply, and of
course there was no more to be said.   There were other
stories current in Oriel, which need not be repeated here,
showing that, in spite of a certain old-world courtesy
of manner, his way of addressing undergraduates, and
especially freshmen, was not conciliatory ; there was something cold, incisive, and at times sarcastic about it, as may
also be said *mutatis mutandis* of his style of reading
prayers and preaching in the College Chapel.   Nor was he
very tolerant of deflections in those under his control from
his own somewhat rigid standard of practice and opinion
in matters academical or religious.   He was himself a
double first—there were only two schools in that day—and
one of his theories, not generally accepted, was that any-
body who took classical might also, if he pleased, take
mathematical honours, as the study of mathematics would
supply the requisite relaxation for the mind from classical
reading.   It was more from critical distrust of new ideas
and an instinctive dislike of enthusiasm, than from any
special reverence for the past, that, without being what is
commonly called narrow-minded, he was in all his feelings
and habits of thought cautiously conservative. *Ne quid
nimis* was a principle deeply ingrained in his moral and
intellectual nature.   Those acquainted with him will
recollect, as an instance rather of his courtesy than of the
exactness Dr. Newman ascribes to him, that, at whatever
hour they happened to meet him in the street, though it
was eleven o'clock at night, he never failed to say " Good
morning, Mr. ——," as he lifted his cap in passing.

That a man thus minded would have quite as little sympathy with the complete transformation which has passed over Oxford life during the last quarter of a century as with the great religious movement which agitated it to its depths during the quarter of a century before, will be readily understood. It is not merely that all religious tests and clerical restrictions have been swept away, though that is a reform Dr. Hawkins could not be expected to approve. But other changes, which perhaps cut still deeper, have made the Oxford of to-day a totally different place— whether better or worse there is no need here to discuss, but at least radically different—from the Oxford of 1828 or even of 1850. So vast indeed is the revolution that it is difficult to realise its having come to pass, not only within a single lifetime, but during the official rule of the same Head of a College. When Dr. Hawkins became Provost the first faint whispers of the Tractarian controversy had not yet been heard, and the great leader of the movement, which was so powerfully to affect both Oxford and England, was known only as an active College tutor of intellectual promise and Evangelical opinions. He was Provost still when that movement was succeeded by another of a very different kind which, through the instrumentality of three successive Commissions, has revolutionized the whole discipline and life of Oxford. The system both of teaching and of examination has been completely remodelled, and a new professoriate created ; the University has in various ways been developed at the expense of the Colleges, and a new element independent of Colleges altogether, in the person of the "unattached," called or recalled into academical existence,

which had its place indeed in mediæval Oxford, but has
been unknown there for the last three centuries; the
internal government and mutual relations of the Colleges
to each other have undergone important modifications,
while they have lost or are losing much of their old individuality of character and *esprit de corps*, through the
introduction of married Fellows and other causes, the full
result of which yet remains to be worked out. All these
changes the late Provost lived to witness, and in the carrying out of the greater part of them he was called to take
an active, though often perhaps an unwilling, part. And
the first ominous signs had already become manifest, after
his withdrawal from Oxford, but before his death, of a
yet more startling and sweeping revolution, not only in
academic but social life in England, which threatens to
reproduce in sober earnest on the banks of the Isis and
the Cam the poet's satiric dream of " prudes for proctors,
dowagers for deans, and sweet girl graduates ; " but with
a view the precise opposite of the Princess Ida's, who
"would make it death for any male thing but to peep at "
them, whereas "mixed education," in a sense our fathers
would have shuddered at, is now the central aim.[1] What
Provost Hawkins would have thought of such a programme
it is not difficult to conceive. He probably too during his
later years was inclined to fear, with the last of that
illustrious Oriel phalanx who still survives him, that
" Phaeton had got into the chariot of the sun " ; but so

---

[1] It is significant that an English dean, wiser in his generation than
St. Paul, has recently advocated the right of women to enter the
Christian ministry and to preach; whether they are also to administer
Sacraments is not yet explained.

long as health and strength remained to him for the administration of his Collegiate office—and he was eighty-five before he dropped the reins—he acquiesced calmly, if not cheerfully, in the new condition of things, which reduced the Provost from almost an autocrat into little more than *primus inter pares*. It was a trying ordeal for one of his temperament and antecedents, and we have the testimony of those who knew him best during those latter years at Oxford that he bore the trial well. It may even have served to evoke and strengthen those nobler elements of his nature, which had not always been so manifest on the surface, but which in earlier days had attracted, as Cardinal Newman assures us, his hearty love. He was the last survivor, not only of a generation, but of a class which has passed away. For the Heads of Houses, as he had known them, were a class who dwelt apart, like the denizens of the Homeric Olympus, in an awful solitude, and wielded a power that could not easily be reckoned with or restrained. It would be a libel to say of them—least of all could it be said of a man so energetic as Dr. Hawkins —that they " lay beside their nectar," but there was about them as a class a stately and somewhat frigid grandeur, an air of *otium cum dignitate*, though it was often a learned leisure, which seemed to belong to a bygone day. At all events, whether we regret it or not, that peculiar type of academical dignity, with which many still in middle life were once familiar, and which was not without its merits or its charm, is extinct in modern Oxford. Its last representative was laid to his rest, on one of the closing days of November, 1882, under the shadow of Rochester Cathedral.

XLII

ARCHBISHOP TAIT.

IT has been said, and said truly, that Archbishop Tait, though not a great theologian, or a great statesman, or a great bishop, was yet a great man. And it is also true that he has left his mark on the Church of England more really than any primate since the time of Laud, who in all other respects was sufficiently unlike him. It cannot therefore be objected that the commendation bestowed on him by a writer in the *Quarterly Review* (for January 1883), who somewhat ostentatiously posed as the representative of "the old High Church Party," as "opposed to the Ritualists," is too high; but his panegyrist praises him, if not too well, not too wisely either; his least estimable peculiarities are exalted into virtues, while his real merits are to a large extent overlooked. Both in matters great and small the reviewer seems to have misconceived the character and aims of the late Archbishop. Neither in his line of action nor of thought can he be called "the pupil of Arnold"—and he was of course not Arnold's pupil in any more literal sense—nor can he be said, except in the most vague and general way, to have been engaged in "carrying into effect the spirit of Arnold's life." He was indeed a warm admirer of Arnold, but a paper he

C C

contributed shortly before his death to *Macmillan* shows
how entirely he had miscalculated both the nature and
range of Arnold's influence, which, considerable as it
was, was always purely personal. It is odd again to
select as one of his distinctive excellences " an eye for
the humorous aspect of any situation," which the
reviewer no less oddly holds to be eminently the privilege of Scotchmen, forgetful apparently of a familiar
proverb on the subject, which points quite the other way ;
that he " did not exhibit," and did not possess, " the high
logical and speculative power characteristic of the Scottish
race" is perfectly true, as also that he did possess a tact
and strong common sense which for practical purposes
might often stand him in better stead. The article throughout, in spite of several rather too studied disclaimers,
betrays a manifest tendency to represent the suppression
of Ritualism as the crowning aim and glory of his episcopate and primacy, and to slur over or minimize the virtual
acknowledgment he made, with characteristic candour and
generosity, on his death-bed, that in the legislative action
which he had promoted with that view some years before
he had fallen into a serious mistake. It sounds rather
strange, by the by, after the revelations on the subject,
however indiscreetly published, in the *Life of Bishop
Wilberforce,* to say that " Mr. Disraeli, in nominating
Bishop Tait, who had been a decided Liberal in politics (to
the primacy), set an honourable example of subordinating
political to religious considerations in ecclesiastical appointments." That is precisely what, if we may trust Bishop
Wilberforce's testimony, he would not have done if he had
been allowed his own way in the matter, and certainly was

not in the habit of doing. On one point, however, it is pleasant to be able to agree with the reviewer, when he speaks of the universal "expression of admiration, affection, and profound regret, on the part of the Church and nation at large," evoked by the death of the late Primate ; and the tribute was not undeserved. In the main, and putting aside the silly sneer at the party which is the *bête noir* of the writer, the following statement is a just one :—

By common consent, not excluding that of the narrow clique who alone expressed any hostile feelings towards him, he asserted the influence and dignity of the great office with which he was entrusted, with a success which few of his predecessors, and none of his immediate predecessors, had attained. They had, indeed, all been men of beautiful personal character, of mild wisdom, and of laborious devotion to their duties. But Archbishop Tait added to all these excellences, by a touch like that of genius, something which at once raised the office to a higher point of influence. He was felt not merely to be the official head of the Church, but to be the true representative of the Church to the nation at large. He was a leader as well as a ruler ; and the Church in his person exerted an influence which awakened a friendly response from every class of his countrymen, whether members of its communion or not. He was not merely a living power himself; he made his office a living power, and animated it with a new spirit.

But the chief interest of the article lies in a question which the writer asks, but scarcely attempts to answer, and certainly fails to answer at all to the purpose ; "What was the secret of this remarkable achievement ?" It did not at all events consist in the alleged fact that "Archbishop Tait had been almost a Primate in the post from which he was translated "—namely, the bishopric of London ; for, in the first place, this is not a fact ; and secondly, if it had been, so far from explaining his subsequent influence,

it would itself require explanation.   Laud, during his
tenure of the see of London, was "almost Primate" under
the feeble rule of Abbot, and there is quite enough in his
character and antecedents to account for it.   But the only
person who during Bishop Tait's episcopate at London,
and indeed during the earlier years of his archiepiscopate,
could with any accuracy be called "almost Primate" was
Bishop Wilberforce.   And nobody, to his credit be it
spoken, was readier than himself to admit it.   There is
excellent authority for saying that, when the late Canon
Ashwell, in preparing the first volume of the *Life*, applied
to the Archbishop for any letters he might have of Bishop
Wilberforce's, promising of course to publish nothing without his sanction, the answer was a free permission to make
any use of the correspondence he pleased, coupled with the
observation, "I wish it to be clearly understood who was
the true primate of the Church of England while Bishop
Wilberforce lived."   The reply illustrates a side of the late
Archbishop's character, not perhaps always as fully recognised as it deserved to be, but which could not fail to
impress all who were brought into personal contact with
him, and must have had something to do with the universal
respect and confidence he inspired.   Under a cold and
somewhat stern exterior—more commonly associated with
the Scotch temperament than a sense of humour—he concealed a warmth and generosity of heart, the more admirable
from his lack of imaginative power ;   for sympathy is of
course more natural to men of a lively imagination, who
can readily enter into a state of mind different from their
own.   His friendships were warm and constant ; little or
nothing has been heard of his enmities.   Two of his old

Oxford friends, whose religious opinions he not only did not agree with, but could hardly even understand—for his religious sentiment was very much of the Presbyterian type, as was natural from his early training—became Roman Catholics ; but neither their change of communion, nor his own subsequent elevation to high ecclesiastical dignity, led to any interruption of friendship or friendly intercourse between them. It was due to the same habit of mind that he had a sincere respect and love of goodness in his own Church, even when it took a shape quite out of harmony with his personal convictions. And hence, in spite of the trenchant denunciations of Ritualism both in his London and Canterbury Charges, to which the reviewer refers with so much satisfaction, he was throughout tolerant, and more than tolerant, of individual Ritualists, whom he knew to be zealous, as he would say, in preaching " the great Gospel truths " and earnestly labouring for the souls of men. No Ritualist prosecution was ever, it is said, instituted with his sanction in the diocese either of London or of Canterbury. Mr. Mackonochie, for one, has publicly acknowledged, in terms honourable alike to the Archbishop and to himself, the kindness and sympathy he always received from him as his diocesan. Nor was it possible for any one brought into intimate relations with him, whether agreeing or not with his opinions, to doubt the reality of his piety. On the other hand, he had a breadth of view and discernment of the vast possibilities of his high office, not common of late among Anglican prelates, which is indicated in a remarkable passage the reviewer cites from his last Charge in London, but was far more prominently shown after his translation to the primacy ; and he was probably the first Bishop of London who did not think his dignity compromised by going to preach to the religious pariahs of his huge diocese in an omnibus yard :—

How far is the national Church of England, and especially the Church of this Diocese, fulfilling the work which Christ has committed to it, and how are we each of us fulfilling our own part ? The national Church and the Church of this Diocese—for, indeed, it is as difficult to separate the two as it is to separate the diocese from its particular parishes, and the parishes from those who minister in them. *London, above all other dioceses, must be indissolubly connected with the whole national Church.* We do not ignore those powerful elements of the softening influences of country life, not found among ourselves ; nor the effect of the position, so different from ours, in which the country Clergy stand to their flocks ; nor the vast power of University life, moulding the thoughts of our rising youth. But still London is the centre : to London flows yearly, in a steady tide, a large body of persons of all classes from every county : from London the stream of influence, however unobserved, sets in irresistibly, through newspapers, books, letters, the converse of friends, to hall, parsonage, farmhouse, and cottage, in the remotest country districts. If we in London are faithless, all England suffers. If London could but become the really Christian centre of the nation, how would our national Christianity grow !

One sentence is here italicized, by way both of emphasis and of contrast. If Bishop Tait regarded the see of London as in one sense the centre of the life of the National Church, he learnt afterwards to regard the see of Canterbury as the centre of a still wider organization. From the first he had insisted that the Primate required the aid of a Suffragan, because of his immense correspondence from all parts of the world, and "the care of all the Churches" in communion with the see of Canterbury, which was in some sort laid upon him ; it would be curious, indeed, to compare his language on the subject with that of some of the most eminent of the early and mediæval Popes. Nor would it be too much to say that there was about his conception of his primatial office a certain Hildebrandine element, in the best sense of the term, in spite of his entire absence of sympathy with mediævalism. The Archbishop of Canterbury has sometimes been designated, whether in jest or earnest, *alterius orbis Papa*, but until the last half-century, when an Anglican Colonial episcopate began to be formed, such a title could have little meaning. It is anyhow certain that, although the phrase may never have occurred to him, Archbishop Tait was the first to seize the situation, with what looks like an intuition of genius. And it is the more remarkable, considering his somewhat Presbyterian type of mind, that he should have been so forward, not indeed to magnify himself—that was not at all his way —but to magnify his office. This estimate of its grandeur was most emphatically proclaimed when, in 1878, he addressed "from the chair of St. Augustine" in his metropolitan Cathedral the prelates assembled from all parts of the world in the second Pananglican Conference, who found, as the *Church Quarterly* expressed it at the time, their "natural Patriarchate at Canterbury."

It is not intended here to offer any complete reply to the question which the *Quarterly Review* leaves unanswered, as to the secret of Archbishop Tait's extensive influence. Nor would it indeed be easy to define with any precision how it came to pass that one, who was not a learned theologian, or a deep thinker, or a born ruler of men, conciliated to himself in his lifetime so general a homage from different

parties in the Church of England and from some outside
its pale, as was testified by an exceptional unanimity in
the effort to pay honour to his memory. That there were
weak points in his character and his policy few of his
admirers would deny. He never understood the importance
of dogma, and was thus quite incapable of appreciating the
value of such a document *e. g.* as the Athanasian Creed, of
which another Broad Church prelate of more philosophical
mind, Bishop Cotton of Calcutta, had learnt to form a juster
estimate. It was due to the same defect of intellectual
insight, not to any intentional unfairness, still less to .any
personal jealousies or caprice, that his whole view of the
Oxford movement, which he expounded in an article already
mentioned in *Macmillan's Magazine*, was both superficial
and inexact. The paper reveals throughout at once the
nobility of his nature, and his inaptitude for speculative
discussion. His notion that the Tractarians are responsible
for the scepticism of modern Oxford—which they alone
foresaw, and did their best to guard against—and that it
might have been averted by a wider acceptance of Dr.
Arnold's "reasonable and large-hearted *system of Christian
teaching*"—when in fact he had no system at all—is curiously
characteristic. It is perfectly true that Arnold is unjustly
charged with being himself a sceptic, or "the father of
scepticism," but the notorious scepticism of some of his
leading disciples is not unjustly attributed, in part at least,
to his entire want of any theological system. To return
to the Archbishop ;—many, no doubt, in the words of the
Quarterly reviewer, did not consider "that he duly appreciated the importance of the Apostolic organization which
the Church of England inherits, or the extent to which

her just claims on the nation are founded upon it."
Others thought he did not go far enough in a contrary
direction. But the conviction was shared alike by men of
the most opposite schools, by those who agreed and those
who disagreed with him—by Archdeacon Denison, who
has taken a prominent part in the movement for organizing
a memorial fund, no less than by Dean Stanley—that he
had at heart the best interests of his Church as he understood them, and that there was nothing mean or petty or
personal about his aims. They felt that he was, in
Scripture phrase, "a good man and a just." In spite of
some conspicuous mistakes, chiefly in the earlier period
of his episcopal career, which he would probably have
afterwards himself acknowledged and deplored, he was
generous in his estimates of his clergy and of their work.
He was not one of those men who are made great by their
office, but one of those who make their office great; and
the dignity of a grand position, too often feebly sustained,
has undoubtedly been enhanced in his hands. He did
much to recover for it the influence and prestige which had
been seriously compromised by the otiose incompetence,
diversified by some rather ludicrous blunders, of his penul-
timate predecessor. He was more than liberal in his
charities, and nobly upheld the traditional repute of Lam-
beth for a dignified and gracious hospitality. Thus much
will be admitted on all sides. While it is difficult to
analyse more exactly the secret of his power, it remains
true that he had in him the elements both of moral and
intellectual greatness.

XLIII

DEAN CLOSE AND THE EVANGELICALS.

THE death of Dean Close, in December 1882, removed not exactly the last of the Evangelicals—for Bishop Ryle still lives and reigns at Liverpool—but the last surviving patriarch of the old Evangelical party. When we reflect that Dr. Close was born before the end of the last century, and took his degree in 1820 at Cambridge, where he was the contemporary of Thirlwall, Hare, and Whewell, and a disciple of Simeon, it will be perceived at once that he lived to witness the triumph and the decline of what in his earlier years was the rising, and became afterwards for a time the dominant, party in the Church of England, as well as the origin and gradual increase of the great religious movement destined to supersede it. When he was ordained, the old High Church party was supposed to be in its dotage ; a leading bishop of the day was credibly reported to have said he could count on his fingers the men who believed in its most distinctive tenet. High Churchmanship had come in fact to be generally looked upon as little else than a negative protest against " Methodism," which loved orthodoxy less than it hated enthusiasm, and cared more for port wine than for either its hatreds or its loves, while of the future Tractarian school there was as yet no sign or surmise. And yet Dr. Close outlived one venerable leader of the movement, who passed away three months before him amid the universal regrets of the Church he had so long and so faithfully served, while another, who had once taken a still more prominent part in its guidance, survives him as an octogenarian Cardinal. It is in truth in the historical review it inevitably suggests, rather than in any special significance attaching to his own career, that the main interest of Dr. Close's life is to be sought. He was for above thirty years the incumbent of Cheltenham, where he gained his reputation as a leading Evangelical preacher, and is said to have ruled the town with a rod of iron. Mr. Clough, when Tutor of Oriel, used to illustrate a passage in the *Clouds* of Aristophanes by the "1700 pairs of slippers," which Dr. Close was said to receive annually from his female devotees. It is curious that one of his Evangelical colleagues at Cheltenham, the late Dr. Boyd, like himself, became a dean; curious, because, if there is one position more than another where an Evangelical preacher would seem to be the wrong man in the wrong place, that position is a deanery. One naturally associates with the idea of a Cathedral a stately edifice, solemn ritual, choral worship, and frequent services, and these are precisely the things against which Evangelicalism has raised a constant and angry protest. One of Dr. Close's most famous sermons bore the ominous title of *Restoration of Churches the Restoration of Popery*, and yet nearly all our old English Cathedrals—not indeed including that over which he was afterwards called to preside— have undergone during the last few decades this Popish process of restoration. It looked like a kind of irony of· fate when it fell to Dean Boyd's lot to figure as the official apologist for the "idolatrous" images in the new Exeter

reredos, which a more consistent representative of his party
had vainly striven to abolish.   It is not recorded that any
such incongruous task devolved on Dean Close, or indeed
that the twenty-five years of dignified repose, which Lord
Palmerston's bestowal of the post secured for him at
"merry Carlisle," were otherwise signalized than by his
adding to his lifelong denunciations of "Tractarianism,
Ritualism, and Rationalism," a fresh and still fiercer philip-
pic against "those twin vampires of human existence, beer
and tobacco."   The nave and cloisters of Carlisle were
destroyed by the Puritans during the wars of the Commonwealth, and Dean Close was hardly the man to undertake
to rebuild them, even supposing such an enterprise to
be feasible.   Nor was it likely that the choral arrangements, for which the Cathedral had not before been
remarkable, would specially prosper in his hands; in that,
as in other respects, he left the task of reform to his
successors.   But Lord Palmerston's premiership was distinguished by a wholesale promotion of Evangelical deans
and Bishops—a circumstance remembered for good by the
Record, when after his death some *advocatus diaboli* thought
proper, with questionable taste, to raise a discussion in its
columns as to the religious character and "eternal prospects" of their patron.   And Dr. Close and Dr. Hugh
McNeile, who passed away before him, were the two most
conspicuous, and therefore most conspicuously misplaced,
among the Palmerstonian Deans.

It is difficult for the present generation to realise the
Evangelicalism of fifty or sixty years ago.   It has been
photographed, or rather daguerrotyped, with the touch of
a keen, if by no means sympathetic, observer in Mozley's
Reminiscences; and thousands of readers probably have

sighed or smiled over his typical portrait of the Evangelical
Vicar of St. Werburgh's, Derby, who " resided in a pretty
villa, surrounded by extensive grounds, out of his parish,
and a good step out of the town "; was never seen in his
parish except on Sundays, and " knew absolutely nothing
of his parishioners ; " while he " deputed to a wealthy
tradesman of the strongest and bitterest Evangelical principles the selection of his curates," who preached, like
their vicar, " nothing more than the coarse blasphemies of
the market-place put into longer words and strung into
sentences," and were never supposed to let " their tone falter
into mercy and grace." That is one side of the picture,
and no doubt Mr. Mozley may be trusted for the accuracy
of his personal recollections ; but there is also another side
to it, which ought in fairness to be kept in mind. Whatever they may have afterwards become, the Evangelicals in
their origin were the religious party of the day, who strove,
according to their lights, to revive a spirit of devotion in a
cold and apathetic age, and in certain respects their position
may be compared *mutatis mutandis*—though Dr. Close
would have recoiled in horror from the suggestion—to that
of the modern Ritualists. Each party in turn has drawn
on itself not only the rancorous abuse of theological opponents, but the still more indiscriminate and often calumnious
censure of a class of critics, whose one religious maxim is
to shun the danger of being righteous overmuch, and who
mentally translate the old saying that the cowl does not
make the monk into the portentous aphorism that all
religious professors, if you scratch the surface, will be found
to be hypocrites at bottom. There are, perhaps, not many
of this generation who ever read, and there may be some
who never heard of, a tale which had a great run in its day,

by Mrs. Trollope, mother of the brilliant novelist whose loss all England was not long ago deploring, published about half a century ago under the title of *The Vicar of Wrexhill*. It was almost avowedly designed as a caricature of a well-known Evangelical clergyman of the day, not free indeed from some of the little weaknesses of his school, who has long since gone to his rest justly honoured by all who knew him, and whom it is impossible to believe that the authoress—who had herself known him well—can have really identified with the coarse and sanctimonious villain depicted as the hero of her story.   However, the book was intended, and accepted at the time, as at worst a perfectly legitimate caricature, by that section of society which Evangelicals designate "the world."   And it is curious to observe how strikingly its tone is recalled to memory, in spite of the utter unlikeness of all the details, by a stupid and offensive anti-Ritualist novel published some years ago, entitled *Under which Lord?*   The Ritualistic vicar is not, like his predecessor of Wrexhill, represented as a downright swindler and profligate—that in the present day would hardly have been tolerated—but each alike is a monster of spiritual pride and oleaginous hypocrisy, leading captive silly women, whom for his own selfish purposes he entices into his net ; and each alike too is reproached, though of course for very opposite reasons, with unfaithfulness to his own Church.   The Evangelicals were not really to blame for raising a higher standard of devotion in a singularly worldly and apathetic age, nor even exactly for the indisputable "simplicity" or "scantiness" of the message which, as Mr. Mozley justly complains, comprised their very defective and arbitrary summary of Scripture teaching, but because, when its meagreness and inadequacy had been demonstrated, they persistently refused to abandon or correct their *mumpsimus*. Justification by faith only and personal assurance might or might not be theological truths—we are not concerned with that question here—but a doctrine which came to be virtually embodied in the popular doggerel, "Doing, deadly doing, doing ends in death," was clearly shown to be a practical falsehood. "As to the effect of this preaching repeated Sunday after Sunday," says Mr. Mozley, speaking from his own experience, "it was simply none. . . . As often as not everybody was asleep, except a few too stupid to be ever quite awake or quite asleep. The sermon was *brutum fulmen*." And hence the sceptre gradually passed from the grasp of the Evangelical school to those who had studied not Scripture only, but Church history and human nature, more deeply than their teachers. Or it would perhaps be more correct to say that a change passed over the spirit of the party, viewed not as a religious system but as a body of living men, for with only two exceptions—Mr. Keble and Mr. Isaac Williams—every one of the Tractarian leaders, and without an exception every single leading convert, had been brought up an Evangelical; and the same might be said of many who are prominent among the Ritualists of our own day.

From the standpoint of their rivals, the collapse of the Evangelical movement was explicable enough, for whereas Christianity is summed up in Scripture under the attributes of grace and truth, Evangelicalism ignored or rejected the ecclesiastical authority of faith and the sacramental channels of grace, and therefore it only needed the lapse of time to exhibit the radical defects of the system. The startling divergence *e.g.* between the career of Mr. Wilberforce and of those who were trained under his roof, but were afterwards "scattered far and wide," might be considered to illustrate at once the reality of his faith and the deficiencies of his creed.   Be that as it may, no religious man can well refuse his sympathy to what took rise in a reaction from the cold indifferentism of the "*sæculum rationalisticum*," which had Cornwallis and Hoadley for its representative prelates. Something is due to the piety which roused itself at such a period of spiritual stagnation to form the Church Missionary.Society and abolish the Slave Trade, and whose earliest protest was not directed against any form of Catholic principle, but against a negation of all Christian principle, whether of faith or life.   Wesleyanism had been cast out of the Establishment, not so much for the errors with which it was legitimately chargeable as for the moral earnestness intolerable to "a Church dying of dignity," as some of its most zealous champions afterwards confessed ; but Evangelicalism succeeded in making good its footing within the pale.   Where it failed was at a subsequent stage, when the negative and antagonistic elements became, in fact, the determining characteristics of the school.   The diminutive washing-stand, which served as a font, wheeled into the darkest corner of the church, or the tiny slop-basin, placed on "the communion-table," when required for use, while the old font was perhaps relegated to uses vile in the vicarage garden ; the table itself, covered with a worm-eaten cloth, and concealed behind the hideous three-decker which descended in stories, "small by degrees and beautifully less," from preacher to parson, and from parson to clerk, and sometimes used as a receptacle for the hats of contiguous sitters—kneeling was out of fashion then ;—such phenomena outraged alike all sense of æsthetic fitness and of religious reverence.   And the teaching became gradually

as meagre and negative as the ritual.   Much of the earlier
zeal of the movement had been drained off into Tractarian
channels, and much of its intelligence was merged in the
Broad Church theology which consistent " Recordites," like
the late Dr. Close, abhorred.   The residuum presented the
ungracious appearance of a party clinging to the letter but
unmindful of the spirit of its traditionary past ; loud in
invective, but feeble in argument ; desperately striving to
maintain its popularity, not so much by raising the world
to the level of the Gospel as by accommodating the Gospel
to the standard of the world ; which had lost the original
fervour of its preaching, without reforming the coldness of
its worship, and would fain compensate for the poverty of
its theology by the narrow exclusiveness of its creed.   This
was the spectacle presented as time went on to external
observers by the party, which had thriven under neglect
and persecution, but proved unequal to the subtler trial of
prosperity and the fatal temptation to persecute in its turn.
It triumphed, when struggling to vindicate the powers of a
paralysed Christianity ; it failed in the suicidal effort to
arrest a larger movement, springing from its midst, in
vindication of the rights and functions of the Christian
Church.   It is a far cry from William Wilberforce and
"Fletcher of Madeley" to the Church Association, and
" the three aggrieved " in buckram.   There is no need now
to reopen the discussion raised by Dean Close himself in
the *Times* a year or two before his death, whether the
Evangelical party as such has ceased to exist.   It is quite
certain that it has ceased to dominate, and that it has supplied abundant recruits to the rival forces of " Ritualism "
and " Rationalism ", against which he made it his life's

D D

business to contend. If it be true that " he was the Pope of Cheltenham, with pontifical prerogatives from which the temporal had not been severed," there can be no sort of doubt that in the absolutism of that Protestant pontificate, neither at Cheltenham nor elsewhere, has he any success- ors. He was not exactly "the last of the Mohicans," but he was the last surviving representative of an age when Broad Church as yet was not, and when his party held their own on equal terms against their High Church rivals. Few men in their early career took a more active part in resistance to Tractarianism than the great prelate who preceded Dr. Close by a fortnight in his passage to the grave ; it must have been a painful, if not instructive, reflection to him in his last hours on earth, that Archbishop Tait had laboured almost with his dying breath to recon- cile the feuds he had once deemed to be irreconcilable. There could hardly have been a more significant announce- ment, not perhaps that the Evangelical party is extinct, but that the cause, which Dean Close had learnt virtually to identify with the Gospel, has become a thing of the past. Evangelicalism did its work when that work was needed; the grand mistake of its professors was their inability to understand that others had entered into their labours and their task was done.

THE END.

11, *Henrietta Street, Covent Garden, W.C.*
(*Late* 193, *Piccadilly, W.*)

March, 1884.

CATALOGUE OF BOOKS

.

PUBLISHED BY

CHAPMAN & HALL,

LIMITED,

INCLUDING

DRAWING EXAMPLES, DIAGRAMS, MODELS, INSTRUMENTS, ETC.

ISSUED UNDER THE AUTHORITY OF

THE SCIENCE AND ART DEPARTMENT, SOUTH KENSINGTON,

FOR THE USE OF SCHOOLS AND ART AND SCIENCE CLASSES.

MILITARY BIOGRAPHIES.

Messrs. CHAPMAN & HALL are preparing for publication a Series of Volumes dedicated to the Lives of Great Military Commanders.

The volumes are designed to form a set of critical Biographies, illustrative of the operations and the art of war, by writers of distinction in the profession of arms, whose competence to weigh the military qualities and deeds of the Chiefs can be accepted. Maps will, when necessary, accompany the volumes, for the convenience of students.

The aim of these volumes is to be both popular and scientific, combining the narrative of the most romantic and instructive of human lives with a clear examination of the genius of the soldier.

The first volume, "FREDERICK THE GREAT," by Col. C. B. BRACKENBURY, containing Maps, will appear in March.

"MARSHAL LOUDON," by Col. MALLESON, C.S.I., will follow it; the two Lives presenting the opposing aspects of the Seven Years' War.

BOOKS

PUBLISHED BY

CHAPMAN & HALL, LIMITED.

ABBOTT (*EDWIN*), *formerly Head Master of the Philological School*—
A CONCORDANCE OF THE ORIGINAL POETICAL
WORKS OF ALEXANDER POPE. Medium 8vo, 21s.

ADAMS (*FRANCIS*)—
HISTORY OF THE ELEMENTARY SCHOOL CON-
TEST IN ENGLAND. Demy 8vo, 6s.

BADEN-POWELL (*GEORGE*)—
STATE AID AND STATE INTERFERENCE. Illus-
trated by Results in Commerce and Industry. Crown 8vo, 9s.

BARTLEY (*G. C. T.*)—
A HANDY BOOK FOR GUARDIANS OF THE POOR.
Crown 8vo, cloth, 3s.
THE PARISH NET: HOW IT'S DRAGGED AND
WHAT IT CATCHES. Crown 8vo, cloth, 7s. 6d.
THE SEVEN AGES OF A VILLAGE PAUPER. Crown
8vo, cloth, 5s.

BAYARD: HISTORY OF THE GOOD CHEVALIER,
SANS PEUR ET SANS REPROCHE. Compiled by the LOYAL SERVITEUR;
translated into English from the French of Loredan Larchey. With over 200
Illustrations. Royal 8vo, 21s.

BEESLEY (*EDWARD SPENCER*)—
CATILINE, CLODIUS, AND TIBERIUS. Large crown
8vo, 6s.

BELL (*DR. JAMES*), *Principal of the Somerset House Laboratory*—
THE CHEMISTRY OF FOODS. With Microscopic
Illustrations.
PART I. TEA, COFFEE, SUGAR, ETC. Large crown 8vo, 2s. 6d.
PART II. MILK, BUTTER, CEREALS, PREPARED STARCHES, ETC.
Large Crown 8vo, 3s.

BENNET (*WILLIAM*) *The Late*—
KING OF THE PEAK: a Romance. With Portrait.
Crown 8vo, 6s.

BENSON (*W.*)—
MANUAL OF THE SCIENCE OF COLOUR. Coloured
Frontispiece and Illustrations. 12mo, cloth, 2s. 6d.
PRINCIPLES OF THE SCIENCE OF COLOUR. Small
4to, cloth, 15s.

BINGHAM (*CAPT. THE HON. D.*)—
NAPOLEON'S DESPATCHES. 3 vols. demy 8vo. [*In the Press.*

BIRDWOOD (*SIR GEORGE C. M.*), *C.S.I.*—
THE INDUSTRIAL ARTS OF INDIA. With Map and
174 Illustrations. New Edition. Demy 8vo, 14s.

BLACKIE (*JOHN STUART*) *F.R.S.E.*—
ALTAVONA: FACT AND FICTION FROM MY LIFE
IN THE HIGHLANDS. Third Edition. Crown 8vo, 6s.

BLAKE (*EDITH OSBORNE*)—
THE REALITIES OF FREEMASONRY. Demy 8vo, 9s.

BLATHERWICK (*DR.*)—
PERSONAL RECOLLECTIONS OF PETER STONNOR,
Esq. With Illustrations by JAMES GUTHRIE and A. S. BOYD. Crown 8vo, 6s.

BOYLE (FREDERICK)—
ON THE BORDERLAND—BETWIXT THE REALMS
OF FACT AND FANCY. Crown 8vo, 10s. 6d.

BRADLEY (THOMAS), of the Royal Military Academy, Woolwich—
ELEMENTS OF GEOMETRICAL DRAWING. In Two
Parts, with Sixty Plates. Oblong folio, half bound, each Part 16s.

BRAY (MRS.)—
AUTOBIOGRAPHY OF (born 1789, died 1883).
Author of the "Life of Thomas Stothard, R.A.," "The White Hoods," &c.
Edited by JOHN A. KEMPE. With Portraits. Crown 8vo, 10s. 6d.

MRS. BRAY'S NOVELS AND ROMANCES.
New and Revised Editions, with Frontispieces.

THE WHITE HOODS; a Romance of Flanders.	THE TALBA; or, The Moor of Portugal.
DE FOIX; a Romance of Bearn.	THE PROTESTANT; a Tale of the Times of Queen Mary.

NOVELS FOUNDED ON TRADITIONS OF DEVON AND
CORNWALL.

FITZ OF FITZFORD; a Tale of Destiny.	WARLEIGH; or, The Fatal Oak.
HENRY DE POMEROY.	COURTENAY OF WALREDDON.
	HARTLAND FOREST AND ROSE-
TRELAWNY OF TRELAWNE.	TEAGUE.

MISCELLANEOUS TALES.
A FATHER'S CURSE AND A DAUGHTER'S SACRIFICE.
TRIALS OF THE HEART.

BROADLEY (A. M.)—
HOW WE DEFENDED ARABI AND HIS FRIENDS.
A Story of Egypt and the Egyptians. Illustrated by FREDERICK VILLIERS.
Second Edition. Demy 8vo. 12s.

BUCKLAND (FRANK)—
LOG-BOOK OF A FISHERMAN AND ZOOLOGIST.
Third Edition. With numerous Illustrations. Crown 8vo, 5s.

BURCHETT (R.)—
DEFINITIONS OF GEOMETRY. New Edition. 24mo,
cloth, 5d.
LINEAR PERSPECTIVE, for the Use of Schools of Art.
Twenty-first Thousand. With Illustrations. Post 8vo, cloth, 7s.
PRACTICAL GEOMETRY: The Course of Construction
of Plane Geometrical Figures. With 137 Diagrams. Eighteenth Edition. Post
8vo, cloth, 5s.

BURNAND (F. C.), B.A., Trin. Coll. Camb.—
THE "A. D. C.;" being Personal Reminiscences of the
University Amateur Dramatic Club, Cambridge. Second Edition. Demy 8vo, 12s.

CAMPION (J. S.).—
ON THE FRONTIER. Reminiscences of Wild Sports,
Personal Adventures, and Strange Scenes. With Illustrations. Second Edition.
Demy 8vo, 16s.
ON FOOT IN SPAIN. With Illustrations. Second Edition.
Demy 8vo, 16s.

CARLYLE (THOMAS)—See pages 18 and 19.
CARLYLE BIRTHDAY BOOK (THE). Prepared by
Permission of Mr. THOMAS CARLYLE. Small crown, 3s.

CHAMPEAUX (ALFRED)—
TAPESTRY. With Woodcuts. Cloth, 2s. 6d.

CHRISTIANITY AND COMMON SENSE. A Plea for the
Worship of our Heavenly Father, and also for the Opening of Museums and
Galleries on Sundays. By a BARRISTER. Demy 8vo, 7s. 6d.

CHURCH (A. H.), M.A., Oxon.—

PLAIN WORDS ABOUT WATER. Illustrated. Large
crown 8vo, sewed, 6d.

FOOD: A Short Account of the Sources, Constituents,
and Uses of Food. Large crown 8vo, cloth, 3s.

PRECIOUS STONES: considered in their Scientific and
Artistic Relations. With Illustrations. Large crown 8vo, 2s. 6d.

CLINTON (R. H.)—

A COMPENDIUM OF ENGLISH HISTORY, from the
Earliest Times to A.D. 1872. With Copious Quotations on the Leading Events and
the Constitutional History, together with Appendices. Post 8vo, 7s. 6d.

COBDEN, RICHARD, LIFE OF. By John Morley. With Portrait. In 2 vols., demy 8vo, 32s.

New Edition. Portrait. Large crown 8vo, 7s. 6d.

Popular Edition, with Portrait, sewed, 1s.; cloth, 2s.

CHAPMAN & HALL'S SIX SHILLING NOVELS:
New and Cheaper Editions of Popular Novels.

FAUCIT OF BALLIOL. By Herman Merivale.
AYALA'S ANGEL. By Anthony Trollope.
THE VICAR'S PEOPLE. By G. Manville Fenn.
AUNT HEPSY'S FOUNDLING. By Mrs. Leith Adams.
AN AUSTRALIAN HEROINE. By Mrs. Campbell Praed.
FASHION AND PASSION, OR LIFE IN MAYFAIR. By the Duke de Pomar.
HARD LINES. By Hawley Smart.

COLENSO (FRANCES E.)—

HISTORY OF THE ZULU WAR AND ITS ORIGIN.
Assisted in those portions of the work which touch upon Military Matters by
Lieut.-Colonel Edward Durnford. Demy 8vo, 18s.

COOKERY—

OFFICIAL HANDBOOK FOR THE NATIONAL
TRAINING SCHOOL FOR COOKERY. Containing Lessons on Cookery;
forming the Course of Instruction in the School. Compiled by "R. O. C."
Tenth Thousand. Large crown 8vo, 8s.

HOW TO COOK FISH. A Series of Lessons in Cookery,
from the Official Handbook to the National Training School for Cookery, South
Kensington. Compiled by "R. O. C." Crown 8vo, sewed. 3d.

SICK-ROOM COOKERY. From the Official Handbook
for the National School for Cookery, South Kensington. Compiled by "R. O. C."
Crown 8vo, sewed, 6d.

CRAIK (GEORGE LILLIE)—

ENGLISH OF SHAKESPEARE. Illustrated in a Philo-
logical Commentary on his Julius Cæsar. Sixth Edition. Post 8vo, cloth, 5s.

OUTLINES OF THE HISTORY OF THE ENGLISH
LANGUAGE. Ninth Edition. Post 8vo, cloth, 2s. 6d.

CRAWFORD (F. MARION)—

TO LEEWARD. New Edition. Crown 8vo, 5s.

CRIPPS (WILFRED)—

COLLEGE AND CORPORATION PLATE. With
numerous Illustrations. Large crown 8vo, cloth, 2s. 6d.

DAME TROT AND HER PIG (The Wonderful History of).
With Coloured Illustrations. Crown 4to, 3s. 6d.

DAUBOURG (E.)—

INTERIOR ARCHITECTURE. Doors, Vestibules, Stair-
cases, Anterooms, Drawing, Dining, and Bed Rooms, Libraries, Bank and Newspaper Offices, Shop Fronts and Interiors. Half-imperial, cloth, £2 12s. 6d.

DAVIDSON (ELLIS A.)—
PRETTY ARTS FOR THE EMPLOYMENT OF
LEISURE HOURS. A Book for Ladies. With Illustrations. Demy 8vo, 6s.

THE AMATEUR HOUSE CARPENTER: a Guide in
Building, Making, and Repairing. With numerous Illustrations, drawn on Wood by the Author. Royal 8vo, 10s. 6d.

DAVISON (THE MISSES)—
TRIQUETI MARBLES IN THE ALBERT MEMORIAL
CHAPEL, WINDSOR. A Series of Photographs. Dedicated by express permission to Her Majesty the Queen. The Work consists of 117 Photographs, with descriptive Letterpress, mounted on 49 sheets of cardboard, half-imperial. £10 10s.

DAY (WILLIAM)—
THE RACEHORSE IN TRAINING, with Hints on
Racing and Racing Reform, to which is added a Chapter on Shoeing. Fourth Edition. Demy 8vo, 12s.

D'HAUSSONVILLE (VICOMTE)—
SALON OF MADAME NECKER. Translated by H. M.
TROLLOPE. 2 vols. Crown 8vo, 18s.

DE KONINCK (L. L.) and DIETZ (E.)—
PRACTICAL MANUAL OF CHEMICAL ASSAYING,
as applied to the Manufacture of Iron. Edited, with notes, by ROBERT MALLET. Post 8vo, cloth, 6s.

DICKENS (CHARLES)—See pages 20-24.
THE LETTERS OF CHARLES DICKENS. Edited
by his Sister-in-Law and his Eldest Daughter. Two vols. uniform with "The Charles Dickens Edition" of his Works. Crown 8vo, 8s.

THE CHARLES DICKENS BIRTHDAY BOOK.
Compiled and Edited by his Eldest Daughter. With Five Illustrations by his Youngest Daughter. In a handsome fcap. 4to volume, 12s.

DIXON (W. HEPWORTH)—
BRITISH CYPRUS. With Frontispiece. Demy 8vo, 15s.

DRAYSON (LIEUT.-COL. A. W.)—
THE CAUSE OF THE SUPPOSED PROPER MOTION
OF THE FIXED STARS. Demy 8vo, cloth, 10s.

THE CAUSE, DATE, AND DURATION OF THE
LAST GLACIAL EPOCH OF GEOLOGY. Demy 8vo, cloth, 10s.

PRACTICAL MILITARY SURVEYING AND
SKETCHING. Fifth Edition. Post 8vo, cloth, 4s. 6d.

DYCE'S COLLECTION. A Catalogue of Printed Books and Manuscripts bequeathed by the REV. ALEXANDER DYCE to the South Kensington Museum. 2 vols. Royal 8vo, half-morocco, 14s.

A Collection of Paintings, Miniatures, Drawings, Engravings, Rings, and Miscellaneous Objects, bequeathed by the REV. ALEXANDER DYCE to the South Kensington Museum. Royal 8vo, half-morocco, 6s. 6d.

DYCE (WILLIAM), R.A.—
DRAWING-BOOK OF THE GOVERNMENT SCHOOL
OF DESIGN; OR, ELEMENTARY OUTLINES OF ORNAMENT. Fifty selected Plates. Folio, sewed, 5s.; mounted, 18s.
Text to Ditto. Sewed, 6d.

EGYPTIAN ART—
A HISTORY OF ART IN ANCIENT EGYPT. By
G. PERROT and C. CHIPIEZ. Translated by WALTER ARMSTRONG. With over 600 Illustrations. 2 vols. Royal 8vo, £2 2s.

ELLIOT (FRANCES)—
PICTURES OF OLD ROME. New Edition. Post 8vo,
cloth, 6s.

ELLIS (CAPTAIN A. B.)—
THE LAND OF FETISH. Demy 8vo. 12s.

ENGEL (CARL)—
A DESCRIPTIVE AND ILLUSTRATED CATALOGUE
OF THE MUSICAL INSTRUMENTS in the SOUTH KENSINGTON
MUSEUM, preceded by an Essay on the History of Musical Instruments. Second
Edition. Royal 8vo, half-morocco, 12s.

MUSICAL INSTRUMENTS. With numerous Woodcuts.
Large crown 8vo, cloth, 2s. 6d.

ESCOTT (T. H. S.)—
PILLARS OF THE EMPIRE: Short Biographical
Sketches. Demy 8vo, 10s. 6d.

EWALD (ALEXANDER CHARLES), F.S.A.—
REPRESENTATIVE STATESMEN: Political Studies.
2 vols. Large crown 8vo, £1 4s.

SIR ROBERT WALPOLE. A Political Biography,
1676-1745. Demy 8vo, 18s.

FANE (VIOLET)—
QUEEN OF THE FAIRIES (A Village Story), and other ‛
Poems. Crown 8vo, 6s.

ANTHONY BABINGTON: a Drama. Crown 8vo, 6s.

FEARNLEY (W.)—
LESSONS IN HORSE JUDGING, AND THE SUM·
MERING OF HUNTERS. With Illustrations. Crown 8vo, 4s.

FITZ-PATRICK (W. J.)—
LIFE OF CHARLES LEVER. 2 vols. Demy 8vo, 30s.

FLEMING (GEORGE), F.R.C.S.—
ANIMAL PLAGUES: THEIR HISTORY, NATURE,
AND PREVENTION. 8vo, cloth, 15s.

PRACTICAL HORSE-SHOEING. With 37 Illustrations.
Second Edition, enlarged. 8vo, sewed, 2s.

RABIES AND HYDROPHOBIA: THEIR HISTORY,
NATURE, CAUSES, SYMPTOMS, AND PREVENTION. With 8 Illustrations. 8vo, cloth, 15s.

A MANUAL OF VETERINARY SANITARY SCIENCE
AND POLICE. With 33 Illustrations. 2 vols. Demy 8vo, 36s.

FORSTER (JOHN), M.P. for Berwick—
THE CHRONICLE OF JAMES I., KING OF ARAGON,
SURNAMED THE CONQUEROR. Written by Himself. Translated from
the Catalan by the late JOHN FORSTER, M.P. for Berwick. With an Historical
Introduction by DON PASCUAL DE GAYANGOS. 2 vols. Royal 8vo, 28s.

FORSTER (JOHN)—
THE LIFE OF CHARLES DICKENS. With Portraits
and other Illustrations. 15th Thousand. 3 vols. 8vo, cloth, £2 2s.

THE LIFE OF CHARLES DICKENS. Uniform with
the Illustrated Library Edition of Dickens's Works. 2 vols. Demy 8vo, £1 8s.

THE LIFE OF CHARLES DICKENS. Uniform with
the Library Edition. Post 8vo, 10s. 6d.

THE LIFE OF CHARLES DICKENS. Uniform with
the "C. D." Edition. With Numerous Illustrations. 2 vols. 7s.

THE LIFE OF CHARLES DICKENS. Uniform with
the Household Edition. With Illustrations by F. BARNARD. Crown 4to, cloth, 5s.

WALTER SAVAGE LANDOR: a Biography, 1775–1864.
With Portrait. A New and Revised Edition. Demy 8vo, 12s.

FORTNIGHTLY REVIEW—
FORTNIGHTLY REVIEW.—First Series, May, 1865, to
Dec. 1866. 6 vols. Cloth, 13s. each.
New Series, 1867 to 1872. In Half-yearly Volumes. Cloth,
13s. each.
From January, 1873, to the present time, in Half-yearly
Volumes. Cloth, 16s. each.
CONTENTS OF FORTNIGHTLY REVIEW. From
the commencement to end of 1878. Sewed, 2s.

FORTNUM (C. D. E.)—
A DESCRIPTIVE AND ILLUSTRATED CATALOGUE
OF THE BRONZES OF EUROPEAN ORIGIN in the SOUTH KEN-
SINGTON MUSEUM, with an Introductory Notice. Royal 8vo, half-morocco,
£1 10s.
A DESCRIPTIVE AND ILLUSTRATED CATALOGUE
OF MAIOLICA, HISPANO-MORESCO, PERSIAN, DAMASCUS, AND
RHODIAN WARES in the SOUTH KENSINGTON MUSEUM. Royal
8vo, half-morocco, £2.
MAIOLICA. With numerous Woodcuts. Large crown
8vo, cloth, 2s. 6d.
BRONZES. With numerous Woodcuts. Large crown
8vo, cloth, 2s. 6d.

FRANCATELLI (C. E.)—
ROYAL CONFECTIONER: English and Foreign. A
Practical Treatise. New and Cheap Edition. With Illustrations. Crown 8vo, 5s.

FRANKS (A. W.)—
JAPANESE POTTERY. Being a Native Report. Numerous Illustrations and Marks. Large crown 8vo, cloth, 2s. 6d.

GALLENGA (ANTONIO)—
IBERIAN REMINISCENCES. Fifteen Years' Travelling
Impressions of Spain and Portugal. With a Map. 2 vols. Demy 8vo, 32s.
A SUMMER TOUR IN RUSSIA. With a Map.
Demy 8vo, 14s.
DEMOCRACY ACROSS THE CHANNEL. Crown
8vo, 3s.

GORST (J. E.), Q.C., M.P.—
An ELECTION MANUAL. Containing the Parliamentary
Elections (Corrupt and Illegal Practices) Act, 1883, with Notes. Crown 8vo, 2s. 6d.

GRIFFITHS (MAJOR ARTHUR), H.M. Inspector of Prisons—
CHRONICLES OF NEWGATE. Illustrated. New
Edition in 1 vol. Demy 8vo.   *[In March.*

HALL (SIDNEY)—
A TRAVELLING ATLAS OF THE ENGLISH COUN-
TIES. Fifty Maps, coloured. New Edition, including the Railways, corrected
up to the present date. Demy 8vo, in roan tuck, 10s. 6d.

HARDY (LADY DUFFUS)—
DOWN SOUTH. Demy 8vo. 14s.
THROUGH CITIES AND PRAIRIE LANDS. Sketches
of an American Tour. Demy 8vo, 14s.

HATTON (JOSEPH) and HARVEY (REV. M.)—
NEWFOUNDLAND. The Oldest British Colony. Its
History, Past and Present, and its Prospects in the Future. Illustrated from
Photographs and Sketches specially made for this work. Demy 8vo, 18s.
TO-DAY IN AMERICA. Studies for the Old World and
the New. 2 vols. Crown 8vo, 18s.

HEAPHY (MUSGRAVE)—
GLIMPSES AND GLEAMS. Crown 8vo, 5s.

HILDEBRAND (HANS)—
INDUSTRIAL ARTS OF SCANDINAVIA IN THE
PAGAN TIME. Illustrated. Large crown 8vo, 2s. 6d.

HILL (MISS G.)—
THE PLEASURES AND PROFITS OF OUR LITTLE
POULTRY FARM. Small crown 8vo, 3s.

HITCHMAN (FRANCIS)—
THE PUBLIC LIFE OF THE EARL OF BEACONS-
FIELD. 2 vols. Demy 8vo, £1 12s.

HOLBEIN—
TWELVE HEADS AFTER HOLBEIN. Selected from
Drawings in Her Majesty's Collection at Windsor. Reproduced in Autotype, in portfolio. £1 16s.

HOLLINGSHEAD (JOHN)—
FOOTLIGHTS. Crown 8vo. 7s. 6d.

HOVELACQUE (ABEL)—
THE SCIENCE OF LANGUAGE: LINGUISTICS,
PHILOLOGY, AND ETYMOLOGY. With Maps. Large crown 8vo, cloth, 5s.

HOW I BECAME A SPORTSMAN. By "AVON." Illustrated. Crown
8vo. 6s.

HUMPHRIS (H. D.)—
PRINCIPLES OF PERSPECTIVE. Illustrated in a
Series of Examples. Oblong folio, half-bound, and Text 8vo, cloth, £1 1s.

IRON (RALPH)—
THE STORY OF AN AFRICAN FARM. New Edition.
Crown 8vo, 5s.

JAMES I., KING OF ARAGON (THE CHRONICLE OF),
SURNAMED THE CONQUEROR. Written by Himself. Translated from the Catalan by the late JOHN FORSTER, M.P. for Berwick. With an Historical Introduction by DON PASCUAL DE GAYANGOS. 2 vols. Royal 8vo. 28s.

JARRY (GENERAL)—
OUTPOST DUTY. Translated, with TREATISES ON
MILITARY RECONNAISSANCE AND ON ROAD-MAKING. By Major-Gen. W. C. E. NAPIER. Third Edition. Crown 8vo, 5s.

JEANS (W. T.)—
CREATORS OF THE AGE OF STEEL. Memoirs of
Sir W. Siemens, Sir H. Bessemer, Sir J. Whitworth, Sir J. Brown, and other Inventors. Crown 8vo, 7s. 6d.

JOHNSON (DR. SAMUEL)—
LIFE AND CONVERSATIONS. By A. MAIN. Crown
8vo, 10s. 6d.

JONES (CAPTAIN DOUGLAS), R.A.—
NOTES ON MILITARY LAW. Crown 8vo, 4s.

JONES COLLECTION (HANDBOOK OF THE) IN THE SOUTH
KENSINGTON MUSEUM. Illustrated. Large crown 8vo, 2s. 6d.

KEMPIS (THOMAS À)—
OF THE IMITATION OF CHRIST. Four Books.
Beautifully Illustrated Edition. Demy 8vo, 16s.

KENT (CHARLES)—
HUMOUR AND PATHOS OF CHARLES DICKENS,
WITH ILLUSTRATIONS OF HIS MASTERY OF THE TERRIBLE AND PICTURESQUE. Portrait. Crown 8vo. 6s.

KLACZKO (M. JULIAN)—
TWO CHANCELLORS: PRINCE GORTCHAKOF AND
PRINCE BISMARCK. Translated by MRS. TAIT. New and cheaper Edition, 6s.

LACORDAIRE'S CONFERENCES. JESUS CHRIST, GOD,
AND GOD AND MAN. New Edition in 1 vol. Crown 8vo, 6s.

LAVELEYE (EMILE DE)—
THE ELEMENTS OF POLITICAL ECONOMY.
Translated by W. POLLARD, B.A., St. John's College, Oxford. Crown 8vo, 6s.

LEFÈVRE (ANDRÉ)—
PHILOSOPHY, Historical and Critical. Translated, with
an Introduction, by A. W. KEANE, B.A. Large crown 8vo, 7s. 6d.

LETOURNEAU (DR. CHARLES)—
SOCIOLOGY. Based upon Ethnology. Translated by
HENRY M. TROLLOPE. Large crown 8vo, 10s.

BIOLOGY. Translated by WILLIAM MacCALL. With Illustrations. Large crown 8vo, 6s.

LILLY (W. S.)—
ANCIENT RELIGION AND MODERN THOUGHT.
One vol. demy 8vo.   [*In the Press.*

LOW (C. R.)—
SOLDIERS OF THE VICTORIAN AGE. 2 vols. Demy
8vo, £1 10s.

LUCAS (CAPTAIN)—
THE ZULUS AND THE BRITISH FRONTIER.
Demy 8vo, 16s.

CAMP LIFE AND SPORT IN SOUTH AFRICA.
With Episodes in Kaffir Warfare. With Illustrations. Demy 8vo. 12s.

LYTTON (ROBERT, EARL)—
POETICAL WORKS—
FABLES IN SONG. 2 vols. Fcap. 8vo, 12s.
THE WANDERER. Fcap. 8vo, 6s.
POEMS, HISTORICAL AND CHARACTERISTIC. Fcap. 6s.

MACEWEN (CONSTANCE)—
ROUGH DIAMONDS; OR, SKETCHES FROM REAL
LIFE. Crown 8vo, 3s. 6d.

MALLET (DR. J. W.)—
COTTON: THE CHEMICAL, &c., CONDITIONS OF
ITS SUCCESSFUL CULTIVATION. Post 8vo, cloth, 7s. 6d.

MALLET (ROBERT)—
PRACTICAL MANUAL OF CHEMICAL ASSAYING,
as applied to the Manufacture of Iron. By L. L. DE KONINCK and E. DIETZ.
Edited, with notes, by ROBERT MALLET. Post 8vo, cloth, 6s.

GREAT NEAPOLITAN EARTHQUAKE OF 1857.
First Principles of Observational Seismology, as developed in the Report to the
Royal Society of London. Maps and numerous Illustrations. 2 vols. Royal 8vo,
cloth, £3 3s.

MASKELL (WILLIAM)—
A DESCRIPTION OF THE IVORIES, ANCIENT AND
MEDIÆVAL, in the SOUTH KENSINGTON MUSEUM, with a Preface.
With numerous Photographs and Woodcuts. Royal 8vo, half-morocco, £1 1s.

IVORIES: ANCIENT AND MEDIÆVAL. With numerous Woodcuts. Large crown 8vo, cloth, 2s. 6d.

HANDBOOK TO THE DYCE AND FORSTER COL-
LECTIONS. With Illustrations. Large crown 8vo, cloth, 2s. 6d.

McCOAN (J. CARLILE)—
OUR NEW PROTECTORATE. TURKEY IN ASIA: ITS
GEOGRAPHY, RACES, RESOURCES, AND GOVERNMENT. With Map. 2 vols.
Large crown 8vo, £1 4s.

MEREDITH (GEORGE)—
MODERN LOVE AND POEMS OF THE ENGLISH
ROADSIDE, WITH POEMS AND BALLADS. Fcap. cloth, 6s.

MERIVALE (HERMAN CHARLES)—
BINKO'S BLUES. A Tale for Children of all Growths.
Illustrated by EDGAR GIBERNE. Small crown 8vo. *[In the Press.*

THE WHITE PILGRIM, and other Poems. Crown 8vo, 9s.

FAUCIT OF BALLIOL. Crown 8vo, 6s.

MOLESWORTH (W. NASSAU)—
HISTORY OF ENGLAND FROM THE YEAR 1830
TO THE RESIGNATION OF THE GLADSTONE MINISTRY, 1874. 3 vols.
Crown 8vo, 18s.

ABRIDGED EDITION. Large crown, 7s. 6d.

MORLEY (HENRY)—
ENGLISH WRITERS. Vol. I. Part I. THE CELTS
AND ANGLO-SAXONS. With an Introductory Sketch of the Four Periods of
English Literature. Part II. FROM THE CONQUEST TO CHAUCER.
(Making 2 vols.) 8vo, cloth, £1 2s.

Vol. II. Part I. FROM CHAUCER TO DUNBAR.
8vo, cloth, 12s.

TABLES OF ENGLISH LITERATURE. Containing
20 Charts. Second Edition, with Index. Royal 4to, cloth, 12s.
   In Three Parts. Parts I. and II., containing Three Charts, each 1s. 6d.
   Part III., containing 14 Charts, 7s. Part III. also kept in Sections, 1, 2, and 5.
   1s. 6d. each ; 3 and 4 together, 3s. *₊* The Charts sold separately.

MORLEY (JOHN)—
LIFE OF RICHARD COBDEN. With Portrait. Popular
Edition. 4to, sewed, 1s. Bound in cloth, 2s.

LIFE AND CORRESPONDENCE OF RICHARD
COBDEN. Fourth Thousand. 2 vols. Demy 8vo, £1 12s.

DIDEROT AND THE ENCYCLOPÆDISTS. 2 vols.
Demy 8vo, £1 6s.

NEW UNIFORM EDITION.

LIFE OF RICHARD COBDEN. With Portrait. Large
crown 8vo, 7s. 6d.

VOLTAIRE. Large crown 8vo, 6s.

ROUSSEAU. Large crown 8vo, 9s.

DIDEROT AND THE ENCYCLOPÆDISTS. Large
crown 8vo, 12s.

CRITICAL MISCELLANIES. First Series. Large crown
8vo, 6s.

CRITICAL MISCELLANIES. Second Series. *[In the Press.*

ON COMPROMISE. New Edition. Large crown 8vo, 3s. 6d.

STRUGGLE FOR NATIONAL EDUCATION. Third
Edition. Demy 8vo, cloth, 3s.

MUNTZ (EUGÈNE), From the French of—
RAPHAEL : HIS LIFE, WORKS, AND TIMES.
Edited by W. ARMSTRONG. Illustrated with 155 Wood Engravings and 41 Full-
page Plates. Imperial 8vo, 36s.

MURPHY (J. M.)—
RAMBLES IN NORTH-WEST AMERICA. With
Frontispiece and Map. 8vo, 16s.
MURRAY (ANDREW), F.L.S.—
ECONOMIC ENTOMOLOGY. Aptera. With nume-
rous Illustrations. Large crown 8vo, 7s. 6d.
NAPIER (MAJ.-GEN. W. C. E.)—
TRANSLATION OF GEN. JARRY'S OUTPOST DUTY.
With TREATISES ON MILITARY RECONNAISSANCE AND ON
ROAD-MAKING. Third Edition. Crown 8vo, 5s.
NECKER (MADAME)—
THE SALON OF MADAME NECKER. By Vicomte
D'Haussonville. Translated by H. M. Trollope. 2 vols. Crown 8vo, 18s.
NESBITT (ALEXANDER)—
GLASS. Illustrated. Large crown 8vo, cloth, 2s. 6d.
NEVINSON (HENRY)—
A SKETCH OF HERDER AND HIS TIMES. With
a Portrait. Demy 8vo, 14s.
NEWTON (E. TULLEY), F.G.S.—
THE TYPICAL PARTS IN THE SKELETONS OF
A CAT, DUCK, AND CODFISH, being a Catalogue with Comparative
Description arranged in a Tabular form. Demy 8vo, cloth, 3s.
NORMAN (C. B.), late of the 90th Light Infantry and Bengal Staff Corps—
TONKIN; OR, FRANCE IN THE FAR EAST. Demy
8vo, with Maps, 14s.
OLIVER (PROFESSOR), F.R.S., &c.—
ILLUSTRATIONS OF THE PRINCIPAL NATURAL
ORDERS OF THE VEGETABLE KINGDOM, PREPARED FOR THE
SCIENCE AND ART DEPARTMENT, SOUTH KENSINGTON. With
109 Plates. Oblong 8vo, plain, 16s.; coloured, £1 6s.
PERROT (GEORGES) and CHIPIEZ (CHARLES)—
CHALDÆA AND ASSYRIA, A HISTORY OF ART IN.
Translated by Walter Armstrong, B.A. Oxon. With 452 Illustrations. 2 vols.
Demy 8vo. Uniform with "Ancient Egyptian Art." 42s.
ANCIENT EGYPT, A HISTORY OF ART IN. Trans-
lated from the French by W. Armstrong. With over 600 Illustrations. 2 vols.
Imperial 8vo, 42s.
POLLEN (J. H.)—
ANCIENT AND MODERN FURNITURE AND
WOODWORK IN THE SOUTH KENSINGTON MUSEUM. With an
Introduction, and Illustrated with numerous Coloured Photographs and Woodcuts.
Royal 8vo, half-morocco, £1 1s.
GOLD AND SILVER SMITH'S WORK. With nume-
rous Woodcuts. Large crown 8vo, cloth, 2s. 6d.
ANCIENT AND MODERN FURNITURE AND
WOODWORK. With numerous Woodcuts. Large crown 8vo, cloth, 2s. 6d.
POLLOK (LIEUT.-COLONEL)—
SPORT IN BRITISH BURMAH, ASSAM, AND THE
CASSYAH AND JYNTIAH HILLS. With Notes of Sport in the Hilly Dis-
tricts of the Northern Division, Madras Presidency. With Illustrations and 2
Maps. 2 vols. Demy 8vo, £1 4s.
POYNTER (E. J.), R.A.—
TEN LECTURES ON ART. Second Edition. Large
crown 8vo, 9s.
PRAED (MRS. CAMPBELL)—
AN AUSTRALIAN HEROINE. Cheap Edition. Crown
8vo, 6s.
NADINE. Cheap Edition. Crown 8vo, 5s.
MOLOCH. Cheap Edition.
[In the Press.

PRINSEP (VAL), A.R.A.—

IMPERIAL INDIA. Containing numerous Illustrations
and Maps made during a Tour to the Courts of the Principal Rajahs and Princes
of India. Second Edition. Demy 8vo, £1 1s.

PUCKETT (R. CAMPBELL), Ph.D., Bonn University—

SCIOGRAPHY; or, Radial Projection of Shadows. Third
Edition. Crown 8vo, cloth, 6s.

RAMSDEN (LADY GWENDOLEN)—

A BIRTHDAY BOOK. Illustrated. Containing 46 Illustra-
tions from Original Drawings, and numerous other Illustrations. Royal 8vo, 21s.

REDGRAVE (GILBERT)—

PRE-CHRISTIAN ORNAMENTATION. Translated
from the German and edited. With numerous Illustrations. Crown 8vo.
[In the Press.

REDGRAVE (GILBERT R.)—

MANUAL OF DESIGN, compiled from the Writings and
Addresses of RICHARD REDGRAVE, R.A. With Woodcuts. Large crown 8vo, cloth,
2s. 6d.

REDGRAVE (RICHARD)—

MANUAL AND CATECHISM ON COLOUR. 24mo,
cloth, 9d.

REDGRAVE (SAMUEL)—

A DESCRIPTIVE CATALOGUE OF THE HIS-
TORICAL COLLECTION OF WATER-COLOUR PAINTINGS IN THE
SOUTH KENSINGTON MUSEUM. With numerous Chromo-lithographs and
other Illustrations. Royal 8vo, £1 1s.

RENAN (ERNEST)—

RECOLLECTIONS OF MY YOUTH. Translated from
the original French by C. B. PITMAN, and revised by MADAME RENAN. Crown
8vo, 8s.

RIANO (JUAN F.)—

THE INDUSTRIAL ARTS IN SPAIN. Illustrated. Large
crown 8vo, cloth, 4s.

ROBINSON (JAMES F.)—

BRITISH BEE FARMING. Its Profits and Pleasures.
Large crown 8vo, 5s.

ROBINSON (J. C.)—

ITALIAN SCULPTURE OF THE MIDDLE AGES
AND PERIOD OF THE REVIVAL OF ART. With 20 Engravings. Royal
8vo, cloth, 7s. 6d.

ROBSON (GEORGE)—

ELEMENTARY BUILDING CONSTRUCTION. Illus-
trated by a Design for an Entrance Lodge and Gate. 15 Plates. Oblong folio,
sewed, 8s.

ROBSON (REV. J. H.), M.A., LL.M.—

AN ELEMENTARY TREATISE ON ALGEBRA.
Post 8vo, 6s.

ROCK (THE VERY REV. CANON), D.D.—

ON TEXTILE FABRICS. A Descriptive and Illustrated
Catalogue of the Collection of Church Vestments, Dresses, Silk Stuffs, Needlework,
and Tapestries in the South Kensington Museum. Royal 8vo, half-morocco,
£1 11s. 6d.

TEXTILE FABRICS. With numerous Woodcuts. Large
crown 8vo, cloth, 2s. 6d.

ROLAND (ARTHUR)—

FARMING FOR PLEASURE AND PROFIT. Edited
by WILLIAM ABLETT. 8 vols. Large crown 8vo, 5s. each.
DAIRY-FARMING, MANAGEMENT OF COWS, &c.
POULTRY-KEEPING.
TREE-PLANTING, FOR ORNAMENTATION OR PROFIT.
STOCK-KEEPING AND CATTLE-REARING.
DRAINAGE OF LAND, IRRIGATION, MANURES, &c.
ROOT-GROWING, HOPS, &c.
MANAGEMENT OF GRASS LANDS.
MARKET GARDENING.

RUSDEN (G. W.), for many years Clerk of the Parliament in Victoria—

A HISTORY OF AUSTRALIA. With a Coloured Map.
3 Vols. Demy 8vo, 50s.

A HISTORY OF NEW ZEALAND. 3 vols. Demy 8vo.
with Maps, 50s.

SALUSBURY (PHILIP H. B.)—

TWO MONTHS WITH TCHERNAIEFF IN SERVIA.
Large crown 8vo, 9s.

SCOTT-STEVENSON (MRS.)—

ON SUMMER SEAS. Including the Mediterranean, the
Ægean, the Ionian, and the Euxine, and a voyage down the Danube. With a
Map. Demy 8vo, 16s.

OUR HOME IN CYPRUS. With a Map and Illustrations. Third Edition. Demy 8vo, 14s.

OUR RIDE THROUGH ASIA MINOR. With Map.
Demy 8vo, 18s.

SIMMONDS (T. L.)—

ANIMAL PRODUCTS: their Preparation, Commercial
Uses, and Value. With numerous Illustrations. Large crown 8vo, 7s. 6d.

SMART (HAWLEY)—

SALVAGE. A Collection of Stories. Crown 8vo, 10s. 6d.

HARD LINES. 1 vol. Crown 8vo, 6s.

SMITH (MAJOR R. MURDOCK), R.E.—

PERSIAN ART. Second Edition, with additional Illustrations. Large crown 8vo, 2s.

ST. CLAIR (S. G. B.)—

TWELVE YEARS' RESIDENCE IN BULGARIA.
Revised Edition. Crown 8vo, 9s.

STORY (W. W.)—

ROBA DI ROMA. Seventh Edition, with Additions and
Portrait. Crown 8vo, cloth, 10s. 6d.

CASTLE ST. ANGELO. With Illustrations. Crown
8vo, 10s. 6d.

SUTCLIFFE (JOHN)—

THE SCULPTOR AND ART STUDENT'S GUIDE
to the Proportions of the Human Form, with Measurements in feet and inches of
Full-Grown Figures of Both Sexes and of Various Ages. By Dr. G. SCHADOW,
Member of the Academies, Stockholm, Dresden, Rome, &c. &c. Translated by
J. J. WRIGHT. Plates reproduced by J. SUTCLIFFE. Oblong folio, 31s. 6d.

TANNER (PROFESSOR), F.C.S.—

HOLT CASTLE; or, Threefold Interest in Land. Crown
8vo, 4s. 6d.

JACK'S EDUCATION; OR, HOW HE LEARNT
FARMING. Second Edition. Crown 8vo, 3s. 6d.

TOPINARD (DR. PAUL)—

ANTHROPOLOGY. With a Preface by Professor PAUL
BROCA. With numerous Illustrations. Large crown 8vo, 7s. 6d.

TRAILL (H. D.)—
THE NEW LUCIAN. Being a Series of Dialogues of the
Dead. Demy 8vo, 12s.

TROLLOPE (ANTHONY)—
AYALA'S ANGEL. Crown 8vo. 6s.

LIFE OF CICERO. 2 vols. 8vo. £1 4s.

THE CHRONICLES OF BARSETSHIRE. A Uniform
Edition, in 8 vols., large crown 8vo, handsomely printed, each vol. containing
Frontispiece. 6s. each.

THE WARDEN and BAR- CHESTER TOWERS. 2 vols.	THE SMALL HOUSE AT ALLINGTON. 2 vols.
DR. THORNE.	LAST CHRONICLE OF
FRAMLEY PARSONAGE.	BARSET. 2 vols.

TROLLOPE (MR. and MRS. THOMAS ADOLPHUS)—
HOMES AND HAUNTS OF ITALIAN POETS. 2 vols.
Crown 8vo, 18s.

UNIVERSAL—
UNIVERSAL CATALOGUE OF BOOKS ON ART.
Compiled for the use of the National Art Library, and the Schools of Art in the
United Kingdom. In 2 vols. Crown 4to, half-morocco, £2 2s.

Supplemental Volume to Ditto.

VERON (EUGENE)—
ÆSTHETICS. Translated by W. H. ARMSTRONG. Large
crown 8vo, 7s. 6d.

WALE (REV. HENRY JOHN), M.A.—
MY GRANDFATHER'S POCKET BOOK, from 1701 to
1796. Author of "Sword and Surplice." Demy 8vo, 12s.

WATSON (ALFRED E. T.)
SKETCHES IN THE HUNTING FIELD. Illustrated
by JOHN STURGESS. Cheap Edition. Crown 8vo, 6s.

WESTWOOD (J. O.), M.A., F.L.S., &c.—
CATALOGUE OF THE FICTILE IVORIES IN THE
SOUTH KENSINGTON MUSEUM. With an Account of the Continental
Collections of Classical and Mediæval Ivories. Royal 8vo, half-morocco, £1 4s.

WHEELER (G. P.)—
VISIT OF THE PRINCE OF WALES. A Chronicle of
H.R.H.'s Journeyings in India, Ceylon, Spain, and Portugal. Large crown 8vo, 12s.

WHITE (WALTER)—
HOLIDAYS IN TYROL: Kufstein, Klobenstein, and
Paneveggio. Large crown 8vo, 14s.

A MONTH IN YORKSHIRE. Post 8vo. With a Map.
Fifth Edition. 4s.

A LONDONER'S WALK TO THE LAND'S END, AND
A TRIP TO THE SCILLY ISLES. Post 8vo. With 4 Maps. Third Edition. 4s.

WILDFOWLER—
SHOOTING, YACHTING, AND SEA-FISHING TRIPS,
at Home and on the Continent. Second Series. By "WILDFOWLER," "SNAP-
SHOT." 2 vols. Crown 8vo, £1 1s.

SHOOTING AND FISHING TRIPS IN ENGLAND,
FRANCE, ALSACE, BELGIUM, HOLLAND, AND BAVARIA. New
Edition, with Illustrations. Large crown 8vo, 8s.

WILL-O'-THE-WISPS, THE. Translated from the German
of Marie Petersen by CHARLOTTE J. HART. With Illustrations. Crown 8vo,
7s. 6d.

WORNUM (R. N.)—
ANALYSIS OF ORNAMENT: THE CHARACTER-
ISTICS OF STYLES. An Introduction to the Study of the History of Orna-
· mental Art. With many Illustrations. Ninth Edition. Royal 8vo, cloth, 8s.

WORSAAE (J. J. A.)—
INDUSTRIAL ARTS OF DENMARK, FROM THE
EARLIEST TIMES TO THE DANISH CONQUEST OF ENGLAND.
With Maps and Illustrations. Crown 8vo, 3s. 6d.

WYLDE (ATHERTON)—
MY CHIEF AND I; OR, SIX MONTHS IN NATAL
AFTER THE LANGALIBALELE OUTBREAK. With Portrait of Colonel
Durnford, and Illustrations. Demy 8vo, 14s.

YEO (DR. J. BURNEY)—
HEALTH RESORTS AND THEIR USES: BEING
Vacation Studies in various Health Resorts. Crown 8vo, 8s. ·

YOUNGE (C. D.)—
PARALLEL LIVES OF ANCIENT AND MODERN
HEROES. New Edition. 12mo, cloth, 4s. 6d.

SOUTH KENSINGTON MUSEUM DESCRIPTIVE AND
. ILLUSTRATED CATALOGUES.

Royal 8vo, half-bound.

BRONZES OF EUROPEAN ORIGIN. By C. D. E. Fortnum.
£1 10s.

DYCE'S COLLECTION OF PRINTED BOOKS AND
MANUSCRIPTS. 2 vols. 14s.

DYCE'S COLLECTION OF PAINTINGS, ENGRAVINGS,
&c. 6s. 6d.

FURNITURE AND WOODWORK, ANCIENT AND
MODERN. By J. H. Pollen. £1 1s.

GLASS VESSELS. By A. Nesbitt. 18s.

GOLD AND SILVER SMITH'S WORK. By J. G. Pollen.
£1 6s.

IVORIES, ANCIENT AND MEDIÆVAL. By W. Maskell.
21s.

IVORIES, FICTILE. By J. O. Westwood. £1 4s.

MAIOLICA, HISPANO-MORESCO, PERSIAN, DAMAS-
CUS AND RHODIAN WARES. By C. D. E. Fortnum. £2.

MUSICAL INSTRUMENTS. By C. Engel. 12s.

SCULPTURE, ITALIAN SCULPTURE OF THE MIDDLE
AGES. By J. C. Robinson. Cloth, 7s. 6d.

SWISS COINS. By R. S. Poole. £2 10s.

TEXTILE FABRICS. By Rev. D. Rock. £1 11s. 6d.

WATER-COLOUR PAINTING. By S. Redgrave. £1 1s.

UNIVERSAL CATALOGUE OF WORKS OF ART. 2 vols.
Small 4to, £1 1s. each.

UNIVERSAL CATALOGUE OF WORKS OF ART. Supple-
mentary vol.

SOUTH KENSINGTON MUSEUM SCIENCE AND ART HANDBOOKS.

Published for the Committee of the Council on Education.

ART IN RUSSIA. Forming a New Volume of the South Kensington Art Handbooks. With numerous Illustrations. Crown 8vo. [*In the Press.*

FRENCH POTTERY. Forming a New Volume of the South Kensington Art Handbooks. With Illustrations. Crown 8vo. [*In the Press.*

INDUSTRIAL ARTS OF DENMARK. From the Earliest Times to the Danish Conquest of England. By J. J. A. WORSAAE, Hon. F.S.A., M.R.I.A., &c. &c. With Map and Woodcuts. Large crown 8vo, 3s. 6d.

INDUSTRIAL ARTS OF SCANDINAVIA IN THE PAGAN TIME. By HANS HILDEBRAND, Royal Antiquary of Sweden. Woodcuts. Large crown 8vo, 2s. 6d.

PRECIOUS STONES. By PROFESSOR CHURCH. With Illustrations. Large crown 8vo, 2s. 6d.

INDUSTRIAL ARTS OF INDIA. By Sir GEORGE C. M. BIRDWOOD, C.S.I. With Map and 174 Illustrations. Demy 8vo, 14s.

HANDBOOK TO THE DYCE AND FORSTER COLLECTIONS. By W. MASKELL. With Illustrations. Large crown 8vo, 2s. 6d.

INDUSTRIAL ARTS IN SPAIN. By JUAN F. RIANO. Illustrated. Large crown 8vo, 4s.

GLASS. By ALEXANDER NESBITT. Illustrated. Large crown 8vo, 2s. 6d.

GOLD AND SILVER SMITH'S WORK. By JOHN HUNGERFORD POLLEN. With numerous Woodcuts. Large crown 8vo, 2s. 6d.

TAPESTRY. By ALFRED CHAMPEAUX. With Woodcuts. 2s. 6d.

BRONZES. By C. DRURY E. FORTNUM, F.S.A. With numerous Woodcuts. Large crown 8vo, 2s. 6d.

PLAIN WORDS ABOUT WATER. By A. H. CHURCH, M.A., Oxon. Illustrated. Large crown 8vo, sewed, 6d.

ANIMAL PRODUCTS : their Preparation, Commercial Uses, and Value. By T. L. SIMMONDS. With numerous Illustrations. Large crown 8vo, 7s. 6d.

FOOD : A Short Account of the Sources, Constituents, and Uses of Food ; intended chiefly as a Guide to the Food Collection in the Bethnal Green Museum. By A. H. CHURCH, M.A., Oxon. Large crown 8vo, 3s.

SCIENCE CONFERENCES. Delivered at the South Kensington Museum. 2 vols. Crown 8vo, 6s. each.
VOL. I.—Physics and Mechanics.
VOL. II.—Chemistry, Biology, Physical Geography, Geology, Mineralogy, and Meteorology.

ECONOMIC ENTOMOLOGY. By ANDREW MURRAY, F.L.S. APTERA. With numerous Illustrations. Large crown 8vo, 7s. 6d.

JAPANESE POTTERY. Being a Native Report. Edited by A. W. FRANKS. Numerous Illustrations and Marks. Large crown 8vo, 2s. 6d.

HANDBOOK TO THE SPECIAL LOAN COLLECTION of Scientific Apparatus. Large crown 8vo, 3s.

INDUSTRIAL ARTS : Historical Sketches. With 242 Illustrations. Large crown 8vo, 3s.

TEXTILE FABRICS. By the Very Rev. DANIEL ROCK, D.D. With numerous Woodcuts. Large crown 8vo, 2s. 6d.

JONES COLLECTION IN THE SOUTH KENSINGTON MUSEUM. With Portrait and Illustrations. Large crown 8vo, 2s. 6d.

B

SOUTH KENSINGTON MUSEUM SCIENCE & ART HANDBOOKS—*Continued.*

COLLEGE AND CORPORATION PLATE. By WILFRED
CRIPPS. With numerous Illustrations. Large crown 8vo, cloth, 2s. 6d.

IVORIES: ANCIENT AND MEDIÆVAL. By WILLIAM
MASKELL. With numerous Woodcuts. Large crown 8vo, 2s. 6d.

ANCIENT AND MODERN FURNITURE AND WOOD-
WORK. By JOHN HUNGERFORD POLLEN. With numerous Woodcuts. Large
crown 8vo, 2s. 6d.

MAIOLICA. By C. DRURY E. FORTNUM, F.S.A. With numerous
Woodcuts. Large crown 8vo, 2s. 6d.

THE CHEMISTRY OF FOODS. With Microscopic Illus-
trations. By JAMES BELL, Principal of the Somerset House Laboratory.
Part I.—Tea, Coffee, Cocoa, Sugar, &c. Large crown 8vo, 2s. 6d.
Part II.—Milk, Butter, Cereals, Prepared Starches, &c. Large crown 8vo, 2s. 6d.

MUSICAL INSTRUMENTS. By CARL ENGEL. With numerous
Woodcuts. Large crown 8vo, 2s. 6d.

MANUAL OF DESIGN, compiled from the Writings and
Addresses of RICHARD REDGRAVE, R.A. By GILBERT R. REDGRAVE. With
Woodcuts. Large crown 8vo, 2s. 6d.

PERSIAN ART. By MAJOR R. MURDOCK SMITH, R.E. Second
Edition, with additional Illustrations. Large crown 8vo, 2s.

FREE EVENING LECTURES. Delivered in connection with
the Special Loan Collection of Scientific Apparatus, 1876. Large crown 8vo, 8s.

CARLYLE'S (THOMAS) WORKS.
CHEAP AND UNIFORM EDITION.
In 23 vols., Crown 8vo, cloth, £7 5s.

THE FRENCH REVOLUTION:
A History. 2 vols., 12s.

OLIVER CROMWELL'S LET-
TERS AND SPEECHES, with Eluci-
dations, &c. 3 vols., 18s.

LIVES OF SCHILLER AND
JOHN STERLING. 1 vol., 6s.

CRITICAL AND MISCELLA-
NEOUS ESSAYS. 4 vols., £1 4s.

SARTOR RESARTUS AND
LECTURES ON HEROES. 1 vol., 6s.

LATTER-DAY PAMPHLETS.
1 vol., 6s.

CHARTISM AND PAST AND
PRESENT. 1 vol., 6s.

TRANSLATIONS FROM THE
GERMAN OF MUSÆUS, TIECK,
AND RICHTER. 1 vol., 6s.

WILHELM MEISTER, by Göthe.
A Translation 2 vols., 12s.

HISTORY OF FRIEDRICH THE
SECOND, called Frederick the Great.
7 vols., £2 9s.

LIBRARY EDITION COMPLETE.
Handsomely printed in 34 vols., demy 8vo, cloth, £15.

SARTOR RESARTUS. The Life and Opinions of Herr
Teufelsdröckh. With a Portrait, 7s. 6d.

THE FRENCH REVOLUTION. A History. 3 vols., each 9s.

CARLYLE'S (THOMAS) WORKS—*Continued.*

LIFE OF FREDERICK SCHILLER AND EXAMINATION
OF HIS WORKS. With Supplement of 1872. Portrait and Plates, 9s.

CRITICAL AND MISCELLANEOUS ESSAYS. With Portrait.
6 vols., each 9s.

ON HEROES, HERO WORSHIP, AND THE HEROIC
IN HISTORY. 7s. 6d.

PAST AND PRESENT. 9s.

OLIVER CROMWELL'S LETTERS AND SPEECHES. With
Portraits. 5 vols., each 9s.

LATTER-DAY PAMPHLETS. 9s.

LIFE OF JOHN STERLING. With Portrait, 9s.

HISTORY OF FREDERICK THE SECOND. 10 vols.,
each 9s.

TRANSLATIONS FROM THE GERMAN. 3 vols., each 9s.

EARLY KINGS OF NORWAY; ESSAY ON THE POR-
TRAITS OF JOHN KNOX; AND GENERAL INDEX. With Portrait
Illustrations. 8vo, cloth, 9s.

EARLY KINGS OF NORWAY : also AN ESSAY ON THE
PORTRAITS OF JOHN KNOX. Crown 8vo, with Portrait Illustrations,
7s. 6d.

PEOPLE'S EDITION.

*In 37 vols., small Crown 8vo. Price 2s. each vol., bound in cloth ; or in sets of
37 vols. in 19, cloth gilt, for £3 14s.*

SARTOR RESARTUS.
FRENCH REVOLUTION. 3 vols.
LIFE OF JOHN STERLING.
OLIVER CROMWELL'S LET-
TERS AND SPEECHES. 5 vols.
ON HEROES AND HERO
WORSHIP.
PAST AND PRESENT.
CRITICAL AND MISCELLA-
NEOUS ESSAYS. 7 vols.

LATTER-DAY PAMPHLETS.
LIFE OF SCHILLER.
FREDERICK THE GREAT.
10 vols.
WILHELM MEISTER. 3 vols.
TRANSLATIONS FROM MU-
SÆUS, TIECK, AND RICHTER.
2 vols.
THE EARLY KINGS OF NOR-
WAY ; Essay on the Portraits of Knox ;
and General Index.

SIXPENNY EDITION.
4to, sewed.

SARTOR RESARTUS. Eightieth Thousand.

HEROES AND HERO WORSHIP.

ESSAYS : BURNS, JOHNSON, SCOTT, THE DIAMOND
NECKLACE.

The above are also to be had in 1 vol., 2s. 6d.

B 2

DICKENS'S (CHARLES) WORKS.

ORIGINAL EDITIONS.

In Demy 8vo.

THE MYSTERY OF EDWIN DROOD. With Illustrations
by S. L. Fildes, and a Portrait engraved by Baker. Cloth, 7s. 6d.

OUR MUTUAL FRIEND. With Forty Illustrations by Marcus
Stone. Cloth, £1 1s.

THE PICKWICK PAPERS. With Forty-three Illustrations
by Seymour and Phiz. Cloth, £1 1s.

NICHOLAS NICKLEBY. With Forty Illustrations by Phiz.
Cloth, £1 1s.

SKETCHES BY "BOZ." With Forty Illustrations by George
Cruikshank. Cloth, £1 1s.

MARTIN CHUZZLEWIT. With Forty Illustrations by Phiz.
Cloth, £1 1s.

DOMBEY AND SON. With Forty Illustrations by Phiz.
Cloth, £1 1s.

DAVID COPPERFIELD. With Forty Illustrations by Phiz.
Cloth, £1 1s.

BLEAK HOUSE. With Forty Illustrations by Phiz. Cloth,
£1 1s.

LITTLE DORRIT. With Forty Illustrations by Phiz. Cloth,
£1 1s.

THE OLD CURIOSITY SHOP. With Seventy-five Illus-
trations by George Cattermole and H. K. Browne. A New Edition. Uniform with
the other volumes, £1 1s.

BARNABY RUDGE: a Tale of the Riots of 'Eighty. With
Seventy-eight Illustrations by George Cattermole and H. K. Browne. Uniform with
the other volumes, £1 1s.

CHRISTMAS BOOKS: Containing—The Christmas Carol;
The Cricket on the Hearth; The Chimes; The Battle of Life; The Haunted House.
With all the original Illustrations. Cloth, 12s.

OLIVER TWIST and TALE OF TWO CITIES. In one
volume. Cloth, £1 1s.

OLIVER TWIST. Separately. With Twenty-four Illustrations
by George Cruikshank. Cloth, 11s.

A TALE OF TWO CITIES. Separately. With Sixteen Illustrations by Phiz. Cloth, 9s.

** *The remainder of Dickens's Works were not originally printed in Demy 8vo.*

DICKENS'S (CHARLES) WORKS— *Continued.*

LIBRARY EDITION.

In Post 8vo. With the Original Illustrations, 30 vols., cloth, £12.

				s.	d.
PICKWICK PAPERS	43	Illustrns.,	2 vols.	16	0
NICHOLAS NICKLEBY	39	,,	2 vols.	16	0
MARTIN CHUZZLEWIT	40	,,	2 vols.	16	0
OLD CURIOSITY SHOP & REPRINTED PIECES	36	,,	2 vols.	16	0
BARNABY RUDGE and HARD TIMES	36	,,	2 vols.	16	0
BLEAK HOUSE...	40	,,	2 vols.	16	0
LITTLE DORRIT	40	,,	2 vols.	16	0
DOMBEY AND SON	38	,,	2 vols.	16	0
DAVID COPPERFIELD	38	,,	2 vols.	16	0
OUR MUTUAL FRIEND	40	,,	2 vols.	16	0
SKETCHES BY "BOZ"	39	,,	1 vol.	8	0
OLIVER TWIST	24	,,	1 vol.	8	0
CHRISTMAS BOOKS	17	,,	1 vol.	8	0
A TALE OF TWO CITIES	16	,,	1 vol.	8	0
GREAT EXPECTATIONS	8	,,	1 vol.	8	0
PICTURES FROM ITALY & AMERICAN NOTES	8	,,	1 vol.	8	0
UNCOMMERCIAL TRAVELLER	8	,,	1 vol.	8	0
CHILD'S HISTORY OF ENGLAND	8	,,	1 vol.	8	0
EDWIN DROOD and MISCELLANIES	12	,,	1 vol.	8	0
CHRISTMAS STORIES from "Household Words," &c.	14	,,	1 vol.	8	0

THE LIFE OF CHARLES DICKENS. By JOHN FORSTER. With Illustrations.
Uniform with this Edition. 1 vol. 10s. 6d.

THE "CHARLES DICKENS" EDITION.

In Crown 8vo. In 21 vols., cloth, with Illustrations, £3 16s.

			s.	d.
PICKWICK PAPERS	8	Illustrations ...	4	0
MARTIN CHUZZLEWIT	8	,, ...	4	0
DOMBEY AND SON	8	,, ...	4	0
NICHOLAS NICKLEBY	8	,, ...	4	0
DAVID COPPERFIELD	8	,, ...	4	0
BLEAK HOUSE	8	,, ...	4	0
LITTLE DORRIT	8	,, ...	4	0
OUR MUTUAL FRIEND...	8	,, ...	4	0
BARNABY RUDGE...	8	,, ...	3	6
OLD CURIOSITY SHOP	8	,, ...	3	6
A CHILD'S HISTORY OF ENGLAND	4	,, ...	3	6
EDWIN DROOD and OTHER STORIES	8	,, ...	3	6
CHRISTMAS STORIES, from "Household Words" ...	8	,, ...	3	6
SKETCHES BY "BOZ"	8	,, ...	3	6
AMERICAN NOTES and REPRINTED PIECES ...	8	,, ...	3	6
CHRISTMAS BOOKS	8	,, ...	3	6
OLIVER TWIST	8	,, ...	3	6
GREAT EXPECTATIONS...	8	,, ...	3	6
TALE OF TWO CITIES	8	,, ...	3	0
HARD TIMES and PICTURES FROM ITALY ...	8	,, ...	3	0
UNCOMMERCIAL TRAVELLER	4	,, ...	3	0
THE LIFE OF CHARLES DICKENS. Numerous Illustrations.			2 vols. 7	0
THE LETTERS OF CHARLES DICKENS...		...	2 vols. 8	0

DICKENS'S (CHARLES) WORKS—*Continued.*

THE ILLUSTRATED LIBRARY EDITION.

Complete in 30 Volumes. Demy 8vo, 10s. each; or set, £15.

This Edition is printed on a finer paper and in a larger type than has been employed in any previous edition. The type has been cast especially for it, and the page is of a size to admit of the introduction of all the original illustrations.

No such attractive issue has been made of the writings of Mr. Dickens, which, various as have been the forms of publication adapted to the demands of an ever widely-increasing popularity, have never yet been worthily presented in a really handsome library form.

The collection comprises all the minor writings it was Mr. Dickens's wish to preserve.

SKETCHES BY "BOZ." With 40 Illustrations by George Cruikshank.

PICKWICK PAPERS. 2 vols. With 42 Illustrations by Phiz.

OLIVER TWIST. With 24 Illustrations by Cruikshank.

NICHOLAS NICKLEBY. 2 vols. With 40 Illustrations by Phiz.

OLD CURIOSITY SHOP and REPRINTED PIECES. 2 vols. With Illustrations by Cattermole, &c.

BARNABY RUDGE and HARD TIMES. 2 vols. With Illustrations by Cattermole, &c.

MARTIN CHUZZLEWIT. 2 vols. With 4 Illustrations by Phiz.

AMERICAN NOTES and PICTURES FROM ITALY. 1 vol. With 8 Illustrations.

DOMBEY AND SON. 2 vols. With 40 Illustrations by Phiz.

DAVID COPPERFIELD. 2 vols. With 40 Illustrations by Phiz.

BLEAK HOUSE. 2 vols. With 40 Illustrations by Phiz.

LITTLE DORRIT. 2 vols. With 40 Illustrations by Phiz.

A TALE OF TWO CITIES. With 16 Illustrations by Phiz.

THE UNCOMMERCIAL TRAVELLER. With 8 Illustrations by Marcus Stone.

GREAT EXPECTATIONS. With 8 Illustrations by Marcus Stone.

OUR MUTUAL FRIEND. 2 vols. With 40 Illustrations by Marcus Stone.

CHRISTMAS BOOKS. With 17 Illustrations by Sir Edwin Landseer, R.A., Maclise, R.A., &c. &c.

HISTORY OF ENGLAND. With 8 Illustrations by Marcus Stone.

CHRISTMAS STORIES. (From "Household Words" and "All the Year Round.") With 14 Illustrations.

EDWIN DROOD AND OTHER STORIES. With 12 Illustrations by S. L. Fildes.

DICKENS'S (CHARLES) WORKS—*Continued.*

HOUSEHOLD EDITION.

Complete in 22 Volumes.   Crown 4to, cloth, £4 8s. 6d.

MARTIN CHUZZLEWIT, with 59 Illustrations, cloth, 5s.

DAVID COPPERFIELD, with 60 Illustrations and a Portrait, cloth, 5s.

BLEAK HOUSE, with 61 Illustrations, cloth, 5s.

LITTLE DORRIT, with 58 Illustrations, cloth, 5s.

PICKWICK PAPERS, with 56 Illustrations, cloth, 5s.

OUR MUTUAL FRIEND, with 58 Illustrations, cloth, 5s.

NICHOLAS NICKLEBY, with 59 Illustrations, cloth, 5s.

DOMBEY AND SON, with 61 Illustrations, cloth, 5s.

EDWIN DROOD; REPRINTED PIECES; and other Stories, with 30 Illustrations, cloth, 5s.

THE LIFE OF DICKENS. By JOHN FORSTER. With 40 Illustrations. Cloth, 5s.

BARNABY RUDGE, with 46 Illustrations, cloth, 4s.

OLD CURIOSITY SHOP, with 32 Illustrations, cloth, 4s.

CHRISTMAS STORIES, with 23 Illustrations, cloth, 4s.

OLIVER TWIST, with 28 Illustrations, cloth, 3s.

GREAT EXPECTATIONS, with 26 Illustrations, cloth, 3s.

SKETCHES BY "BOZ," with 36 Illustrations, cloth, 3s.

UNCOMMERCIAL TRAVELLER, with 26 Illustrations, cloth, 3s.

CHRISTMAS BOOKS, with 28 Illustrations, cloth, 3s.

THE HISTORY OF ENGLAND, with 15 Illustrations, cloth, 3s.

AMERICAN NOTES and PICTURES FROM ITALY, with 18 Illustrations, cloth, 3s.

A TALE OF TWO CITIES, with 25 Illustrations, cloth, 3s.

HARD TIMES, with 20 Illustrations, cloth, 2s. 6d.

MR. DICKENS'S READINGS.

Fcap. 8vo, sewed.

CHRISTMAS CAROL IN PROSE. 1s.

CRICKET ON THE HEARTH. 1s.

CHIMES: A GOBLIN STORY. 1s.

STORY OF LITTLE DOMBEY. 1s.

POOR TRAVELLER, BOOTS AT THE HOLLY-TREE INN, and MRS. GAMP. 1s.

A CHRISTMAS CAROL, with the Original Coloured Plates, being a reprint of the Original Edition.   Small 8vo, red cloth, gilt edges, 5s.

DICKENS'S (CHARLES) WORKS—*Continued.*

THE POPULAR LIBRARY EDITION
OF THE WORKS OF
CHARLES DICKENS,
In 30 Vols., large crown 8vo, price £6; separate Vols. 4s. each.

An Edition printed on good paper, containing Illustrations selected from the Household Edition, on Plate Paper. Each Volume has about 450 pages and 16 full-page Illustrations.

SKETCHES BY "BOZ."	OLD CURIOSITY SHOP AND REPRINTED PIECES. 2 vols.
PICKWICK. 2 vols.	
OLIVER TWIST.	BARNABY RUDGE. 2 vols.
NICHOLAS NICKLEBY. 2 vols.	UNCOMMERCIAL TRAVEL-LER.
MARTIN CHUZZLEWIT. 2 vols.	
DOMBEY AND SON. 2 vols.	GREAT EXPECTATIONS.
DAVID COPPERFIELD. 2 vols.	TALE OF TWO CITIES.
CHRISTMAS BOOKS.	CHILD'S HISTORY OF ENG-LAND.
OUR MUTUAL FRIEND. 2 vols.	EDWIN DROOD AND MISCEL-LANIES.
CHRISTMAS STORIES.	
BLEAK HOUSE. 2 vols.	PICTURES FROM ITALY AND AMERICAN NOTES.
LITTLE DORRIT. 2 vols.	

The Cheapest and Handiest Edition of
THE WORKS OF CHARLES DICKENS.
The Pocket-Volume Edition of Charles Dickens's Works.
In 30 Vols. small fcap. 8vo, £2 5s.

New and Cheap Issue of
THE WORKS OF CHARLES DICKENS.
In pocket volumes.

PICKWICK PAPERS, with 8 Illustrations, cloth, 2s.
NICHOLAS NICKLEBY, with 8 Illustrations, cloth, 2s.
OLIVER TWIST, with 8 Illustrations, cloth, 1s.
SKETCHES BY "BOZ," with 8 Illustrations, cloth, 1s.
OLD CURIOSITY SHOP, with 8 Illustrations, cloth, 2s.
BARNABY RUDGE, with 16 Illustrations, cloth, 2s.
AMERICAN NOTES AND PICTURES FROM ITALY, with 8 Illustrations, cloth, 1s.6d.
CHRISTMAS BOOKS with 8 Illustrations, cloth, 1s. 6d.

SIXPENNY REPRINTS.
(I.)
A CHRISTMAS CAROL AND THE HAUNTED MAN.
By CHARLES DICKENS. Illustrated.

(II.)
READINGS FROM THE WORKS OF CHARLES DICKENS.
As selected and read by himself and now published for the first time. Illustrated.

(III.)
THE CHIMES: A GOBLIN STORY, AND THE CRICKET ON THE HEARTH.
Illustrated.

List of Books, Drawing Examples, Diagrams, Models,
Instruments, etc.,

INCLUDING

THOSE ISSUED UNDER THE AUTHORITY OF THE SCIENCE
AND ART DEPARTMENT, SOUTH KENSINGTON, FOR THE
USE OF SCHOOLS AND ART AND SCIENCE CLASSES.

CATALOGUE OF MODERN WORKS ON SCIENCE
AND TECHNOLOGY. 8vo, sewed, 1s.

BENSON (W.)—
PRINCIPLES OF THE SCIENCE OF COLOUR.
Small 4to, cloth, 15s.

MANUAL OF THE SCIENCE OF COLOUR. Coloured
Frontispiece and Illustrations. 12mo, cloth, 2s. 6d.

BRADLEY (THOMAS), of the Royal Military Academy, Woolwich—
ELEMENTS OF GEOMETRICAL DRAWING. In Two
Parts, with 60 Plates. Oblong folio, half-bound, each part 16s.
Selections (from the above) of 20 Plates, for the use of the Royal Military
Academy, Woolwich. Oblong folio, half-bound, 16s.

BURCHETT—
LINEAR PERSPECTIVE. With Illustrations. Post 8vo, 7s.

PRACTICAL GEOMETRY. Post 8vo, 5s.

DEFINITIONS OF GEOMETRY. Third Edition. 24mo,
sewed, 5d.

CARROLL (JOHN)—
FREEHAND DRAWING LESSONS FOR THE BLACK
BOARD. 6s.

CUBLEY (W. H.)—
A SYSTEM OF ELEMENTARY DRAWING. With
Illustrations and Examples. Imperial 4to, sewed, 8s.

DAVISON (ELLIS A.)—
DRAWING FOR ELEMENTARY SCHOOLS. Post
8vo, 3s.

MODEL DRAWING. 12mo, 3s.

THE AMATEUR HOUSE CARPENTER: A Guide in
Building, Making, and Repairing. With numerous Illustrations, drawn on Wood
by the Author. Demy 8vo, 10s. 6d.

DELAMOTTE (P. H.)—

PROGRESSIVE DRAWING-BOOK FOR BEGINNERS.
12mo, 3s. 6d.

DYCE—

DRAWING-BOOK OF THE GOVERNMENT SCHOOL
OF DESIGN: ELEMENTARY OUTLINES OF ORNAMENT. 50 Plates.
Small folio, sewed, 5s.: mounted, 18s.

INTRODUCTION TO DITTO. Fcap. 8vo, 6d.

FOSTER (VERE)—

DRAWING-BOOKS:
(*a*) Forty-two Numbers, at 1d. each.
(*b*) Forty-six Numbers, at d. each. The set *b* includes the subjects in *a*.

DRAWING-CARDS:
Freehand Drawing: First Grade, Sets I., II., III., price 1s. each.
Second Grade, Set I., price 2s.

HENSLOW (PROFESSOR)—

ILLUSTRATIONS TO BE EMPLOYED IN THE
PRACTICAL LESSONS ON BOTANY. Prepared for South Kensington
Museum. Post 8vo, sewed, 6d.

JACOBSTHAL (E.)—

GRAMMATIK DER ORNAMENTE, in 7 Parts of 20
Plates each. Price, unmounted, £3 13s. 6d.; mounted on cardboard, £11 4s.
The Parts can be had separately.

JEWITT—

HANDBOOK OF PRACTICAL PERSPECTIVE. 18mo,
cloth, 1s. 6d.

KENNEDY (JOHN)—

FIRST GRADE PRACTICAL GEOMETRY. 12mo, 6d.

FREEHAND DRAWING-BOOK. 16mo, 1s.

LINDLEY (JOHN)—

SYMMETRY OF VEGETATION: Principles to be
Observed in the Delineation of Plants. 12mo, sewed, 1s.

MARSHALL—

HUMAN BODY. Text and Plates reduced from the large
Diagrams. 2 vols., £1 1s.

NEWTON (E. TULLEY), F.G.S.—

THE TYPICAL PARTS IN THE SKELETONS OF A
CAT, DUCK, AND CODFISH, being a Catalogue with Comparative De-
scriptions arranged in a Tabular Form. Demy 8vo, 3s.

OLIVER (PROFESSOR)—

ILLUSTRATIONS OF THE VEGETABLE KINGDOM.
109 Plates. Oblong 8vo, cloth. Plain, 16s.; coloured, £1 6s.

POYNTER (E. J.), R.A., issued under the superintendence of—

ELEMENTARY, FREEHAND, ORNAMENT:
Book I. Simple Geometrical Forms, 6d.
„ II. Conventionalised Floral Forms, &c., 6d.

POYNTER (E. J.), R.A.—Continued.

FREEHAND—FIRST GRADE:

Book I. Simple Objects and Ornament, 6d.
„ II. Various Objects, 6d.
„ III. Objects and Architectural Ornaments, 6d.
„ IV. Architectural Ornament, 6d.
„ V. Objects of Glass and Pottery, 6d.
„ VI. Common Objects, 6d.

FREEHAND—SECOND GRADE:

Book I. Various Forms of Anthermion, &c., 1s.
„ II. Greek, Roman, and Venetian, 1s.
„ III. Italian Renaissance, 1s.
„ IV. Roman, Italian, Japanese, &c. 1s.

THE SOUTH KENSINGTON DRAWING CARDS,

Containing the same examples as the books:
Elementary Freehand Cards. Four packets, 9d. each.
First Grade Freehand Cards. Six packets, 1s. each.
Second Grade Freehand Cards. Four packets, 1s. 6d. each

REDGRAVE—

MANUAL AND CATECHISM ON COLOUR. Fifth
Edition. 24mo, sewed, 9d.

ROBSON (GEORGE)—

ELEMENTARY BUILDING CONSTRUCTION. Oblong
folio, sewed, 8s.

WALLIS (GEORGE)—

DRAWING-BOOK. Oblong, sewed, 3s. 6d.; mounted, 8s.

WORNUM (R. N.)—

THE CHARACTERISTICS OF STYLES: An Introduction to the Study of the History of Ornamental Art. Royal 8vo, 8s.

DRAWING FOR YOUNG CHILDREN. Containing 150
Copies. 16mo, cloth, 3s. 6d.

EDUCATIONAL DIVISION OF SOUTH KENSINGTON
MUSEUM: CLASSIFIED CATALOGUE OF. Ninth Edition. 8vo, 7s.

ELEMENTARY DRAWING COPY-BOOKS, for the Use of
Children from four years old and upwards, in Schools and Families. Compiled by a Student certificated by the Science and Art Department as an Art Teacher. Seven Books in 4to, sewed:

Book I. Letters, 8d.
„ II. Ditto, 8d.
„ III. Geometrical and Ornamental Forms, 8d.
Book IV. Objects, 8d.
„ V. Leaves, 8d.
„ VI. Birds, Animals, &c., 8d.
„ VII. Leaves, Flowers, and Sprays, 8d.

*** Or in Sets of Seven Books, 4s. 6d.

ENGINEER AND MACHINIST DRAWING-BOOK, 16 Parts,
71 Plates. Folio, £1 12s.; mounted, £3 4s.

PRINCIPLES OF DECORATIVE ART. Folio, sewed, 1s.

DIAGRAM OF THE COLOURS OF THE SPECTRUM,
with Explanatory Letterpress, on roller, 10s. 6d.

COPIES FOR OUTLINE DRAWING :

DYCE'S ELEMENTARY OUTLINES OF ORNAMENT, 50 Selected Plates, mounted back and front, 18s. ; unmounted, sewed, 5s.

WEITBRICHT'S OUTLINES OF ORNAMENT, reproduced by Herman, 12 Plates, mounted back and front, 8s. 6d. ; unmounted, 2s.

MORGHEN'S OUTLINES OF THE HUMAN FIGURE, reproduced by Herman, 20 Plates, mounted back and front, 15s. ; unmounted, 3s. 4d.

OUTLINES OF TARSIA, from Gruner, Four Plates, mounted, 3s. 6d., unmounted, 7d.

ALBERTOLLI'S FOLIAGE, Four Plates, mounted, 3s. 6d. ; unmounted, 5d.

OUTLINE OF TRAJAN FRIEZE, mounted, 1s.

WALLIS'S DRAWING-BOOK, mounted, 8s., unmounted, 3s. 6d.

OUTLINE DRAWINGS OF FLOWERS, Eight Plates, mounted, 3s. 6d.; unmounted, 8d.

COPIES FOR SHADED DRAWING :

COURSE OF DESIGN. By CH. BARGUE (French), 20 Selected Sheets, 11 at 2s. and 9 at 3s. each. £2 9s.

ARCHITECTURAL STUDIES. By J. B. TRIPON. 10 Plates, £1.

MECHANICAL STUDIES. By J. B. TRIPON. 15s. per dozen.

FOLIATED SCROLL FROM THE VATICAN, unmounted, 5d.; mounted, 1s. 3d.

TWELVE HEADS after Holbein, selected from his Drawings in Her Majesty's Collection at Windsor. Reproduced in Autotype. Half imperial, £1 16s.

LESSONS IN SEPIA, 9s. per dozen, or 1s. each.

COLOURED EXAMPLES :

A SMALL DIAGRAM OF COLOUR, mounted, 1s. 6d.; unmounted, 9d.

CAMELLIA, mounted, 3s. 9d.

COTMAN'S PENCIL LANDSCAPES (set of 9), mounted, 15s.

„ SEPIA DRAWINGS (set of 5), mounted, £1.

ALLONGE'S LANDSCAPES IN CHARCOAL (Six), at 4s. each, or the set, £1 4s.

SOLID MODELS, &c. :

*Box of Models, £1 4s.

A Stand with a universal joint, to show the solid models, &c., £1 18s.

*One Wire Quadrangle, with a circle and cross within it, and one straight wire. One solid cube. One Skeleton Wire Cube. One Sphere. One Cone. One Cylinder. One Hexagonal Prism. £2 2s.

Skeleton Cube in wood, 3s. 6d.

18-inch Skeleton Cube in wood, 12s.

*Three objects of *form* in Pottery :
    Indian Jar,
    Celadon Jar, } 18s. 6d.
    Bottle,

*Five selected Vases in Majolica Ware, £2 11s.

*Three selected Vases in Earthenware, 18s.

Imperial Deal Frames, glazed, without sunk rings, 10s. each.

*Davidson's Smaller Solid Models, in Box, £2, containing—

2 Square Slabs.	Octagon Prism.	Triangular Prism
9 Oblong Blocks (steps).	Cylinder.	Pyramid, Equilateral.
2 Cubes.	Cone.	Pyramid, Isosceles.
Square Blocks.	Jointed Cross.	Square Block.

* Models, &c., entered as sets, can only be supplied in sets.

SOLID MODELS, &c.—*Continued.*

* Davidson's Advanced Drawing Models, £9.—The following is a brief description of the Models:—An Obelisk—composed of 2 Octagonal Slabs, 26 and 20 inches across, and each 3 inches high; 1 Cube, 12 inches edge; 1 Monolith (forming the body of the obelisk) 3 feet high; 1 Pyramid, 6 inches base; the complete object is thus nearly 5 feet high. A Market Cross—composed of 3 Slabs, 24, 18, and 12 inches across, and each 3 inches high; 1 Upright, 3 feet high; 2 Cross Arms, united by mortise and tenon joints; complete height, 3 feet 9 inches. A Step-Ladder, 23 inches high. A Kitchen Table, 14½ inches high. A Chair to correspond. A Four-legged Stool, with projecting top and cross rails, height 14 inches. A Tub, with handles and projecting hoops, and the divisions between the staves plainly marked. A strong Trestle, 18 inches high. A Hollow Cylinder, 9 inches in diameter, and 12 inches long, divided lengthwise. A Hollow Sphere, 9 inches in diameter, divided into semi-spheres, one of which is again divided into quarters; the semi-sphere, when placed on the cylinder, gives the form and principles of shading a dome, whilst one of the quarters placed on half the cylinder forms a niche.

*Davidson's Apparatus for Teaching Practical Geometry (22 models), £5.

*Binn's Models for Illustrating the Elementary Principles of Orthographic Projection as applied to Mechanical Drawing, in box, £1 10s.

Miller's Class Drawing Models.—These Models are particularly adapted for teaching large classes; the stand is very strong, and the universal joint will hold the Models in any position. *Wood Models*: Square Prism, 12 inches side, 18 inches high; Hexagonal Prism, 14 inches side, 18 inches high; Cube, 14 inches side: Cylinder, 13 inches diameter, 16 inches high; Hexagon Pyramid, 14 inches diameter, 22½ inches side; Square Pyramid, 14 inches side, 22½ inches side; Cone, 13 inches diameter, 22½ inches side; Skeleton Cube, 19 inches solid wood 1¾ inch square; Intersecting Circles, 19 inches solid wood 2¼ by 1½ inches. *Wire Models*: Triangular Prism, 17 inches side, 22 inches high; Square Prism, 14 inches side, 20 inches high; Hexagonal Prism, 21 inches diameter, 21 inches high; Cylinder, 14 inches diameter, 21 inches high; Hexagon Pyramid, 18 inches diameter, 24 inches high; Square Pyramid, 17 inches side, 24 inches high; Cone, 17 inches side, 24 inches high; Skeleton Cube, 19 inches side; Intersecting Circles 19 inches side; Plain Circle, 19 inches side; Plain Square, 19 inches side. Table, 27 inches by 21½ inches. Stand. The set complete, £14 13s.

Vulcanite Set Square, 5s.

Large Compasses, with chalk-holder, 5s.

*Slip, two set squares and **T** square, 5s.

*Parkes's Case of Instruments, containing 6-inch compasses with pen and pencil leg, 5s.

*Prize Instrument Case, with 6-inch compasses pen and pencil leg, 2 small compasses, pen and scale, 18s.

6-inch Compasses, with shifting pen and point, 4s. 6d.

LARGE DIAGRAMS.

ASTRONOMICAL:

TWELVE SHEETS. By JOHN DREW, Ph. Dr., F.R.S.A. Prepared for the Committee of Council on Education. Sheets, £2 8s.; on rollers and varnished, £4 4s.

BOTANICAL:

NINE SHEETS. Illustrating a Practical Method of Teaching Botany. By Professor HENSLOW, F.L.S. £2; on rollers and varnished, £3 3s.

CLASS.		DIVISION.		SECTION.		DIAGRAM.
Dicotyledon ..	..	Angiospermous	..	Thalamifloral ..	..	1
				Calycifloral ..	..	2 & 3
				Corollifloral ..	..	4
				Incomplete ..	..	5
		Gymnospermous ..			..	6
Monocotyledons	..	Petaloid ..	..	Superior ..	..	7
				Inferior ..	..	8
		Glumaceous	..	.. ..	..	9

* Models, &c., entered as sets, can only be supplied in sets.

BUILDING CONSTRUCTION:

TEN SHEETS. By WILLIAM J. GLENNY, Professor of Drawing, King's College. In sets, £1 1s.

LAXTON'S EXAMPLES OF BUILDING CONSTRUCTION IN TWO DIVISIONS, containing 32 Imperial Plates, £1.

BUSBRIDGE'S DRAWINGS OF BUILDING CONSTRUCTION. 11 Sheets. 2s. 9d. Mounted, 5s. 6d.

GEOLOGICAL:

DIAGRAM OF BRITISH STRATA. By H. W. BRISTOW, F.R.S., F.G.S. A Sheet, 4s.; on roller and varnished, 7s. 6d.

MECHANICAL:

DIAGRAMS OF THE MECHANICAL POWERS, AND THEIR APPLICATIONS IN MACHINERY AND THE ARTS GENERALLY. By Dr. JOHN ANDERSON.

8 Diagrams, highly coloured on stout paper, 3 feet 6 inches by 2 feet 6 inches. Sheets £1 per set ; mounted on rollers, £2.

DIAGRAMS OF THE STEAM-ENGINE. By Professor GOODEVE and Professor SHELLEY. Stout paper, 40 inches by 27 inches, highly coloured.

Sets of 41 Diagrams (52½ Sheets), £6 6s. ; varnished and mounted on rollers, £11 11s.

MACHINE DETAILS. By Professor UNWIN. 16 Coloured Diagrams. Sheets, £2 2s.; mounted on rollers and varnished, £3 14s.

SELECTED EXAMPLES OF MACHINES, OF IRON AND WOOD (French). By STANISLAS PETTIT. 60 Sheets, £3 5s.; 13s. per dozen.

BUSBRIDGE'S DRAWINGS OF MACHINE CONSTRUCTION. 50 Sheets, 12s. 6d. Mounted, £1 5s.

PHYSIOLOGICAL:

ELEVEN SHEETS. Illustrating Human Physiology, Life Size and Coloured from Nature. Prepared under the direction of JOHN MARSHALL, F.R.S., F.R.C.S., &c. Each Sheet, 12s. 6d. On canvas and rollers, varnished, £1 1s.

1. THE SKELETON AND LIGAMENTS.
2. THE MUSCLES, JOINTS, AND ANIMAL MECHANICS.
3. THE VISCERA IN POSITION.—THE STRUCTURE OF THE LUNGS.
4. THE ORGANS OF CIRCULATION.
5. THE LYMPHATICS OR ABSORBENTS.
6. THE ORGANS OF DIGESTION.
7. THE BRAIN AND NERVES.—THE ORGANS OF THE VOICE.
8. THE ORGANS OF THE SENSES.
9. THE ORGANS OF THE SENSES.
10. THE MICROSCOPIC STRUCTURE OF THE TEXTURES AND ORGANS.
11. THE MICROSCOPIC STRUCTURE OF THE TEXTURES AND ORGANS.

HUMAN BODY, LIFE SIZE. By JOHN MARSHALL, F.R.S., F.R.C.S. Each Sheet, 12s. 6d.; on canvas and rollers, varnished, £1 1s. Explanatory Key, 1s.

1. THE SKELETON, Front View.
2. THE MUSCLES, Front View.
3. THE SKELETON, Back View.
4. THE MUSCLES, Back View

5. THE SKELETON, Side View.
6. THE MUSCLES, Side View.
7. THE FEMALE SKELETON, Front View.

ZOOLOGICAL:

TEN SHEETS. Illustrating the Classification of Animals. By ROBERT PATTERSON. £2 ; on canvas and rollers, varnished, £3 10s. The same, reduced in size on Royal paper, in 9 Sheets, uncoloured, 12s.

PHYSIOLOGY AND ANATOMY OF THE HONEY BEE.

Two Diagrams. 7s. 6d.

A History of Art in Chaldæa & Assyria.

By GEORGES PERROT AND CHARLES CHIPIEZ.

Translated by WALTER ARMSTRONG, B.A., Oxon.　With 452 Illustrations.
2 vols. royal 8vo, £2 2s.

"It is profusely illustrated, not merely with representations of the actual remains preserved in the British Museum, the Louvre, and elsewhere, but also with ingenious conjectural representations of the principal buildings from which those remains have been taken. To Englishmen familiar with the magnificent collection of Assyrian antiquities preserved in the British Museum the volume should be especially welcome. We may further mention that an English translation by Mr. Walter Armstrong, with the numerous illustrations of the original, has just been published by Messrs. Chapman and Hall."—*Times.*

"The only dissatisfaction that we can feel in turning over the two beautiful volumes in illustration of Chaldæan and Assyrian Art, by MM. Perrot and Chipiez, is in the reflection, that in this, as in so many other publications of a similar scope and nature, it is a foreign name that we see on the title page, and a translation only which we can lay to our national credit. The predominance of really important works on Archæology which have to be translated for the larger reading public of England, and the comparative scarcity of original English works of a similar calibre, is a reproach to us which we would fain see removed . . . it is most frequently to French and German writers that we are indebted for the best light and the most interesting criticisms on the arts of antiquity. Mr. Armstrong's translation is very well done.'—*Builder.*

"The work is a valuable addition to archæological literature, and the thanks of the whole civilised world are due to the authors who have so carefully compiled the history of the arts of two peoples, often forgotten, but who were in reality the founders of Western civilisation."—*Graphic.*

History of Ancient Egyptian Art.

By GEORGES PERROT AND CHARLES CHIPIEZ.

Translated from the French by W. ARMSTRONG.　Containing 616 Engravings, drawn after the Original, or from Authentic Documents. 2 vols. imperial 8vo, £2 2s.

"The study of Egyptology is one which grows from day to day, and which has now reached such proportions as to demand arrangement and selection almost more than increased collection of material. The well-known volumes of MM. Perrot and Chipiez supply this requirement to an extent which had never hitherto been attempted, and which, before the latest researches of Mariette and Maspero, would have been impossible. Without waiting for the illustrious authors to complete their great undertaking, Mr. W. Armstrong has very properly seized their first instalment, and has presented to the English public all that has yet appeared of a most useful and fascinating work. To translate such a book, however, is a task that needs the revision of a specialist, and this Mr. Armstrong has felt, for he has not sent out his version to the world without the sanction of Dr. Birch and Mr. Reginald Stuart Poole. The result is in every way satisfactory to his readers. Mr. Armstrong adds, in an appendix, a description of that startling discovery which occurred just after the French original of these volumes left the press—namely, the finding of 38 royal mummies, with their sepulchral furniture, in a subterranean chamber at Thebes. It forms a brilliant ending to a work of great value and beauty."—*Pall Mall Gazette.*

The *Saturday Review*, speaking of the French edition, says : "To say that this magnificent work is the best history of Egyptian art that we possess, is to state one of the least of its titles to the admiration of all lovers of antiquity, Egyptian or other. No previous work can be compared with it for method or completeness. . . . . Not only are the best engravings from the older authorities utilised, but numerous unpublished designs have been inserted. M. Chipiez has added greatly to the value of a work, in which the trained eye of the architect is everywhere visible, by his restorations of various buildings and modes of construction ; and the engravings in colours of the wall paintings are a noticeable feature in a work which is in every way remarkable. This history of Egyptian art is an invaluable treasure-house for the student ; and, we may add, there are few more delightful volumes for the cultivated idle who live at ease to turn over—every page is full of artistic interest."

THE FORTNIGHTLY REVIEW.

Edited by T. H. S. ESCOTT.

THE FORTNIGHTLY REVIEW is published on the 1st of every month, and a Volume is completed every Six Months.

The following are among the Contributors:—

SIR RUTHERFORD ALCOCK.
MATHEW ARNOLD.
PROFESSOR BAIN.
SIR SAMUEL BAKER.
PROFESSOR BEESLY.
PAUL BERT.
BARON GEORGETON BUNSEN.
DR. BRIDGES.
HON. GEORGE C. BRODRICK.
JAMES BRYCE, M.P.
THOMAS BURT, M.P.
SIR GEORGE CAMPBELL, M.P.
THE EARL OF CARNARVON.
EMILIO CASTELAR.
RT. HON. J. CHAMBERLAIN, M.P.
PROFESSOR SIDNEY COLVIN.
MONTAGUE COOKSON, Q.C.
L. H. COURTNEY, M.P.
G. H. DARWIN.
SIR GEORGE W. DASENT.
PROFESSOR A. V. DICEY.
RIGHT HON. H. FAWCETT, M.P.
EDWARD A. FREEMAN.
SIR BARTLE FRERE, BART.
J. A. FROUDE.
MRS. GARRET-ANDERSON.
J. W. L. GLAISHER, F.R.S.
M. E. GRANT DUFF, M.P.
THOMAS HARE.
F. HARRISON.
LORD HOUGHTON.
PROFESSOR HUXLEY.
PROFESSOR R. C. JEBB.
PROFESSOR JEVONS.
ANDREW LANG.
ÉMILE DE LAVELEYE.

T. E. CLIFFE LESLIE
SIR JOHN LUBBOCK, M.P.
THE EARL LYTTON.
SIR H. S. MAINE.
DR. MAUDSLEY.
PROFESSOR MAX MÜLLER.
G. OSBORNE MORGAN, Q.C., M.P.
PROFESSOR HENRY MORLEY.
WILLIAM MORRIS.
PROFESSOR H. N. MOSELEY.
F. W. H. MYERS.
F. W. NEWMAN.
PROFESSOR JOHN NICHOL.
W. G. PALGRAVE.
WALTER H. PATER.
RT. HON. LYON PLAYFAIR, M.P.
DANTE GABRIEL ROSSETTI.
LORD SHERBROOKE.
HERBERT SPENCER.
HON. E. L. STANLEY.
SIR J. FITZJAMES STEPHEN, Q.C.
LESLIE STEPHEN.
J. HUTCHISON STIRLING.
A. C. SWINBURNE.
DR. VON SYBEL.
J. A. SYMONDS.
THE REV. EDWARD F. TALBOT
    (WARDEN OF KEBLE COLLEGE).
SIR RICHARD TEMPLE, BART.
W. T. THORNTON.
HON. LIONEL A. TOLLEMACHE.
H. D. TRAILL.
ANTHONY TROLLOPE.
PROFESSOR TYNDALL.
A. J. WILSON.
THE EDITOR.

&c. &c. &c.

THE FORTNIGHTLY REVIEW *is published at 2s. 6d.*

CHAPMAN & HALL, LIMITED, 11, HENRIETTA STREET, COVENT GARDEN, W.C.

. CHARLES DICKENS AND EVANS,]   [CRYSTAL PALACE PRESS.